the entire series is not to be missed—and this last book ties it all together in stunning fashion."

—RT Book Reviews, 4 stars

"The story highlights friendship, loyalty, and perseverance with likable characters and engaging writing."

—World for Unbreakable

"Ella masterfully creates a realistic fantasy world, a story . . . filled with excellent narratives, engaging characters, and truths—and plenty of plot twists!"

—Christian Library Journal for Unbreakable

"*Unblemished* may have set the stage, but *Unraveling* will forever bind you to this story like a Kiss of Accord. Sara Ella's exquisite writing left me gasping at new revelations and rereading whole chapters just because. *Unraveling* is a sequel that outshines its already brilliant predecessor. Read it. Now. Then come fangirl with me."

—Nadine Brandes, award-winning author of the Out of Time trilogy and *Fawkes*

"With plenty of YA crossover appeal, this engaging and suspenseful debut urban fantasy features superb world building and a tightly paced story line. Reading groups will find plenty to discuss concerning self-image, the nature of good vs. evil, and the power of the marginalized to change the world."

—Library Journal, starred review for *Unblemished*

"Sara Ella's debut novel is a stunning journey into a fascinating new world of reflections. Intricately plotted, the story is complex, but not difficult to follow. Eliyana is a strong heroine, yet also has a vulnerable side that readers will definitely identify with. The other characters are also well-developed and have many hidden secrets revealed throughout the course of the tale . . . It will be fascinating to see where the author takes the characters next."

—*RT Book Reviews*, 4½ stars, TOP PICK! for *Unblemished*

"Ella has created a captivating, relatable protagonist and never hesitates as she keeps things moving briskly through the many twists and turns."

—*Publishers Weekly* for *Unblemished*

"A breathtaking fantasy set in an extraordinary fairy-tale world, with deceptive twists and an addictively adorable cast who are illusory to the end. Just when I thought I'd figured each out, Sara Ella sent me for another ride. A wholly original story, *Unblemished* begins as a sweet melody and quickly becomes an anthem of the heart. And I'm singing my soul out. Fans of *Once Upon a Time* and Julie Kagawa, brace yourselves."

—Mary Weber, award-winning author
of the Storm Siren trilogy

"Lyrically written and achingly romantic—*Unblemished* will tug your heartstrings!"

—Melissa Landers, author of *Alienated*, *Invaded*, and *Starflight*

"Self-worth and destiny collide in this twisty-turny fantasy full of surprise and heart. With charm and wit, Sara Ella delivers *Unblemished*, a magical story with a compelling message and a unique take on the perils of Central Park."

—Shannon Dittemore, author of the Angel Eyes trilogy

"*Unblemished* is an enchanting, beautifully written adventure with a pitch-perfect blend of fantasy, realism, and romance. Move this one to the top of your TBR pile and clear your schedule—you won't want to put it down!"

—Lorie Langdon, author of the Amazon
bestselling DOON series

Coral

OTHER BOOKS BY SARA ELLA

THE UNBLEMISHED TRILOGY
Unblemished
Unraveling
Unbreakable

Coral

SARA ELLA

THOMAS NELSON
Since 1798

Coral

© 2019 by Sara Carrington

Published in Nashville, Tennessee, by Thomas Nelson. Thomas Nelson is a registered trademark of HarperCollins Christian Publishing, Inc.

Published in association with Hartline Literary Agency, Pittsburgh, PA 15235

Interior design by Mallory Collins

Thomas Nelson titles may be purchased in bulk for educational, business, fundraising, or sales promotional use. For information, please email SpecialMarkets@ThomasNelson.com.

Publisher's Note: This novel is a work of fiction. Names, characters, places, and incidents are either products of the author's imagination or used fictitiously. All characters are fictional, and any similarity to people living or dead is purely coincidental.

ISBN 978-0-7852-2446-4 (e-book)
ISBN 978-0-7852-3238-4 (audio download)

Library of Congress Cataloging-in-Publication Data

Names: Carrington, Sara, 1985- author.
Title: Coral : The little mermaid reimagined / Sara Ella.
Description: Nashville, Tennessee : Thomas Nelson, [2019] | Audience: Ages 13+ | Audience: Grades 10-12 | Summary: The worlds of Coral, Brooke, and Merrick, teens wounded by mental illness and family problems, collide and they must choose what to leave behind in order to survive and start fresh.
Identifiers: LCCN 2019026469 (print) | LCCN 2019026470 (ebook) | ISBN 9780785224457 (hardcover) | ISBN 9780785224464 (epub) | ISBN 9780785232384 (epub)
Subjects: CYAC: Loss (Psychology)--Fiction. | Mental illness--Fiction. | Suicide--Fiction. | Family problems--Fiction. | Love--Fiction. | Mermaids--Fiction.
Classification: LCC PZ7.1.E435 Cor 2019 (print) | LCC PZ7.1.E435 (ebook) | DDC [Fic]--dc23 LC record available at https://lccn.loc.gov/2019026469
LC ebook record available at https://lccn.loc.gov/2019026470

Printed in the United States of America

19 20 21 22 23 LSC 5 4 3 2 1

This story is dedicated to anyone who has ever
encouraged, or listened, or understood.
And to anyone who needs encouragement. Or to be heard. Or to be understood.
This one is for you.
As well as:
For my husband, Caiden—
Because you accept my tears and love me, emotions and all.
And for Brooke—
You are my sister always.
Thank you for letting me borrow your name . . . and for everything else.
And for Janalyn—
A sunshine heroine for my beautiful sunshine friend.
I hope she's everything you wanted and more.
And for Mary—
For understanding. For empathy. But mostly for your heart.
And for my sister, Madisyn—
You are one of the strongest people I know.
I hope you know how much your strength continues to inspire me.
And in loving memory of Angela (Coffee & Chapters)—
You were a light in the darkness.
Your story lives on through the lives you touched.
Can't wait to see you again, my friend.
And for Mandi—
Your heart and courage amaze me.
Your authenticity resonates with me more than I can say.
And for Kayla—
You've been with this story from day one.
For that and so much more, this one's for you.
And for Gabrial—
From beginning to end, you have always been right here.
You remind me why I write even when I want to quit.
And for Nadine—
Because you walked me through this Abyss.
And you brought light when I couldn't find my way.

"Life itself is the most wonderful fairy tale."

—Hans Christian Andersen

A NOTE TO MY READERS

(TRIGGER WARNING)

For my friends who have experienced trauma, a warning—this story may be triggering. I have done my best to approach the mental health topics addressed in this book in the most sensitive and caring way possible. But even all the research and sensitivity readers in the world would never make it so I could approach every aspect of mental health from every perspective. Your experience is unique to you.

Potential triggers include suicide, self-harm, emotional abuse, anxiety, depression, eating disorders, PTSD, and unwanted advances.

With that said, while some of what I have written comes from research and some from the caring eyes of readers who have lived through many of these experiences, other pieces come from my own personal experience with emotional trauma. If you have lost a loved one, I'm with you. If you face depression or anxiety, my heart aches with you in a truly personal way. If you have ever felt misunderstood for these things or simply wanted to escape altogether—I understand.

For the girl who is not okay. For the boy who wonders if it will ever get better. This story is for you.

My hope is that Coral's tale may be a small pinprick of light in your darkness—a reminder that you are seen. You are loved. You are *not* alone. You are not nothing, my friend. And neither am I.

Sincerely,

Sara Ella

BEFORE

Her soul was bleeding.

The sand beneath her was cool and damp, the high tide from last evening lingering between the grains. The water would turn red soon, transforming into a bloody, poisonous mess. Red Tide called for her.

Maybe it always had.

She buried her feet, allowing them to take refuge as a hermit crab does on a summer day. She could sit here forever, listening to the ocean's song as she sprayed her melody onto the shore. The ocean beckoned her as a mother to a child, pleading with her to return to her bosom. To her heart.

But she could never go back. Not now. It was a strange feeling. Longing for something she'd never have again. Hoping for the past, while at once realizing there was nothing she could do to change it.

Hope. A foolish girl's dream. Time. An unavoidable monster.

Time was a ribbon. She could fold it and tie it, bend it, lose it. Cut it. But if she cut it, she could never piece it back together the way it was before. She could never get it back. All she had left was after.

And after was never the same.

After was full of regret and remorse, fear and doubt. It was the era of shoulda, coulda, woulda. The evolution of "Hi. This is me." And that was it. Nothing. Because she'd given herself away time and time again, in each instance losing the very fibers that made her who she was inside. And outside. And every in-between. The fibers that made up the soul she longed for and at once wished she never had.

She rubbed her feet. Curled and stretched her toes.

A broken shell tore into the skin of her left foot. She winced and withdrew. Blood, red and angry, *drip, drip, dripped* onto the sand, dissolving in an instant. As if it never was.

Better a bleeding sole than a tortured soul.

A soul that was nothing now. Because before preluded after.

And after. Was never as it was. Before.

Winter

"But a mermaid has no tears, and therefore she suffers so much more."

—Hans Christian Andersen,
"The Little Mermaid"

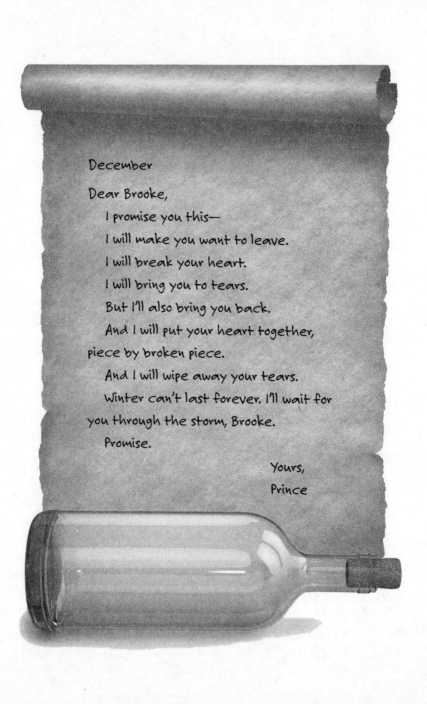

December

Dear Brooke,

I promise you this—

I will make you want to leave.

I will break your heart.

I will bring you to tears.

But I'll also bring you back.

And I will put your heart together, piece by broken piece.

And I will wipe away your tears.

Winter can't last forever. I'll wait for you through the storm, Brooke.

Promise.

Yours,
Prince

ONE

Coral

She's not sick. She's not.

Coral repeated the idea over and over in her head, clinging to the hope her belief would become truth if she willed it so.

But as her oldest sister's tearless weeping carried on a steady current from down the palace hall, the idea she was, in fact, not sick became all the more a fantasy. Her sister's once upon a time now led to an unhappily ever after, forever looming in the shadows of the end.

Coral's oldest sister—the crown princess—was Diseased.

The Disease hung over their family, their people, following them in all they did. It was a spell that held them under. An illness from which their kind could not hide.

Coral would not allow it to drown her too.

She cursed her constricting throat and shuddering fins. Her palpating pulse, as thunderous as the red flashing before her eyes, could take a swim in the Abyss as far as she was concerned.

Coral longed to swim to her oldest sister's chambers and comfort her, but how could she? Any show of emotion might mean Coral carried the illness her sister bore.

"Father will calm her." Their middle sister, Jordan, tightened her grip on Coral's shoulders, her dainty, silken hands stronger than they appeared. "Trust me." Jordan's whisper did nothing to abate Coral's anxiety. "He knows what he's doing." Her voice was slick and silver and sleepy, the same muted hue as her tail.

Coral bit her trembling lower lip, wished upon a sea star that she might shed even a single tear. She shook her head. "Father never calms her." Nothing did.

"Bite your tongue." Jordan's voice changed from silver to red with three words.

Red was poison. Red was pain.

Coral ripped out of Jordan's grasp, the forceful jerk out of character but necessary. She may have been small for her age, but Coral more than made up for it with the feisty tenacity their grandmother had quietly encouraged. When Coral whirled to face Jordan, her sister's expression appeared as smooth as a pearl.

But this did nothing to quench the fire inside. "If stoicism is equal to soothing," Coral said, "then I'm an electric eel."

The crown princess's sobs increased, coloring the water around them in faded shades of taupe and gray.

Coral pictured her oldest sister. She imagined Father floating there, watching. Staring through his first daughter as if she were nothing. Contaminated. As if she would make him ill too.

But she wouldn't. Mermen were immune to the Disease. Deep, soul-wrenching emotions were not something they could fall prey to.

Especially not the great King of the Seas.

"I'd be careful with that temper of yours, baby sister," Jordan said.

"I'll be sixteen in three days." Didn't that count for something? "I don't need you to chastise me."

Jordan blinked but did not waver from her spot three shark fins away. "You're too emotional for your own good. Dramatic. Sensitive. Let those feelings hook you, and you'll end up just. Like. Her. Sunken and unsalvageable." She jammed a finger toward Coral's chest, slid her gaze sideways to the portrait of their trio on the nightstand. When Jordan's gaze found hers again, it dared the little mermaid to react. To respond and prove her theory true. "You *are* like her, you know."

Coral stuffed her thoughts into a bottle at the back of her mind, corked the glass tight for good measure. Why must Jordan remind her? Did she think Coral was oblivious to the signs of the Disease?

"It's only a disease if you allow it to be one . . ." Their grandmother's words swam back to her on a wave. They'd never made much sense. Still, they comforted. Giving her the confidence she needed to say, "You're wrong."

"We shall see." Jordan considered her complexion in the mirror that stretched from the stone ceiling to the straw-colored sand. She fussed over her silver hair. Examined the bridge of her refined nose. "You're weaker than she is. What makes you think you are immune?"

"What makes you think *you* are?" The quip was ill formed but quick enough.

Jordan eyed her through the mirror's reflection, clearly considering her response.

Coral bit her lower lip until it bled, tasting of brine and rust.

Curse my overactive tongue.

"*I* am not the one raising my voice or turning so red in the face I'd be mistaken for a lobster." Jordan's breaths didn't hasten and her eyelashes didn't bat.

Coral forced a matching calm into her features. Relaxing her coral-hued tail from scales to fins. For once, she had no words. Her. The mermaid whose life was a run-on sentence.

"You are young, baby sister. One day you'll understand."

Coral almost believed she detected a hint of softness in Jordan's tone, but then it drifted away as easily as sea foam across the surface of the water.

And then the cries grew louder.

Jordan rolled her eyes, crossed to the heavy chamber door carved from old ship wood, and shut it.

The action muffled their sister's heartbreak, but this didn't change the true volume of the situation. "You can't pretend this isn't happening. She needs help."

"Mind your own business, *Cor.*"

Ugh. Coral hated when Jordan called her that. But two could play at that game. "Our sister *is* my business, *Jor.*"

"These episodes are nothing new." Jordan rolled her eyes again, her signature expression. "She's had them since Mother died—giving birth to *you*, I might add."

Guilt blossomed. Shame had hung over Coral since she understood they once had a mother who was not their grandmother or her oldest sister—who had both helped raise them.

She allowed the argument to drop to the golden-grained seabed. Then she floated to the closed door. Coral cracked it an inch as more cries filtered down the hall. When she was younger, the crown princess's episodes were few and far between. Only recently had they become more frequent. A constant they could no longer ignore.

The future queen was Diseased. Her sobs were an unbearable, Abyss-worthy black.

Something slammed. A door? A chest? Father's voice—tinged with deep magenta—released low and forced. While their sister's words came through as clear as tropical water, Father's were more difficult to decipher.

Coral strained to listen.

"How many times must we go through this?" Father grew louder, then eased again. "You will sing. And that is final."

"I won't," the crown princess snapped. "I don't *feel* it anymore."

"You know very well *that* word is forbidden in this household."

Coral pictured the lines creasing on her father's forehead. She imagined his dark eyes attempting to force their sister's emotions away.

"Feelings are devious," Father said. "They are deceitful. They are *human.* Use your head, Daughter. Your feelings are deceiving you into betraying your family. You know how much we depend on your voice. We have a contract. It is binding. And that is final."

The crown princess moaned.

"Stop this. You are being dramatic."

She moaned all the more. "This isn't helping me, Father."

"What would help, then? The truth?"

Silence. Then sobs. "Your truth and my truth are very different things."

"There you go again with your nonsense. There is only black or white."

"Except for when there is gray," the crown princess said.

Coral pictured their oldest sister, gracious and poised, reining in her heart before their father crushed it again.

"I cannot do it any longer." Defeat weighted their sister's faded ash words. "If Mother were here—"

"Do not bring your mother into this," Father barked. "She is gone. She's been gone for nearly sixteen years."

Coral's eyes burned with each retort. Her throat tightened.

Their sister grew quieter. Withdrawing. Sinking into herself until she was drowning inside.

"Why won't you listen?" the crown princess asked.

Father's response, ever the same, ramped Coral's irritation. She didn't need to listen to hear him say, "Why won't you obey?"

But the little mermaid did listen. And this time, their father kept silent.

Coral opened the door wide enough to swim a few feet into the corridor outside the bedchamber.

"What are you doing?" Jordan spat, swimming up behind her. "If Father were to catch you—"

"Shhhh." Coral waved her off. Now was not the time to suddenly care if she got caught. This was the part where Father would ask his question, then leave their sister be. But . . .

"I'm sick, Father." Her sister's words became stones, weighing on Coral's heart. "I feel like I'm dying. Please, don't make me sing. Jordan can do it solo."

Their defenses lowered. Jordan reached out and grasped Coral's hand. A split second of unity, maybe even love.

Coral squeezed her hand, wishing their temporary bond would last.

"You are fine." Father's resignation was an iron anchor. "You'd be fine if you'd only choose to be."

Choose? Does he believe the Disease is a choice?

"It isn't so simple," the crown princess said.

"But it is. You're making yourself sick. The Disease takes those who are too weak to rise above their *feelings*. This is all in your head."

"Maybe." The answer bled of resolve. "But the Disease affects the heart, Father. And mine is breaking. If only you could understand—"

"You will sing, Daughter. *Tonight.*"

The crown princess did not respond to his final word. He'd silenced her. She would sing. Then she wouldn't speak again until morning.

It took everything in Coral's deepest fathoms not to swim down the hall, barge into the sitting room, and defend their oldest sister. She hated that they weren't even allowed to use her given name anymore. She was simply "the crown princess" or "the future queen."

The king was detaching himself. They all were.

"Will Father sit by and wait for Red Tide to come as it has for others before her?" Coral whispered. "We've heard the stories. The Disease spares no one who contracts it. If our sister is ill, if she's getting worse . . . How long before Red Tide takes her too?"

Was that disappointment lingering behind Jordan's gaze? "I told you he'd calm her." She released Coral's hand, backed away, and found the sand-length mirror as if it had been waiting all along.

"You *wanted* the solo. You were *hoping* Father would allow our sister's request." Coral's ears burned. How could Jordan be so selfish?

"There you go again with your make-believe ideas." The middle mersister combed her fingers through her hair, then touched her fingertips to the corners of her eyes, lifting the skin at the nonexistent creases ever so slightly. "You worry too much, little sister. The crown princess has her spirals, but she comes back. She'll be fine. We'll all be fine."

Fine. A word Coral had come to loathe. A word so yellow, so cowardly, it couldn't carry its weight in goldfish.

She released a long sigh. Bubbles rose. *One, two, three, four . . .*

Jordan lowered her hands and smoothed them over the scales on her tail. "What you should be worried about is *your* performance." Her deadpan expression chilled the room. She eyed Coral through her reflection. "Or have you forgotten what's expected of you?"

Coral broke eye contact. "Of course I haven't forgotten." Jordan would never let her. "I know my place."

"Good." Jordan's gaze shifted and shadows lay to rest across her lashes. "We've waited a long time to show off that pretty little voice of yours. We are our father's daughters. And so we sing."

Her voice. Her vice. A curse of its own. Coral swam to her pallet, sat, and drew her tail to her chest. The bedclothes were wrinkled and her pillow slept in the sand. She shuddered. When had the water grown so cold?

"Have you thought of what you will sing for your first concert? We've traveled all the way here to our Pacific palace for the occasion." Jordan twirled before the mirror, a whirlpool of muted silver and green. With each swirl burst a symphony. Silver was the spray of a whale at the surface. Green became fins grazing grains of sand.

"I have a few selections in mind." The lie was easy, another added to the bucket of fibs Coral had learned to tell over the years.

Jordan joined her on the pallet, plucked a red flower from a pore in the wall, and stuck it into the hair tucked behind her right ear. Jordan may have seen the color, but she had no idea what sound it produced.

Another curse, but this one extended to Coral alone.

Her senses intertwined, two playing as one. The colors made sounds and the sounds created colors. Yet another oddity that would only serve to raise suspicion. Every shade had a note, a melody distinguished by its particular hue.

The Diseased were different, as unique and one of a kind as a mermaid out of water.

11

"I hope, for your sake, the song you choose is one approved by Father." Jordan plucked another red flower from the wall and placed it between her silvery locks.

With every wave of the flower's delicate petals, Coral heard a clap of rolling thunder.

This sort of red boomed. Even with the melodic differences between hues, every shade of red was brash. "I aim to please. I'd never dream of singing something forbidden." No romance ballads. No heartfelt limericks. Nothing too emotional. Or moving. Or goose-bump inducing.

A simple song to draw sailors to her father's waters. To drown them in her voice and make them forget who they were. *Where* they were. Just as they threw themselves at Coral's sisters each time, along with any treasures they possessed. The sailors belonged to the merfolk before the concert was finished.

Coral was permitted to do whatever it took to keep the humans trapped within their depths.

She was not, however, allowed to speak to them. Or touch them. Or breathe near them. Or do anything with them. Not if her father had anything to say about it.

Draw them in, then leave them stranded. Always wanting more.

"May I tell you a secret?" Jordan's monotone played in harmony with her somber personality. Her gaze relaxed then, her gray eyes appearing almost blue.

The shift in color played a calming cadence across Coral's vision. She watched. Waited. Glanced in the mirror. Her own Eyris pearl eyes—not quite green nor blue nor violet—widened in anticipation. Just once she wanted Jordan to admit she, too, hid symptoms of the Disease. Coral would never tell Father. No. But if Jordan shared her secret, then Coral would know for certain.

The Disease was not as much of an anomaly as everyone said.

And everything she'd ever been taught was a lie.

But Jordan never failed to disappoint. "As long as you get past that first note, it's all downstream from there. Easy as a kelp pie." She drew in three long breaths and her shoulders visibly relaxed. Grandmother had taught them this technique to prepare for their debuts.

"Calms the nerves . . . and the fins," she had said in her soothing voice the color of a winter sky.

Only a few sunsets left.

Coral tugged on a strand of her spun-gold hair. *There must be more to life than fearing the Disease and singing like my sisters before me.*

What if she didn't *want* to sing?

What if she wanted something different? A life outside her family's fame and expectations?

Jordan drew three more long breaths before she rose and swam to the archway. She paused. Did she expect Coral to say more?

Coral's mouth bowed and her insides turned to jellyfish. She didn't want Jordan to go, despite how she tended to get under Coral's scales more often than not. Having either of her sisters near almost made up for their mother's absence.

Almost.

Coral opened her mouth to ask Jordan to stay, then snapped it closed. She ought to practice, prepare for what was to come. Jordan was closest to her in age and knew how to keep what their grandmother called "balance" better than anyone. Never too high or too low, Jordan had mastered the art of in-between. She didn't keep quiet about her suspicions of Coral when they were alone. Still, Jordan never spoke of it beyond their private conversations. She must have cared for Coral more than she let on.

"Coral." Jordan sighed, her voice lifeless. She pinched the bridge of her nose and rubbed tiny circles into her skin. "You must learn your place in this family, as I had to." Her words were gentle, reminding Coral of how their oldest sister used to be. "Otherwise you'll end up like her."

Coral's lower lip quivered. *How can she speak of our sister this way? The crown princess practically raised us. I don't understand it.*

Jordan shook her head. "Do what's expected, little sister. You'll be better off. I promise."

Her words latched on to Coral's heart. "Of course. My only wish is to be your equal." The half lie grated her teeth like chewed sand. "The Disease is poison. The Disease is death."

The speech was practiced, precise, clever even. Words she'd been made to repeat year after year. With each season, she'd learned she was different. Once, as a child, she told a schoolmate her voice was the color of a sea turtle's shell. The mermaid had cried to their teacher, and Coral was sent home for poor behavior.

She never mentioned her gift again.

After that she observed Jordan and the other merfolk her age from a distance. They didn't respond to things the way Coral did. Soon she learned they didn't see or hear the same way either. Her world produced the brightest, most brilliant shades of turquoise and aqua and sapphire blue, all mixed with harmonies she couldn't begin to describe. Blues composed the prettiest sounds. Soft but full of life. Soothing but awakening too.

Jordan hovered between chamber and hall. "Three more days, Sister." Her tone exuded no malice. Only fact. "Then you must take your proper place beside us." She floated through the open arch of their shared chamber.

Coral often wished she roomed with her oldest sister instead. But as heiress to the throne, the crown princess had her own private chambers. Yet, until she found a suitor, she'd never be given the crown. Father had brought in many mermen, but the future queen refused them all.

Maybe when she finds a match, she can stop singing. When she no longer requires Father to provide.

Coral freed the bubbles she'd been holding as she examined herself in the mirror. Father's approval was everything. Without it, they'd be left to the wayside. No home. No protection. No longer a part of the family.

Jordan had already been paired with a merman of Father's liking.

They weren't yet betrothed, but the formalities were only a matter of time. When Jordan turned eighteen before the year's end, the wedding date would be set.

How long before Father starts bringing suitors around for me?

Coral shuddered, shoving the thought away, refusing to think on it. She was hardly ready to be married.

Coral's reflection stared back at her. She knew this girl. She saw her every day. But then, in that moment, she hardly recognized herself. Almost as if she weren't real. "Who are you?"

The mermaid in the mirror did not answer. Coral abandoned the stranger and swam to catch up with her sisters, darkness following close behind. Her heart pounded with each flick of her misfit tail as she glanced back at her namesake.

"Coral," her grandmother used to croon. *"My sweet little Coral with the coral-colored tail."*

Coral had loved looking at her tail because of that. Its hue stood out among the rest, singing a tune of life and joy.

Now she frowned. Because, for the first time, the color was silent.

She ignored the irregularity and swam faster. Hoping in her depths that she was simply too tired to see the song.

At the palace's broad arched entrance, Jordan joined the crown princess in the courtyard. They paid respects to the memorial paving with their mother's and four lost sisters' names inscribed. The queen's miscarriages were rarely talked about—two before their oldest sister, then one before Jordan. The final preceded Coral. It was said the Disease took them before they inhaled their first bubbled breaths. Coral lagged behind and offered her own salutations, bowing her head as each of their names surfaced in her mind.

Queen Oceane.

Hudson.

Pearl.

Aqua.

Isla.

Coral drowned her emotions and opened her eyes after a spell. She focused on the mermaid who would be queen. The first daughter. Her best friend and forever confidant. Her oldest sister stared toward the surface, brow knit in waiting. The way she could so easily switch from pained to poised fascinated Coral. Like night and day. One minute the sun shone brightly, and the next it was drowned by night's blanket of gloom.

A broad shadow passed overhead, the signal her sisters had been awaiting. Every time it was the same. Sailors crossed through their waters and, drawn by her sisters' duet, they became lost. Forgetting the cares and worries of their human lives, leaving them behind for the empty promises of shallow words playing on practiced melodies.

Coral's entire existence was torn between who she was supposed to be and who she truly was.

A mermaid whose sole purpose was to drown every sailor who crossed her path?

Or a girl who felt things she shouldn't but longed to experience at the same time? A girl who wondered if the dreaded illness her family feared was dwelling within at that moment?

The raging war inside burned and bruised, each day wearing on her resolve to act the part she was expected to play.

As her sisters rose, Coral neared the memorial stone. She removed the flower from her hair, kissed it once before she placed it upon the raised gray rock. The colors contrasted, but their songs synced.

Gray was tragedy. Red was agony.

She swam double-time back through the palace halls. The remnants of a sunken city, years before her time, sang a sad melody of loss and regret. Stone columns and archways led to hundreds of identical rooms, all lamenting the deaths of merfolk long passed. Rooms filled with nothing. No life. No song aside from that which brought lives to an end.

What would her father say if he knew she could see and hear every color she swam across? What would he do if he learned his youngest had no desire to follow the path he'd set before her?

He'll treat me like the crown princess. Then at least we'll be united. Maybe together we can sway him.

It didn't matter.

Because Father never looked at her.

Coral was a reminder of all he'd lost. A torch carrying the weight of the deceased queen and the four merbabies who could have been but never were.

Emotions rose but she shut them down. At the point beyond the southern palace gate, Coral swam ever faster. Past the three pointed rocks with their constant foreboding. Beyond the reef comprised of colors so vivid, her tail faded in comparison. Over the sunken ship that arrived when she was three. And there, just there at the edge of the wood, waited a cliff. And in the heart of that cliff lurked a dark cave. An ominous cave. A cave into which no merman, maid, or child would dare venture.

Coral lifted her head and entered. She'd escaped here a hundred times before.

She held no fear of darkness.

Light always awaited her at the other end.

Black and cool for but a fleeting moment, the interior of the cave gave way to luminous moonlight. She swam upward, flipping and tumbling in momentary freedom. She wasn't actually disobeying any rules. While she was forbidden to break the surface until the day she turned sixteen, this seemed different. No human would find her here, hidden among the jagged rocks far enough from shore it appeared blurred.

The evening air chilled her face. Coral pushed herself up onto the ledge of a low rock and wrung out her hair, a crazy mess of coarse tangles. Spear-like stones surrounded her as a circular fortress. Waves kissed the walls from the other side, spraying her face with salt and foam. She inhaled the fresh air that seemed to lift her higher. While the water weighted her when she breathed it in labor, the air seemed to relieve every ache brought by her sister's sobs. By Father's lack of concern.

Coral's tail rested in the water below, swaying this way and that. The sea garden she'd tended sprang forth from the nooks and crevices of the rocks in every shade. Deep-green sea grass. Bright-pink hibiscus with its sun-yellow tongue. And purple sea hollies. Spiked and menacing, but a beautiful sight to behold. She grazed one with her fingertips, absorbing the song their rainbow produced.

A sound she didn't recognize beckoned her from beyond the rocks. She startled and slipped, splashing back into the deep pool.

The sound echoed.

The urge to peek over her stone fortress seeped into every hidden crevice within. The moon shone high above the ocean waters. Soon her sisters would make themselves known. She should go. She should . . .

The song resounded a third time. Gold, pure, and shimmering.

What would one glance harm? Even if the sound was human, they were far enough away. No one would see her. Her sisters would be preoccupied and Father would never know. Coral had been here before. No one had ever noticed the glances she'd stolen from her secret place.

Coral pulled herself up enough to peer over the closest rock. In the distance, stars twinkled, blowing her kisses from the heavens. The moonlight lit the coast, illuminating the land palaces beyond. They were smaller than her palace, but somehow so much more inviting. Entirely white with warm yellow windows that called "hello." With stairs descending to the shore, the palaces stood nestled in so many shades of C-sharp green and lullaby periwinkle. The vision was glorious.

Beautiful.

And that song. It wasn't grandiose like the concerts her sisters often gave.

It was lovely. Simple. And oh so warm.

But the beauty of that simple harmony was quickly destroyed by her sisters' song.

Coral covered her ears and shut her eyes, diving beneath the surface to avoid the chilling sound. A sound so black it terrified her as much as the Abyss. Their call meant death, and she could not cope. The feeling inside grew hotter.

Mermaids. Cold. Death. Destruction.

Humans. Warmth and color and life.

Everything was backward.

Maybe the cure for the Disease was nowhere in the ocean.

Could humans hold the key to a cure the merfolk never imagined existed? Father might be in denial about his oldest daughter's illness, but he couldn't ignore her pleas forever.

Coral dove into darkness, swam toward home.

She must do whatever it took to stop the Disease from destroying her sister.

And she must do so before Red Tide came again.

TWO

Brooke

After

This is not my home.

This is not my bed.

After all this time, it's finally come to this. A facility. A treatment plan.

A nightmare lurking in the day.

Why did I agree to this?

Three blinks and a gulp of oxygen open my eyes to a shard of light slicing the puffy bedcovers. Vague snippets of memory piece together in a rough outline, reminding me how I got here. One word, maybe two, for each bullet point. The in-betweens remain intentionally blank. Too many triggers in those middle spaces. Glass half empty? No, but thanks. I'll take it completely hollow if it means I can avoid drowning.

The heater shuts off, making way for new sounds. Water trickling. And steam? I crane my neck. A miniature stone fountain and a diffuser, spraying something smelling of citrus and lavender. The effect soothes but also stirs a familiar warning. One that says these are devices used to manipulate. To make me feel safe and comfortable so they can get whatever it is they want.

Nice try. Not gonna work, though. I've only agreed to come here out of desperation. At a loss for anywhere else to go. This is my cliff. My deserted island. My means to an end.

I sit and take in the room I have all to myself. I arrived late last night and immediately crashed. Exhausted from the good-bye I wasn't quite ready to say. Now, in the light of day, this isn't what I expected. No sterile hospital bed or cold linoleum floor. Instead, the room is homey, cozy even. Everything in me wants to sleep for days. The fatigue never falters. There have been times I've slept eighteen hours and still didn't feel rested. Other times I'm awake all night, unable to calm my thoughts.

Now, my mind swims, sparking a manic energy that makes me want to move. Moving equals distraction. And distractions keep me from filling in those blanks. From thoughts that spiral out of control.

I force myself to stretch, to fully wake. My glazed eyes find a clock beside the full-size bed. The lit numbers blur, and I rub my eyes to focus.

5:53 a.m.

A knock sounds from the other side of the wall behind me. The creak of a bed frame. The opening of a door. Shuffling feet. Another door closing.

I'm not the only one here. Of course not. Somehow this does nothing to calm my nerves.

A yawn escapes, full and free as the sliver of sun widens, casting an earnest shadow across the room with walls that are probably blue but appear more gray through my lens. Everything is as gray as California fog these days. When was the last time I came across a color that stood out amid dull hues and their muted undertones? My life is a black-and-white film, one lost and forgotten, overlooked for more vibrant, exciting tales.

Pipes squeal and water runs. A girl's muffled voice finds its way through the walls. Her concert for one is a strange sound, a disconcerting one. She belts a show tune and I wonder what meds she's on.

Despite the pleasant feel of the room that pretends to be my friend, I can't be fooled. This is a facility. I am here to be treated, psycho-analyzed, and sent on my way. At the year's end I'll be eighteen, with nowhere to go but a shelter, the streets, or—

No. Never. Never in a thousand sunsets. That is a last resort. "I'd rather die," I say to the walls. They don't respond, instead offering a blank stare as empty as my soul.

The water shuts off and the girl's song ceases as more sounds awaken beyond the bedroom door. Creaking floorboards and pad-ding footsteps. I pull my covers up to my neck, wrap them around my shoulders, and burrow down, kicking the top sheet to the foot of the bed. I didn't get nearly enough sleep and my body moans in protest for it. But I couldn't sleep now if I tried.

"Thank you, Anxiety."

My anxiety responds in amped fashion. Typical.

Ignoring the sandpaper grate of my nerves, I take an inventory of the small space I occupy. *Occupy* because I am just *here*. Existing until I'm gone and the next person rolls in. None of this is mine. Not the lamp with its gray base and off-white shade. Nor the desk that was clearly salvaged from a yard sale. The plastic cups filled with pens and pencils at the desk's upper-right-hand corner stir a longing inside. I shut it down and move on.

A vase of fake white flowers mocks me. They laugh at my reality while resting in their artificial existence. What is this, a funeral?

Maybe. Not yet, but soon enough. Probably.

P. L. Travers said it best—"Once we have accepted the story, we cannot escape the story's fate."

I've accepted my story *and* my fate. Now it's a matter of time before the two collide. To think I never believed in fate. Ha. Guess some things do change after all.

My gaze lingers on the flowers too long, then shifts back to the first item that caught my eye—an item I promptly avoided but can no longer ignore.

The journal, leather-bound with a ribbon tie, taunts me. The images of seaweed and seashells impressed into its cover bring back days long past. I rise, keeping the comforter around my shoulders like a cape. My fingers graze the lines and edges of the leather. The images are immersed in life, but blank pages wait within. Pages I refuse to fill. Leather cover or paper, it doesn't matter. They can pretend this place is a haven all they want. But I know the truth.

And the truth is *nothing* is safe. No matter how many words I write, they can never understand. Pouring one's soul into ink and paper does nothing aside from bleed you dry until there's nothing left to give.

The smell of something foodish attacks my senses as I begin unpacking my suitcase. I open the dresser drawers and lay my scant wardrobe within. A couple pairs of jeans. A handful of solid tees. An unopened package of below-ankle socks. One hoodie. A week's worth of underwear. I place my toiletries, a brush and comb, and makeup in the top drawer. A powder compact, mascara, clear lip gloss. I don't know why I bothered to pack these. Who needs makeup when no one else is looking?

At the bottom of my suitcase rests a single piece of jewelry. A pearl bracelet. A gift. A curse. I take it out and toss it in a drawer. I never want to see it again.

The food smell grows stronger, though I can't quite pinpoint the source. The scent is faded, dull, indistinct. I cross the room to bolt the door and find it has no lock. I look around. No closet either? Guess I'll be dressing under the covers. So much for the show of privacy. Fake, fakety, fake.

As I reach into a drawer for my favorite pair of distressed jeans and a white ruched tee, the alarm clock blares. My muscles tighten. Six in the morning. Great. Whoever set the thing wants me on a schedule. A routine. Better get this over with.

I toss the clothes on the bed and move to shut off the alarm but can't find the right button in the shadows. Panic starts to rise as the alarm *ent, ent, ennnts.*

Stop. Be quiet. Shut up. My fingers fumble and shake. I switch on the lamp opposite the bed, but it's too late.

The sound becomes a siren. A siren racing closer, ready to swallow me whole.

It batters me before I can fend off the blow. My body reacts outside all reason. Outside the logic that says this is an alarm clock. *Just* an alarm clock. *Chill out already.*

This is not *just* an alarm clock.

This is death's anthem. An anthem that all too often calls when I'm around.

I tear the cord from the wall. Collapse to the floor. Hug my knees to my chest. *Oh my word, would you breathe already? Pathetic. Can't even handle an alarm, how do you expect to handle the real world?*

This is *the real world. Stop living in a fantasy.*

Trigger. Trigger. Bang. Bang.

"Get over it. Just get over it! Why can't you get over it?"

The bulleted voice hits its mark. Straight through my chest, lodging deep down where the light can't see.

Slowly, the spiral dies. Time passes. I stare at the dead clock. I know I should get up. *Get up*, my mind says. But my legs won't move. They tingle. And twitch. The restlessness inside my unmoving muscles brings with it exhaustion and an awareness of isolation. Defeat. I'm not here anymore. Not at all.

When the fog beyond the curtained window burns off, the unwelcome sunshine says time has passed well into the late morning. I finally find the will to move. Pain and ice bite my soles where I stand, gnawing at my arches like tiny shards of glass. I curl and wiggle my toes, willing the sleep to leave my body as circulation returns.

Once feeling finds my feet, I cross to the dresser again. Razor pain shoots through me. My stubbed toe throbs. My cry echoes around the tiny square of space.

"You okay?" a voice asks.

I whip my head toward the door to find a girl several years younger than I am standing in its frame. She has one of those faces. The kind that makes you feel like you've met this person but can't figure out where.

Her expression relays genuine concern.

I don't trust her one teensy bit.

She's twelve? Thirteen, maybe? Wearing a pair of black leggings and a long-sleeved tunic sweatshirt. Her hair, the color of changing maple leaves, is swept into two messy buns that look like teddy bear ears. She's disgustingly adorable and so not what I need right now.

She is my torturous reminder.

A reminder who is carrying a plate of food.

I sit on the bed and examine my aching toe.

"First day's the hardest." The girl shuffles toward me, sets the plate on the desk. "I'm on day ten." My wide eyes must give away my uncertainty because she adds, "I don't mind it here so far." Her shoulders sink.

I ignore my own sinking feeling. The one that tells me she's not being entirely honest. Instead, I glance sideways at the half tuna salad sandwich, apple, bag of Fritos, and can of lemonade. "I'm not hungry."

She reaches over and squeezes my hand as if we're old friends.

I flinch at the uninvited touch. "Don't."

She steps back, lifts her palms in surrender. "Sorry." She sighs. "Sometimes I forget—" She shakes her head. "I'm supposed to ask before I touch." Her arms cross over her flat chest. "Rules and consent and stuff. Anyway, you don't talk much, do you?"

"I talk." I scowl at my toe, which is now turning two shades darker than the surrounding skin. Nice. "Maybe I don't want to talk to *you*." Ouch. Harsh. Whatever. It's not as if she and I could ever have a relationship outside of this place. It wouldn't last. And more than likely, one of us will commit suicide eventually. Statistics don't lie. "You can go now."

But she doesn't leave. "That's okay. I didn't talk at first either. But you'll see. This place is different." She moves to sit beside me. "You should see the grounds. They have horses and hiking trails and there's even an indoor swimming pool."

I peer up at her, skepticism keeping my shoulders rigid and my eyes narrowed. "A swimming pool?" Right. Funny. If there's a swimming pool it's not ours. Unless they want us to clean it.

The girl smiles. "Food here's decent too," she says. "They have a nutritionist on staff who creates an individual meal plan for you. Your lunch won't always look so—"

"Pitiful?"

"Bland."

Sounds too good to be true. I'm not buying the nice place act, though. Not for one second. "I'm not going to be here long." I decide.

"But you're here today." Who is this girl? The positive pill is going to get old. Fast.

"'Kay, bye, then." My dismissal sounds as if spoken by someone else. I'm an observer outside my body, frowning down at this bitter, hollowed-out creature I've become.

She shifts but doesn't leave. She shoves her right sleeve up to scratch her arm, then quickly pulls it down. The movement was quick but I saw them. Her arm is covered in scars.

Trigger.

She is no stranger to darkness.

Bang.

I shake off the déjà vu feeling once more.

"I know my way around, which makes me super useful." She hitches a thumb over her shoulder. "Bathroom's right outside your door and to the left. Kitchen and dining are downstairs. Gathering room is at the front. It's the one with the big bay window."

"Gathering room?"

"It has a nice ring, don't you think? 'Cuz we don't really live there and we're not exactly a family, you know? But we do gather there for group therapy and stuff . . ."

The girl goes on and on about schedules and sessions and anger management and mindfulness exercises and chores and homework. I'm more overwhelmed with every word and I haven't even gotten dressed yet. I hold my head between my hands, thoughts swimming toward that familiar spiral again.

"Hey." The girl kneels beside me, placing a hand on the bed inches from my knee. She doesn't touch me this time, and I am grateful for the respect of personal space. "I talk too much, I'm sorry. It's . . . the only way I know how to distract myself, you know?"

My shoulders relax and the spiral slows. I do know. I swallow. "I'm Brooke." I stand, fighting the cold that seems to grow from the inside out.

"See, you're adjusting already. That wasn't so hard, was it?" She sits on the bed and pulls some of my blanket over her legs. "Call me Hope." A striking grin grows across her porcelain features, lifting the freckles on her cheeks to her salted-sea eyes. "I prefer to go by my middle name, if you don't mind. One of the few things I can control around here. Plus, every time someone says my name, I remember I don't have an excuse to give up, you know?" She winks.

Before I know what's happening, my throat constricts and my eyes burn. The sudden swell of emotion comes uninvited. This girl is trying so hard to be nice. All I want to do is tell her to go. Leave. And don't come back.

"Look, Hope? I appreciate you wanting to help me, but seriously, you're, what? Eleven?"

"And a half." She rises. Crosses her arms over her chest once more.

I roll my eyes. "Yeah, well, same difference. Anyway, I'm seventeen, so we probably aren't even in the same group. You're a kid. You don't have a clue what real problems are yet." Why did I say that? Where did that come from? Am I really such a witch?

Her expression shifts from amused to shell-shocked. She finds her way to the door. "You're mean."

Now it's my turn to be shell-shocked. At least she's honest. "Yeah. I guess I am." I've accepted my story. She should accept hers as well.

Hope grazes the doorframe with her fingertips. Then she says the last thing I'd ever expect. "I'm sorry. For whatever happened to you. I'm sorry."

The apology I don't deserve stirs me. This kid is something else. This place. I don't dare hope it might be different too.

When she's out of sight, I bolt for the door and shut it. Slide down the length of it until I'm hugging my knees again.

Wish granted. I wanted to be alone.

So why, then, do I wait? Listening intently for Hope's too-young-to-understand footsteps to return?

THREE

Merrick

This was total and complete capital *B* capital *S* if someone asked Merrick.

Which no one ever did.

He'd been arguing with his father for the past ten minutes. An argument that had taken a one-way train to nowhere.

Why couldn't the man get it through his head? Nikki Owens was great. *Perfect*, Merrick believed, was the word she often used to describe herself. She wasn't wrong.

Confidence was a rare trait. She was smart too. She *was* perfect.

Just not perfect for *him*.

Not that such a thing existed. Did he know what he wanted? What he sought in a relationship? To be honest, Merrick didn't have any life goals in general. He'd graduated last year and hadn't filled out a single college application.

"You're going. That's final." His father didn't even bother to set down his copy of the *Wall Street Journal* as he said it.

Typical Dad. CEO of the big-shot company everyone was talking about. San Francisco's golden boy and everyone's most likely to succeed.

"I'm not." Merrick was eighteen. His father couldn't tell him what to do. Besides, it wasn't as if he needed to please his dad to protect anyone these days. His sister, Amaya, was tackling fifth grade like a boss, already taking a few middle school classes, well past her juvenile peers in, well, everything. She was good. His mom smiled more now. They were 90 percent okay.

"You are." This time his father peered at him over the top of his paper. His obsidian eyes stared right through Merrick, disdain apparent across his stoic brow.

Merrick crossed his arms. Leaned back against the frame of the arch separating the formal dining room from the modern kitchen, all sharp angles and black granite countertops. An oval mirror on the opposite wall reflected back what he didn't care to see.

He was the spitting image of the man he couldn't stand. Narrow gaze as dark but not as cruel. Black hair. Attenuated jaw. Eyes that tapered on either end. But this was where their similarities died.

"Oh," Merrick replied. "But I'm not."

His father heaved a sigh. Folded his paper in that precise way of his. Intertwined his fingers on the antique oak table before him. "Oh, but you are."

It was a stare-down. And Merrick was determined to come out the champion. He refused to let his father control him for one more day. "Nikki and I have nothing in common."

"Except, you do. I am in the process of merging with her father's company. Now, her father has been"—he steepled his fingers and tapped them against the cleft in his chin—"difficult. He's not so sure about the merger. He's resisting. He thinks he can continue to 'make it' on his own. I am trying to correct that serious error in judgment. And the shareholders are watching."

Merrick rolled his eyes. Ah, the shareholders. How could he forget about *them*? As the founder of one of the most successful tech companies on the West Coast, his father should have felt accomplished. He was right up there with Apple and Google, for goodness' sake. Merrick thought his father would retire when he reached the top. Go fishing or something. Join a fantasy football club.

Yeah, right. Nothing was ever good enough for this man. *More* was his favorite word. Anything less was settling. And the man didn't settle. The idea wasn't in his vocabulary.

"I don't give a rip about your business deals." Merrick scooted to the left, just enough so the mirror no longer reflected his scowl. "Get one of your interns to take her out. I'm done playing your corporate mind games." He would pay for that one. His father might cut off his allowance for a week. So what? He had seventeen years of the man's garbage. Merrick had no problem paying a fine if it meant putting the dictator in his place.

His father's jaw worked, the muscle in his right cheek twitching. But he remained calm, which made it worse. Nothing seemed to faze him during their arguments. No matter how hard Merrick tried to solicit a reaction, to get him to care, the man remained placid as ever. Maybe if he could provoke him to get physical, just once, he'd—

"Need I remind you that *you* should be one of my interns? I offered an apprenticeship the day you graduated, but you refused and spent the entire summer partying. You don't deserve to set foot in this house after you squandered your graduation gift."

"Give me what's mine and I'll leave." The challenge was one Merrick had offered a thousand times over.

"The money I've saved for you is meant to be invested. In school. In your future." His father's single arched brow was a challenge all its own. "After your recent behavior I cannot, in good conscience, give you a dime until you start acting more responsibly."

He was stuck. A rat in his trap. His father wanted control. Power. Why would Merrick enroll in school and waste money on courses that might not apply five or ten years down the road? He was doing his father a favor by taking time to figure things out.

"Nikki fancies you." The man's change to the original subject interrupted Merrick's thought train. "She is her father's weak spot. And you are hers." He glanced at his watch. "A car will be here in . . . twenty-nine minutes to retrieve you. I suggest you be ready on time." With a firm glare, he resumed his paper perusal. "Put on an ironed shirt.

Maybe a clean pair of slacks? I'm sure that's a lot to ask, considering, but I have faith you can accomplish as much."

Merrick had half a mind to stand there. To wait and see what might happen if he was not, in fact, on time. If he didn't bother to change at all. But then his mother entered the room.

And everything altered.

"You boys getting along, Hiro?" She called his father by the shortened version of his first name—Hiroshi—taking her place behind him. She rubbed his shoulders.

The sight made Merrick physically ill.

His father was a villain. To call him "hero" sounded wrong.

Hiroshi patted her freckled hand and the stoicism melted away. Merrick's mother was the only one who inspired the man to feel something other than disdain.

Merrick shoved his hands into the pockets of his two-day-old jeans and clenched his fingers.

"Yes, of course, Lyn." His father cleared his throat. His tone softened. "We were discussing a certain date with a certain daughter of Marcus Owens."

The setting sunlight shone through the western window of their house. Merrick's mom blushed at the exact moment the rays hit her cheeks. Her strawberry freckles, the same shade of her hair and eyelashes, seemed to catch fire. "Nikole?" The way his mom said Nikki's name made her sound not so bad. "She's lovely. Where are y'all going?" His mother's southern accent slipped through her syllables as it so often did.

His father eyed him and Merrick cleared his throat. "Gary Danko."

She arched a brow. "Do you have a reservation?"

Merrick wasn't much of a planner, and Mom probably suspected he'd dropped the ball on this one.

She knew him too well.

"I took care of it." His overly organized father patted her hand again. A seemingly kind gesture, but one that would lead to manipulation.

If tonight went poorly, his father would find a way to blame her. She was too soft on Merrick, Hiroshi would say. He would beat her down with his words until she eventually became little more than a puddle of tears in the bathroom. Never screaming. But quiet condescension was worse.

Merrick clenched his fists again, this time so hard he could feel the white reach his knuckles.

He hated that sound. The sound of the heartbroken sobs she tried to hide beneath the noise of a running shower. It had been months since he'd heard it, but he would do anything to avoid it, even if it meant bending to his father's will. Again.

The man checked his custom-made Rolex for the second time. "Twenty-two minutes now, Son. Gary Danko will wait for no man. You'd better get changed."

Merrick did as he asked, though his teeth grated and his stomach turned.

Because Mom was right there. Her presence blurred his vision, made him lower his guard. One minute he was drowning, sinking into the whirlpool his shark of a father created every time they spoke.

Then his mother was there, drawing him back out again.

Of the four of them, she was the smartest, the most clever.

She was the one who taught him that if he wanted to avoid the sharks, his only salvation, his only escape, was to swim. Not away but with. Side by side until, eventually, they considered you an equal.

If he wanted to defeat a shark, Merrick would first have to be one.

He swallowed his protests as he trudged upstairs to his room. He found his clean slacks but refused to iron them. Rolled up the sleeves of his collared shirt to his elbows, if only because his father thought the look was lazy. Merrick threw his blazer over one shoulder and checked himself in the mirror.

"We'll see who gets bitten first."

FOUR

Coral

The night's quiet stung, waking her. Sometimes silence was the loudest sound of all.

Coral sat up in bed and tucked her mess of hair behind her ears, only to have it float stubbornly back in her face. She spied Jordan through the darkness. Her sisters must have heard the music at the surface too. Had it moved them the way it had Coral?

She wanted to ask.

She didn't dare.

Her birthday fast approached. She needed to decide what she would perform. Coral would be safe with Father's favorite, of course. A haunting melody that drew the sailors in. But every time she opened her lips to begin the first note, it stuck in her throat.

Coral peered at Jordan again. Sound asleep. What could it hurt?

The tune from the surface found its way deep into the place where her soul would be if she possessed one. It rose up and out, caressing Coral's tongue. Vibrating across the plane of her lips as a gentle hum. The song soothed her fears for the crown princess in a way nothing else had. It made her feel . . .

Warm. Real. Human.

She let the song die as quickly as it had begun. Treachery. What would her father think? Coral's insides mixed with guilt as her gaze found Jordan again.

Her middle sister was none the wiser to the little mermaid's moral dilemma. Jordan was sound asleep on her pallet, her chest rising and falling, mimicking a steady, rolling wave.

Why must Coral hear every swish of a fin or release of a bubble within a league of the palace walls?

A stingray of jealousy speared her straight in the chest as she watched Jordan dream without a care or worry in the sea. Jordan was a true example of what their father wanted in a daughter.

Coral lay back down and closed her eyes. Forced calm and exhaustion into her bones. *One angelfish, two angelfish, three angelfish, four . . .*

Her eyelids snapped up.

Then down.

Then up again.

For the love of pearls, why is it so quiet?

This time when she sat up, Coral flung her seaweed covers off her tail. If she couldn't sleep, she might as well embrace it. She swam to her sister and hovered above her for a beat.

"Jordan." Coral's whisper, the color of an ombre sunset, was the only sound aside from Jordan's steady breathing, which released in flashes of dulled light. "Jordan, are you asleep?"

Jordan didn't move. Not so much as a stir or a roll or a wiggle. She slumbered as if anchors weighted her eyelids. Her delicate hands rested over her middle. Long eyelashes never fluttering.

"Well, Sleeping Beauty . . ." Coral's words brushed the space above Jordan. "I guess it's me, myself, and I."

When Coral was certain Jordan wouldn't notice her absence—which meant she wouldn't tell Father—she moved to the door and grabbed her kelp shawl off a hook on her way out.

The deep greens of seaweed and sea grass produced the same notes. Not a waltz or an upbeat melody. More reminiscent of the droning processional of a mermaid on the wave to her grave.

The dank and quiet corridor sent a shudder up her spine, only adding to the deathly feeling draping her frame. A single lantern fish guarded each alcove she passed. Ugly, mute creatures, and the lot of them blind. Their glow let off just enough light so she could navigate the darkness.

The light did little to make up for their eerie presence.

Coral wrapped her shawl tightly around her shoulders and turned a corner, listening for any sound of life within the palace walls. Something was missing, but what? It wasn't that she heard noises at night. But now the lack of whatever she didn't hear set her on edge.

She rounded another corner and hesitated. The future queen's private chambers loomed before her. The majesty of the entrance alone intimidated the fibers beneath Coral's scales. The arch towered, the surrounding walls inlaid with pearls and sea glass and other natural sea stones. Curtains waved through the water like jellyfish tentacles, inviting her in and warning her to stay away at once.

Coral's chambers would never look so grand or lavish. She didn't mind, of course. Something about luxury made her feel smaller, less. Would she ever shine as brightly as the crown her sister was destined to wear?

What am I doing here? It's late. The crown princess will be asleep. It would be rude to wake her.

Coral bit the inside of her cheek. Hesitated. Now that she floated inches away from her sister's quarters, the absence of what had vanished was a shipwreck. Shattered. Broken.

The crown princess wasn't here.

Coral could almost hear it. The lack of her sister's breathing. The absence of her soothing presence. Her momentary inexistence stopped Coral's heart and shot lightning through her nerves.

Her stomach turned twice over. She swallowed the putrid taste of polluted water that suddenly filled her mouth. She scrunched her nose and rubbed it hard to rid herself of the sour scent. Without another thought, Coral crossed the threshold and entered the room.

Moonlight glimmered in watery waves, spilling over the seabed like pearls in the sand. The first princess's pallet was empty, the covers perfectly laid, though it was well past the midnight hour.

And then a sob harpooned the night.

Coral followed the sudden sound to the archway leading onto the balcony. A winding staircase that once belonged to a thriving, above-water metropolis rose to the surface. Chunks of steps had been broken away as if bitten off by a sea monster. Coral imagined for the tiniest inkling of a second she was a human girl with long, slender legs, gracefully taking each step. Where would she walk? To whom might she run?

Coral swam farther. Faster. A sudden vision captured her. There, at the crest of the stairs where she supposed something grand must have stood. She pressed toward her sister, pausing only a moment for fear she might scold Coral for surfacing before her birthday.

When Coral's face greeted the air, she blinked away ocean droplets and looked up at her sister's face.

The crown princess sat on the broken staircase's ledge, which looked more like a jagged rock piercing the surface than a forgotten piece of a lost city. Her tail bobbed, half in and half out of the sea. She sobbed again and her shoulders shook.

When Coral floated closer, her ears picked up her sister's muffled words.

"My prince never loved me," she said. "He never will."

Her *prince*? Her sister had fallen in love with a prince?

Theirs was the only merdom for thousands of nautical miles. When would she have met a merman from another—

Coral gasped and placed her fingers to her lips. *No.* Her sister *wouldn't.* She *couldn't.* Coral refused to entertain the idea further.

She reached to touch the crown princess, but her hand fell shy of her sister's exposed scales. She removed her shawl and drifted nearer. "Sister." Draping the shawl over her sister's lap, Coral placed her hand there to rest. The situation invited both foreign and familiar feelings.

With her tail covered, the future queen appeared almost human. "Is everything all right?" Coral asked.

Another sob released, this one slow and shuddering. "All right." She patted Coral's hand. But she didn't make eye contact. "Yes, Sister. I'm fine. Okay."

All right. Okay. Fine. Empty words with empty meanings. Words Jordan had said were the quintessence of a mermaid's vocabulary.

"The more you say them, the truer they become," she told Coral for years. *"If you say you're okay, then you are. If you voice you are fine, what's to stop you from being so?"*

Coral had challenged Jordan's view.

"But," she asked the first time Jordan said this, *"what if I'm not fine? What if I'm not . . . okay?"* Coral bit her tongue after the questions spilled forth. Hearing them aloud made them sound ridiculous somehow, though she couldn't pinpoint why.

Jordan glared through the mirror's glass.

At the time Coral squirmed in place, a hooked worm.

Jordan swam to her side, patted her twelve-year-old head. More akin to slaps than kind reassurances, her pats stung. *"There, there, sister dear,"* she crooned. *"We don't speak about such things."*

And they didn't. Ever again. Still, Coral wondered . . .

Did speaking a word to the outside truly change what took place within?

She circled the crown princess now so she could view her fully. The moon washed her sister's Abyss-black hair in an ethereal glow. Coral's vision shifted and the shadows around them altered. For a moment she saw her oldest sister as she had been in their younger years. Sweetly smiling. Rarely bothered by anything.

Now her sister appeared sunken. Her lips relayed she was okay. But her face?

Her face was one belonging to a poor, tortured soul.

Except mermaids didn't have souls.

So why, then, did the emotion behind her sister's expression suggest otherwise?

Coral caressed the crown princess's pale hand as if it were fashioned from sea glass. She squeezed it and her sister's lashes lowered. They stayed there for a moment, just the two of them. When her sister opened her gemstone eyes, she looked straight into Coral's. The crown princess blinked rapidly, and that's when Coral saw it.

A single tear, pooling in the corner of one eye.

Coral backed away and their hands disconnected. She shook her head. "Sister . . ." She had no words. Mermaids *could not* cry. They had no tears to shed. This was impossible. Unfathomable.

Unless . . .

What if the Disease . . .

Could the Disease make a mermaid . . .

Human?

Another shiver racked Coral's being. She swallowed, focused on her sister, studying the way the tear doubled in size, then slipped silently down her cheek and over her delicate jaw.

The crown princess's brows were knit and scrunched, her tail trembling beneath the shawl.

"My prince never loved me," she whispered again. "He never will."

Coral's chest tore in two at the shadowed sound of her brokenhearted words. "Sister . . ." She licked her lips and consumed her fear. Waves lapped against her neck and her hair floated around her. Maybe her sister was referring to Father. He was a prince once, after all. "Father loves you. He means well, he—" Coral couldn't finish the sentence.

The crown princess tilted her head to face Coral. "Not Father."

"Who then?"

"You wouldn't understand. You're too young. What I've done . . . It's forbidden. Now Red Tide comes," she said. "It seeks out those like us."

Coral winced. "Us?"

Her sister cupped her cheek with one palm. "You have remained the sweetest of us three, Coral. The most sensitive. If you are not careful, you will fall prey to the Disease as I have."

"But what if—"

The crown princess hushed Coral again with a single finger to her lips. She shook her head. "I know what you're thinking. Nothing can be done for me now. Red Tide is . . . inevitable."

Coral's lower lip quivered. Why did she feel six instead of nearly sixteen? "You can fight it." Her statement was a plea. *Please fight it, Sister. I can't lose you.* She blew her hair from her eyes, too desperate to bother hiding the fact she had eavesdropped on her sister's earlier conversation. "I know things with Father are tense, but—"

"Tense?" The hollow sound of her sister's laugh caught in her throat. "There is so much you don't know, Coral. Nothing can be done. Father would banish me if he knew. I welcome Red Tide. It's an easier fate than what he would plan."

"No!" Coral's soft cry became a full-on yelp. "I won't let it take you! We will go to Father together. Whatever you've done cannot be as bad as you claim."

Coral's throat tightened. She couldn't find words fitting for the moment. If her sister had lost her hope, what could Coral say to help her find it? She swallowed. "Red Tide. Will. Not. Take. You." Each syllable required extreme effort. "It can have me, but it cannot have you."

"I am afraid"—her sister swept away a lock of hair that had been stuck to Coral's forehead—"you do not have a choice."

Coral's eyes burned, but no tears released. The tear her sister shed had long since dried, but a trail down one side of her face left its mark.

The tear had been real.

When the someday queen placed her arm around Coral's shoulders and drew her in, holding her the way she had so many years ago, the little mermaid wished on every sea star in the ocean that she could cry as humans did.

Perhaps her sister was right. Perhaps Red Tide was inevitable.

Her own hope sank. Was she foolish to believe their curse might be cured or controlled?

"Promise me something." Slender fingers stroked Coral's hair, running through the tangles and loosing them with tiny tugs.

Coral nodded into her sister's embrace. She usually possessed more words than anyone. Now she felt as hollow as an abandoned crab shell.

"If you ever find love, *true* love, hold on to it."

Coral gulped against the lump lodged in her throat. "Why?"

"Because," her sister breathed. "True love makes life, even a broken one, worth fighting for."

Coral turned her face into her sister's shoulder and inhaled her saltwater taffy scent, unsure how to respond or what to ask. Coral's pulse *thump, thump, thumped* against her skin. She wished the sound wasn't so red.

Red brought heartbreak. Red brought doom.

"True love is a rare treasure, as mysterious and unfathomable as life on land." The crown princess tilted Coral's chin with one finger so they were eye to eye again. "But do not be deceived. Not all who claim to love truly do. Be wary to give your heart away, lest it be tossed into the Abyss, never to beat again."

Her words began to piece together in Coral's mind.

"My prince never loved me. He never will."

Coral wanted to shake her sister out of her current state. To assure her that whoever did not love her did not matter as much as the mermaid floating before her now.

Coral's love was true. And nothing could change that.

"I love you, Sister." Why did her words sound halfhearted on her lips? Was it that fear kept her from speaking the mermaid's true name?

Coral opened her mouth to do so. She wanted nothing more than to honor and acknowledge her sister in this way, even if no one else would.

But the crown princess pressed a finger to Coral's lips. "I know." She didn't say Coral's love was not enough. She didn't have to.

"How do you know so much about true love?" Maybe the more Coral knew, the closer she would come to saving her. To saving them both.

"The Sorceress of the Sea told me."

Coral shuddered, but the spasm had nothing to do with the chill of the night air against her clammy skin. They'd heard the tale since they were old enough to swim on their own. Jordan used it to scare Coral before she went to sleep at night. And their father mentioned it to keep his princesses from venturing too far past their bounds. The waters they resided in were tame, with rarely a predator to be seen. Close enough to the shore, but not too close. Far enough out, but not too far. Too far would be the difference between tame and treacherous.

Deep in the darkest depths, near the Abyss where bones collect, lies the cavern of the Sorceress of the Sea. Wickedly clever, the Sorceress is tormented with more emotion than ten humans combined. It is because of this she rarely ventures from her lair. And why she invites those from the outside to become entrapped within her tentacle-like lies.

Mermaids before you have sought her out for knowledge. They seek answers beyond what they have been given. They search for a way to escape Red Tide.

There is no escape, of course. The Sorceress enjoys deception. She would have naïve little mermaids believe she alone holds the power to provide a cure, an end to the curse. The Sorceress claims power is found within her soul, the soul she does not possess. She would tell you human tears are healing, when in truth they are a sorcery of their own. Tears are what separate us from humans. Without them we are safely stored within ourselves.

Without them we are safe.

Without them we remain forever strong.

42

Coral blinked at the memory of the grim tale. The crown princess had tears, or at least one. Did this make her weak?

Or could the Sorceress—should she exist—have it right? What if human tears could heal her sister? What if the more she shed, the closer she'd come to escaping Red Tide for good?

"Have you chosen your song yet?"

An inward moan came to full fruition. "Why does it matter what I sing?"

"A mermaid's song is her life," the crown princess said. Did she believe her own words? They sounded forced, practiced, and not at all genuine. "Sing something for me."

Coral's eyes widened. "I'm not allowed. Not until I'm sixteen."

Her sister chuckled. Shrugged. "Father isn't here. Please? Sing one tune before—"

Her words sank. But she didn't need to speak them for Coral to know where they were headed.

Before. Red Tide. Came.

The ocean lapped against their tails, which bobbed in contrast to one another. The future queen's a deep-sea emerald. Coral's as bright as the warm-water reef.

She sighed.

Her sister nudged her.

Coral blew at her hair again and mentally flipped through the list of approved song choices. Nothing struck her. She didn't want to sing. But she needed to offer her sister something. So she closed her eyes and described the world as she saw it. The words came out on their own rhythm, with a cadence that belonged to Coral alone. A poem of her own creation.

"Red is the sun as it bathes in blue,
Green are the waters when the sky is new,
Yellow is the sand, far out as we can see,
Violet are the eyes of curiosity."

She waited for her sister to respond. To say . . . something. But her eyes were closed. Her calm expression assured Coral she was taking in every word. So the little mermaid continued . . .

"Red sounds a warning, a light I wish would fade.
Green sings a hymn, a harmony of jade.
Yellow squeals of laughter, violet hums of you.
The colors of my world paint my heart sky-blue."

Though Coral's words did not carry on the waves of melody, they were hers. Something Father could not take and Jordan could not control.

"Lovely." Her sister exhaled the word and Coral soaked it in. Then her sister began to sob once more.

"What is it?" Coral asked.

The crown princess shook her head. Before she said anything, Coral knew. She felt it in the way her sister shut down, distancing herself again. "Let Red Tide come for me quickly." She balled up the shawl and shoved it into Coral's arms. With a kiss to her forehead she added, "I refuse to watch it come for you too."

Then she dove. Vanished. For a moment there and at once gone.

Thunder boomed above, warning a storm brewed behind a curtain of clouds.

An invisible anchor confined Coral to her spot on the ledge. She could not move.

"I am alone," she whispered. "Alone . . ."

And Diseased.

FIVE

Brooke

After

Hope does not return.

Do I sit here? Wait for someone to get me? An instruction manual might've helped. Or a schedule. I rise and dress and make my bed. The result is sad, showing no real effort on my part. What's the point of making a first impression when I don't plan on staying long enough to make a second?

A glance at the desk reveals a subtle change. How did I fail to notice Hope had opened the journal? Placed a black pen over the front page? Did she write these words? They slant and flow, waves moving across the top line.

"Life itself is the most wonderful fairy tale."

—Hans Christian Andersen

Pretty writing for an eleven-year-old. The quote is one I've seen many times. Written in glittery paint or plastered onto whimsical memes.

I scowl, snap the cover closed. "What a load of—"

"Making yourself comfortable?"

I whirl, knocking the journal off the desk in the process. It hits the floor with a *thud*, the cover resting open again, mocking me.

"On behalf of Fathoms Ranch, I am pleased to welcome you." The woman standing before me is short, with a kind face and piercing ocean-green eyes. Tattoos climb in sleeves up both her toned arms. She wears sweats, a tank top, despite the fact it's winter, and a ball cap that says "Boss."

"My name is Miss Jacobs, but everyone here calls me Jake."

And I care, why?

"And you are?"

"Don't *you* know?"

"I do but I'm a sucker for proper introductions. I'm sure you understand."

Everything in me wants to come up with something smart or quick in return. Instead, I frown in a moment so anticlimactic, I wish I wasn't part of it. "I'm Brooke, I guess."

"You guess?" Jake steps toward me, picks up the journal, and sets it on the desk, care and purpose driving her every move. "That's perfect, actually. Because it is my job to help you know. To help you discover who you truly are. If given a chance, you'll find this place is incomparable to any other."

I eye her up and down. "I seriously doubt that."

"Fair enough."

"That's it?"

"For now."

Who is this lady? Does Jake think she can trick me into believing she's my friend? "I only agreed to come here because—"

Because why? Because I had nowhere else to go? Because I knew it would make the only person who ever cared for me happy?

I can't fill in my own blank. I drop my gaze, inviting an awkward silence.

"I've been filled in on your backstory," Jake says softly. "I'd prefer to hear you tell it, though, when the timing's right."

I look up. Blink. Why is she being so nice when I've been nothing but rude? This is too much.

"We'll go over the details of your day-to-day routine once you're settled." She eyes the untouched food tray on my bed. "Eating is a requirement here. A pesky rule, I know, but an important one."

"I'm not hungry." My words hang in the air.

"You will be." Jake pivots on her heel and returns the way she came. When she pauses at the door she adds, "Kitchen's downstairs. Mary's a whiz when it comes to finding your stomach's weakness. Ten bucks says you don't stand a chance against her double-fudge brownies."

"I don't have ten bucks."

"Doesn't matter." Jake shrugs. "Loser pays in bites. You finish a brownie and your debt's as good as paid."

This doctor? . . . Nurse? . . . Therapist? . . . Whatever her occupation, she's something else. Is she playing games to get me to confide?

Could she be the real deal?

Nah. No such thing. Learned that the hard way.

"Brownies." She points at me. Rude. "You won't regret it." Another fake smile spreads across her face. "Group dish starts in T-minus thirty minutes." She holds up her phone and shows me the time. "Bring your journal. Schedule is on the bulletin board in the hall. Familiarize yourself with it. You'll get a copy in your packet during our one-on-one this afternoon." She pockets her phone and begins jogging in place, salutes, then she's gone.

Dish? One-on-one? Am I on an episode of reality TV? The care-free terms don't fool me. I know all about group therapy and private counseling sessions.

This is going to be a long afternoon.

It takes me five minutes to run a brush through my hair, throw on some modest makeup, and head out the door. I'll bet brownies are code for pills or something. This Mary person probably administers medication.

I'm halfway down the stairs when—*shoot*—I realize I forgot the journal. I ignore the urge to return for it. What's the big deal? Jake may think I'll have some thoughts to write down, some precious gems to take away from a most enlightening encounter with my depressed and suicidal peers. She needs a reality check.

I don't need a notebook when I have nothing worth saying. Not anymore. To write words that matter, you need something I don't have. Not even Jake with her tough-chick tattoos or that Hope girl with her fake friendship is going to find what's not there.

They can try, but one day with me and they'll see.

Nothing there. Nothing left. Nothing to lose.

All the group therapy in the world—excuse me, *dishes*—eye roll—can't bring a person back from nothing.

When I'm alone in the kitchen, all I can think is that this is super weird and not at all what I expected, which makes me even more suspicious than I was before.

Hello, Sunshine. Did you get those curtains from Target? Because they sure are looking rather Joanna Gaines–approved if you ask me.

I take two steps into the space where Betty Crocker was clearly born and bred. Clean but cozy, with appliances on every surface and a trio of old milk-jug tins holding every spatula and wooden spoon the Pioneer Woman ever made. There are, however, no knives. Surprised? I'm not.

"Anyone here?"

No one answers.

I scoot closer to the kitchen island, eye the cake stand displaying a mountain of brownies beneath a glass dome. It calls to me from its place at the center of the granite countertop. No lineup of pills in medicine cups the way you see in movies. No person in scrubs distributing doses or making notes on a clipboard, watching, waiting for you to swallow and checking under your tongue. Just the brownies and the dull scent of something sweet and fruity wafting from a wax warmer by the window.

Weird.

I make a move to retreat when someone brushes past me. Her nearness makes me flinch, but the light touch isn't enough to warrant going into panic mode.

"Sorry, hon, had to feed the dogs." A tiny woman shorter than I am scurries into the kitchen, washes her hands, then dries them on the dish towel hanging from the oven handle. In one move she swoops her waist-length blond hair into a knot atop her head. Next she ties a half apron over her faded ripped jeans. She's barefoot. The absolute definition of a hot mess. But there's still something so . . . together about her. As if the mess is on purpose and she'd rather keep it that way, thank-you-very-much.

A tattoo below the inside of her wrist says one word that seems to encompass her entire persona.

breathe.

Though the word isn't capitalized and bears a period at the end, it seems profound—once again, a mess on purpose. I open my mouth to ask her about it.

But then she beams at me and I freeze. I'm inclined to resume my backward pace but remember Jake's insistence that I try a brownie. I'm not sure what will happen if I don't. And better a brownie than another gross tuna salad sandwich.

So I opt for a lighter, easier topic. One that won't involve getting to know this woman who will control my food intake for the next however many days.

She mentioned dogs, right? I've never had a dog. Still, the question is easy. Small-talkish and surfacey. "What kinds of dogs do you have here?"

Hot Mess brushes a stray hair from her eyes with the back of her wrist and sets to removing bowls and pans from the cupboards, then proceeds to gather ingredients from the walk-in pantry.

"Goldendoodles, of course," she calls over her shoulder, arms full of baking supplies. "Is there any other kind?" She laughs at her own joke as she takes a carton of eggs from the fridge. Before she closes the door she asks, "Do you want milk with your brownie?" assuming I was planning on having one.

I stare at her far too long for this to be considered an awkward silence. But she just smiles, as if this quiet between us is the most natural thing in the world.

"Do you have almond milk?" The ten bucks Jake bet says they don't. Because that would be a special request.

"Coming right up." She reaches so deep into the massive fridge, the image is somewhat laughable. Stretching on her toes to rearrange containers and bottles, jugs and cartons, she looks more like a little kid than the person in charge of the menu.

"Mary?" The name Jake mentioned surfaces. "Your brownies are double-fudge."

"Yes, they are!" After pulling out a carton of vanilla almond milk— not the off-brand either—she grabs me a glass and fills it halfway. "It's my grandmother's recipe." She pulls the cake stand to the edge of the counter, removes the dome, and sets the biggest brownie on a napkin.

"Oh." A glance toward the clock with coffee cups for numbers and spoons in place of hands tells me I'm going to be late. Not that I care about Jake's schedule, but I also don't want to be the last person to arrive. New introverted girl plus awkward grand entrance do not mix. "Can I take this to-go?"

"Of course!" Mary sets the glass and brownie directly in front of me. "And when you fall head over heels for the chocolaty goodness, which you totally will, FYI, you can come back and get another during downtime."

I wait for her to say more. To tell me it's time for my medication. For there to be some kind of hook to her happily-ever-brownie story. But she resumes her hustle and bustle, then asks a little speaker at one corner of the counter to play the ultimate boy band playlist. The speaker responds with the phoniest love song ever. The singer is a guy, apologizing for breaking some girl's heart.

Classy.

I say nothing as I maneuver around the extra-long dining table and through the rest of the lower floor. Voices carry from a room down the hall. I shove a bite of brownie in my mouth, wishing it didn't taste so bland, and shuffle toward the noise. A giant sliding barn door waits to be moved. I steal a breath, swallow my bite, and slide the barrier aside.

Ten other girls ranging from Hope's age to mine chatter within. Three near the overstuffed bookcase, two on the cushioned window bench, and the remainder spaced across two sectional couches. Lamps on several surfaces emit warm light while a glass pitcher of cucumber water calls my name.

Where's the circle of cold metal chairs? What happened to anxious and stoic expressions? Don't these girls know this "dish" will be jotted and recorded, and whatever they say can and will be used against them in the court of their assigned therapist? How long did it take for Jake to brainwash them into thinking therapy helps and heals?

And how long before she tries to do the same to me?

Newsflash, *Miss Jacobs*. I've been around the psychoanalysis block before. There's no such thing as "better."

There is before.

And there is after.

The.

End.

SIX

Merrick

He couldn't deny it. Nikki looked *good.*

Merrick allowed his gaze to run over her toned legs and arms. Bronze, smooth, you name it. The heiress of the Owens estate had it all. She showed enough skin to make his pulse pound but hid the rest, leaving him to wonder . . .

Ugh. Stop, Merrick. She is not *an object. Plus, we have zilch in common aside from our extremely wealthy fathers. Get a grip, man.*

Still, how could he deny their physical chemistry? Their relationship was easy. Zero work involved.

"You look . . ." Hot? Pretty? Gorgeous? "Nice." He cleared his throat as he slid into the back seat beside her.

Nikki scooted across the leather bench. Her skirt rode up her thighs.

He cleared his throat again. That was two already. He ought to slow down if he was ever going to make it through the date.

The one he didn't want to go on.

Merrick gazed out the privacy glass window after glancing at her legs once more. *Do not be that guy. You're better than that. She deserves more.*

"Where to?" the driver asked from the front. A chauffeur's cap sat low over his eyes and black driving gloves covered his hands. His accent was difficult to place. Polish, if Merrick had to guess. If anything could be said well of his father, it was this—the man didn't discriminate against race, color, ethnicity. He hired based on merit. Prided himself on it too.

Good for you, Dad. Way to keep up those appearances.

Hiroshi loved to remind his son where they'd come from. Telling him how his Japanese great-grandparents pinched every penny and saved every dime for Hiroshi's future.

"They didn't have equal-opportunity employers back then," his father had said. *"Which is why our company will never discriminate."*

Bitterness coated Merrick's tongue and throat. The man had no problem with anyone, no matter where they hailed from or what they believed. But his own son? Merrick could do nothing right. How about an equal-opportunity father? Could he get one of those?

"Um, Mer?" Nikki's silky voice jerked Merrick from his internal stew.

They weren't moving. Why weren't they moving?

Ugh. Right. He leaned forward. "Gary Danko, please. Near Ghirardelli Square."

"I know the place, sir." The driver nodded. Then he pulled into traffic in one effortless glide.

Merrick sat back and relaxed. Clasped his hands behind his head.

"You spoil me." Nikki shifted. She placed a graceful hand on his knee and began tracing little circles with her long, pointed fingernail.

From the corner of his eye, Merrick glanced at her legs. Again. Her skirt had ridden higher. He closed his eyes. *Help me. Help me now.*

She scooted closer and leaned her head on his shoulder. Her dark, curly hair was soft against his cheek.

Merrick let one arm fall around her. Drew her near. Then he inhaled. What line were his mom and sister always quoting from that old Julia Roberts chick flick?

Big mistake. Huge.

He was a goner. Nikki smelled amazing, though he could never place the particular scent. Merrick turned his head. Nikki tilted her face toward his and they began their routine. They'd been here before. Tangled in too much emotion and desire to bother seeing they were completely wrong for one another.

But it felt good.

She felt good.

Merrick ignored the rising guilt. Shoved it out of sight and locked the door. Soon he didn't know where Nikki ended and he began.

Then again, he wasn't sure he ever knew where he began. So he welcomed her touch and tender kisses, not bothering to care how uncomfortable their driver must feel.

Uncomfortable was Merrick's life story. But this?

This was his escape.

This was how he kept his head above water.

When the car reached their final destination in under fifteen minutes, they unlocked lips.

"Your kisses always taste like the first," Nikki breathed.

He nodded but couldn't meet her eyes. He smoothed out his shirt, jacket, and pants while Nikki touched her face and tamed her beautifully wild hair. She closed her palm-size mirror, which served as Merrick's signal that it was safe to get out and open her door.

"We'll be a couple hours," he told the driver. When he attempted to slip the man a tip, the chauffeur waved him off.

"Already covered, sir." He tilted his hat. Adjusted his gloves. "Compliments of your father."

Of course. "Thank you . . . ?"

"Harold, sir."

"Thank you, Harold."

"It is my pleasure, sir."

When Merrick opened Nikki's door, she rose from the car. Practiced royalty. San Francisco's paparazzi princess.

He offered his hand.

Beaming, she took it but barely held on. When they were eye to eye, she kissed him tenderly on the cheek. So innocent. So different from the passion of moments before.

A flash to Merrick's right indicated some tabloid photographer had already spotted them, probably followed them over from Pacific Heights. Paparazzi regularly parked outside their iconic Victorian-style house. Then again, so did social media junkies—forever snapping selfies with the homes straight from old nineties TV shows. This was nothing new.

Nikki and Merrick turned on the charm and angled themselves so the photographer could get a better shot.

"You're so bad," Nikki mumbled under her breath. Then she kissed the spot below his jaw.

Snap, snap, snap.

He nuzzled her dark locks as they walked.

Click, click, click.

This was what his father wanted. For his son to be caught in public with Nikki—correction: *happy* Nikki—so her father would see the papers and social media posts and magazines and be all the more inclined to take Hiroshi's deal. Pictures didn't lie. Merrick's father could woo the CEO of Owens Industries into a merger all he wanted, but images of his daughter on the town with San Francisco's most eligible bachelor? Mr. Owens would see the companies were a perfect match.

Merrick loathed his father's game.

But here he was, playing it. Could he blame the man for his own choices?

"Are you cold?" Merrick whispered in Nikki's ear.

She shivered and nodded.

He removed his blazer and draped it over her glowing bare shoulders. When he led her inside the restaurant with his palm at the small of her back, a few more flashes blinded his peripheral vision.

"Merrick, table for two." He purposely avoided giving the hostess his last name. He hated admitting he was his father's son.

It didn't matter. Everyone knew anyway.

The hostess didn't look up but snatched two menus and led them into the establishment without a word. Her heels *click-clacked* while Nikki somehow managed to walk in her crazy-tall shoes soundlessly. When they reached their table, Merrick pulled out her seat, removed the blazer, and draped it over the back of her chair.

"Thank you." A satisfied blush colored her cheeks.

His stomach soured. This wasn't a stunt to her. "Of course." Merrick took his own seat and smoothed his expression.

Fake, practiced, concealing his shame.

"Your server will be right with you." The hostess pivoted and took her leave.

He'd been to Gary Danko a handful of times but never with Nikki. This was nice. For a minute, he forced himself to forget why he was here and focus on the company. The atmosphere. The high-dollar food they'd be consuming at zero cost to him.

Cost in dollars, anyway.

Beneath the table, Nikki slid her bare foot up his calf.

Be cool. Be cool. He took a deep breath, cleared his throat for the *third* time, and pretended not to notice. "You like risotto?"

She laughed and folded her hands so they concealed a portion of her face. Her doe eyes were the prettiest shade of copper. A man could get lost in those eyes.

As he all too often did.

"Risotto is so cliché," Nikki said.

Amused, Merrick leaned forward. "What would you propose?" He almost offered to take her for pizza, though he couldn't imagine Nikki eating with her hands.

But then she mentioned something about "endives" and "cardamom" and "foie gras" and his hope withered with his appetite. For a second he considered they might have something in common after all.

However, nothing surprised him. "Order whatever you wish," he said and placed his napkin in his lap.

Dad would be so proud. Merrick scowled. He could almost hear the nod of his father's approval beneath the yawn-fest background music.

Dinner was a blur of pretentious foods Merrick hated he knew how to pronounce and too-small portions with some fancy glaze and soufflés and champagne. (No such thing as underage when you had his name.) Merrick's favorite spot at Fisherman's Wharf distracted his thoughts—a place the opposite of Gary Danko. His father would have had a stroke if Merrick had taken the elegant Nikole Owens to get a cheap pretzel and Coke, then invited her to walk Pier 39 barefoot.

Maybe he should have done that after all.

Their usual lip-lock consumed the drive home. Merrick had been so engrossed in Nikki, at first he didn't notice the blue and red flashing lights outside his house.

But then he did notice, and everything else faded with the after-taste of champagne on his tongue.

He didn't feel Nikki squeeze his hand or hear her whisper "I love you" in his ear for the first time as he stumbled out of the car.

He didn't react to his mom's hysterical cries.

He didn't cringe at his father's emotionless expression.

The only thing Merrick saw was Amaya, pale and unmoving on a stretcher, her ginger locks matted to her temples and forehead.

Amaya, too small to fill the stretcher with her frame.

"Son, stay with your mother." His father placed a hand on his shoulder. "You two can ride down to UCSF Benioff Children's when she calms down."

Merrick jerked from his touch. Stumbled.

"Have you been drinking?" Hiroshi asked.

Merrick didn't answer. Instead, he staggered toward the stretcher. "Wait." He held up one hand as rain began to fall.

The paramedics halted, allowing him to see his sister before she was taken.

He uttered a single question through his teeth. The only question that mattered. "What did he do to her?"

The older paramedic returned the question with a furrowed brow.

His father had finally cracked. Finally stopped using his words to make Merrick's sister feel worthless. Now he'd shown his true colors.

Black-eye blue. Bruise purple. Blood red.

Merrick's taut arms and fists shook, his veins close to bursting. He would kill his father for this. He could report him at last. The cops couldn't do much for verbal and emotional abuse. But this? Amaya wasn't even eleven yet. They couldn't stop him from reporting it. Merrick was eighteen. Between him and Mom, his sister would be taken care of. Could this be the final straw that convinced her to leave his father for good?

He hoped so.

"What. Did. He. Do?" Merrick asked again. Cuts covered her arms. Some old. Some new. How long had this been happening? What kind of sick person would—

The paramedic shook his head. "I'm not sure what you mean." A pause. Then, "This was a suicide attempt. If not for your father, your sister would have died."

Merrick's jaw went slack. He examined Amaya more closely. The cuts . . . Most of them were . . . old. Scabbed and scarring. There were some fresh ones too, but nothing that appeared deadly.

He glanced at her right arm. A tight bandage covered a wide space between elbow and wrist. The bandage was soaked with blood and rain.

Suicide? Amaya? The girl who still wore pigtails and slept with a stuffed dog?

This didn't make sense.

He squeezed her freezing hand once, twice, three times. Then he backed away.

They lifted his unconscious sister into the ambulance and his father followed, stepping inside without glancing in his direction once.

Merrick's mother wailed again.

The doors slammed.

He wanted to scream. To pound on those doors until his fists bled.

But he didn't. He had to be calm, collected. If this was their chance to get away from his father, Merrick would have to remain cool.

He gazed up at his mother where she waited on the porch steps. She watched the ambulance as it raced away, sirens fading in the distance. She was no longer crying, just staring. Staring and unmoving. A marble statue, sunken to the bottom of the sea.

He took her hand and led her inside. She didn't say a word as he handed her a towel from the hall closet.

"Get changed, Mom. Maya needs us."

She nodded, looking right through him, and headed upstairs. Once she was out of view, Merrick paused, then did a quarter turn. From the family room, their lit Christmas tree stared back at him, the symbol of hope and light mocking him where he stood. The holiday was over, with New Year's mere hours away. But there would be no more celebration. No chorus of "Auld Lang Syne" or cheers when the ball finally dropped.

He walked to the tree and yanked the cord from the wall. Hard. Then he bolted back outside to let Harold know they'd be needing his services a little later than normal.

"Is Maya okay?" Nikki asked.

"She will be," Merrick said, pushing control into his voice.

Inside was a different story, though.

Inside raged a squall.

Inside, he was undone.

Who knew a person could drown without ever stepping foot off land?

SEVEN

Coral

Parties happened often in the winter palace.

Jellyfish-jar lanterns swung from thick ropes salvaged from sunken ships. Mirrored tabletops reflected the moonlight that shone down through the open rafters, and lavish foods richer than royalty filled every belly. The water smelled of tropical perfumes, imported from warmer waters. The music bore the colors of laughter while the tapestries sang of masked sorrows.

This was King Jonah's favorite game of pretend. Music. Dancing. Delicate foods too pretty to eat. Anything and everything he could use to distract them all from what awaited beneath the surface.

Their people were cursed.

And everyone was talking about it.

One might think after so long they'd grow tired of the same old gossip. But merfolk were nothing without their pristine memories and unrelenting reminders. They were a people divided.

Those who had avoided the Disease.

And those too weak to overcome it.

Coral pushed all thoughts of curious stares aside and tried to focus on this night. Her night. Her excited fins fluttered in synchronicity with her heart. She peered around the stone pillar. After what happened the other evening with the crown princess, Coral was sharp as a swordfish. Her muscles seemed to grate against her bones and her nerves electrified. She hadn't seen or heard her oldest sister since.

A shell horn sounded, announcing the arrival of another guest. "Presenting Lukiss and Laura Lye Dunes of the Northern Shore."

A couple swam forth beneath the main archway, hanging vines of ocean ivy parting in ripples at their entrance. The merman was somewhat slumped over, and a bored look washed his shadowed face. The merwoman was his opposite in every way. Though she showed no teeth, her amber eyes appeared to dance in time with the upbeat tempo of the orchestra. Even from this distance, Coral could hear the refrain those eyes produced—joy.

Emotion. Hidden there beneath the surface where no one wanted to look.

Coral inhaled a breath. Exhaled. A group of merboys and maids her age entered, which made her cheeks warm and her stomach backflip. Why did her father invite them? She didn't even know them. Not that things were much different back in their Atlantic merdom. Coral had never been one to fit in. East or west, north or south, she remained a mermaid out of water.

Once again she found herself wanting to cling to the one person she was most comfortable with. Coral scanned the room for her oldest sister. There must have been dozens of merfolk from every region of the Northern and Southern Shores. More boys than maids, she noticed.

Please don't tell me Father is already searching out a suitor for me.

She gasped, then hiccupped. He was. Why didn't Coral see the signs? His prodding, pushing her to make her debut? All those merboys she didn't know? He was presenting her. This party was more about finding her a match than it had ever been about her birthday.

Of course it was.

The crown princess remained nowhere to be found. Instead, Coral spotted Jordan. She twirled at the center of the sea glass–mosaic dance floor, wrapped in the arms of her chosen suitor, Duke. Neither appeared happy.

Coral was about to make her grand entrance when two familiar faces approached the pillar a few feet from her. Her two favorite mermaids in all the sea.

Coral moved to greet the future queen and their grandmother, thankful she could postpone introducing herself to a stranger for a few more fathoms. But then her sister said her name in a low tone and Coral whirled out of view. The mention was not directed in greeting.

She's talking about me. Curiosity won and she remained hidden.

"Coral knows now," the crown princess said. "I don't know what else to do, Grandmother."

"Your youngest sister is no threat. The question is, does your *father* know yet? Has he figured it out?" Their grandmother tasted her green jellied kelptini, her expression a mixture of amusement and grace.

"I don't think so." Her sister fiddled with the pearl bracelet on her wrist. Her downcast expression matched the inflection in her dreary voice. "But it's only a matter of time, Grandmother."

"You are right about that." Their grandmother had never been one to sail around uncomfortable situations. Now was no different. "Have you considered your options? You could come live with me."

The crown princess smoothed her scales. "I can't go back there. It's too much."

Go back where? What was she talking about?

"I understand." Their grandmother floated a few inches to her left, smiling and looking out at the ballroom. "I am here. I will even go with you to tell the king."

"Father would kill me before Red Tide ever got the chance." The crown princess hung her head.

Coral pressed her back against the stone, pulse pounding and mind racing faster than a runaway current. They stayed quiet for a spell, giving Coral a chance to calm her breathing and collect her scattered nerves. She examined her far-too-glittery skin and touched the updo she'd tried to achieve after Jordan didn't have time to help her get ready. Coral looked a fright. She had never been good at mermaid things—not the way her sisters were.

"Look," their grandmother continued. "Sometimes you have to swim through a bit of darkness . . ."

". . . if you're ever going to surface in the light." Her sister finished the mantra their grandmother often spoke to them. A scraped fin? A bruised scale? This was forever the remedy.

The crown princess laughed then and Coral relished the sound. When was the last time she'd heard her sister laugh?

"You are a captivating beauty," their grandmother said. "You will find love again. And your father will understand."

"And if he doesn't?" The one-day queen's voice rose, and a few dancers nearby stopped to stare. Her next words were softer but remained firm. "If he doesn't, I'll truly have nothing left."

Coral's heart skipped several beats before she found a way to breathe. Her sister's fear ran in scarlet ribbons across her vision. Coral wanted to grasp those ribbons, to rip them apart until her sister felt safe once more.

"You will have me. And your sisters." Taking time with her dessert, their grandmother took plenty of time with her words. To her, words held a magic far greater than anything the Sorceress of the Sea possessed. Finally, after what seemed the remainder of the evening had passed, she said, "I know your heart is broken right now, but have a little faith. Things will get better."

Eyes pleading with the merwoman who'd helped raise them, the crown princess sighed. "How can I have faith when I have seen firsthand what Father will do? If he knew I'd fallen for a human, and then that human abandoned me? He'd banish me to the Abyss."

Coral's fears were at last confirmed, and it was all she could do not to vocalize her internal moan.

"Remember," their grandmother said. "Swim through the darkness, find the light." She touched the crown princess's arm.

A lingering pause. A quick breath. A sigh. "Thank you, Grandmother. For listening."

"Think nothing of it. It is my privilege and my pleasure."

Her sister shifted and Coral mirrored her move, staying out of sight but close enough to catch her next whispered words. "Take care of Coral, okay?" A tear slipped free, falling fast down her right cheek. The crown princess erased it in a heartbeat.

Coral covered her mouth to stifle a gasp. Another tear? How was it even visible at these depths? Were tears so powerful they withstood even the mighty ocean waters?

Their grandmother didn't respond for a fathom. Coral couldn't see her face now, but she imagined her pondering expression. A mixture of darkened conflict worrying her brow and chin, singing the tune of the rolling fog on the water's surface in winter.

When she finally answered, she took a long, deep breath. Then, "I would not dream of doing anything to the contrary."

The crown princess bowed her head and left without another word or tear. Coral expected her to join the party, but instead her sister swam past a pair of palace guards, beyond the entry arch, and into the evening blue.

Coral watched the future queen, her gaze lingering on the arch long after she'd vanished. The little mermaid didn't move. Or blink.

Her sister was in love with a human?

She could hardly process it.

"You can come out now, Coral," her grandmother said, though she made no effort to look at her granddaughter over her shoulder.

The casual way she spoke didn't startle Coral. *How could I have thought she was unaware of my eavesdropping?*

The merwoman made it her job to keep up with the kingdom gossip.

"Good evening, Grandmother." Coral dipped her chin to her chest as she swam up beside her.

Her grandmother waved a waiter over. He nodded and produced a tray of delicacies full to the brim with more jellied kelptinis and a few whipped sunrise brûlées. The waiter handed Coral the latter and quickly swam on to the next group of guests.

She tasted a spoonful of the creamy, tangy concoction. The texture stuck to the roof of her mouth and eased down her throat. The overpowering sweetness of it made her queasy, so Coral resolved to hold the dessert, if only to keep her hands from fidgeting.

Grandmother nodded to a passing nobleman, who bowed his head in return. "Are you enjoying your party?" she asked Coral.

"Well enough." If "well" meant she'd rather be anywhere else.

"I expect you'd enjoy it more if you didn't spend so much time hiding."

The statement could have been harsh, but it wasn't. The sparkle in her grandmother's champagne eyes released a burst of harmonizing notes—encouragement. Understanding. Grace. She didn't mention Coral's oldest sister or bring up their conversation. This was her grandmother's way. She could be trusted with secrets. She would not betray any of her granddaughters by speaking of them behind their backs.

"I expect you're right," Coral said.

"Have you prepared your performance?"

Coral's rib cage closed in, squeezing her lungs and heart until they were ready to burst. *Breathe, Coral. You don't have to sing. Not yet. Maybe there's still a way out of it.*

"Father wants to match me tonight, doesn't he?"

Her grandmother turned to her then, placing her free hand on Coral's cheek and stroking it with a tender thumb. "We're all made for something. And you, my darling, have so much to give."

The answer wasn't an answer. Or maybe it was.

Coral studied her eyes. Her own burned and she blinked the sensation away. "What if I don't want to give it? Not this way—not to someone I do not love."

"If you ever find love, true love, hold on to it."

She clung to her oldest sister's words. There had been an urgency behind her gaze when she shared them. And something told Coral her sister had never shared this belief with anyone.

Which made those words of so much more value and worth than even the pearls adorning her waist.

"You'll find your voice, eventually." One more stroke against her cheek before her grandmother lowered her hand. "And the one who hears it? Who truly stops to listen? He'll be the finest match in all the oceans, won't he?" She winked and sipped her last drop. "Now then, this is a party. I suggest you find a nice young merman to ask you to dance." And just like that, her grandmother switched from profound wisdom-giver to carefree father-supporter.

Was it difficult for her? To have a son as gray as the king and a granddaughter as vibrant as Coral? To love and support them both when they were as different as land and sea?

"Go on," she urged, forehead wrinkles smoothing. "Might as well have some fun if you have to be here."

The thought of joining hand in hand and hip to hip with a stranger gave Coral almost as much anxiety as singing in front of a crowd, especially if it was for the wrong reason. Fun? That was the last word she'd use to describe the situation.

But her grandmother never took no for an answer. "You heard me. Enjoy yourself." She shooed Coral with one hand.

Coral suddenly found herself amid twirling couples. The orchestra struck up a new tune as graceful as a manta ray's glide. Those who danced floated about as if they'd rehearsed in sync for some time. The same moves on repeat. Left, two, three, turn. Right, two, three, turn. Bow, dip, pivot, glide. Coral's pulse accelerated. A merboy around her age caught her eye and began swimming toward her. She avoided his gaze, finding a rather interesting light fixture to study.

A server whipped by, cocktail tray raised with a crooked arm above his head. He didn't even stop to offer her an hors d'oeuvre. Which was fine. She wasn't hungry anyway.

Swallow. Relax. Breathe.

I. Can. Do. This.

How hard could this dancing thing be?

Dishes clattered, rattling Coral's nerves and lighting a blaze of orange before her vision as the merboy moved closer. He wore black and white, same as everyone else. The required attire made the absence of color seem almost purposeful. The lack of hue was a splendor all its own. Despite the muted shades, a rainbow burst before her vision with each key change. New notes invited shifting tones. They darkened, lightened, twinkled, and flashed. This was her world.

And she was drowning in it.

Coral touched her daylight hair. Ran her fingers over her grumbling stomach and traced the edge of her out-of-place tail. The other merwomen wore lengthy skirts of dark, drab seaweed, their hair slicked in tight twists atop their heads.

Coral had tried to fit in, using a bit of Jordan's eel gel to tame her unruly locks. The goo had darkened the strands immensely, making them seem more midnight green than midday gold. A belt of black pearls hung from her waist, matching her necklace and earrings, birthday gifts from her sisters. She'd messed with Jordan's eyeliner, attempting to frame her bright eyes in shadows. The resulting reflection sent chills deep into Coral's marrow.

She closed her eyes. Who was she? Someone her father would approve of? Or merely a pawn in his game? Someone born to play a role she'd never fill?

"Won't you join the festivities, Princess?"

Opening her eyes, Coral prepared to greet the merboy and accept his offer to waltz.

But he was not the one who waited before her.

Jordan's suitor, Duke, floated inches away, smelling of too much cologne and oyster tonic.

Coral raised an eyebrow. "Duke." When she backed away, Coral nearly bumped into another couple. "Nice to see you." The lie almost sounded believable and she smirked. Maybe she was better at smooth speech than she believed.

Duke shook his head. "Is it?" He held out a hand. "Then humor your brother and grace me with a dance."

Ahem. "You're not my brother *yet*." Coral gripped his hand firmly, squeezed, then released. "Perhaps another time. I need to find our future queen." Or anyone, for that matter. Where had the merboy gone? Couldn't he swim faster?

"What better time than at your own ball?" Duke eyed her up and down.

The intrusiveness of his gaze wrapped Coral's nerves in jellyfish tentacles.

He withdrew a small mirror from the inside pocket of his waistcoat. Duke didn't take his eyes off his own reflection as he uttered his next words. "Daddy loves his parties, doesn't he?"

Cringe. She'd almost forgotten he referred to their father as "daddy" when he wasn't around.

Gag me. What could Jordan possibly see in this merman?

Maybe nothing. Because their father had chosen him.

"Where *is* Daddy, anyway?" Duke checked his teeth. Pocketed the mirror once more. "He's missing the celebration."

"I'm sure I don't know." And she wouldn't tell Duke if she did. She narrowed her eyes. "Now, if you'll excuse me."

Before Coral could escape, Duke grabbed her left hand and drew her in. His chest pressed against hers. A wall. A prison. Dark and void of color or sound.

A soundless, inky cloud of nothing exploded before her vision.

"I asked you to dance." His voice warbled, far off, though too close. His tight grip crushed Coral's hand to a near breaking point. "It's rude to decline a gentleman."

Stay here, Coral. Stay now. Don't lose the color. Don't lose the light.

"You're no gentleman." She pulled and tugged, forced herself to rise from the darkness. Whipped at his tail with hers. "And I don't want to dance."

She fought against the shadows. Against the blankness threatening to take her away.

Duke's palms, colder than the water surrounding them, were slime against her skin. "Have I offended you in some way, dear sister?" His wicked grin could slay an army of sea monsters. "A racing pulse." The grin turned ravenous. "Are you nervous? Or perhaps a better word would be . . . Diseased?"

He could sense it? How?

"Do us all a favor, Princess." He released her.

She was shaking. The earthquake inside her bones rivaled a shifting seabed.

"Go for a swim in Red Tide. Maybe then my wife-to-be can stop acting so cold toward me, worrying she's going to end up like your wretched older sister." Duke turned, weaved his way through the crowd, and wiped his hands on his tail.

Did he think she was contagious?

We'll see about that.

"Be bold. Be brave. Even if you don't feel it, act it. This is the way of a true princess."

Stored insights from her grandmother soothed Coral in a way nothing else could.

She straightened, becoming her own calm. Shoulders squared and bubbles in, she followed him despite her fear. Everything in her wanted to jet in the opposite direction.

But Coral had no intention of allowing Duke to believe he held any amount of control over her or her family.

When she reached him at the edge of the ballroom floor, she tapped his shoulder. Hard. Attempted to speak up for herself as their grandmother and the crown princess had both taught her. "Duke. It must have been the band's vibrations you felt. Red Tide is as far from me as the depths of the Abyss. And you'll take care not to speak of your next queen in such a manner. What would *Daddy* think if he heard his almost son-in-law had failed to show respect to one of his daughters? Now, if you'll excuse me."

For once, the color crimson wasn't so menacing. The embarrassment blooming on Duke's cheeks was worth the nausea that rose as she left him in her wake.

She swam around the edge of the ballroom. Purpose and pace drowned her nerves. Keeping with the tempo, she aimed for the row of sand-sculpture chairs one tier below the king's balcony where her sisters would shortly reside.

"Princess, would you mind—"

Coral ignored the address. Stopping for a chat was obviously not a good call. Not after her encounter with Duke. If he could see the Disease, who else might notice it?

"Princess Coral, Princess Coral!" This time it was a child whose attention was piqued by the sight of her. She waved frantically, attempting to pull away from her guardian. "Princess Coral!"

How could she ignore this child? Coral paused midswim, redirected her attention toward the mermaid who couldn't be older than six. Coral laced her fingers and met the little mermaid's eyes. Cleared her throat. "Yes?"

The maid peered up at Coral through big dark eyes the size of sand dollars. "You're pretty. Sparkly. Not like the others."

Coral's pulse picked up again. She self-consciously touched her greased hair. Her glittered skin. "Others?"

"Your sisters. The dark ones." She pointed to Coral's tail. "You're different. You shine." The words rolled off the mermaid's innocent tongue.

And something cracked in the armor Coral had been so careful to construct.

A strange shift took place. Coral's lashes tingled and her lids throbbed. Then a single tear, as real as the heart beating inside her chest, surfaced. She caught it with her knuckle before it slipped past her lid, hoping the small mermaid didn't see.

But the O shape of the child's mouth and the expanse of her gaze told Coral everything she needed.

The mermaid saw. She knew.

"Mama, did you see—"

"Hush, Ellesyn." The mother offered an apologetic look. "I'm so sorry, Princess. She doesn't know any better."

"She's all right." Coral stopped, breathed, looked deeper into the mermaid's eyes. The darkest shade of turquoise she'd ever seen. A hidden gem, but it was there, producing the sweetest, most innocently colored sound Coral had witnessed yet.

This mermaid was not a stranger to tears. A silent secret passed between them as Ellesyn's mouth turned up and her eyes glinted.

Could the Disease be more common than Coral thought? Maybe if they stopped hiding from it, they could begin to understand it like never before.

Coral's mind whirled, hope swelling and thoughts dancing. She had to tell the crown princess. If her sister knew more shared her tears, perhaps she wouldn't feel so alone.

Coral didn't care about the party or her guests or the wrath that would inevitably follow if she missed her debut.

Determination in tow, she aimed for the exit.

She didn't bother glancing back. Not even when the shell horns sounded.

Not even when they announced her name.

EIGHT

Brooke

After

A giant bay window overlooking a stretch of grass allows the sun's natural light to warm the gathering room's cozy space. Silk flowers grace every surface from the bookshelves to the windowsill.

I shield my eyes and find the trash can, picking at my brownie and gulping the milk. Anxiety over having food in my mouth when I'm inevitably called upon begins to fester. I finish my dessert and drink in a rush, then crumple the napkin and toss it into the trash before I place the glass on a low table. I swipe at the corners of my mouth as Jake enters the room.

"Happy Monday, ladies." She closes the sliding door behind her and takes a seat on a poufy ottoman, setting a tote bag on the floor beside her. "Gather 'round, please. We have some fun in store today."

I find a seat on the edge of one couch's chaise, refusing to sit back and get too comfortable. That's what she wants, isn't it? The others may be too naive to see it, but she can't fool me.

"Full disclosure?" Jake says once everyone's seated. "I know it's only January, and Valentine's Day isn't for another month. But for the sake of this exercise, we're putting our hearts on the line."

A few of the girls laugh, but the brownie in my stomach churns. Valentine's Day? Why draw attention to a day that focuses on love when it's merely a fantasy? I glance around, taking in the others' expressions. Most keep their eyes trained on Jake. They've clearly fallen into her trap. The rest avoid eye contact at all costs, staring at the throw pillows in their laps or gazing out the window.

For these, there is still hope. The hope they'll realize such a thing does not exist.

The sliding door opens and closes again, inviting everyone to face in that direction. The effect is one I succeeded in avoiding upon my own entry, though a twinge of pain knots my gut when a blush creeps up Hope's cheeks.

"That's the second day in a row." Jake's words are firm, but kindness coats them. The tone throws me. "It's odd for you to be late. See me after?"

Hope nods and pulls her long sweater sleeves down to cover half her hands. "It won't happen again."

"Good." Jake taps something out on her tablet. "Now then, pass these around." She retrieves a stack of red paper hearts from her tote along with a pencil case. "Take a heart and a pencil each."

Everyone obeys but I'm a statue, staring at Hope where she sits cross-legged on the trellis rug. She's different than she was this morning. The easygoing girl who insisted this place is special now forces a smile. Her crisscrossed legs turn into butterfly wings when she takes a heart and pencil and sets them in her lap. She could fly away. Does she have someone on the outside who would notice if she went missing?

Why do I care?

I take my things without looking, keeping my focus on Hope instead. We are *not* friends and we're never going to be. I don't have time or even the hint of a desire for attachments that won't last. But the piece of me that used to be, the part once whole and unbroken, makes eye contact with the girl I assumed was too young to understand.

You okay? I mouth when she meets my gaze.

Fine, she mouths back, though she's obviously not.

I narrow my eyes. The all-knowing empath in me that surfaces when I'm not numb can sense when someone's lying. My heart screams offense, but my head says we're not as different as I first believed.

Hiding behind practiced expressions and cookie-cutter answers. Never allowing anyone inside because we've done so too many times to count and we're tired. Washed up. Finished.

I bite my tongue and stare at the heart in my hands. A rip in the paper's edge begs me to make the tear deeper, longer. Until the stupid symbol is torn in two and nothing can be done to save it. Tape and glue will never take it back to perfect.

"I want you each to close your eyes and think of some negative words or even phrases you've allowed to define you." Jake closes her own eyes.

Classic fail, lady. Treating us like children isn't going to get us to trust you.

On principle, I keep my eyes wide open. I'm the only one, though. Even Hope obeys despite the edge about her now.

"Maybe these are words you've used for yourself," Jake says. "Ones you've voiced until you've come to believe them so deeply, they're ingrained as truth." Hand to her heart, our leader rolls her shoulders, inhales, and releases the breath. "Or they could be terms or phrases someone else has tagged you with. *Unwanted. Ugly. Unworthy. Waste of time.* Whatever they are, let them appear before your mind's eye."

I have half a mind's eye to slip out of the room, leave my paper heart behind with the rest of this nonsense. But a twitch in Hope's expression catches the corner of my vision. Her chin crinkles and quivers, eyebrows the shade of her freckles and hair pinching the space above her nose.

And something within me cracks, Hope's pain pouring in, becoming my own.

I seal the hole quickly, finally closing my eyes if only to keep from letting her in.

"Do you have your words? Can you picture them?" Jake clears her throat, and I almost get the sense she's choked up.

She's a fine actress. Too bad I don't believe in fiction.

Some girls "mmm-hmm" in response to her question. Hope is the only one who voices a clear "yes."

I peek through my lids.

Jake's satisfaction goes viral across her face. "You can open your eyes," she says, placing a long, carefully chosen pause before continuing. "Now, I want you to take your pencils and write those words and phrases on your paper heart. Take care not to rush. Use flourishes or embellishments. Etch those beliefs into that heart until there's no denying they're there."

I'm almost boiling now, my nerves rattling muscle and bone. "What's the point of this?" I hiss under my breath.

Jake faces me, pouring all her attention and energy into her considering stare. "Brooke." She leans forward slightly. "I was going to save introductions for after our exercise, but maybe you'd prefer to do that now?"

The friendly tactic won't work. I'm on to her methods and this is only day one. "No, thanks."

I expect her to insist. To use her power to force the soul out of me. Never mind the brownie I ate to appease her. I'm not going to let her win this one.

But she only shrugs. "Okay. Where were we?" Fingers combing her short hair, Jake almost appears flustered, absentmindedly regular like anyone else when interrupted.

Another trick? Or a flaw in her façade?

"Right. Words, ladies. I'll give you ten minutes."

The rest of the group begins the assignment. Some scribble feverishly, filling their hearts within a few minutes. I look to Jake, surprised to find her also filling out a paper heart.

What game is she playing?

Hope catches my attention again. She stares at her heart, glancing from it to her hands and back again. Our time's almost up before she writes a single word at the heart's center, then folds it in half, creasing the edge, precision in her gaze.

Ah, a perfectionist. Should have pegged it sooner.

"Great." Jake crosses one leg over the other, taking time to make eye contact with each of us in turn. "We'll divide into pairs now." She turns her heart to face us so we can read the words she wrote. *Underqualified* and *doesn't fit the mold* are two of several definitions displayed on the paper surface.

My invisible wall lowers an inch.

Most of the other girls grab their desired partner, leaving me and Hope the only ones without a match.

Great. New girl and newest girl are stuck with each other. *Can I get a rain check, please?*

"You may find any spot on the grounds you wish. Go for a walk through the gardens," Jake says. "Take a stroll through the stables. Head up the hill, bask in the ocean view."

My ears perk at the word *ocean*.

How long has it been? Months? A year? I can't remember anymore.

"It doesn't matter where you go, so long as you are willing to trust your partner with your heart," Jake goes on. "It's your job to release it. And it's your partner's job to speak truth into you until those words no longer matter. Until you can erase them with full confidence they mean nothing at all." She takes a breath, letting her instructions sink in. "Some words may be erased today. Others may take much longer to remove. Maybe even after you leave here and go home, at which point you would find a new life-giver. A trustworthy friend or family member, a teacher, or even a counselor who can continue to hold you to those truths."

This is all way too touchy-feely for my taste. Can we get to the "dish" or whatever it is already?

"We'll convene back here at the top of the hour. Trust each other, ladies. I can't wait to hear about your journeys whence you return."

Did she say "whence"? Seriously, this woman is too much.

Everyone's on their feet before I can grasp what's happening. When they've all left and Hope stands before me, she offers her heart. The gesture is innocent. Childlike.

I snatch the shape from her hand in a harsh move I regret almost immediately. "Let's get this over with."

"You're supposed to give me yours," she responds, more snap in her voice than I expect.

I shove my own paper into her hands.

She stares down at it, a frown creasing her expression. "It's blank." Her stare mimics her spoken word.

"Yeah." My response presents a challenge, daring her to so much as breathe the wrong way. "So?"

"It's just . . ." Her head tilts. She blinks once. Shakes her head. "You are not nothing. You know? Whether you wrote the word or not, you should know you're not nothing. And whoever made you think you are is a liar."

My jaw goes slack before I can control it. My chest swells and emotion squeezes my throat, choking me until it's nearly impossible to breathe. I don't know why, but I open her folded paper and look over the word on her heart, find the one she did, in fact, write. The one I didn't have the courage to make real.

Nothing

I swallow. Then meet her eyes, my heart softening when I do.

"You're not nothing either," I tell her.

"I guess that makes us both something." Her grin isn't practiced this time.

"I guess so." I almost mean it.

When we walk outside, I follow her to the hill I assume leads to the view of the ocean. As I watch her, the January air nipping at my neck, our words replay in my mind, stirring something unfamiliar and foreign.

A couple of nothings, making their way toward something.

Something beautiful.

Something real.

Something I haven't seen in quite some time.

NINE

Merrick

"Y'all go on in. I'll be right behind you."

Merrick's mom flipped down the visor in the front passenger seat. She checked her face in the small mirror and wiped at her eyelids, rubbing off the black, inky spots her tears had temporarily tattooed onto her skin. She caught his gaze in the mirror's reflection. Her eyes brightened, hinting at a smile though he couldn't see her lips.

"You don't have to come in." Merrick turned toward Nikki, squeezing her hand but avoiding her eyes. Her admission from earlier hung between them, and he couldn't bring himself to meet the questioning look she was probably giving him. "Harold can take you home."

"Do you not want me here?" As confident as she was, even Nikki had her insecurities.

"No!" Merrick's gut clamped at the lie. Worse, his dad's voice took the lead in his mind, telling him what good publicity it would be if Nikki were seen with their family during a crisis. Her father might be swayed to merge companies if he knew Merrick was serious about his daughter.

The thought made him sick.

He opened the door. Stepped out of the car and into the rain.

Drenched instantly, he ducked his head back into the car. "We could be here all night. You should go home, Nik. Get some rest. I'll call you in the morning. Okay?" He flashed his teeth and that seemed to do the trick.

Nikki nodded, seemingly satisfied with his excuse. She was on her phone before he slammed the door.

Beneath the awning of the hospital's entrance, Merrick shook out his hair and wiped his feet. It was New Year's Eve and the hospital's Christmas décor was still up, same as it was at home. Wreaths with giant red bows hung from the glass doors. Twinkle lights wrapped the pillars on either side of the mat where he stood. He was about to go in when a distinct mechanical hum sounded. He turned, found himself eye to eye with his mom behind a half-rolled-down window.

She looked like she was about to say something but didn't.

Her stare left him uneasy. "See you inside?"

She nodded. "See you, baby."

Then she rolled up the window, her face vanishing behind a pane of dark glass.

It had been years since his mother had referred to him as "baby." Merrick resented the sour feeling it left in the pit of his stomach.

"It shouldn't be much longer."

A hand holding a steaming Styrofoam cup hovered an inch from Merrick's face. He looked up to find the nurse—what had she said her name was? Jane? June?—standing in front of him. She wore festive Whoville and Grinch scrubs and a reindeer antler headband that jingled when she moved.

He sighed. Right. This was a children's hospital. No doubt he'd be seeing many a reindeer antler around. He took the cup. Sipped. Hot cocoa. With marshmallows. Of course it was.

She hummed, clearly comfortable in her own skin. Her white

Skechers squeaked on the linoleum floor. "We have family counselors here if you need to talk to someone. They're on call twenty-four-seven."

Oh. Great. We have a talker.

So not what he needed. Someone to tell him it would all be "okay."

He sighed again, louder. Hinting. "Thanks for the drink, but I'm good. Waiting to see my sister."

And this, apparently, was an invitation for her to sit.

Merrick rubbed the bridge of his nose between his thumb and finger. Pinched hard, hoping to wake from what was sure to be a conversational nightmare. When he opened his eyes and she was still there, he saw it would take more than sighs and body language to get his point across.

"Look. My mom will be up any minute." He took another sip, this one coming too fast, burning his tongue, scorching his throat. "She may want one of your counselors, but I'm good."

"You said that."

"I meant it."

"Are you sure?"

She was pushing the boundaries. Crossing the line between professionalism and prying.

"Yep."

She stood and cleared her throat. "Let me know if you or your family need anything. I'll be at the nurses' station all night."

"Will do." He expected her to go then. She didn't.

She sniffled instead.

Merrick cringed. He noticed something he hadn't before. Though she wasn't super pregnant, the bump was definitely there. He didn't have to be a prodigy to figure out she was prone to become an emotional wreck due to the simple fact she was growing a human inside of her.

He looked around, hoping the tough nurse, the one he saw in movies, would walk by and save him.

"My dad died by suicide." Nurse Basket Case shifted from foot to foot. Had she considered she might be the one in need of counseling? "Last year. He . . . jumped off the bridge."

She didn't have to say which bridge. They lived in San Francisco. The bridge meant *the* bridge. Still, the fact that they were both natives didn't make this therapy hour. And it didn't make them friends either.

He glanced at her name tag. Jana. She was pretty, though tired looking. As if time in this place had aged her. What genius thought to give the pregnant lady the graveyard shift anyway?

"Has the doctor talked to you at all? Has he explained what . . . happened?" Jana tilted her head, waiting.

Merrick shook his head. "I'm sure he'll come talk to us when my mom arrives."

Jana's brow pinched. "We've seen a lot of childhood suicide cases and attempts over the past year. It's heartbreaking . . . to see someone so young want to take their own life."

He didn't want to have this conversation. He wasn't ready to wrap his mind around it.

But his lack of preparedness didn't stop the pregnant nurse from going on. "Most of the time, when someone slits their wrists, they bleed out in minutes. There isn't time to save them."

Merrick couldn't face her. He hung his head lower, enough so she couldn't see the pathetic sign of weakness welling in his eyes.

"I'm not allowed to give you medical details or advice, but I can tell you the difference between a true attempted suicide and a cry for help. This is a chance you might not get again. Next time might end differently. Anyway, let me know if you need anything." Jana retreated then, seeming to realize she had, one, already said this and, two, said too much.

Merrick was thankful for her absence and annoyed at the same time. Though he wasn't in the mood to deal with wacky woman hormones, he also didn't want to spend one more moment watching the clock on the wall *tick, tick, tick.* Another second. Another minute. Another hour. A cry for help? A chance we might not get again? Where was his mom? Why wasn't she around to hear this? How long did it take a person to get it together and come inside?

It had been three hours since he'd arrived. And fifty-two minutes. *Seven, eight, nine . . .*

She was in the gift shop.

Or she was getting food. The cafeteria was closed and she'd gone to bring something back. His dad would never approve, but Merrick would give anything for Taco Bell.

It didn't take this long to get Taco Bell.

Maybe she was filling out paperwork.

She could do that up here.

He set his cocoa on the chair beside him, pulled his phone from his pocket. No missed calls. Zero unread texts. The signal in the hospital was probably bad. He powered the device off and then back on, waited a full minute for it to register any new voice mails. Something.

But there was nothing.

Where are you, Mom?

The text said delivered. He waited for it to inform him it had been read. Stared at the screen, as if he were some kind of superhero who could force her to answer with his mind.

"You can go in now."

Merrick swiped at his eyes with the heel of his palm before meeting the gaze of his father across the hall.

Hiroshi stood with one foot still inside Amaya's room, looking a little disheveled but still his regular self. The man's expression gave nothing away as he nodded, then headed down the opposite hall before Merrick could even ask him if he'd heard from Mom.

Amaya's door was cracked when Merrick reached it. One breath. Two. He entered. The heavy door announced his presence, but his sister didn't stir.

The IV *drip, drip, dripped.*

The vitals monitor *beep, beep, beeped.*

He inched closer and finally resolved to sit in a reclining chair at her bedside. An artificial Charlie Brown Christmas tree stood by the window, its lights pale in comparison to those of the city beyond. They probably had these in all the rooms. Merrick angled himself so the tree was nowhere within his line of vision. He didn't need false cheer rubbed in his face. Not now.

"Worst brother ever, huh?" Merrick's hand migrated to Amaya's knee. He shook it awkwardly. "Guess this means you get the top bunk to infinity and beyond."

The odd joke came out of past memories of watching *Toy Story* on *Oba-Chan's* old VHS player. Memories that refused to die. They hadn't shared a room in years. Not since their father lived on base back in his Navy days. Merrick was twelve. Amaya, four. Their small house only had three rooms. One for their parents. One for Hiroshi's office. And one for the kids. They were young enough that privacy wasn't a thing, and it had made no difference that she was a girl and Merrick was a boy. But he was still older and that meant he got the top bunk.

Amaya used to have the biggest meltdowns over it until one night when Mom finally gave in.

Merrick's sister had fallen off the ladder and broken her arm when she woke up to go to the bathroom that night.

Their mom never gave in to Amaya's tantrums after that.

"I should have asked you why you always wore sweaters and stuff." He ran a hand over his face and leaned back. "I should have paid attention."

"You *did* ask. I told you I was cold. Can't blame you for believing me."

He shot forward and grabbed her hand. His sister was only ten, but she was the most honest person he knew. A trait he hoped she would carry as she grew older.

"Hey, watch it!" Amaya pulled her icy fingers away. "I don't want you to accidentally pull out my IV." His sister smoothed the tape on her hand. "Then they'd have to stick me again and it'd be a whole thing. No thanks."

"You don't seem to have a problem with sharp objects." He shifted his gaze to her scraped arms. Pink marks on freckled skin.

They shared a laugh at the dark retort. Amaya rubbed her IV tube between her thumb and forefinger. "It was stupid, okay? I won't do it again."

Merrick arched one eyebrow. "You won't cut again or you won't cut that deep again?"

She squirmed. Her next words would be only half true. "Both, all right? It was an accident."

"Why, Maya? What could possibly be worth losing your life over? Is it something at school? Are you being bullied?" It had happened before and he'd shut it down quickly.

All she has to do is say the word and I'll take care of it.

"No." Her answer was quick. Too quick.

Merrick opened his mouth to refute her, but she rushed on, her words one long, jumbled explanation.

"I just . . . I wanted to see what it would feel like and some of the other kids do it, you know, the eighth graders and stuff, and they said I'd be cool if I did it too." She fiddled with the edge of the bandage on her arm.

He let a low whistle sail through his lips. There had to be more. Her admission was incomplete, but he'd go with it. For now. "Of course popularity and a few eighth graders are worth, um, I don't know, *dying*." Sarcasm dripped from every word, but this was how they were. Bantering back and forth. Never saying anything real.

"I was tired. I couldn't think straight. It was dark in my room. Usually I only slice deep enough to—" She stopped herself, obviously realizing she'd said too much.

A small knock on the door interrupted them. Merrick bolted from his chair. Finally. He didn't even have to check his phone to know it was Mom. She'd make everything okay again. She'd—

The door opened.

His jaw went slack, then clenched so tight he thought his teeth might break.

"Son. Amaya." His father stepped awkwardly into the room. He filled the space in a way that made it feel claustrophobic. Especially with the aftershave he wore. The scent burned.

But nothing like Mom's absence.

Merrick's hands automatically turned into fists at his sides.

"Your mom's gone." No sugarcoating. No prelude. Hiroshi got right to the point. "Harold called and let me know. When she got out of the car, he took Nikki home. Then he returned. He wanted to wait in case we had need of him. Your mom still hadn't gone inside. She sat there, on a bench, in the rain. He thought she might be trying to process things. But when she eventually got into a cab, he followed her to the bus station."

"What'd you say to her now?" Merrick started toward him, but Amaya reached out and caught the corner of his jacket between her fingers.

"Your mother has been looking for a way out for a long time, Son." Hiroshi turned his gaze to Amaya. "She's finally found her chance."

Amaya's lower lip quivered, but she didn't cry. She released Merrick's jacket, scrunched up her bedsheets with her fists, and stared at the wall.

Merrick sank back into the chair and gazed at her too-white sheets.

Nothing in life was ever that white. Things appeared white. Smelled white. But if he held them up in the light and gave them a hard look?

He'd see brown. Yellow. Beige.

Because despite the exterior his father wanted to paint for his perfect family, if Merrick truly looked? He'd see the truth.

Exposed to the light too long, and he'd see. Anyone would.

The dirt.

The muck.

The ugly.

Stains. Yeah, that was the right word.

Stains were all he would see.

TEN

Coral

"Where do you think you're going?"

The king's voice boomed through the hallway. He looked down at his youngest daughter.

With all the courage she could muster, Coral met his gaze. "I'm looking for the crown princess."

"She'll be along shortly." Her father took her arm in a firm but painless grip. Though his touch was different from the way Duke had handled her, that didn't make it welcome.

Coral didn't dare try to escape her father's grasp. She did, however, glance over her shoulder and speak up a second time. "Where is she? Where is my sister?"

King Jonah did not answer. Soon they entered the ballroom together. At the precise moment the light of the grand hall lit her father's face, his stoic expression lifted into one of quiet amusement.

This was the merman the people knew.

Coral wished he was the same one who held her arm now.

The clock at the other end of the ballroom with its gears fashioned from ships' wheels *tick, tick, ticked* in time with the band's blue-hued tempo. The second hand, made of human bone, twitched with the little mermaid's uncollected concerns. *How much longer? A fathom? A bubbled breath?*

When at last the band ceased and the maestro tapped his wand, Coral straightened. The crowd's chatter faded to a low hum the color of mud. The maestro cleared his throat. "Presenting King Jonah . . . and, here she is, the princess Coral Atlantica!"

Urchins. She was trapped now. Coral glanced up at the lower tier to find Jordan and Duke already sitting in their chairs. Jordan caught her stare, then quickly looked away. When Coral sat, Jordan said nothing about the empty chair between them. Was that satisfaction lifting her sister's cheeks?

Their father rose above them to the highest tier, charred crown of deadened coral atop his head, black trident held firmly in his grasp.

Coral's stomach churned.

The crown princess was nowhere to be seen.

When the king tapped his trident, drawing the guests' attention, Coral kept her eyes fixed on the entry arch. Any moment now her oldest sister would make an entrance.

"Mergents and maids," the king began. "I welcome you, one and all, to the inception of my youngest daughter into what has become not only our great tradition but our purpose as the sentinels of the sea. We extend our deepest gratitude to all who have traveled from far and wide to join us for this momentous occasion."

Coral's anxiety was a thrashing hammerhead shark. But not because she was about to make her own debut performance. Those nerves had been replaced by a new sort of unease.

Where. Was. Her. Sister?

"Your crown princess would have loved to join us for the festivities, but I am afraid she has taken ill." A pause. A cough. "I ask that you hold her in your hearts and thoughts as we continue without her."

Wait. What? Coral twisted in her seat, squinted up at the king who'd said her oldest sister was on her way seconds before. When his gaze didn't yield, Coral attempted to exchange glances with Jordan.

Only Duke met her eyes. He winked, then grinned, his crooked teeth glinting.

Eww. Coral tore away her gaze. The merman was the scum of the sea. Why couldn't Jordan see it?

"Now then," their father continued. "Let me put you all at ease. Tonight calls for celebration, not sorrow."

Coral's pulse throbbed in her temples. The merfolk murmured. She glimpsed a few of them whisper behind cupped palms. At last she found her grandmother's knowing gaze.

The corners of her mouth turned toward the sand, though the merwoman didn't flinch.

If anyone knew something, her grandmother certainly did.

The sour feeling returned to Coral's stomach. Something wasn't right. It hadn't been right for some time.

Coral narrowed her eyes at the king once more. Clenched the coarse arms of her chair. How could she celebrate when the crown princess needed her now more than ever?

Heartache, pure and green as sea grass, fell in a swell over Coral's entire body. Her insides writhed. Muscles tensed.

The king raised his burly hands. "Join me in wishing my youngest daughter a happy birthday." One hand swept toward Coral. Eye contact, rare and awkward, made its path between her and the merman who seldom looked her way.

She forced herself to hold his scrutiny.

"Coral." His low voice soothed and terrified. "It is now time for you to rise with your sister to the surface. On this, your first eve as a true merwoman, you shall prove your worth as a member of this family."

Bitterness coated her tongue. Since when did her worth depend on her voice?

"Coral." Her father's tone was firm and final. "Take your place."

She sat tight. The next words Coral uttered released before she could hold them back. "I'll wait for our sister."

Jordan touched her arm. The gesture was so kind, so sisterly, so unlike her that Coral almost freed another tear. "Don't test him. Father's wrath is not something you want to provoke at any cost."

The back of Coral's neck tingled. She swallowed and her eyelids twitched once more. Coral eyed Jordan. Cost? What about the cost of abandoning their oldest sister in her time of need?

"I'll wait for the crown princess," she said again. If Coral didn't stand for her, who would?

Jordan glanced at Father.

"*Coral.*" The king tapped his trident.

Jordan bowed her head.

"Rise. *Now.*"

Coral did as he commanded, but defiance flowed through her veins in full burning crimson now. He wanted a song, he'd get one. But not any tune he'd approved. She drew a breath and recalled the melody from her time at the surface three nights before.

The composition was human. If her father discovered, there was no telling how he'd react. But if no one would speak up for her sister, she would sing until everyone heard.

> "As unforgiving as the stormy waves,
> Your heart of stone digs watery graves.
> She lives in fear while you are near.
> Can't you see what you've done here?
> Your love could be what truly saves."

Coral didn't stop, not even when Jordan began, singing with all her might to drown her youngest sister's song with her own. Jordan grabbed one arm and tugged. Coral fought to free herself, but Father gave her a warning glare and she relented.

Together, she and Jordan rose into the night.

At the surface, the waves were calmer than Coral had ever seen from her hiding place in the rocks. The sea was glass now, the ocean a reflection of the clear and starry-eyed sky above. Stars that appeared as if they might fall, they shone so close. She ripped her arm free, gasping. She wanted to scream at Jordan. To curse her for how she'd disregarded what was happening.

"Did you have to make a scene?" Jordan said, control leaving her voice with every word. "Father went to great lengths to throw you that party. How can you be so ungrateful?"

All Coral could say was, "*Me*? How could you be on his side? Our older sister needs us. Something's wrong."

Jordan rolled her eyes. "When is something not wrong with her?"

"This is different."

"Don't be so dramatic."

"*Enough.*" Coral couldn't take it anymore. "I'm tired of you speaking to me like a child."

"That's what you are, isn't it? Our sister favored you, Coral. And Grandmother too."

Coral caught a glimpse of her reflection in the water. Her expression was a mixture of shock. Understanding. Realization. Was this why Jordan acted so hostile toward her? Had she always felt so . . . unloved? Left out? Alone?

Jordan turned away, shoulders shaking.

The Disease, not overpowering but still present, rose to Jordan's surface.

Coral's heart twisted. The Disease affected all three of them? Why didn't they talk about it? Why did everyone act as if discussing it was treason?

"Jordan." Coral touched her shoulder, feeling like the older one, like their roles were reversed. "It's okay to feel this way. You're not alone. I'm sorry I never—"

Jordan shrugged her off. "Don't presume to know how I—" She stopped. Caught a breath. "Don't presume to know *anything*. Don't you dare. You are nothing to me. *Nothing.*" The middle mersister dove beneath the water, swimming away, escaping before things turned too serious. Coral used to believe it was because of her sister's cold heart. But it was precisely the opposite.

Did Jordan possess a hidden tear too?

The little mermaid collected her scattered emotions as her life played in scenes of color and sound through her memory.

Jordan, putting Coral down, trying to make her feel unworthy of her own station.

The crown princess, holding Coral close as Jordan looked on.

Their grandmother with one arm around Coral and the other around—

"Oh, Jordan." Coral was about to follow her when fire illuminated the night sky. The vision reflected off the ocean's surface, thousands of sparkling gemstones ready to become sunken treasure.

Boom, boom, boom.

The sight was glorious and mesmerizing and captivating. A grand orchestra of her own brilliant hues played in flourishes across her vision. Coral forgot the squall that waited below. She took in the beauty of the evening. And then, as quickly as they had begun, the sky bursts died, glittering in descending sparks that disappeared as each one kissed the water.

A new sound played out into the serene night. A sound so beautiful it lit the dark night, splashing the air with gold.

She'd heard that sound—that song—before.

Coral turned every direction, seeking the source. She swam closer to shore, and then closer still. And . . . *there* . . . on the sandy beach, a small boat rested. A single sailor sat within, a hand-size instrument pressed to his lips.

"Drown him," Jordan would say.

"End him," her father would urge.

"He's a human," the merfolk would titter. "A worthless, good-for-nothing human."

But then her oldest sister's voice—her very real and present voice—said, "Be careful."

Coral whirled in the water.

The crown princess, pale complexion aglow beneath the moonlight, stared back at her.

Coral flung her arms around her sister. Skin like ice, the crown princess was a sculpture, frozen in time. And yet, it seemed her frail frame could break at any moment. "I was trying to get to you. I wanted to tell you—"

"Hush." The crown princess caressed the little mermaid's cheek with her thumb. "It's nearly time."

Fear wrapped itself around Coral's heart, threatening to crush it. She needn't ask to know what her sister referred to.

Red Tide. Was. Coming.

"No," Coral said, panic striking her center. "Wait." She wanted to tell her sister everything. About the tear. About Jordan. And the young mermaid at the ball with the secret behind her eyes. "You're not alone," was all she could manage.

But her sister's downcast gaze and quiet resolve spoke volumes, though she said nothing at all. She'd accepted her fate, sure as the tides would change.

The human's soft, melodious tune played in the background. Soothing the ache inside.

"Humans are not to be trusted," the crown princess said. "Give your heart to one and you can never go back." She removed the pearl bracelet she wore and slipped it over Coral's wrist.

Coral heaved, her calm waning. She had no interest in humans and she didn't want her sister's favorite treasure. Not after hearing of her heartbreak. That, at least, was where their father had been right. Coral only wanted things to be as they had been. Exactly as they had been. Before.

Her sister stiffened her upper lip and stared toward shore.

Coral followed her gaze. The human's music had ceased. He stood now, one foot outside the beached boat, watching them. His pointed gaze expressed concern, while his rigid stance showed a protectiveness Coral hadn't expected.

"He'll hurt you," the crown princess said. "He'll break you."

Strange. The human didn't look menacing. He seemed . . .

Apprehensive. Worried. Afraid?

A part of Coral wanted to find out the truth for herself. But she couldn't let go of the future queen. Not yet. If she could find the right words and the perfect way to say them, her sister would understand. Red Tide didn't have to be the end. Coral was sure of it. Her sister might have been ready to give up. But that was why she needed a sister who wouldn't.

"I'm here," Coral said, ignoring her own longing to discover a new world. With fresh words and reassurances on the tip of her tongue, she faced her sister once more.

The crown princess floated across the glassy surface, unmoving and facedown. When Coral turned her sister over, her expression appeared serene, happy even.

Someone shouted. The human pushed the small boat into the water, then climbed aboard.

Coral took her sister's cold, lifeless hand. "Sister," she said, her voice lost. She swallowed and cleared her throat. "Crown Princess?"

The last was a question that would never be answered. Her sister's skin was colder now. Lacking the warmth of life.

A hundred soundless things happened at once.

The human rowed to her side. He spoke but Coral couldn't hear.

Her instinct was to protect herself. To swim away before this boy could do harm.

But then a hand grabbed Coral's wrist. Duke. He glared, murder in his eyes. His mouth moved but made no sound, at least none Coral could distinguish. She slapped him hard with her tail, tried to cry out, but her voice would not emerge.

The boy raised his oar in the air and swung it at Duke. The boat rocked. The merman's eyes went wide. He released Coral and swam off.

Coward.

Conflicting emotions and thoughts tore her heart in two.

When she looked up at the human, she found fear in his expression. He breathed so hard his back rose and fell. He blinked and shook his head. As if steeling himself, the human boy reached down and lifted her sister into the boat.

Horror overcame Coral. But not because of the human or even due to the confrontation with Duke.

Her sister's tail was gone, vanished, replaced with a pair of legs.

Coral recoiled, a net of fear trapping her in place.

For the first and last time, she saw her sister as human. Did the crown princess's love for a human change her? Had she been human all along?

The boy reached for Coral next, offering a hand. Compassion shone in his dark gaze. The sight was nearly foreign. So foreign that all Coral could do was stare into his eyes for a few extra fathoms.

His black irises were the most beautiful she had ever seen. Dark but warm. Deep as the uncharted sea. So different from the terrifying black of the Abyss.

Temptation urged her to take his hand. But then she looked at the crown princess. At her lifeless human body that had seen so much pain.

Pain at human hands. At a prince's hands, no less.

And Coral backed away.

She noticed for the first time that the water around them had turned to blood.

Her own blood drained from her head. It had finally happened.

Red Tide had come.

A fragment permanently broke from Coral's heart. The emptiness it left behind turned gray, leaving a procession of dread in its place. She twisted the pearls on her wrist, vowed never to take them off. Coral would wear the bracelet as a constant reminder.

Her sister was gone.

The future queen was no more.

ELEVEN

Brooke

After

"Come on, Brooke. It's not much farther."

Hope says my name as if we've been friends for years. She's beginning to act like a pesky little sister, something I'll need to nip if she grows too clingy.

I don't want a sister. And I don't need one. Hope with all her innocence will never change that.

The trek up the hill takes longer than I expect. Sweat sticks to the small of my back. Cooling me to the bone. Making me wish for a jacket. Though warmer than usual for winter, the wind still bites. I pant and my side cramps, reminders I'm too out of shape for this.

Hope, however, has clearly made this hike recently. She's all confidence and determination, a kid at recess, excited for her chance to play outdoors.

We pass several adults on our way. They nod as we walk by, smiling. Watching.

Babysitting.

"Don't mind them." Hope spins and skips backward. "They're here to make sure we don't—"

"Kill ourselves? Run away?"

"Something like that." She winks. Runs ahead. Rather than letting me make her uncomfortable, she appears to take my bluntness as playful teasing.

But we both know those are real possibilities for this place. For people like us. I don't know Hope's story, but I do know mine.

I'm not afraid of death. For more reasons than I care to remember.

"Can I ask you something?" I say when I catch up, out of breath and aching.

"Anything," she says.

I hate that I believe she means it. "Are you on meds?"

She nods. "I'm not afraid to say I need them. It's okay to need them, Brooke. It doesn't make you weird. I've learned that at least— that I can talk about it and it's not weird. Being able to say, 'Hi, I'm Hope and I take medication for depression.'" The way she says *depression* makes it sound like she's discussing something as common as the weather. "Your meds don't define you. They're your normal, you know? Everyone needs a normal."

I want to tell her I don't need anything and I don't want to talk about it. That I've avoided taking my own meds off and on for months. I'm tired of feeling like an experiment.

I'm about to snuff out her "normal" theory when we approach one of the babysitters about halfway up the hill. The grandmotherly woman wears a lanyard with the word *volunteer* stitched into it. The handwritten name tag at the lanyard's end says *Beck.*

"Mornin', girls." Beck offers a salute that would make any Girl Scout proud. Though her weathered face tips off her age, she matches our upward pace without hesitation, falling into step on Hope's other side. "Headed to see the view?"

"We promise to be good, Beck." The ease with which Hope speaks to the woman at least six times her age lets on they've made this walk together before. On more than one occasion. "Brooke here hasn't had the grand tour yet."

Beck picks up speed, her smile as long as her stride. "Allow me, then. It isn't much farther. You're a lucky one, by the way," Beck says to me. "This girl's special. Hold on to her."

I frown but follow, purposely falling behind. How could I have thought for a minute we'd be able to roam without supervision? Maybe Hope needs a sitter, but I'm almost an adult.

Ha, some adult I'll make. No job. No home. Nowhere to go but nowhere at all.

This is it for me. The end. Last page. Final word. Jake and Hope and Beck . . . They can try all they want. But the truth is my time here is only prolonging the inevitable.

At the hill's crest, a breeze greets us, spraying us with salty air from the ocean. It's several miles off, the peaks of the cypress trees between here and there standing like sentinels, guarding the precious secret the water seems to hold.

"Return to me," she calls. *"Remember."*

I give her the cold shoulder. Find a rather interesting rock to study.

"Storm's comin' soon." Beck rocks back on her heels and whistles. "We probably shouldn't stay out here too long, girls."

I scoot toward the ledge, hyperaware of Beck's close eye. The fall would be a long way down. I'd hit branches and needles before I met the out-of-sight ground below. It might not even kill me. I'd suffer. Maybe live.

I'm not okay with that.

"Isn't that smell amazing?" Hope flings her arms wide, offering herself with abandon to the view. "I wish we could go down there."

I almost say what I'm thinking but bite the inside of my cheek instead.

"As a matter of fact, I think Jake's cookin' up a field trip to do just that." Beck takes out her phone, scrolls, and taps. "Yep. In March. Should be fun." She pockets the device and closes her eyes, basking in the beauty.

I picture myself plummeting with nothing but the wind in my face and life at my back. Who would notice? Who would care?

"You are not nothing." Hope repeats the words from earlier. They etch themselves into my skin.

Resentment traps me in silence. She doesn't know me. This place is temporary. The people, seasonal. I stick to my guns. Lifelong friendships cannot be formed. Things do not get better. I'm about to say as much, but then the wind whips around my head, brushing against my ears, urging me to look up.

And there she is again, the one who will not be ignored. Her water is so blue, the waves ebbing and flowing, inviting the storm in, welcoming the clouds to do its bidding. The ocean is not afraid.

And neither am I.

An ache inside threatens to break open the cracks I've worked to fill. I look away, back toward the ranch. Seeing the ocean, so close but a million miles away, is a pain I cannot endure. I don't want to wait anymore. The hurt is a death of its own.

"You okay, dear?" Beck doesn't touch me, but her compassionate voice wraps my heart, offering a place to rest. An invitation to confide.

"Fine." I cross my arms. Inch away. Out of reach. "It's too cold up here. Can we go back?"

"I thought you wanted to see the view." Hope lowers her arms and faces me. Her innocent question makes her sound even younger. What could've happened to bring her to this point? To make a child need this place?

"Changed my mind." I don't look back as I begin my descent. "You two can stay. I'm going."

Hope and Beck follow but keep their distance. Twigs snap and the dirt path turns to mud as rain begins to pour like a crashing tidal wave. Every step grows hindered. My shoes suck and slip with each step forward. Still, I continue faster, pushing through the weather that seems to have a vendetta against me. My walk turns into a jog, then a run. I drop the paper heart I'd been holding for Hope, abandon it in the mud where the hill's path meets leveled grass.

When I reach the ranch house, I take the steps up the wraparound porch, wring out the hem of my shirt, rainwater *drip, drip, dripping* onto my already soaked shoes. Everything in my aching bones wants to head inside, to hop in a hot shower and stay there for days.

But Jake is in there. And the other girls. The thought of returning to the group, of introductions and trying to keep everyone's name straight, overwhelms me to the point of a fatigue so cumbersome, I think I might be sick.

I can't people right now. No matter how frozen I am.

I veer left, retreat to the side of the house. My sneakers squeak and my drenched hair hangs straight, sticking to my cheeks and neck. Maybe I can slip in through a back door. Avoid the group at least until someone comes to search for me.

Volunteers and staff members run for the ranch house from all angles. A few twentysomethings emerge from a massive barn, covering their heads with pieces of cardboard. Several more middle-aged women join them, sweatshirt hoods their only armor. I spot Beck and Hope too.

Everyone is taking shelter.

If I ever had a chance to escape, now would be the time.

I don't think. I run. Down the porch steps and across the wide field. I slip on the grass twice, land straight on my rear. I came so close to letting Hope in today. She peered deep into a place I keep hidden. Where no one is allowed. She wasn't welcome, but she found her window. Nearly made me reconsider—

What's the point in postponing? Nothing ever lasts. Nothing.

"You are not nothing."

"Get out of my head!" I push Hope's voice away and press forward. My shout is drowned by the storm's call.

When I reach the hill we hiked, I catch my breath. Fold in half and brace my hands on my thighs. A wooden sign on a stake that reads

"Beachfront—2 miles" stares back at me. How did I miss it earlier? I glance up the muddy hill that might as well be a landslide, then down the level path ahead. How fitting.

I take the low road and never glance back.

Soon I find myself encompassed by sky-high cypress trees and the sky's thunderous soundtrack fades. Branches wave and whip, fighting off the wind. The battering rain transforms to a bearable sprinkle. I slow my pace, inhale the wet dirt and bark scent. Wings flap somewhere in the distance and a critter scampers into a nearby bush.

This is how it should be. Inhale. Exhale. This is my send-off.

My joints relax with each new step. The more ground I gain, the less anxiety I feel. A longing deep within pushes me closer to the world I've missed. The leveled path begins its descent, a steady decline to sea level. The trees thin. I smell it now. Though my senses have dulled over the past year, this one never dwindles.

The ocean. Angry and heartbroken. Tossing and turning, high tide unforgiving, leaving little left of the shore.

The muddy path meets a knee-high barrier of smooth stones. Their slick, rough surfaces buffed by seawater and sand. I swing one leg over, then the other. My soles sink deep. My left shoe comes off first, then my right. The walk is painful, the white sand littered with shells and rocks and bark.

But there she is. The ocean I once loved.

And soon my pain will be no more.

TWELVE

Merrick

Merrick stared after the ambulance. After the second set of sirens he'd seen in less than a week.

He'd come to the seaside town where he'd spent summers as a kid to get away from everything. To clear his head following his sister's episode and his mom's disappearance. But he couldn't escape any of it. His problems followed him even here.

"Your mother has been looking for a way out for a long time, Son . . . She's finally found her chance."

Merrick combed his fingers through his hair and tried to shake off the feeling of dread that coursed through his veins. More than that, he needed to drown the sound of Hiroshi's voice, forever stagnant in his mind.

That woman from the water had died in Merrick's arms. And there was nothing he could do to stop it. What were the chances he'd encounter this sort of thing twice in such a short period of time? First Amaya, and now this stranger?

And the girl with her. Those eyes. They looked straight into his soul.

By the time his boat had reached shore with the older girl and he'd called 911, it was too late. He'd taken off his shirt and attempted to stop the bleeding, but he didn't know where to begin. Her blood had been everywhere and nowhere. When the paramedics arrived and took over, the woman was nothing but a ghost.

That could have been Amaya.

"A cry for help," that nurse had called it. Now all Merrick wanted to do was get back to the city so he could be that help his sister needed.

"Son, we need to ask you some questions." A police officer approached Merrick, jarring his thoughts, apology and compassion unspoken in his gaze. "Would you mind coming down to the station with us?"

Merrick swallowed and followed the officer to his patrol car. He had taken the two-and-a-half-hour bus ride from the city down to the coastal tourist trap nestled near Monterey and Pebble Beach three days before. Slept in a cheap hotel, nothing but the clothes on his back and the harmonica in his pocket. Which of course meant he didn't even have his own way of transportation. When he sat in the back of the car and watched the ocean disappear from view, he couldn't help but feel as if he were the criminal here.

Not because of the woman. But the other girl in the water, the younger one. And that man. He'd tried to grab her. Somehow it was all related. Was that girl in danger? Where had she gone after Merrick had taken the woman ashore?

"Come on in." The officer opened his door.

Merrick shielded his eyes from the bright streetlight above. They'd arrived already? He followed the officer up the station steps. Once they were inside, he said, "Wait here."

Unlike what Merrick had seen on TV shows, the lobby area of the station was empty. No criminals with handcuffs waited to be booked. No one screamed profanity as they were dragged back to a jail cell. It was quiet. A popular talent show played on the TV hung high in one corner, and a half-full coffeepot sat on a table with some Styrofoam cups, stirrers, and packets of sugar and dry creamer.

Merrick moved to make himself a hot drink when the woman at the front desk said, "You can come back now."

He followed her to a small room that did not have a two-way mirror as he'd expected. The room did have a wall of regular windows. It was just a big office, not all that different from the ones in his dad's building.

"Have a seat . . ."

"Merrick."

The officer wrote down his name, then proceeded to ask him a series of questions before Merrick's rear even hit the chair.

"We need you to fill out a statement before you leave since you're eighteen," the officer explained after Merrick had given his last name and date of birth. His phone buzzed in his pocket. That would be Nikki. Again. Wondering where he'd disappeared to.

"Now, did you know the woman who committed suicide this evening?"

Suicide. A word Merrick had heard too often recently. The way the officer said it, so matter-of-factly, caught Merrick off guard. Maybe it wouldn't have if his sister hadn't attempted it three days before. Or maybe it was that no one ever talked about this kind of stuff. Not until it happened to them.

"No, I didn't."

"What happened? In your own words. Take your time."

Merrick leaned back in his chair and blew a puff of air through his lips. He blinked up at the fluorescent light overhead and ran through the events, frame by frame, in his mind. Then he leaned forward, hung his clasped hands between his knees, and told the officer everything.

Had it only been a couple hours since he held a lifeless girl in his arms?

The sun had barely set when he left his hotel that afternoon, the lingering scent of salted sea air before him.

Merrick hadn't intended to end up here, exactly. And he certainly hadn't planned to stay more than one night. But somehow, after wandering around the small beach town's historic area of shops and restaurants that first day, he'd found his way to the shoreline. The same shoreline where he spent so many summers as a child. It had been years since his family came for a season here. They used to come the weekend after school let out.

Those summers were the best. Merrick and Amaya and Mom. His father would come on weekends, only to be pulled away for work by noon on Saturday. Then he'd commute back to the city, Bluetooth glued to his ear.

Watching him drive away brought Merrick true relief.

He'd wished Hiroshi would never come back.

Merrick glanced at his phone. One missed call from Amaya. He made sure to call her each day since he left the city. He tapped on her name and pressed Call.

"Hey, dork," she said after one ring. "Still MIA?"

He shook his head. The girl was ten going on twenty-two. "I told you, I needed to clear my mind. You're still in the hospital a few more days, right?"

"Unfortunately, yes. Dad says I have to stay until Doctor What's-His-Name with the black hair who totally looks like Professor Snape, FYI, says I'm free to go."

Merrick laughed and a weight lifted. She was already her normal self. He needed to get back before Maya was sent home. He'd be there for that. Then together they'd work out a plan to find Mom and start over.

Dad not required.

"Where are you, anyway?" Maya asked, as she had each day since he left. He could hear the noise of some television show in the background.

She'd sense a lie in a second. He exhaled. "Remember that beach town Mom used to take us to as kids?"

"The one where Mom and Dad met?"

"That's the one."

"That's like . . ." He could almost see her doing the math in her head. "Two hours south of here."

"Do you think this is where she came? Harold said he followed her to a bus station."

"Harold who?" Amaya asked. "Does he have a purple crayon?"

Her reference to the children's book reminded Merrick how young she was.

"Funny, but no. He's Dad's new chauffeur. Drove me and Mom to the hospital the night—" He cut himself off. "Do you think Mom could have come here?"

"I don't know." Maya got quiet. The TV chatter ceased. "Maybe."

"Don't worry, Maya. We'll figure this out. We'll find Mom. I'm sure she would have taken us with her if Dad hadn't threatened her."

"You heard him threaten her?"

He toed the sand with his shoe. "Well, no, but c'mon. Mom wouldn't leave. Dad probably blamed her for what happened to you." Why did he feel he needed to defend himself to his little sister?

"Um, I have to go," she said. "The nurse is here to check my vitals. Don't be gone too long, okay?"

"I won't."

"Pinky promise?"

"Pinky promise."

She hung up first, then Merrick hit End. The conversation left him hollow. Amaya wasn't defending their father. She knew what kind of man Hiroshi was. They both did.

Merrick took off his shoes and walked down the beach. Trees, a playground, and a few fallen logs cluttered the area. Driftwood used as makeshift benches added to the laid-back feel. The place was mostly abandoned this time of year. His favorite spot would be his for the taking.

It took him longer than it should have to find the old abandoned rowboat he used to play in as a boy. The sun was setting when Merrick climbed inside and sat, picturing the days he and his best friend, Nigel Grimsby, had played pirates. He and Grim hadn't spoken or seen each other in years. Merrick hadn't thought much about the guy until now. Did he and his family still spend summers here?

Their mothers had grown up together. Merrick used to call Grim's mom "*Aunt* Ashley," even though they weren't related. There had also been a woman his mom worked for when she was younger, but Merrick had never met her. What was her name?

Man. The past was getting to him, as if it had been stored right here in this boat, waiting for him to peruse it like an old photo album.

Would Aunt Ashley be able to give him clues about his mom's past? Or maybe that older woman still lived here. If he could track them down, he might be able to uncover some clues. His dad wasn't giving anything away, and Merrick had already spent the previous day stalking his mom's social media. She didn't have any living relatives that he was aware of, and her city friends were more like convenient acquaintances. None of them knew the real Lyn. Not in the way Merrick did.

He pulled out his great-grandfather's—Ojii-Chan's—old harmonica as the sky turned a deep night blue. He messed around with a few chords until he got into his own rhythm. Merrick didn't care much for jazz or the blues. He preferred to play his own songs, as his great-grandfather had taught him.

He sat that way for a while, playing the instrument Ojii-Chan once said was the most American thing he'd ever owned. An ache grew inside him. Merrick missed his great-grandparents. They were gone before he could learn all he'd wanted to from them. He was only ten the year they died, first Ojii-Chan, then Oba-Chan—his great-grandmother—shortly after. They had been married fifty-one years. They came to the States from Japan together, raising Hiroshi as their own after his mother was killed in a car crash. The man had never known his American father, who left before Hiroshi was born.

The harmonica turned cold between Merrick's fingers. He paused, took a breath, then out of nowhere, fireworks blew up the sky above him. How could he forget? This place had fireworks for every holiday. He'd only ever seen the ones on Memorial Day and the Fourth of July, but these weren't much different. New Year's Eve was three nights ago. Had the festivities been delayed by the storm?

The ocean's surface came alive. Merrick blinked. Two figures—a girl and a woman—stood waist deep in the water maybe fifteen feet out.

He stood, set one foot outside the beached boat. *Where did they come from?*

From the corner of his eye, he saw another figure. Merrick turned his head. A man. On the beach. Watching the young woman and the girl.

The girl stared toward Merrick.

The woman sank. Then floated to the surface. Facedown.

Merrick didn't think, he moved. He got behind the beached boat and tried to push. It budged an inch. Two. *This will never work. Of all the times not to know how to swim.*

The man walked toward the water now. That look in his eyes . . . It rubbed Merrick the wrong way. *Come on, stupid boat. Come on.* He dug some sand out from around its sides, then tried again. Finally he gained some momentum and gravity did the rest. He didn't know if it was the sudden adrenaline or the sand-digging or both. Whatever it was, Merrick found himself seabound with one paddle and no experience in an old boat that might sink.

What have I gotten myself into?

"Is that everything?" The officer's hand flew across his notes.

Merrick nodded, then noticed the officer wasn't looking at him. "Yes."

He didn't mention the part about beating that man off the girl when he'd grabbed her.

He also didn't tell the officer how much her gaze still haunted him. It was clear the woman had been someone close to her. A mother? An aunt? A sister?

"I've gotten everything I need. We'll still need you to fill out your own statement and sign it for our records. Then you can go. Do you have someone who can pick you up?"

Merrick was eighteen, but he lacked transportation and his shallow pockets proved he needed his father to bail him out. Not an option.

"Yeah, I can call someone."

As he headed to the lobby to finish up his paperwork, Merrick pulled out his phone and scrolled through his contacts. He was taking a chance on the old number, but he hit Call anyway, his chest pounding.

After three rings, a voice he hadn't heard since he was twelve sounded through his speaker. "Grimsby residence, how may we serve you?"

"Hey, Grim. It's me."

Merrick didn't even have to tell his friend who "me" was before he heard a car engine roar to life in the background.

THIRTEEN

Coral

An eerie silence draped the palace like a funeral garment on a mourn-ing widow. Which was appropriate, of course, as the crown princess's farewell procession had taken place that very morning.

The guests had long since been ushered away. Now all that re-mained was family. The palace staff cleared the buffet table, and the musicians packed up to take their leave. It was all too . . . normal. Routine. And far too quiet. Where was the heart in any of it? Where was the soul?

Jordan floated beside Duke in the now-empty grand hall. The same hall that had been used for Coral's celebration two days prior. Coral lingered at the center of it all. Staring.

How is this real? My oldest sister can't be gone.

It was as if it had happened to someone else. As if Coral was removed from it all and simply watched these horrific events unfold within the timeline of another's story. Except . . .

This happened to me. *So why can't I feel anything?*

Jordan hadn't spoken a word to her since Red Tide came and left. Her last words echoed in Coral's mind.

"You are nothing to me. Nothing."

The king avoided her.

Coral was completely and utterly alone.

Still, she couldn't let go of what she'd witnessed.

My sister had legs. She was mermaid. She was human.

How was it possible? Could the crown princess have found a way to possess a human soul?

"Mermaids do not have souls," Jordan had said once. *"We become as the foam of the sea when we die. And then we are no more."*

Did they really . . . stop existing? Coral couldn't quite wrap her mind around the idea. If there was a before, a now, there must be an after.

Right?

The human boy. Where had he taken her sister? And why did no one speak of the matter?

"I'm ready to go." Duke's irritated tone drew Coral from her musings.

She peered through a slit between her lashes.

Arms crossed and face pinched, Duke resembled a sour-faced guppy more than a merman. "I've been here all day. Staying longer won't make her less dead."

Anger boiled. How dare he. How *dare* he. Coral opened her eyes fully and whipped her head left and right, hoping her father had heard the despicable comment. But . . .

Oh.

Right.

The king had been the last to arrive and the first to leave.

Duke opened his mouth to speak again but Jordan eyed him in warning. While the merman made Jordan out to be weak, terrified the cursed Disease would come for her, she showed herself to be quite the opposite.

Jordan approached Coral then. She lifted a hand toward Coral's shoulder, then pulled back. "Duke will be staying in the palace for a while. Father needs all the support he can get. He hired Duke as second in command."

Coral's jaw dropped. Behind her sister, Duke caught her eye. The way he'd held on to her the other night—it wasn't the end. If given the chance, Duke would take everything.

The thought invited the shadows. A shudder raised her scales. She hadn't told anyone how Duke had grabbed her twice in one night. Nor had she said a word about the human scaring him off. Would anyone believe her if she did?

Jordan would marry Duke eventually. If Coral said something now, accused him of . . . What? *Almost* harming her? No. She couldn't risk that he'd take it out on Jordan when they were alone.

"Now that I'm the oldest, the new crown princess," Jordan continued, "whomever I marry will be next in line to the throne. Duke will need to begin training as Father's heir."

Coral had a wicked wish then. An evil, guilt-inducing wish she at once regretted and longed to be true.

I wish that human had ended Duke for good.

The human. Why couldn't she get him out of her head?

Because, when all others ignored her, in the end, the human was the one to help, to hear her sister's cry.

The same inky darkness of nothing that had threatened to take over at Duke's touch encroached now. Colors blurred together until all became black. Their sounds faded. The music of her constant rainbow died. Not one hue could be distinguished from another.

Coral felt. Nothing.

I am. Nothing.

It was in these nothing moments she believed the Disease had taken over.

And there was nothing under the sea she could do to stop it.

She blinked and blinked and blinked again. Harder. Swifter. A tear never came. Had she imagined them before?

She glanced at Jordan, retreating quietly to Duke's side.

"Jordan." Coral swam after her sister and took her hand, ignoring Duke. "What about Red Tide?" The burning under her eyelids returned. She wanted to rub at them but pinned her arms at her sides instead. "Our sister knew it was coming. Almost as if it was her . . ." Coral swallowed. She'd sound crazy but she had to know. "Her choice. As if she invited it."

A quiet gasp released from Jordan's lips.

Duke's upper lip curled.

"Coral . . ." Jordan sighed. "That is nonsense and extremely childish. Red Tide is a result of the Disease."

"What if the Disease doesn't have to end with Red Tide? What if there is a way to overcome it? What if—"

"Don't be absurd," Jordan said. "Red Tide wins. Every time." Her glare said everything her words did not. Coral's sister saw her as the little mermaid. It didn't matter that she was sixteen now. Jordan wouldn't listen to anything she had to say.

"Isn't it past your bedtime?" Duke said, poking an invisible knife into Coral's insecurities. "Do you need someone to tuck you in?"

"No. I do not." Coral's voice quavered. Her eyes stung. She couldn't let them see her inner defeat.

She turned to address Jordan. "Shall we swim to our chambers together?" Coral eyed Duke. If he was staying, she would not make herself vulnerable.

Jordan shook her head. "Father has given me our sister's private suite. I *am* the oldest unmarried daughter now, after all. The suite is in a completely separate wing. It wouldn't make sense for us to swim together."

Her sister had no idea how much this newfound information sank Coral's heart. Not only with the sense of abandonment, but part of Coral also wished to have the private suite herself. She and her oldest sister had been close. She didn't want Jordan messing with her things before Coral had a chance to go through them.

"I have inherited her belongings as well," Jordan added. "I will, however, be so gracious as to allow you to keep her pearls in your possession." She eyed Coral's wrist.

"Thank you for your kindness, *Your Majesty*."

If Jordan detected the sarcasm in her sister's tone, she didn't show it. "Think nothing of it. Good night."

Coral hesitated, but she would not beg for an escort. Not in front of Duke. Her fear would only encourage him. "Good night."

Duke was nothing more than a sardine in merman's clothing. A coward. And he would not make her afraid in her own home.

Coral's lashes descended to her cheeks. She bowed her head and exited the hall. When she was out of sight, she swam as fast as she could to her now-private bedchamber. Maybe she could ask for a personal guard at her door. That wasn't too grand a request, was it?

Down the long corridors she swam. Through the many arches and around the bends of halls. The eyes of her ancestors followed her, watching from their painted portraits. Some were old, with dull eyes void of life. Others were depicted in their youth, captured in candid action. Twirling at a ball. Rising to the surface.

Most portrayed mermen or maids she'd never met in her lifetime. The awareness was a fin slap to her face.

Few renderings existed of their family all together. Hardly any at all.

No portrait of her parents on their wedding day. There was a single painting of the king, of course, all majestic on his throne.

Then there was one of the crown princess, Jordan, and Coral. She was a baby in this one. The oldest held Coral in her arms while Jordan sat poised and separate, inches away from them as if she were sitting for an individual portrait. Even then, Coral's sunny strands looked out of place next to Jordan's silver hair and their oldest sister's night-sky locks.

When she reached her chambers, muffled voices floated from inside. Coral floated closer to the ajar door and pressed her back against the wall.

"She can stay with me," her grandmother said.

"I don't care where she goes," the king snapped. "She defied me. Shamed me in front of my own people. She has betrayed her family. She has betrayed us all."

Coral covered her heart with one hand. The unexpected pain that rose at her father's harsh words cut deeply. Though they were not close, and never had been, this final rejection crushed her. Would he have no compassion in the wake of his oldest daughter's death?

The argument ceased and Coral retreated into the shadows, keeping as close to the wall as possible so the king wouldn't see her when he passed. She watched him go and said a silent good-bye to the merman who didn't want her.

She was . . . *alone.*

When she was certain he would not return, Coral took a breath and entered her chamber. Her grandmother floated here and there, gathering Coral's things. The old merwoman did not look up when Coral entered. "It's better this way," she said, as if she knew her granddaughter had heard the previous exchange.

Relief and longing filled her heart at once. Coral loved her grandmother. The merwoman understood her more than anyone. But to leave this way? Rejected, unwanted, and full of unanswered questions? It didn't seem right.

She wanted an explanation. Why had Red Tide turned her sister human? What about becoming as the foam of the sea? Coral could still feel the crimson water surrounding her. Thick like blood and smelling of something acrid. There had been no foam. Only death and the vision of her sister drifting away.

"Now then," her grandmother said, snapping Coral's trunk closed and tugging it behind her. "We'd best be on our way, dear. It will be dark soon."

Without another word, her grandmother exited the empty bed-chamber.

Coral examined the space, allowing it to sink in that she might never see the place again. She focused on Jordan's pallet, then looked toward the sand-length mirror they had shared. Coral glanced at her own pallet then. The shawl she had worn the night with the crown princess at the surface rested across her pillow. She retrieved it, then swam through the arched doorframe.

Resolve hardened with each stroke of her tail.

She wouldn't look back.

Her family had failed her. Only her grandmother and the human had bothered to care. Once they were safely out of earshot of the palace, hopefully her grandmother would have the answers Coral sought.

And if not?

Then I'll have to find that human again.

FOURTEEN

Brooke

After

Thunder booms and lightning flashes, as if snapping a photo of the grave end scene. I sit on the shore with my back to a fallen log, hugging my knees to my chest, allowing myself the time I need to say good-bye.

I have all the time in the world now. This is my epilogue. Might as well make it mean something.

I'll leave no note. No farewell video or parting voice mail. The single soul who might care I'm gone will forgive me. Someday.

"I guess this is good-bye," I say to the wind while tossing a rock down shore.

The wind answers in whistles and gusts. As tormenting as it is to be near the sea, it's far more devastating to be apart from it. This is where it happened. Not this particular beach, but the ocean is the ocean.

Whether here or there, she saw everything. She knows my secret. And she remembers that it's all my fault.

I'm freezing. Soaked to the bone from the rain. Good. I deserve it. I let the pain sink in. I have to suffer a little longer before I can be set free.

The breeze that followed me here catches my exposed skin, shooting chills up my arms and down my spine. I blow hot air onto my hands as I resolve to follow through. To sit here, unmoving.

The tide creeps closer. Higher.

Questions rise uninvited. Doubts sail forth, making me second-guess my decision.

Why?

Why am I here?

Is Fathoms for real? Too good to be true?

What happens next?

"Nothing," I say, stopping my doubts in their tracks. "You know there's no use in hoping anymore."

Other questions rise too, ones from the past I don't wish to revisit. But they force their way in.

"What do you want from me?" I cry to the sky.

It answers with a flash of lightning. A flash so close and so bright, it electrifies the clouds, turning them white for a split second before abandoning the world.

I swipe at the rain on my cheeks. As wet as they are, I know the moisture stems from the storm and nothing more.

Daylight soon becomes twilight. Thoughts swirl until they spiral. They leave me a blank and empty mess, more confused than ever.

Get up, Brooke. Leave. Give life another chance.

"And if I do? What then?"

No answer. No guidance.

If anyone cared, they'd have come to look for me by now. So I stay. Past dark. The storm abates, and the clouds clear. The air grows too cold to endure as the stars make their debut. I sniff and cough, a headache taking up residence between my brows. Every muscle aches. I can hardly keep my eyes open.

I rise on shaking legs. It's time. "I'm sorry." I stare down at my bare feet. Examine my shaking hands. "I'm so sorry."

Grief, fresh and new, washes over me as I step toward the sea. I'm to blame for everyone's heartache as well as my own. It would be easier if I were gone. With this truth solidified in my mind, I take another step, allowing the frigid water to wrap my ankles. I'm ready. I welcome the pain, knowing it will be fleeting.

That's when a sound so hauntingly beautiful pierces the night.

I stop. *Impossible.*

Sea foam washes over my feet, inviting me deeper. I hiss, gritting my teeth at the icy salt water stinging my skin.

The sound ceases. My mind must be playing tricks.

I almost don't notice my chattering teeth. The way my fingers change color as I stroke the ocean's surface. Surrounded by her now almost feels like being enveloped by an old friend.

The sound rises again. A tune so desperate and weak it could be a cry for help.

I see it then. The giant yellow life raft, standing out in the dusk as a beacon, headed straight for a rocky cliff.

Ignore it, my mind says.

Not your problem, the waves seem to echo.

Come to me, the sea calls.

I take another step. Hypothermia may set in before I have the chance to drown. But the sound stops me again. That tune. It reminds me of . . .

Go, a voice from the past seems to say. *Save them.*

I'm frozen and aching. My mind spins. Breaths build, one upon another. They grow frantic, panicked, dreading the pain that comes from living another second in this life. I need this.

But a more urgent need inside says I have to help—save—whoever is in that raft.

Something hard and heavy knocks against my elbow. A bottle?

Shaking, I draw it from the water. It's corked, frosted. Sea glass? Did the person in the raft send this? What are the odds it would find me? I glance from the bottle to the raft and back again.

What's one more day going to change?

"Absolutely nothing," I say. Speaking the words aloud makes this a concrete, inarguable truth.

I reverse and speak again, this time loud enough so the sea with all her fathoms below will hear. "This changes nothing."

I'll join her depths soon. Because this changes *nothing*.

Nothing.

At.

All.

Abandoning the sea, I retreat toward shore, bottle in hand.

About a hundred feet to my left, a sandy dune rises, transforming into rocks and ridges. This might once have been a climbing course or even a hiking trail. An adventure for the more dangerous at heart. I face that danger now, my heart *pump, pump, pumping*, blood *rush, rush, rushing*.

When I reach the rocks, I begin my course, though my muscles beg me to turn back. Up and down, back and forth. At times I'm sure I might fall. Then I'm enclosed, stone rising on either side, leaving me unable to view the ocean at all. It's dark now, and the clouds have started to clear. The full moon and stars do little to illuminate my path. But adrenaline fuels a high I've never experienced. A rush that only comes from attempting to tackle the impossible.

When at last I've made my way through the rocky course and down to sea level, hidden tide pools to my left and a shallow cave at my back, I sweep my gaze to and fro.

Where is the raft?

Did I lose it? Did the tide pull it too far down the coast? What if the waves slammed it into the rocks and—

There! I climb down as low as I can. The raft floats ten, maybe fifteen feet away. The gap would mean nothing on land. But a watery gap this wide could be the difference between life and death.

"Hey!" I stand and flail my arms. "Over here."

The drifter's harmonic tune ceases. A flashlight beam illuminates the night.

A voice echoes. Male? Female? Too faint to tell. They're alive, though. Alive is a good sign.

The irony of the situation is not lost on me.

I'm down on my knees. If I reach, I can touch the water with my fingertips. It splashes and sprays. Do I swim to the raft? I might make it. But then how would we get back? If they had a rope or a life preserver—

That's it! I cup my hands around my mouth. "Do you have a life preserver you can toss?"

A holler. A wave of light. I almost detect the words. *"Hold on"*?

Adrenaline vibrates through every muscle. I feel a warmth I know won't last but cling to it all the same.

The flashlight beam bounces. The drifter lifts a white ring in the air. Perfect. We've got one shot at this. *Don't blow it, Brooke.*

"Toss it here!" I call through cupped hands.

The drifter seems to catch on to my idea. My heart pounds as I brace myself.

Ready.

Three, two, one . . .

The ring sails toward me through the air. *Splash!* A few more feet and I would have been able to reach down and grab the thing. Crud.

The drifter tugs the ring back toward the raft, fishes it from the water, and readies to toss it again.

And again it fails.

A third time we try this. And a third time it doesn't work.

Is the rope too short? Or is the raft drifting farther out? We can keep going this route, but then we risk losing our chance.

"One more time," I call.

The drifter obeys and the ring lands in the water a few feet from the rocks.

I suck in a breath, close my eyes, release. Then I turn and attempt to gain a firm grip on a vertical section of rock close to the ledge. My hands are icicles and the stone is far too wet and cold. I frown, remove my tee, and thank the stars I chose to layer today. The tank top underneath wouldn't be my first choice of attire, but it'll do for now.

My removed shirt becomes an anchor. I loop it around the pointed rock and knot it once, tugging to make sure it holds. No way the hack will last long. I'll have to be quick.

I wrap the end of the stretched shirt once around my wrist and grip it tight before easing my legs down over the low ledge. My soles meet frigid sea, followed by my calves and thighs. I gulp oxygen. How is it possible to be colder than I am already?

Once I'm waist deep, I glance over my shoulder. My right leg stretches as far as it can while my left thigh and knee brace against stone. The position is equal parts awkward and painful. The sea weighs me down and then . . .

My toe catches something! *Yes!* I strain for another inch. My biceps shake. My wrist cramps. My breath hitches. But . . . got it!

I pull myself back up, tugging the preserver along. The feat isn't easy and it takes several minutes before I'm flat on the ledge. I pull the preserver in, gathering the attached rope foot by foot by foot. The raft nears. Closer, closer. The figure inside comes into clear view. A boy. With dark hair and broad shoulders that accent his narrow hips.

A boy so familiar, I almost drop the rope.

A boy I know so well, I nearly tumble to the sea.

This can't be happening.

My heart can't take it.

FIFTEEN

Merrick

The car idled at the corner of two major cross streets—if they could be called that. This town could fit inside San Fran's little finger.

Merrick stared at the longest traffic light in history. Maybe his glare would force it to turn green.

"Patience, compadre." Grim clapped Merrick's shoulder, then slouched low in the driver's seat of his '89 Chevy Camaro.

The thing was ancient and Merrick was pretty sure his friend used burger grease to wipe the leather seats, but it was more than Merrick had to his name.

"What do you need a car for, Son?" Ah, the wise words of San Francisco's king. *"We have chauffeurs."*

For a man who claimed to believe in hard work, Merrick wondered if the man ever lifted a thumbnail for himself.

The light blinked a green eye and Grim eased onto the gas, the exhaust spitting out a motorcycle-like noise. An elderly woman with an umbrella in one hand and a hankie in the other glared their way from her perch on the sidewalk corner.

Merrick slunk down. "How long have you had this thing?"

Grim honked and rolled down his window. "Good evening, Mrs. Oliver!"

Mrs. Oliver eyed them as they passed. Was she familiar? No. At this point Merrick would have thought—or hoped—everyone looked familiar. The more people from his past he could find, the closer he would come to his mom.

"Don't judge an old lady by her grumpiness, comrade. You never know what's going on behind her cold gaze."

Sure enough, a quick peek back at the woman revealed where she was headed. Merrick watched her amble, slow and sure, toward the town cemetery. It was dark, but Merrick thought he caught a glimpse of flowers in her hand.

The sight stung and a thought he'd be ashamed to speak aloud rose to the surface. *Better to have someone die, to leave you behind against their will, than to abandon you on purpose.*

The beach town's sidewalks were barren aside from dog-walking, night-jogging locals. Things wouldn't pick up again until late May when Memorial Day flags flew and ice cream shops had lines out the doors.

"So why'd you guys stop coming to my beach?" Grim had a way of reading his mind.

Even after so many years, Merrick had to smirk when his friend called it *his* beach. "It's complicated."

"Our summer parties aren't the same without you, *mon frère*. I've had to set off fireworks from the beach all by my lonesome. It's a shame."

Merrick's laugh shook his shoulders. "Not much of an interesting story, I'm afraid. Same old Hiroshi for you."

"Ah." Flipping the blinker, Grim changed lanes without a glance. "That's right. I saw your summer property in the local ads. Sold for, what, a few million?"

"Yeah. He said the money could be invested in more important things than a vacation home."

"Such as . . . ?"

"Education. Other businesses. Elbow rubbing and behind kissing." Nikki's face appeared in his mind. The dinner at Gary Danko had been several hundred, easy. Chump change to his father. An easy spend for a big deal.

One hand on the wheel, Merrick's oldest friend drove as if he didn't have a care in the world. "You know, just because he doesn't show up doesn't mean you have to follow in his footsteps."

There he was. Grim had never been one to hold back his thoughts.

"I'm not like him," Merrick said.

"Hate to break it to you, pal, but you are."

Merrick pressed his lips and ground his teeth. He was exhausted and he wasn't going to argue. "I appreciate everything. I only need a place to crash tonight. Then I'm gone." He would have gone back to the hotel or even hopped a bus back home tonight, but he could barely keep his eyes open. After the day he'd had, all he wanted was sleep.

At a four-way stop, Grim turned to face him. "Stay as long as you please. Invite Amaya if you want. How old is she now?"

"Ten."

"Whoa. Already?"

"Yeah."

"Cool." A car pulled up behind them and honked. Grim eased on the gas after looking both ways. "My mom is abroad for a while. Paris, Italy, the works. She's wanted to travel for years, and I'm not a kid anymore. So I have the castle to myself and nothing but sunshine days ahead, my friend."

Merrick laughed. "I almost forgot you call the beach house a castle."

"Make no mistake, mate—that's what she is." He turned the knob on the radio, raising the volume more on static than melody. *"Mi castle es su castle."*

Merrick considered the offer.

Grim had the beach house to himself. His mom was gone.

It was too perfect.

"Tell me about your girl." Grim changed lanes as quickly as he changed the subject. The car's blinker sounded like a dying cricket.

"My girl?"

"Yeah, the one I see you with online and stuff. And in those grocery store checkout lanes. The magazines."

Magazines. Right. *Tabloids* was more appropriate. News they were not. But gossip? Bingo. "Not much to tell, I guess."

Grim whistled. "I don't know, *Romeo*. You two looked pretty cozy in those pictures."

Merrick scratched the back of his head, wishing to the king of the ocean, if there was such a thing, they could talk about anything else. "Looks can deceive."

Grim waited.

Merrick tugged on the seat belt. Was it trying to strangle him? "I don't know, man. Nikki's nice. Great legs. Pretty smile."

"Good kisser?" Grim elbowed him.

Ha. Understatement of the year. "Yeah. But she's . . ."

"Not your *one*."

His *one*. As nonexistent as mermaids. He was about to tell Grim everything. About Nikki's "I love you" and Amaya's ambulance ride. But then Merrick's phone buzzed. He slipped it from his pocket and stared at the name that flashed across the screen.

Dad.

"You need to answer that?" Grim asked.

"Nope."

When it buzzed again, Merrick set the vibrate setting to silent.

He'd talk to his father eventually. But only after he got Maya out of there.

"Did you mean what you said? The whole *mi castle es su castle* thing?"

Grim feigned offense. "Would I lead you on, my friend?"

"That's what I thought you'd say." The plan turned to action. "In that case, I'll need to borrow your car."

SIXTEEN

Coral

Something sour and tasting of polluted water burned in Coral's throat.

The farther they swam from the palace, the more an invisible anchor weighted her. Where she thought she might feel freedom, she only felt more pain.

What would the crown princess think of all this?

Coral had always gone to her oldest sister for answers. Advice. Wisdom. Now a hollowness expanded her chest, and it was all she could do to just keep swimming before that feeling consumed her.

It seemed a century had passed before she and her grandmother reached Last Village—the one situated at their merdom's easternmost edge. Coral had never ventured here—to the last signs of life before the Abyss. There had never been a need. Where moonlight pierced the depths in scarce columns moments before, darkness now dwelled. Black, ink-drenched ocean stretched as far as she could see. No seabed. No surface. Oblivion. The beginning of the end. A few more miles and they'd be lost. Never able to find their way back.

Coral shifted her focus to the small village nestled before them. Whoever thought to build homes here must have enjoyed solitude. Or shadows. Or privacy.

All of the above.

Shoulders taut and eyes ahead, Coral searched the homes for signs of life. A few windows glowed with the soft light of a captive crystal jellyfish. With her grandmother in the lead, they made their way through the forgotten village. Past dilapidated old homes built from shipwreck remnants. So different from her regal palace accommodations. Some doors appeared to hang on their hinges, the wood planks rotting with wide cracks or holes in between. Helms acted as window coverings. Masts stood as signposts. Rudders played as fences or gates.

The path took some work to navigate. With little light and zero familiarity with this place, Coral would have gotten lost had it not been for her grandmother. When their way turned into a dead end, Coral stopped.

"What now?"

Her grandmother turned, setting Coral's trunk down in the sand. "My sweet Coral. There is so much to tell you now that you are finally free of your cage."

My cage? "What do you mean?"

The old merwoman approached her, smoothed her hair back, then cupped Coral's face between her palms. "Oh, I have waited for this day, my special girl. The day I could reveal the truth of who you are. And who I am."

Coral couldn't speak. Or breathe. With the Abyss looming in the background, she wasn't sure if she wanted to know what came next. But deep inside she could sense it. She thought of the dark tunnel she swam through to get to her secret place in the rocks. Coral had never feared that darkness.

Light always waits on the other end.

"What is beyond the Abyss, Grandmother?"

The merwoman's face lit up. Had she been waiting for Coral to ask this very question? "The only way to know that, my darling, is to swim through it. For it is only in darkness that one is forced to seek the light. Many Diseased before you have been offered the chance. Now I will ask you—will you trust me enough to follow me through this darkness?" She offered her hand.

Coral blinked. Swim through the Abyss? How? It was said to be never-ending. They could get lost for an eternity. "Grandmother, we should turn back. What you're asking me to do . . ." It sounded like a trick. It sounded like—

Coral gasped.

Her grandmother nodded.

Only one in all the ocean was said to be powerful enough to survive the Abyss.

Coral's pulse throttled.

Her grandmother leaned near. Whispered, "Indeed. Now you will either believe what others have said, or trust me. The choice is yours." She retrieved Coral's trunk and floated away until she vanished into the shadows.

The merwoman who helped raise Coral was more than even Father knew. Her grandmother was the Sorceress of the Sea.

If Father were here, he'd forbid Coral from going anywhere near her presence.

Which is precisely why I have to see it through.

With all her courage plus a splash of defiance, the little mermaid followed the Sorceress into the Abyss.

SEVENTEEN

Brooke

After

When the boy's raft meets stone, he hoists himself onto the ledge without my help.

For several seconds he stares at me, mouth open. When I ignore him and attempt to retrieve the raft, he assists. Together we draw it up in silence, drag it into the cave at our rear.

I stagger and hold on to the rock wall for support, my body catching up to my mind. The shivers come full and harsh and battering. I'm shaking uncontrollably and *ack*! Why can't I stop?

"Hi." His voice sounds like that of a classic movie star. Cary Grant or Rock Hudson. It's a recordable voice. One you'd want to narrate audiobooks so you could listen to it all day.

I wish I could cover my ears and drown out the sound.

He shuffles, his flashlight bouncing with each movement.

My vision blurs. I might throw up. Or pass out. I vote for the second. At least then I'd escape this misery.

When he nears, I stiffen and recoil.

But then something that feels like a blanket wraps my shoulders.

His hands rub against my arms over the material. I'm chattering and shivering and unable to stop when my body falls against his. He wraps me, then removes his coat and helps me put my arms into the sleeves. It's damp but warm. Next he's leading me to the raft and helping me sit, tucking the blanket around my legs like a burrito.

"Th-th-thanks," I say between chatters.

"I should be the one thanking you." He stands his flashlight straight up, then riffles through what appears to be an emergency supply kit attached to the raft. "All this high-end survival stuff and not a single cheese pizza in here."

The joke catches me off guard and I release a clipped laugh.

My vision may not be the best right now, but his satisfied half smile does not escape my notice. I blink and focus. Close the distance between us with my gaze.

There's something so . . . What's the word? . . . *intriguing* about watching a person who doesn't realize they're being watched. I consider him across the space. Face pale when he arrived, the color has begun to return to his cheeks. He's angular, every point of his elbows and bow of his knees revealing a purpose, a destination, a plan.

"Wh-what were you d-doing out th-there?" Curiosity wins against my will.

"It's complicated." He exhales and his shoulders quake. When he looks up, eyes locking with mine, I retreat into myself. "What were you doing?"

"Looking for you. Or wasn't that obvious?"

Lightning flashes over the water, thunder rolling and echoing around the cave. "I h-have t-to g-go." Even as I speak, the idea sounds absurd.

The boy chuckles, echoing my thoughts. "Neither of us is going anywhere tonight. We'll have to wait for morning. It's too dark and the storm's picking up again. And you are in no condition to move, let alone make the climb back."

He's right, but the idea of staying here all night in a cave with him, even if we do know each other, amps my anxiety. What was I thinking? Why here? Why now?

"If you're worried about me hurting you, you should know I wouldn't." How does he read me so easily? Is that regret I hear in his tone?

I hide the grin that threatens to betray my attempt to hate him. "You kn-know that's exactly wh-what a c-creeper would say, r-r-right?"

The amusement in his voice is evident when he replies, "I am definitely not a creeper."

An awkward silence ensues. The worst kind of torture.

"What's y-your n-name?" There. I said it. Now he can know for sure I've forgotten all about him.

He doesn't answer right away, then, "You don't know?"

Frustration flares. "Should I?" I peek at him through my lashes. We're playing a childish game, but somehow it succeeds in making my cheeks burn in a nonchildish way. Ugh. Can I keep nothing to myself?

He presses his lips, clearly considering his next move. Is he going to call me out?

I stare back at him, our eye contact too easy.

"I have an idea."

"Go for it." My pulse speeds. What's wrong with me? Why does he make me feel so comfortable? Make me act at ease and normal? Understood?

"We'll guess each other's names."

The chatters die off one by one. "Excuse me?" My panting slows. I'm far from warm but at least the jacket, the blanket, the cave . . . all work together to ward off the cold.

"Oh, c'mon." He unwraps some kind of protein bar thing and hands it over, then grabs another for himself. After two bites he says, "Don't tell me you've never done this ice-breaker exercise before."

I shrug. "Sorry." I nibble at the fake-tasting chocolate. Best fake chocolate ever.

He shoves the rest of his bar into his mouth, then jumps to his feet.

I flinch.

He makes no comment about my obvious jitters, or my refusal to acknowledge the past. Instead, he sits beside me. "We're stuck here, at least for tonight. Might as well make the most out of it, eh, Katie?"

My nose wrinkles. I bite another corner off the bar.

He laughs again. Lifts both hands in mock surrender. "Okay, okay. Not Katie. It was my first guess. Give a guy a break."

I glance at the rain falling in sheets. A curtain between cave and sea. My anxiety fails to win this one. We have no choice.

We'll stay.

He must catch the surrender in my sunken expression because he says, "Welcome to my humble abode." His voice projects and he sweeps a hand wide as if showing off a loaded bachelor pad. "Now, rules." He rubs his hands together. Scoots closer.

Must he insist on torturing me? I want to widen the gap between our shoulders. But his nearness adds warmth. The tension in my muscles, in my clenched fists, eases.

"We get five guesses each." He holds up a hand, all fingers displayed. "Whoever's guess is closest gets to give the other person a nickname."

If he remembers me, he knows I despise nicknames. Which is precisely the reason I say, "Sounds good."

"Let me see . . ." He taps his chin and stares up at the ceiling.

"Not so fast. You had your first guess. It's my turn."

"That was my practice guess."

"If you get a practice, isn't it only fair to give me one too?"

He shrugs. "I suppose."

"Good." Except I have no idea what I'm going to say. I blurt the first name that comes to mind. "Caiden."

Not-Caiden shakes his head. "Nice try, but you're way off. Now, for the real guesses. Five each. You look like an . . . Hmmm . . . Your hair is so long. And your eyes, what color is that exactly?"

I look down at my lap. This conversation is way too familiar. "Blue."

"No. Not quite." He nears me and I have nowhere to go except into the raft's inflated side. "You're quiet," he says. "How about . . . Serene?"

I scrunch my face and stick out my tongue. That's his guess? What if . . . Maybe he doesn't remember me? I don't know if that would be better or worse.

"Yeah. You're right. Not you at all." His serious words don't match his light tone. He rubs his chin and scoots closer.

Guilt chafes. I'm wearing his coat while he has none. Could he need my warmth as much as I need his?

"Your turn." His shoulder rolls.

His inability to sit still sends an unrecognizable sensation vibrating into my chest and up my neck and face. Why can't I think straight? "Um . . ."

"*Ennnt*, wrong. My name, most fortunately, is not 'Um.'"

I slap him on the arm and immediately regret the acquainted gesture. If I scoot away now, he'll know he's making me uncomfortable. If I don't, I'll be uncomfortable. Gah! Why is this so weird?

"Sorry, sorry," he says. "Go on."

I bite my lower lip, consider using his tactic to make an educated guess. "Alec," I say, a foreign grin spreading across my face.

"Why Alec?"

I sit a little taller. "Because you're kind of a smart Alec. Get it?"

"Ha-ha. Touché."

That same blush from before returns. I only hope he can't see it through the shadows.

As if reading my mind, he leans forward and retrieves the flashlight, shines it on the cave wall. It bounces off the slick stone, reflecting back into his gaze.

"Back to those eyes of yours." He tilts his head to face me. "They actually remind me of these pearls my grandmother used to wear. You could be a Pearl."

My gut pinches at the word *grandmother*. I suddenly feel too tired for games. "Not Pearl." How long can we keep this up? I don't even bother trying on the next one. "Zach."

He lifts a brow. "With an *h* or a *k*?"

"Either."

There's that half smile again. "Nope."

Two guesses later each, we still haven't said the other's name. "What if we both lose?" I ask, because I do not intend to win.

"Then we both get to give each other nicknames." He seems excited at the notion, bouncing where he sits, his shoulder rubbing against mine.

I ignore the butterflies taking flight in my stomach, make my final guess. "Peter." Because I'm so tired I feel far away in Neverland. In that scene when Captain Hook has kidnapped Tiger Lily and Peter swoops in to save her. Except, I saved him. So why does it feel like he's the one with the power here?

"Not a Peter," he says.

"'To die will be an awfully big adventure.'" The quote slips before I can stop it.

"J. M. Barrie. Nice. You enjoy reading?"

He knows I do. "I did. Once."

"No more of this 'once' business. We're getting out of here and it's my turn." He faces me full-on. His features soften and his eyes search mine. "Brooke."

Why did he have to ruin it? "No." I morph back into the me who is more familiar. The me I became after him. "Wrong."

He eyes me but doesn't call me out. "I guess it's nickname time. You first."

This feels too intimate. Still, I say, "Drifter."

"Good one, but a little cliché. You're lucky I like it or I'd make you think of something else."

"If that were the case, we might be here forever."

"Is that such a bad thing?" He elbows my side.

After some time, when he hasn't spoken, I wonder if he's fallen asleep. But a glance at his dimly lit expression reveals he's putting some thought into this. I suddenly regret being so quick to choose my nickname for him.

I don't care. I don't.

"You saved my life," he says, his words a thoughtful whisper. "You brought color back to me when everything seemed gray."

His profound statements open old wounds. Why do I get the notion he's not referring to tonight alone?

"I have a name," he says, shifting where he sits. "But I'm not going to give it to you yet."

I frown. "Why?"

"Because it's not the right time." His self-assurance is incredibly infuriating.

"When is the right time?" What is it about him that makes me say all the words?

"Trust me. You'll know."

I have no idea what that means or why he's acting this way. My heart wants to build walls, to block him at all entrances. I'd made myself forget him. But I'm so tired and cold I can't think. Before I can press him further, my eyelids betray me.

When his arms fall around me, I don't fight it. This boy—this drifter—smells of summer. When the sun hits the rocks just so at about midday in July and everything feels yellow. A poppied hue that complements the blue of the sea in a way that makes their duet sing. Warmth envelops my body despite the chill.

In my sleep, the nightmares never come.

And this, I realize, is even more terrifying than the darkness.

EIGHTEEN

Merrick

The drive back to the city took them less than two hours the next morning. They'd left early enough to beat the rush-hour traffic. So much faster than the bus with all its stops.

"Thanks for coming with, man. You didn't have to." What else could Merrick say? Grim hadn't heard from him since middle school and now he was dropping everything to help Amaya.

"Think nothing of it, my friend." Grim slowed the car as he pulled into the hospital's parking lot.

Merrick dialed his sister's cell. He tried to call her back last night, but it went straight to voice mail. When the same thing happened now, he hung up without leaving a message and looked up the hospital's main line. He pressed Call and waited.

"UCSF Benioff Children's, how may I direct your call?"

"Can you transfer me to room 301, please?"

"One moment."

That moment lasted way too long and Merrick's morning coffee quickly turned to acid in his gut. Maybe she was sleeping. Or eating. Or having her vitals checked again. When the call was sent back to the operator, he asked for the nurses' station on the third floor.

"This is Jana."

Merrick cleared his throat. "Hi, Jana. This is Merrick. I don't know if you remember me, but my sister, Amaya, is there in room 301. I'm trying to get ahold of her."

"Of course I remember you," the overly chipper pregnant woman said. "How are you holding up?"

"I'm good. No complaints. Can I speak to Amaya?"

"Oh, sorry." She laughed. "She was discharged this morning. I believe your father came to pick her up."

Or his chauffeur. Merrick rolled his eyes. If his father could send someone else to do his work for him, he would.

"Okay, thanks."

"Anytime."

Merrick hung up and stared at his phone's still-lit screen.

"Everything all right?" Grim's car had been idling. He put it in park and turned off the ignition. "Are we staying? Going?"

"Do you mind taking me to my house?" It took everything in Merrick not to call Amaya's number again. "I'm sure my sister's there."

"I am at your service, my liege." Grim turned the key and backed out.

Merrick entered the route into his GPS and a female voice led the way. The morning fog stayed low until they reached the city limits, as if issuing a warning of what lay ahead. When Grim pulled up to the curb across the street from the home where Merrick grew up, the place looked different. Empty. He inhaled, closed his eyes, and set one foot on the pavement. But then the front door of his house opened and he ducked back into the car.

"What's up?" Grim asked.

"That's my father." Merrick squinted, keeping his head low so his father wouldn't see.

Hiroshi descended the steps and slid into the back seat of a black luxury sedan. Harold drove the car onto the road and they were gone.

"Keep the car running."

"Sure thing, buddy."

This time when Merrick got out, he sprinted across the street, nearly getting hit by a car he failed to notice. The driver honked and

Merrick waved a halfhearted apology. When he entered the house, classic rock met him where he stood.

It was Tuesday. Of course. The maids were here.

It had been this way every Tuesday for years. Three women—a grandmother, her daughter, and *her* daughter—came to clean their house from floor to ceiling fan. His father could afford it, of course, and his mom said the house was too big to clean by herself. When the oldest of the three stepped from the dining room into the foyer, where Merrick stood, she screamed.

"Goodness gracious, Mr. Merrick. You about gave this old woman a heart attack."

He slumped against the wall. "Sorry, Mrs. H. I'm looking for Amaya."

"She's upstairs in her room. I'm sure she'll be happy to see you before she leaves."

Before she leaves? Merrick took the stairs two at a time and found his sister exactly where Mrs. H said she was. A rolling suitcase lay open on her bed, and Maya was tossing unfolded pieces of clothing from her dresser into the bag. The bed was stripped bare and a shudder ran up Merrick's spine.

It's because the sheets had blood on them.

"Hey," he said. "What's going on? I thought you weren't being discharged yet. I tried to call you."

"Dad took my phone." Maya rolled her eyes. "He said he decided ten wasn't old enough to have my own device. Can you believe that?"

He could but refrained from saying so. Maya spent way too much time on the thing, especially for someone her age. Their father hated social media for anything other than marketing and business purposes, but Mom had convinced him to let Maya get an account on all the main platforms.

"My friends all have accounts!" Maya had argued. When that hadn't worked, she'd taken an alternate route. *"All my classes are in private groups. The teachers post extra credit and give a heads-up on due dates and when there's going to be a quiz."*

That had done it. From then on Merrick's sister had been glued to her phone, checking her likes and friends' status updates every second of the day. She'd gotten tons of new followers as the daughter of a business tycoon. Their father had his money in so many businesses at this point, it was difficult to keep track of exactly what the man did and didn't own.

"So he has your phone." Merrick glanced around her pristine room. Not a thing stood out of place. The white furniture matched the white curtains. A single painting hung on the wall above Maya's desk—a lighthouse that reminded him of childhood and made him wish for clearer answers. "Are you guys going on vacation or something?"

Maya moved to her closet and started pulling things off hangers. "Guess again, big brother. Your crazy sister's being sent away."

Something cold and sharp sliced through him. "Does Mom know?"

His sister emitted a dark laugh. "Her number's been changed. All her social media accounts have been deleted."

Merrick cursed under his breath. He'd checked his mom's accounts yesterday. What could their father have said to make her abandon her own children? The more Merrick thought about it, the hotter his blood simmered. If Hiroshi didn't want their mom found, that gave Merrick all the more reason to find her. He'd convince her they would be safe together. That man would never hurt her with his words, his power, again.

"Get what you need," Merrick said. "Change of plans."

Maya jumped up and down, then ran to him and threw her arms around his neck. "You mean it?"

"I do. But hurry before he gets back."

He left her to finish packing and entered his own room. His duffel bag waited under his perfectly made bed, and his neatly folded clothes were stacked in color-coded order. This had not been the maid's doing. They were not allowed to touch his room upon his father's instructions.

"If I could keep my barracks shipshape, you can do the same with your own space," Hiroshi had said.

It wasn't that Merrick minded being tidy. But he wanted to do it on his own terms, in his own ways. His father's constant military-style inspections were enough to make Merrick hate his room. It had never belonged to him. A mere holding place until freedom came.

He grabbed some shirts, pants, underwear, and socks from the drawers. A hoodie and jacket from the closet. A few necessities from the connecting bathroom he and Amaya shared. He knocked on her door from inside the bathroom and said, "Five minutes," then headed downstairs.

The song had changed from classic rock to an upbeat dance tune. Mrs. H stood on a step stool in the family room, dusting the bookshelves and mantel. Her daughter was in the kitchen and the granddaughter must have been cleaning the bathroom for all the loud singing coming from that direction.

When Mrs. H spotted him, she climbed down and wiped her brow with the back of her hand. "Leaving so soon, Mr. Merrick?"

"Yeah. Don't want to be in your way."

"I thought Mr. Hiro was coming back for Miss Maya. He asked us to keep an eye—"

"I've got it from here, Mrs. H. No worries." Merrick cringed. He didn't want to lie to the kind old woman, but he also didn't need her nosing around or calling his father. And Hiroshi wouldn't have let Maya out of his sight unless he knew Mrs. H would watch out for her.

The last thing he wanted was for her to get fired. So Merrick grabbed a pen and pad of paper from the old rolltop desk drawer in the foyer and scrawled out a quick note. Then he handed it to Mrs. H. "Give this to him when he gets here, okay?"

"But, Mr. Merrick—"

"Ready!" Maya hauled her bag down the stairs. It *clunk, clunk, clunked* behind her. "Thanks, Mrs. H!" Maya hugged her as if the situation was perfectly normal and headed out the front door.

"I'm sorry," Merrick said and followed his sister before he could change his mind.

He ran through the note he'd written in his head as Grim pulled out into traffic and Maya messed with the radio station.

"Doesn't this car have Bluetooth?"

"Sorry, kiddo." Grim roughed up her hair. "We do things old school where I'm from."

Maya found the least static-filled station she could and began talking Grim's ear off. Merrick wondered if his friend would be sick of them by the time they reached his beach house.

He stared out the window from his spot in the back seat, saying a silent good-bye to the life he had. Not that he'd miss it, but still. What else did he know? His phone vibrated in his pocket, but Merrick ignored it. It would be his father, furious with the note he had written.

His own self-satisfaction lifted his mood. The man's face would have been priceless. He couldn't stand to lose control.

To Whom It May Concern,

I'm taking Maya to find Mom. Wish us luck! And hey, don't blame Mrs. H. It's not her fault we never want to see you again.

—Your most disappointing son,

Merrick

NINETEEN

Coral

Coral thought she'd met darkness. She believed they were acquainted.

She was wrong.

Those long nights staring into deep blue while Jordan tossed in her sleep were nothing compared to this. And Duke's hungry stare when the shadows threatened to steal life and sound from color? Mere shadows in contrast to this place.

The Abyss was a typhoon.

A numbing Coral couldn't begin to explain encased her heart. No light. No sound. She couldn't even tell if she had a body, a tail. Torture. Were her eyes open? Closed? Halfway between awake and asleep? She no longer sensed her grandmother's—the Sorceress's—presence. Had she abandoned Coral, deceived her into trusting her as the story said?

The Sorceress enjoys deception. She would have naive little mermaids believe she alone holds the power to provide a cure, an end to the curse.

Why would her grandmother keep this from her? How could Coral trust a mermaid who willingly swam in darkness?

I have chosen to swim through darkness too. Maybe she is more than the stories claim.

The colorless nothing around Coral left her mind to wander. To fill in the blanks of every conversation she never had.

The fight she and her father never shared. All the things Coral was certain he thought but never said.

"You're cursed, Coral. Like your sister. Weak. Pathetic. Diseased. I never loved her and I never loved you."

Then there were the unspoken thoughts of her sister Jordan.

"She looks nothing like me," Jordan might say. *"She can't possibly be my sister."*

And Duke. He'd certainly have an opinion and he wouldn't be afraid to share it.

"She will infect us all," he'd jeer. *"She deserves to drown in Red Tide."*

Coral would reach for her ears to shut out the voices that weren't there, but she couldn't feel her hands anymore.

Her oldest sister, her best friend, was gone.

Her family looked at her as they would a stranger.

"If I am nothing to no one," she said to the black, "am I anyone at all?"

The silence that met her question encased her heart in ice.

The darkness of the Abyss seeped into her pores. Mixed with her blood. Flowed through her veins.

And.

Then.

It.

Awakened.

Coral opened her eyes. She released the bubbles she'd held in for far too long, then shielded her vision. But where she expected light, there were only shadows. Where she'd hoped to see color, only gray remained.

Ready to drown, Coral shook and shivered. She focused on the Sorceress—the human—before her.

"Welcome to the other side," her grandmother—the Sorceress—said with a tip of her chin.

Coral narrowed her eyes and followed her grandmother's gaze down the length of her own body. Her tail, scales, fins . . . vanished.

She stood on two shaky legs, water dripping from the skin that now matched her torso.

"What have you done to me?"

"We all have a little human in us, dear. You just have to know where to find it."

As Coral stepped forward on her newfound limbs, she stopped to look back at the sea, at the darkness that had consumed her.

It consumed her still.

"There is nothing left but death for you there," her grandmother said.

Emotions more powerful than any Coral had ever experienced rose, and temptation pulled her toward the nothing. She'd forgotten about her sister and Red Tide, about Jordan's rejection and her father's hatred. In the Abyss, there was no Duke. No Disease.

She put her own longing for nothing aside and focused on a new-found desire. One that blossomed within her every new second she spent as a human. And her certainty on one matter grew.

The Abyss was not a place. It was the Disease.

Coral was sick. Her insides were as black as the revenge she sought.

"You tricked me," Coral said. "You are a sorceress."

"I have never liked the term *sorceress*. It is far too foreboding." Her grandmother offered a mischievous grin followed by a wink. "Who comes up with these things, I'll never know. The storytellers like to elaborate. Perhaps because what I am is not so interesting."

"What are you, then? A witch?"

"Some call me *guardian*. But by others I have been referred to as *friend*."

"You are no friend to me." A war raged inside Coral. She couldn't cope with any of it. Not without her sister. "How do I go back?" She didn't care if her family didn't want her. She only wished to return to the safety of the cold, dark sea. It was familiar. It was home.

"There is only one way back, though I don't recommend it. It's best you find a way on legs. Trust me on this."

The little mermaid—no—*girl*. The girl had no idea what to do with her grandmother's vague answers. Still, she'd decided. "I'll stay." There was so much her sister had kept from her. Coral wanted to know it all.

Her grandmother led her up the shore, toward a small cottage that looked out over a flower garden and the sea. None of the colors stood out to Coral. All were silent, their song left behind with Coral's innocence.

She would remain human, for now.

The crown princess needn't have worried about her baby sister's heart, though. Once curious about humanity, now Coral sought only one thing. She stared at the pearl bracelet on her wrist with newfound resolve.

She would find the human who had brought Red Tide upon her sister.

Then Coral would make him drown.

TWENTY

Brooke

After

The first light after a storm is the most beautiful.

When I open my eyes, free from the exhaustion that usually plagues me after a long night of tossing and turning, I don't remember where I am. I haven't slept so well in ages. I inhale and take in the scent of the ocean, the feel of something warm and solid wrapped around me. I lean into that feeling. The comfort of home.

"Mmmm," I sigh aloud. *Summer.* Forever my favorite—

I stiffen. Inhale again. All at once the warmth I woke with flickers. Dies. I blink and look up. The cave. The storm. Winter.

Panic overwhelms every other emotion.

He's gone.

And here I thought this would change nothing. That this wouldn't have to hurt at all.

"Over here!" a voice calls in the distance, a mere faded echo beyond the cave's walls.

I still feel his embrace around me. His summer scent remains. He's taken everything. And nothing. He was never—

"Hurry!" A woman's voice. "I found her!"

I try to move, but the feat proves impossible. Try to inhale again, but the task is more than I can bear.

I wish I hadn't fallen for him. I wish we'd never met at all.

"Brooke," Jake says. "Can you hear me?"

Yes, I think.

"She's hypothermic. Get Search and Rescue up here *now*." Static crackles.

A muffled male voice sounds through a speaker.

I don't register his words or see what happens next. I don't care. I'm so tired and cold and I suddenly feel everything and it hurts and he hurts and this *hurts*.

"Hold on, hon. We've got you."

The bottle. What happened to my bottle?

I keep my eyes open long enough to glimpse the ocean once more. Her waves push and pull, playing a tug-o-war with my heart. *"Let go,"* she seems to say.

If I could spring to my feet and run into her arms, forget everything, I would. But a stiller, smaller voice sweeps across my heart. One I remember from before.

"True love makes life, even a broken one, worth fighting for."

Do the words belong to me? Or were they spoken by another? Someone stronger. Braver.

"Hold on," Jake says again as I'm lifted off the ground. "You've got this. Fight, Brooke. *Fight.*"

I've decided my ending, my mind tells the sea.

I don't want to live anymore, my heart reminds the waves.

There's nothing left for me here, my soul reminds my depths.

I don't know why. It doesn't make sense. But Jake's voice is the one that rises above all else. When she grabs my hand, I feel her warmth. And something cracks deep inside.

No, not cracks. Fills in.

So I hold on.

Even if only for a season.

Spring

"When words fail, sounds
can often speak."

—Hans Christian Andersen,
What the Moon Saw

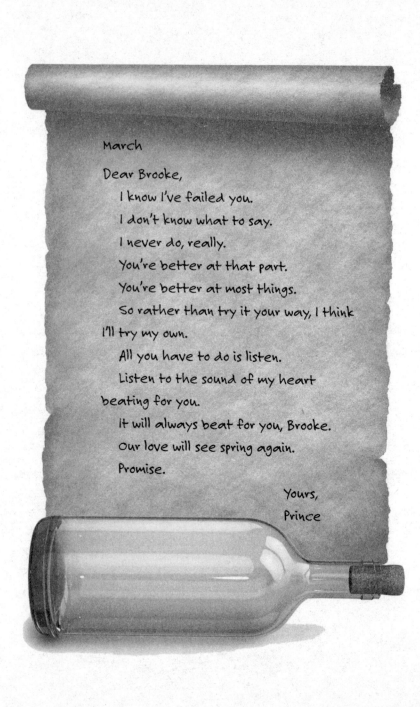

March

Dear Brooke,

I know I've failed you.

I don't know what to say.

I never do, really.

You're better at that part.

You're better at most things.

So rather than try it your way, I think I'll try my own.

All you have to do is listen.

Listen to the sound of my heart beating for you.

It will always beat for you, Brooke.

Our love will see spring again.

Promise.

Yours,
Prince

TWENTY-ONE

Merrick

That was close. Too close. *Extremely* close.

Merrick stepped into the large meeting room at the library and peered through the window on the door. He'd become paranoid. For a split second, he believed he saw his father. In this measly little ocean-town-slash-tourist-trap where the man hadn't set foot in years. Merrick's head spun. They'd survived a few months without raising suspicion. If Hiroshi found them now, he'd ruin everything.

Merrick still hadn't tracked down his mom.

A text chimed from the phone in his pocket as Merrick set up the metal chairs in a circle.

The librarian poked her head in the room and eyed the space. She looked up at the clock and said, "Five minutes."

He nodded and went to check the refreshment table. Coffee and tea, check. Donuts, cookies, brownies, check, check, and check. The suicide survivors group that met every Wednesday evening would be here any minute. This was possibly his favorite thing about his part-time job at the library. Maybe it was that he got to listen in on the session. He never spoke up, but hearing the others' stories made him feel a sense of belonging. They'd all been through something similar. Maya hadn't died, but Merrick had been affected. It helped to know he wasn't alone in that.

The phone pinged again. He'd left his smartphone on his bed at the house in San Francisco, bought a cheap prepaid one with a new number. He'd taken what was left of his cash stash at home too. The money he made at the library wouldn't provide for both him and Amaya. If not for Grim, he didn't know what they'd do. Merrick had promised to pay him back.

"You'd do the same for me," was all Grim had said.

Merrick frowned and flipped open his phone. He hoped that was true.

I'm kind of a jerk. I didn't tell Nikki where I went. I didn't even give her the decency of a good-bye.

He tried to set his guilt aside and focus. Nikki would have gotten over him by now, moved on.

He glanced at the clock. Two minutes. A few people started to file in. They mingled and grabbed snacks and drinks. The real stuff wouldn't actually start for another ten minutes or so. He double-checked that everything was in place, slipped into the library, and hopped on the nearest computer.

Rarely a free minute passed that wasn't dedicated to finding his mom. The fake online profiles he'd created had been of zero use in tracking her down. The few leads he'd found at the beginning of March sped toward dead ends. Now it was the last day of April and still nothing.

How does a person just vanish?

His phone lit up and Amaya's name flashed in the blue window. Merrick flipped it open and whispered, "Hey, I'm at work. You can't keep calling me at work unless it's an emergency, Maya."

"Oh really, *Nigel*?" He could hear the sarcasm in her voice. Amaya loved to tease him about the fact that he was working here under Grim's name. Since it was a small town, he hadn't even been asked to show a picture ID with the paper application he'd filled out. And since he had Grim's permission, it wasn't identity theft either.

"I'm bored," Maya whined. "Grim keeps letting me win Scrabble."

"I do not!" his friend shouted in the background. "This girl's a cheater! Tell her *quixotic* isn't a real word!"

"Why can't I come hang out with you?" Maya said, ignoring Grim's complaints.

Merrick gripped the phone so hard he thought it might break. He closed his eyes and swallowed his panic. How was he supposed to explain to his ten-year-old sister that he was probably wanted for kidnapping? That he could literally go to jail for what he'd done? He'd already seen their names on the government's Amber Alert site. Yes, he'd checked. Not that anyone here paid much attention. Here, time stopped. Here, he could hide in plain sight and no one gave him a second glance.

"It's safer for you at the house," was all Merrick said, tugging his fedora lower over his brow. "Isn't it past your bedtime?"

"Whatever." He could practically see his sister's pout through the phone. "Just bring me a new book to read."

He rolled his eyes and shook his head. *"Prisoner of Azkaban?"*

"Order of the Phoenix. I'm in a broody teenager mood tonight."

"You're not even eleven yet."

"Just over a month and counting, big brother."

He chuckled. Amaya had discovered the first Harry Potter book when she was seven and devoured the series once every year since. She started reading them based on mood. He didn't know how she kept track of the story out of order but said in a bad attempt at a British accent, "Your wish is my command."

Merrick hung up before she could ask for anything else, but he made a note to grab the book before he closed up.

After scanning social media, again, he headed back to the meeting room. It was a larger group tonight with a few new faces ranging from teens to elderly adults. Some came back every week and others filtered in and out. No matter who showed up, the moderator, Miss Brandes, led a good discussion.

And, if he was being honest, Merrick held on to the unrealistic but idealistic hope his mom might show up one night too. It was a long shot, but she'd loved this town when he and Amaya were kids. Maybe she would end up here again and find this group as a way to cope with her own feelings about Maya's attempted suicide.

He still had no clue what he would say to her if by chance that ever happened.

Merrick took a seat on his corner stool, doing a quick check to make sure all was well in the food and beverage department.

"Good evening, everyone. For those of you who are new, I am Miss Brandes. I work full time as the counselor over at the high school and have ten years' experience with grief- and suicide-survivor counseling. As with every session, I'd like to begin by having you turn to the person on your right and say the words, 'You are not alone.'"

The group did as she said, then followed her next instruction to do the same with the person on their left.

"We don't want to put any pressure on our new attendees to speak. You don't even have to introduce yourself. But if you do decide to share, please start by giving us your name so we can get to know you a little better. Sound good?"

Everyone nodded.

The door opened and Merrick cringed. He hated when people showed up late because there was always that awkward moment when everyone turned and stared. He felt for this girl standing in the doorframe now, looking as if she didn't want to be here at all.

Miss Brandes's expression brightened. "I'm so glad you decided to come."

The girl shrugged. She hugged a plain brown paper notebook to her chest. He also noted she was barefoot. Not extremely odd for a beach town but a little less common inside the library. "My grandmother made me," was all she said before walking to the circle.

Merrick moved quickly to add another chair for her while a couple of people scooted out of the way to make room. She met his eyes briefly, an instant that captured the oxygen from his lungs.

Her eyes. Memorable. Distinct. Where had he seen them before?

Merrick had the sudden urge to shield the girl from anything and everything that might harm her.

He shook it off. Ignored the instinct. *Where did that come from?*

Miss Brandes finally turned her attention to the rest of the group and went into her spiel about calling the suicide hotline or 911 in the case of a life-threatening emergency. Then she opened up the floor.

One of the veteran attendees, a middle-aged guy, raised his hand. "I guess I'll start. Hey, guys. Name's Bastian. Most of you know my wife, Emma, took her life about a year ago."

Several in the group nodded, and an elderly woman next to Bastian even reached over and put her hand on his knee as he talked about his four-year-old daughter and how she kept asking when her mom was coming home. Bastian got choked up and Merrick found his own emotions wavering. Hiroshi said it wasn't manly to cry.

But here was this man, this father, who was learning to cope following the loss of his wife and the mother of his child. This, in Merrick's opinion, was the manliest thing he had ever witnessed.

"Thank you, Bastian," Miss Brandes said when he was done. Before she could even ask, a woman who looked to be in her forties raised her hand, introduced herself, and went on to offer some kind words for the grieving man. She had also lost a spouse, though several more years back. She even offered to babysit for Bastian if he needed a break.

After an hour had passed, Miss Brandes offered her closing remarks and encouraged the attendees to stay and talk and exchange numbers or emails. The idea of the get-together was never so much about counseling as it was about coping together. Confiding and relating and being understood.

He rose from his stool and left to make a fresh pot of coffee. When he returned, he noticed most of the group remained, chatting and hugging. But the girl was gone. She hadn't said a word.

Her notebook rested on a chair.

Merrick could give it to Miss Brandes. She *did* work at the school and would have no problem returning it. He could also place it in the lost and found, which was what he was supposed to do in the event someone left a belonging behind. It was his job. He'd have done it with anyone else and forgotten about it.

Before he could change his mind, Merrick snatched up the notebook and peeked inside the cover. He smiled at the name penned there in practiced cursive, then snapped it closed and sprinted for the exit. She'd probably already left. It wasn't like she would be waiting around for him, her knight in shining armor, to return her beloved pages.

When he reached the curb beside the parking lot, Merrick scanned the area. The night lamps had come on, washing the asphalt in yellow light. And there, on a bench between two hydrangea bushes, sat the girl. She didn't seem to notice him. She was too engrossed in whatever she was doing on her phone.

He approached and cleared his throat. At the risk of coming off as a total creep, he said, "Hi."

She didn't look up. Kept scrolling through social media.

Merrick swallowed hard. Was she ignoring him? Lost in thought? He stepped closer and peered over her shoulder. She had done a word search for *princes in the United States*, which pulled up some interesting profiles.

"Hi," he said again.

She jumped this time, pressed the phone to her chest.

He held in a laugh. Though she was older, the girl reminded him a little bit of his sister. Amaya was easily startled too when focused on a particular thing.

"Sorry," Merrick said. "I saw you inside. At the meeting? I'm Merrick."

Not an ounce of recognition altered her expression.

"Anyway . . ." He dragged out the word. This was not going well. Merrick needed to redeem himself. He offered the notebook. "You left this . . ." Was she going to tell him her name?

No. She wasn't. Her eyes widened. "Did you read it?"

Merrick blinked. He wasn't the greatest guy in the world, but did he strike her as someone who would read someone else's private whatever it was? Looking inside for her name didn't count. "No. Of course not." He shuffled from foot to foot. What was it about this girl that made him nervous? "I didn't get your name back there." If she knew he'd opened it, he'd never stand a chance. Better to let her give an introduction.

"I didn't give it," she said, deadpan.

He chuckled. Kicked a small pebble by his shoe. "Right . . ." He dragged the word out. "Well, then, you leave me no choice but to guess . . . Anna?"

The girl rose, pocketed her phone, and tucked the notebook under one arm. She was short, her forehead only reaching Merrick's chin, he guessed. He'd have to get closer to know for sure.

She looked him straight on as if assessing his truthfulness about the notebook. A pearl bracelet on her wrist caught his eye.

Where had he seen it before?

He abandoned his game and said, "I promise." He held up his hands in surrender. "I didn't read it." Merrick made an X over his heart with one finger the way he used to with Amaya. "I'll pinky promise if you like." Lame. Now she was going to think he was making up an excuse to touch her.

The girl, still nameless, scrunched her eyebrows. "Pinky promise?"

"Aww, seriously? You've never pinky promised anyone?"

She shook her head.

Her naiveté was adorable and Merrick couldn't help himself. "Can I show you?"

She hesitated.

"Please? It'll just take a second." Why did he care if she knew how to pinky promise? They were both way too old for this sort of thing.

"Okay."

"Yeah?" His heart raced faster the longer her eyes remained on his.

This was insane. He'd full on made out with Nikki multiple times. So why did this girl send his confidence packing? They hadn't even touched yet.

"So it's . . . you stick out one pinky finger." He showed her and she copied him. "Then we link." He stepped close enough that he could smell whatever body lotion or shampoo she used. Like sunscreen and pineapple. Vacation. Escape.

The girl stared up at him. She was impossible to read.

Merrick wrapped his pinky finger around hers and shook it gently. How could a touch so slight raise this many feelings at once? He cleared his throat and backed away. "And that's a pinky promise. Now you know I didn't read it."

"Do I?" She raised one eyebrow. Again, adorable. "How so?"

"Because breaking a pinky promise is treason." He toed the ground. He needed to get back inside so he could start breaking down the chairs and cleaning up the food. But this girl was so much more interesting.

"What happens if you break it?"

He'd never been asked this before. He and Amaya knew there was no way around the pinky. "I guess if I break it then I have to give you something."

"Like what?"

His phone vibrated. He ignored it. "What do you want?"

She tilted her head. The longer he studied her, the more he was sure this wasn't their first meeting. At the same time she said, "A prince," Merrick asked, "Have we met before?"

"No," she said almost immediately.

"Are you sure?" He racked his brain. It wasn't every day he saw eyes like hers. Violet mixed with ocean blue. "I'm pretty sure . . . Wait—" He tried to read the creases in her forehead and the unsure way in which she held herself.

The image of where he'd seen her became clear. It was the reason she'd come to the meeting tonight.

He dropped his gaze.

The first time they'd met had lasted mere seconds, but however short-lived, all he cared to do was forget that night ever happened.

But here she was. In his life again. "I've always believed in fate." Now he was sure it existed.

"Fate is for fairy tales. It doesn't exist."

We'll see about that. "I was there. That night." He didn't explain or give more of a reference. When he found her gaze again, he had everything he needed.

The girl blinked, then took a step back, recognition a swirling storm in her eyes.

Everything in him wanted to quiet that storm.

A few people walked past them, talking and chatting. Bastian even waved a thanks to Merrick before he got into his car.

But Merrick kept his eyes on the girl without a name. Not even he thought he was ready to understand everything she had bottled inside. But, for some reason he couldn't figure, he wanted to. And he told her as much when he said, "I know a prince."

Her eyes held an ocean of pain, confusion, and maybe even hope?

If it took every last promise he had in him, Merrick was determined to do whatever it took to set that ocean free.

TWENTY-TWO

Coral

Coral could hardly believe he was real.

The human who had taken her sister. He'd been here all along.

And he claimed he knew a prince.

Did she dare believe him? A human? Her grandmother hoped going to the meeting would help her move past her pain. It was pain that drove Coral toward her goal. Was she supposed to ignore what happened to her sister?

No. She would never forget. Not in a hundred mermaid years.

When the boy didn't stop staring, she crossed her arms and searched for the anger that eternally lingered an inch beneath her surface.

"There is goodness in them," the Sorceress had said. *"Give them a chance."*

"They've had their chance." Coral was tired of having the same argument. Why couldn't her grandmother see humans for what they were? *"They wasted their chance and now the crown princess is gone."*

Her father had been right all along. And Jordan.

Coral hated them for it.

"I'm Merrick, by the way."

"You said that. Merrick," she repeated. Why did this name taste different from all the others?

"Be careful."

The once–future queen's words rose, and Coral made them her own. She had no intention of falling for a human as her sister had, no matter how nice he seemed. Coral would get her revenge and return to the sea. That was the plan.

And nothing would alter it.

But he'd said he knew a prince.

"Where can I find him? The prince."

"I looked for you afterward. That night."

Was he avoiding her question? "Okay. Thank you?"

He scratched the back of his head.

A car pulled up to the curb.

"Coral," she said quickly.

"Coral?"

"My name."

Now it was Merrick's turn to eye her. Did he think she was lying?

The car's passenger-side window rolled down. "Hi, dear, did you have a good time?"

Coral looked at her grandmother, then back at Merrick.

"Who's this nice young man?" her grandmother asked.

Merrick opened his mouth at the same time Coral said, "No one. Let's go." She winced at her own harsh words. Then winced again for caring. What was wrong with her? She shouldn't care what this human felt.

"Okay." Merrick opened the door for her. "I'll see you next week then?"

"She'll be back, son. Don't you worry." Her grandmother winked at him and heat rose to Coral's cheeks as she climbed inside the car.

Merrick closed the door and leaned down. He offered his pinky. "I'll tell you about the prince next time?" He waited there with his elbow on the open window frame. Whispered, "Coral."

She looked back at her grandmother who pretended not to notice their exchange. She didn't want anyone to get the wrong idea. She only wanted to use the human to find the prince her sister had mentioned.

She linked her pinky with his and shook it once, then released. Coral would not let it go past that. No doubt he wanted the same thing her sister's prince had taken. This boy hoped to crush her heart and leave her in time for Red Tide to rear its ugly crest.

He reached out to me. He cared when no one else—

No. She would not allow herself to return to that naive way of thinking. That had been before the Abyss. Before the crown princess's tears and human legs and Red Tide and Duke's glare and Jordan's disregard and Father's—

Coral blinked away the sting in her eyes. She pulled the button on the door and the window rose.

The boy watched her through the glass. She could feel his gaze even after they drove away.

"He seemed nice," her grandmother said when they pulled onto Main Street.

Coral offered no comment. She was tired of everything. She was . . . tired. Beyond the glass, streetlights winked and shop lights blinked off for the evening. She clutched her notebook. These pages were the only ones who understood.

Coral had taken to writing down whatever she could, whenever she could. The words found her in the middle of the night. When the nightmares surfaced and the ache for her oldest sister flourished. She opened to a blank page and removed the pen that had been clipped to the back cover. With the streetlights as her guide, she bled fresh words in black ink, forcing herself to relive the pain, a reminder of why she had chosen humanity in the first place.

I've discovered the secret to breathing underwater, she wrote.

Don't.

Hold your breath as long as you can.

Count to ten, then twenty, then thirty.

Don't breathe. Don't surface until the nothing comes . . .

"Do you want to talk about it?" her grandmother asked when they turned onto the dark, winding road that led to their cottage.

"No."

Her grandmother sighed. "Your sister would have wanted—"

"Don't you dare presume to know what she wanted." Coral's hands shook and the pen dropped, leaving a long, ugly, permanent mark across the page.

"I know more than you think," the Sorceress said. "She was my granddaughter before she was your sister." Her voice sounded hurt, choked and strangled.

Coral had no words. She'd been cruel and longed for who she had once been. The optimistic little mermaid who believed the right words could fix anything. That the light was always there, waiting for her to find it.

Now Coral lived for darkness. She survived on it. Drank it in until it filled every crevice and grotto inside. Each day that passed without the crown princess acted as a dagger to her spine, paralyzing her until she couldn't move. She would find the prince.

And she would destroy him.

As they pulled into the driveway behind the cottage, all Coral could think about was Merrick's promise.

She smirked, a plan forming in her mind.

Her grandmother was right. Coral would return to the library next week. She was a princess. And a princess never broke a promise.

Besides, who better to help her catch a prince than a human boy who would drown her if he ever got the chance?

TWENTY-THREE

Brooke

After

I never dreamed I'd find my way back here. After three months of recovery and suicide watch at a traditional psychiatric facility, Fathoms Ranch never looked so good.

This is what home is meant to feel like.

I watch Jake from my place in the passenger seat. She has the window rolled down and one arm out, surfing the breeze.

We drove the coast highway, cruising for hours with the sea to the west and the hills to the east. We didn't talk much and I didn't mind. What do I say to the woman who saved my life after I tried to end it?

I can't gather the words, so I keep quiet and hold fast to the stuffed tote bag full of belongings in my lap. The tote bag I have because Jake brought it to me when I was being treated for hypothermia. A popular book quote graces one side.

"That's the thing about pain. It demands to be felt."

—John Green

I'd ignored—or tried to ignore—whatever message Jake wanted to send with her not-so-subtle gift. But then she produced the bottle.

My beautiful, stupid bottle.

When I'd finally opened my eyes after a week in the intensive care unit, the doctors said it was a miracle I'd survived. Jake's was the first face I recognized.

"You gave us quite the scare." She set the corked, frosted, blue sea glass bottle on the table beside my hospital bed.

I stared at it. Why had she saved it? Amid the vases of flowers and balloon bouquets and the dozen cards from the girls at the ranch, it looked . . .

Ordinary.

"You have a visitor," Jake said that first day I sat up without help.

I knew who she meant, but I'd been too prideful to face the one who'd sent me away. "I don't want any visitors."

"Understood," Jake conceded, palms raised.

She didn't push me or prod me or try to guilt me into changing my mind.

Which was why I didn't refuse *her* visits. Jake showed up every Saturday for the past three months. I didn't say much and she didn't ask. When she picked me up this morning, I didn't question her.

"Hope's been asking about you," Jake says now, turning off the ignition and shifting the van into park. "She's calling you a mermaid. They all are. I'm still stunned you survived those temperatures for that long. The ocean was watching out for you."

I shoulder my tote bag and exit the car at the same time she does. How do I respond? I still don't know what to make of all this. Of my vivid hallucination or why I survived. I stick with the safety of my silence and follow Jake inside.

The moment we cross the threshold, a whirlwind of commotion ensues. Two Goldendoodle dogs greet me, jumping and pouncing and licking my hands. Mary shoos them away and hands me a cup of hot cocoa. The girls gather around. A few I recognize from the group session, but new faces have been added to the mix as well.

When Hope, the smallest of all, presses through them, she offers me a dried, wrinkled, and faded paper heart. "You dropped this. I saved it."

I try to deny it, but even the ocean in all her vast depths doesn't have as much soul as this little girl has with her genuine tenacity and very real heart.

I clear my throat and meet her eyes. "You saved it all this time? Why?"

She exchanges a knowing look with Jake. "I had a feeling you'd be back." Hope winks. "Wanted to make sure you remembered."

She doesn't have to continue. Because despite my hypothermic hallucinations and the craziness of that January day, Hope's words stayed with me.

I am not nothing.

"Thank you," I say. Then, "I'm sorry."

She shakes her head. "You can be sorry for dropping my heart. You can even be sorry for running away and almost dying. But you don't get to be sorry for existing anymore. Okay?"

My chest grows tight. My eyes sting. I have no profound words to match her eleven-year-old wisdom, so I nod and repeat, "Okay."

How fitting this one little word feels as I clutch my quote tote and head upstairs.

When I'm under the spray of the warm shower, alone with nothing but the artificial rain as my soundtrack, I say it again. "Okay."

And when I'm lying in bed? I breathe the word. Nod as I drift off to sleep. Speak it again.

"Okay."

TWENTY-FOUR

Merrick

Anxiety grated Merrick's nerves all the way back to Grim's.

Coral sought a prince.

He'd given her his word. Promised to help her find one. But as he walked home, doubts weighed in, making Merrick question their entire conversation.

What if his father had sent her? Would Hiroshi send a teenager as a spy? Maybe she wasn't a teenager. What if she just looked young? Had his father somehow discovered the police report from that terrible January night? If Hiroshi had tracked Merrick down, why didn't he act?

Merrick frowned as he entered the dark beach house. His first instinct was to check on Maya. He crept upstairs, where he found her sound asleep in Grim's guest bedroom. Merrick exhaled and made his way back down to the kitchen.

He cursed. Too loudly for this time of night, but who cared? His father *would* pull a stunt like this. To make Merrick go insane. Leave him wondering if he was being watched or followed.

Eventually, he'd snap.

But that day was not today.

Whoever Coral was, Merrick would find out. If she was a spy, he'd—

"What am I doing?" He hung his head and massaged the bridge of his nose. "This is crazy." He spoke the words aloud because somehow it made them more concrete. He'd let his father get into his head. Maybe in the city, Merrick had been a hotshot bachelor. Here he was a nobody. It made things simple. Something he'd never experienced.

Grim's laptop sat on the counter and Merrick pulled it toward him. He logged in to several social media platforms in different tabs and started his nightly keyword search.

"It's late, man," a groggy Grim said from the couch. "You should get some shut-eye."

Merrick picked up the laptop and moved toward the stairs. "Sorry. Didn't realize you'd fallen asleep down here."

Grim sat up, rubbed his eyes, and waved him off. "Sit down." He walked to the kitchen and opened the fridge. "Hungry?"

"I'm good. How was tutoring?"

"Can't complain, my friend." Grim took a swig of OJ straight from the carton, then wiped his mouth with the back of his arm. "Job's a job, am I right?"

Merrick nodded and found his place at the counter again. His eyes were dry and he could feel the lack of rest wearing on him. But he didn't have time to waste. He'd sleep after he found their mom. She would understand what Maya needed and she wouldn't send her away, like his father had wanted to.

Grim pulled up a bar stool and joined Merrick at the counter. "You forgot the book, didn't you?"

Merrick winced. "I'll grab it tomorrow."

"Can I ask you something?"

Merrick opened a new tab and typed in the address for the next social media platform. "Yeah."

"Maya's cuts?"

An inward groan rumbled through him. "Not this again. They're old." The site opened and Merrick's eyes widened. The person who used the device last hadn't logged out. His sister's profile photo stared back at him. "Has Maya been on here?"

Grim shrugged. "She wanted to see her friends. I swear, she didn't post anything."

Merrick swabbed a hand over his face and scanned her profile. Then he checked her messenger box. Her search history. All looked untouched. Or she'd covered her tracks. "I don't want her on here." Merrick couldn't prove it, but he'd had a sinking suspicion his sister's "friends" were part of the problem back home.

"You're avoiding the question." Grim nudged him.

Merrick looked up from the screen. "We've had this conversation. She's not cutting. She's taking classes online under a fake name and address. As soon as I find our mom, we'll be out of your hair and Maya can get treatment close to home. She's *fine*."

"Hey now, friend, you know this isn't about that. I have no problem with you staying here or being your wingman when it comes to running from the law. I know your intentions are good. So I've taken a risk. And gladly. But your mom—"

"What about her?"

"Did you consider maybe she doesn't want to be found?"

The question stilled Merrick's fingers over the keys. "This is my father's doing." He resumed typing. Clicked through a few profiles of women who fit his mom's demographic. Nothing.

"I don't know, compadre." Grim rose and returned the carton of OJ to the fridge. "Looks to me like your mom's the one—"

Merrick logged out and snapped the laptop closed. "You're right. I should go to bed."

Grim sighed. "Good night, man. I'm here if you need anything."

Merrick grumbled a pathetic "Night" and walked upstairs to his futon in the den. When his head hit the pillow, he almost immediately passed out.

He found his mom there in his nightmares—running. Every time he'd catch up to her, she'd back away. He grabbed hold, but she vanished beneath his touch.

When the sun shone through a screen of fog in the morning, a new strategy found him. He needed someone on the inside.

He picked up his phone and dialed the number he'd thankfully memorized.

Merrick could only hope Nikki wouldn't hate him too much.

TWENTY-FIVE

Coral

If humanity was Coral's prison, high school was her torture chamber.

She slammed her locker and ducked her head, wishing this place were made of sand. Longing for it to be filled with water so she could swim her way free.

But these walls were concrete and the people between them were stone. Coral had learned how to make herself small and insignificant as the little mermaid she'd once been. But even this didn't stop some people from blocking her way to the exit.

"Hey, what's the rush?" some stupid boy with his stupid grin said. Typical human. How could her sister have fallen for one?

Coral tried to distinguish which boy in particular this was. She couldn't. They were all the same, of course. Each and every one of them were Dukes or princes or kings, or some other version of the men, both below and above, she had grown to loathe.

At least one thing she'd been told about the Disease rang true.

The male species was immune. Deep, soul-worthy emotions they could not fathom.

"I saw your sister the other day," the boy said, hanging an arm around Coral's shoulders though she tried to keep walking. "She's got quite the voice."

Had he been out on a boat? How did he know about Jordan? Her family's reputation preceded her when all she wanted to do was disappear. But what did she expect? Jordan's voice *was* beautiful. She was famous, as the crown princess had been before her.

"Too bad your other sister offed herself," the boy added.

Coral spun on him then. "What do you know about it, you worthless urchin?" She spat in his face and stomped on his flip-flopped toe, immediately regretting the action.

Some princess she was. What had she become? Human or not, she had no excuse for acting so improper. She was above this.

"You little witch." He grabbed her hair and yanked hard.

She jerked, but his grip was too tight.

His bony fingers latched on to her wrist. "What's this?" He tugged her sister's pearl bracelet free and held it high in the air. "Looks like money to me."

"Give that back." Hysterics threatened to break her. The bracelet was the only thing she had left of the crown princess. "Please."

"Nah, I think I might take these to the pawn shop. See what they're—"

"Hey!" Another boy with sloppy clothes but kind eyes jogged toward them from the hallway's opposite end. This boy was older. Coral guessed he was one of the after-school tutors from the community college.

"Are you looking to be thrown into moving traffic, my friend?" His voice carried through the long corridor. "Because I can certainly make that happen."

The bully released her as Mr. Tall, Bright, and Lanky approached. He wore a laid-back grin and had shaggy brown hair. He didn't boast the build of an athlete, but his presence made the hallway feel much smaller.

"Just having a bit of fun." He dropped the bracelet.

Coral snatched it off the floor and slipped it over her hand, then tugged her sweater sleeve down to cover her wrist.

"I like fun, amigo." Coral's hero clapped a hand on the coward's shoulder and squeezed hard. "How about I have the same kind of fun with you?"

The urchin shrugged him off and stormed away, giving the finger and tugging on the collar of his letterman jacket.

"You all right, ma'am?" The kind boy swept his arm in a horizontal arc and gave a chivalrous bow.

Coral had never been called "ma'am" before, but she had a feeling this guy addressed everyone the same way. With terms of endearment or friendship or respect.

"Yes, I'm fine."

"Be careful." He wagged a finger. "That word is often misused. Name's Nigel. Can I walk you somewhere, Miss . . . ?" He offered his arm.

"No." She took a quick step back, not giving her name in return. "I'll be fine."

He straightened. "Again with that word."

She avoided his gaze.

"Okay . . . well, I'm around if you ever need a bodyguard." He saluted and they went their separate ways.

Soon Coral found herself soaking up the sun on the sidewalk outside the school. The *only* good thing about the school was that it was situated exactly three blocks from the beach. It was so close, in fact, that grains of sand lingered on the pavement where the humans had tracked it over time. She wanted to run there. But it was May now, and she was no closer to finding her sister's prince than when she'd started.

"Coral?"

An inner groan ensued. So close, yet so far. She turned to find Miss Brandes with hair piled high and glasses thick as bottles looking right at her.

"Do you have a few minutes to talk?"

No. She didn't. There were bigger things at stake here. This woman could talk all she wanted, but what would it help? Absolutely nothing. "I came to your group." What else did she want?

"Yes, and I'm so glad you did. I promise this isn't about that." Miss Brandes turned as if Coral had already agreed to follow.

She did, of course. The last thing she needed was her grandmother's chiding.

Might as well get this over with.

The office was as bland as any other. Cluttered and filled with drab, muted shades of brown and taupe and manila. Coral sat in the seat before the metal desk. Her leg shook and she stilled it with one hand.

"How are you liking your classes?" Miss Brandes asked.

Coral shrugged. She'd spent her entire life splitting time between a class full of students and her private studies at home in the palace. Now that she attended school full time, she longed for the solitude a private tutor brought.

"Your teachers say you've been . . . distracted. Want to talk about that?"

"Nope."

"And your family? Any updates? Have you spoken to them since we talked last?"

Coral eyed her through narrow slits. This woman was venturing dangerously close to the place Coral kept under tight lock and key. "No."

"I only want to help."

Why did everyone keep trying to help her? The Sorceress bringing her here. Then Merrick with his pinky promises. Now Miss Brandes. The only thing that would help Coral was out of reach.

"Your English teacher says you're quite the writer. He showed me some of your class work."

A new emotion lowered Coral's guard. She sat back in her seat. Waited.

Miss Brandes took out a file and opened it flat on the desk before her. She thumbed through some pages and pulled one free. "This piece is particularly good. So good, I'd like to encourage you to submit it to the district-wide Young Literary contest."

Coral's ears perked. She sat straighter in her chair. She searched for malice in Miss Brandes's eyes but found only eagerness.

This human was complimenting her? What was the catch?

"The winning entry goes on to the state competition. From there, first place would get your work published in a nationwide anthology."

What did Coral care about contests and anthologies? She'd never been good enough to fit within her own family. How was this different?

Miss Brandes closed the file and laced her fingers over it. "You have a chance to start fresh here. Your grandmother filled me in on some things."

Of course she had. More distrust grew for the woman who'd helped raise her.

"I wonder how you'd feel about me referring you to a therapist. She travels, but she's in town the second and fourth Tuesday of every month. She also does video chat sessions if that works better for you. Your grandmother says you deal with anxiety? Is that why you didn't share last night?"

Why must they insist on meddling? Didn't they know there was no cure for the Disease?

Coral shook her head. "I didn't want to share." What would she say? That her sister had been taken by Red Tide and now Coral wished it had taken her instead?

"I see," Miss Brandes said. "You know, a lot of writers deal with anxiety when speaking in a large group. They find it much easier to express their voices on the page." She backed away from the desk and rose to her feet. "Consider the contest, okay? I'm here to talk if you need me. And if you change your mind about the therapist, here's her card."

Coral took the small piece of cardstock and stuffed it in her bag without a glance. "May I go now?" She couldn't stay in that office one more minute. It was too much to try to understand why this strange woman was being so kind.

"My door is open."

When she was free, Coral swiped at her dry eyes and ran to the coastline. Shells bit at her soles and the water tugged at her ankles. She looked up at the white houses along the hills with walls of windows and balconies that overlooked the ocean. Then she wrote. She wrote until she couldn't write any more.

For an afternoon, Coral forgot about the prince she was supposed to find and the hatred she was meant to have.

Instead, she thought of colors, and the music they once made.

TWENTY-SIX

Brooke

After

I find Jake alone in the gathering room.

It's different, warmer than my previous venture here. Another two months until summer, but I can already feel the new season inside this room. Yellow daisies dress the windowsill and the heat from the afternoon sun bathes every surface in an orange hue.

I welcome the colors that have started to grow vibrant again with winter's end.

"Our first real one-on-one." Jake draws my attention away. "I can hardly believe it."

"Me either." Nerves unearth old insecurities. I find my neutral perch on the chaise I sat on my first day. This time I fold my legs beneath me and sit back, allowing myself to get comfortable.

Jake sits across from me, and I brace for the thousand questions she's kept at bay these months.

I fidget with the tassel on a throw pillow.

"Nice bracelet," Jake says. "Is that new?"

The question takes me aback. I glance at my wrist. At the pearls

I'd tossed in a drawer earlier this year. Why did I put them on this morning? Nostalgia?

"They were a gift." I don't elaborate.

She doesn't push me. "You must have so many stories, Brooke."

I start, stare. This is the part where I'd normally let off a smart remark, up my defense. But I'm tired, and despite the fact that freezing to death is months behind me, I've never quite been able to shake off the cold. I tuck my socked feet in between the cushions and sigh.

"Whenever you're ready."

I avoid her gaze, but a glance sideways reveals she holds no tablet. No clipboard. No recorder. I'm still skeptical, but . . .

Has Jake ever given me a reason not to trust her?

"Why did you save me? You knew I wanted to die."

"I knew you *thought* you wanted to die."

"Same thing."

"Is it?"

I rub my arms, shift so the sun finds my skin. "I don't know."

Jake stands. She lifts the lid off the ottoman a few feet away, withdraws a knit blanket. She sets it on the edge of the chaise, a few inches from my thigh. An invitation.

Finding her seat again, she nods. "It's okay not to know, Brooke. That's the first step toward healing. Knowing that we don't have all the answers all the time. Understanding there isn't always a why and sometimes we feel the way we feel because we do. And that's okay."

I want to believe her. So. Much. I've been prodded with questions from the doctors at the hospital. People from my past told me to move on. But Jake has allowed me to be exactly where I am.

And here I wanted to believe she was another villain in this tragic tale.

"What do you want, Brooke? Right now. Right here. Do you want to die?" Her forward question holds nothing back, but a sensitivity lingers there too.

I don't respond for a stretch. Then, "I want to start over." It isn't until I say the words aloud that I realize they're true.

"Fathoms is the perfect place to do that. When I received a call about you last fall, asking if we had an opening, I sensed you were someone special."

It's the first time we've talked about it. What brought me here. And who I left behind. "She wanted what was best for me, I think." I only wish I noticed sooner.

"You'll be eighteen in December." Jake clasps her hands between her knees. Hunches her back. "We're here for the now, but we also try to help young women like you who are nearing adulthood. I know the idea of school can be overwhelming, but we have opportunities. College campus visits take place over the summer. We set you up with a student mentor. It's a great experience and one I highly recommend."

A few months ago I would have laughed at the idea. Rolled my eyes. Now expectation and possibility swell, awakening something inside. "Okay."

"Glad to hear it. Course tutors come in on Tuesdays and Thursdays. I'll shoot a message to your tutor and let her know you'd like some program information. Do you have any particular interests?"

"Reading. And writing. Sometimes."

"Have you ever thought about writing down what happened?"

I shrug. I've more than thought about it. "I've tried. But it's like reliving the past. Going through everything all over again. I can't even talk about it. How am I supposed to write it down?"

"That's one way to look at it." Jake taps her lips with one finger, then gestures toward the bookcase. "But what about writing it as if it happened to someone else?"

"Someone else?"

"You know, like a story you're removed from. It still becomes concrete. Valid. Permanent. But putting those experiences on a page, through the eyes of your characters, the control shifts. Rather than those thoughts controlling you, you have the power. You're free."

Free? Impossible. "I'll think about it." I haven't written anything in ages. How will I know where to begin?

"That's all I ask." She rises, then pauses at the sliding barn door. "When you use your voice, whether through speech or the written word, it has a way of healing. And healing is what we're all about here at Fathoms."

Healing? I've been a firm believer there's no coming back—no healing—from what happened.

Now I only want the hope she's offered to be real. And it's in this small admission to myself that I know I trust Jake. It feels like nothing and everything at once.

"It's free time now." She checks her watch. "It's as good a time as any to get started. Maybe even make a phone call to a loved one? There's a landline in your room."

I nod at the hint.

Jake disappears and closes the door softly, leaving me alone with only the folded blanket and my thoughts for company.

The phone. When was the last time I picked one up? I've been so angry with the person who sent me here. And now?

Her voice is the only one I want to hear.

I take the blanket and wrap it around my shoulders. Upstairs, I find my door, my name now written on a hanging chalkboard sign. The familiar handwriting matches the quote in the journal I found on my first day.

I touch the loops and flourishes, tracing the letters that make up me.

"You are not nothing. And neither am I."

Hope's statements sink in as I enter my room. I've never been able to shake them. In a way, it was Hope's words that brought me back. That kept me going when I should have been gone.

I leave the door cracked, close my eyes, and ground my breaths. My memories find me when I'm alone. Sleep is my usual defense. Now Jake's nudges spark and awaken.

I find the phone on my nightstand. I don't have the number memorized, so I dial information. When the operator answers I say, "Ocean Gardens Assisted Living."

She tells me to hold. The seconds stretch to a full minute before she patches me through. When a man answers, "Ocean Gardens, how may I direct your call?" I ask to be connected to room 104.

The line goes silent.

My heart races.

The man comes back on the line. "I'm sorry, there's no answer. Would you like to leave a message?"

I hang up without responding. The past dances before my vision, taunting, teasing. A prelude to the nightmares that will inevitably follow when sleep takes over.

Instead of giving in, I walk to the window and fling the curtains wide, letting all the light in. Then I remove the sea glass bottle from my bag and set it on my desk as a reminder.

I imagined plenty that night.

But finding this bottle? That was real.

I sit and switch on the desk lamp. The leather journal challenges me to open it. To ruin its perfect white pages with my not-so-perfect story.

"It's you and me." I stretch and flex my fingers, choosing a simple black pen from the cup at the corner of the desk. Pen because I can't erase it. Pen because if I'm going to do this, I'm going to make it real. I open the cover and find the quote Hope wrote on my first day. It's been joined by a second, this one perhaps even more prominent than the first.

"Life damages us, every one . . ."

—Veronica Roth

"Hope, how do you know me so well?" I ignore the second part of the quote. I'm not ready to go there yet.

Life does damage us. But I've at least decided to give this damaged life a chance. Fairy tale or not, I flip to a fresh page and put down the first words that come to mind.

"Once upon a time,"

And so my story . . . *her* story . . . begins.

TWENTY-SEVEN

Merrick

"Are you sure this is a good idea?" Grim glanced out the rearview mirror. He kept the car idling, in case they needed to make a quick getaway.

Merrick slunk low in the passenger seat as he had become accustomed to doing the last several months. "No," was all he said. In fact, this was so far from being a good idea he almost told Grim to make a run for it right then.

Almost.

The metered beach parking lot was busy. He didn't dare tell Nikki to meet them at Grim's house—aka the castle, aka the secret hideout. It had taken a fair amount of groveling to get her here. Now he wondered if she was coming at all.

Was this what Merrick had resorted to? Hiding from the law? If his mom hadn't left, they wouldn't be in this situation.

No, he wouldn't blame her. This was his father's doing.

"Is that her?" Grim lowered his sunglasses and jerked his chin toward a red convertible with its top and windows up.

Typical Nikki. She wanted the show car but would never risk ruining her perfect hair. It was part of her charm, of course, and a small piece of Merrick knew he'd missed her, though not in the way she probably missed him.

"Yeah," Merrick said, straightening. "That's her." He checked himself in the sideview mirror to make sure his fedora and Ray-Bans were in place, then he turned up the collar of his jacket.

Grim snorted and shook his head.

"Too much?" Merrick asked.

"All of this is too much, 007. But it's my day off and this is quality entertainment."

Merrick turned his collar back down and headed toward Nikki's car.

When he reached the pristine paint job with custom rims, he knocked on her passenger-side window. The door unlocked with a click and Merrick jumped in. "Did you bring them?"

Nikki lowered her sunglasses and gripped the steering wheel with her perfectly manicured fingers. "I don't hear from you in months and that's the first thing you say to me?"

She was right. He was a real piece of work. "I'm sorry. Hi."

"Hi?" She gripped the wheel tighter. She turned and gave him the face that had gotten him into trouble in the past.

"Nik . . ." He wanted to comfort her, but he didn't want to keep leading her on. He couldn't be that guy anymore.

"Oh please, Merrick. I am so over it. And no, I didn't bring them. Your dad has your house under constant watch. What was I supposed to say? That I needed your old photo albums because I wanted to bring them to his son who had kidnapped his daughter?"

Ouch. Right again.

"I did, however, manage to talk to him."

Merrick swallowed. Whatever came next would let him know if he could trust her or if it was all over. He'd taken a risk and this was the moment of truth. "Okay."

"You doubt my skills?"

"No."

"Whatever. You think because I wear heels and drive this car that I'm an idiot. News flash, Merrick, I was accepted to Berkeley."

"Yeah?" He *was* a jerk. Merrick didn't even know she'd applied. "That's great."

"Thanks."

"What are you studying?"

"I'm going to get my gen eds out of the way, but eventually I plan to go into the medical field. I want to help people."

Wow. He didn't know her at all. He'd judged her by her last name and the way she dressed. He wanted to apologize for all of it but found himself saying, "I'm happy for you," because "Sorry" sounded too easy.

A sense of regret and failure washed over him. He would be nineteen next year and he hadn't applied to a single university. The college brochures collected dust in his desk drawers at home. Every time he'd tried to look at them, an overwhelming pressure set in. A twinge of jealousy hit him. Nikki had it all figured out.

"Anyway, I went to see your dad." She circled back to what they'd been discussing in the first place. "He misses you."

"Fat chance." His father might miss having control, but he certainly didn't miss his disappointment of a son.

"Why do you do that?" Nikki asked.

"Do what?"

"You think your dad's the worst. But, Mer, he's really not."

"Says the girl whose father signed a deal to merge companies."

She looked down at her lap. "You know about that?"

"I keep up with the news."

"That's not why I'm here."

"Sounds to me like you're taking his side. Did he follow you?"

"What?" Her eyes narrowed. Moisture glossed her doe eyes. "No. Of course not . . . I wouldn't betray your trust. I'm not you."

This conversation was going nowhere. "Tell me what he said, Nikki."

"Maybe I shouldn't. You clearly don't trust me and honestly, Mer, I have no reason to trust you."

Merrick waited.

Nikki sighed. "I kept it casual." She rested her forehead on the steering wheel. "We met for lunch and I told him I was going to Berkeley, and he happened to mention your mom went there, you're welcome. I thought it might at least give you a clue to her past. Maybe someone there knows or remembers her."

Merrick wanted to kiss her for how awesome she'd been, but he refrained. No matter the physical attraction between them, his heart wasn't in it.

"I deserve better, Mer." Nikki straightened and checked herself in the visor mirror.

"Yes, you do." Out the window, he saw Grim's car, still idling. He wanted Nikki to be happy. Grim was her opposite in every way. He was a mess, he wore shorts and flip-flops, which Nikki would hate, but they had one thing in common.

They were two of the best people he knew.

"Come on." Merrick reached over, turned off her ignition, and tossed her keys in her purse. "I want you to meet someone." He stepped out of the car and skirted the bumper to open her door.

"I see the gentleman in you hasn't burned off with all this sun."

"Hey, I'm not all bad." He turned on his charm, but this time it meant something. He led her to Grim's car.

His friend promptly rolled down the window. Then he whistled. "Hello, Dolly!"

Oh, man. Merrick scratched the back of his head, waiting for Nikki to react with an eye roll or some sort of snobbish lip curl.

Instead, she batted her eyelashes. Was that a blush? "Are you seriously driving an '89 Camaro?"

"Why yes, ma'am, I believe I am." Grim lowered his sunglasses and winked.

Nikki opened the door for herself and hopped inside the front seat.

"Looks like she's riding shotgun," Grim said to Merrick, but didn't take his eyes off Nikki.

Merrick moved to Grim's side and climbed in behind his seat. He sat back, listening to Nikki and Grim talk shop and cars and horsepower and all the stuff Merrick had never learned or cared about because he'd never needed to. He had a license, passed his driver's test, but he never drove. Anywhere.

As Grim pulled out of the lot and cruised toward the highway, a shift took place inside Merrick. He'd been too quick to judge. Too fast to make assumptions about people based on first impressions and a few trivial facts.

Merrick poked his head between the front seats. "Hey, can you drop me at the high school?"

"Sure." Grim flipped the blinker switch. "Any particular reason why?"

"I need to talk to the counselor who comes to the library on Wednesdays." It wasn't a total lie. He would talk to Miss Brandes. She might know where he could find Coral.

Merrick peeked at the date on his phone. Friday. He couldn't wait almost an entire week to see her again.

He shot a text to his sister. She hadn't checked in yet, but he wasn't too worried. Grim's mom had come back to town for the weekend and offered to hang out with Maya for a bit.

How's it going with Aunt Ashley?

Maya's instant reply helped him release some of the tension he'd been carrying.

We went shopping and she took me for tea and now we're collecting seashells. I don't need a babysitter, as I am almost 11, in case you've forgotten, but if I have to have a nanny I pick her.

Merrick frowned. He'd specifically told Aunt Ashley he preferred his sister hang out at the house. It appeared Maya pulled out all the stops and persuaded her otherwise. He hated that they had to keep Grim's mom in the dark. She was a bit of a free spirit. Didn't believe in television and traveled "wherever the wind took her," as Grim put it. She had no idea they were hiding. She'd learn the truth eventually. She might even figure it out when Merrick got to asking questions about his mom.

Are you wearing a hat and sunglasses?

Maya replied with a selfie. A wide-brimmed beach hat shaded her face and giant, bug-eye sunglasses covered the rest.

Satisfied, Merrick closed his phone and took in the view. *Where are you, Mom? Maya needs you.*

And he needed a time-out. A break from worrying about Maya and wondering if his dad would show up any second.

Maybe Coral could be that break for him.

He let the thought simmer as another one formed.

Maybe she could even be more.

TWENTY-EIGHT

Coral

Spring didn't last. It waved a brief hello, only to be swept up with the heat of summer's breeze. She wouldn't miss it, though. Here, summer meant no school. It meant more time to focus on what mattered.

What *did* matter?

Her sister. *Only* her sister.

Coral scrutinized her Young Literary entry again. If she planned to enter, it needed to be perfect. The longer days called to her. Days spent sleeping in and writing at the beach and figuring out who she was and who she wanted to be.

And her sister's prince. There was still the matter of finding him. Merrick would help her. He'd promised. Maybe she should go back to the library, see if he was working. Not because she wanted to see him. Of course not. He was her sole lead.

Him and this bracelet. She touched the delicate pearls with her fingertips. Her sister had never said so, but Coral suspected the piece had been a gift from the prince himself. What if it was a clue to discovering his identity?

Her phone alarm sounded and Coral silenced it. Then she pulled the medication from her purse and stared at the label. At the name printed there. Her heart raced as she read the directions she'd memorized but felt the need to review anyway. She would not speak to Miss

Brandes's therapist. Coral's grandmother had forced her to see a doctor. He'd prescribed the bottle of pills after asking a handful of questions and not once looking her in the eye.

I don't need this. I'm fine.

She unscrewed the cap and emptied a capsule into the palm of her hand. Her grandmother would check the count. So Coral dropped the pill into the sand and buried it beneath the grains. She hated the way it made her feel. The way it coated everything in sugar when deep down in her bones she knew it wasn't real. The anxiety always came back. The thoughts of death and Red Tide lingered forever at the door of her heart.

A pill changed nothing. It only delayed things for a time.

She returned to the handwritten page before her, making edits with a red pen. Coral had convinced herself she didn't care about the contest. She only wanted to avoid more questions from Miss Brandes or meetings in her office. Still, Coral couldn't turn in a piece of work she wasn't proud of. So she focused on the black letters, reading them aloud to help her set the tone and feel.

"*My soul is bleeding,*" she started.

"*The sand beneath me is cool and damp, the high tide from last evening lingering between the grains. The water will turn ~~red~~ crimson soon, the tide transforming into a bloody, poisonous mess. I feel it. Sense it. Red Tide ~~calls for~~ beckons me.*"

"Maybe it always has," she told the sea. Coral shook her cramping hand, glanced up at the waves for an instant, before she took her red pen to paper again.

"*I bury my feet,*" she read. "*Allowing them to take refuge as a hermit crab does on a summer's day. I could sit here ~~indefinitely~~ forever, listening to the ocean's song as she sprays her melody onto the shore. She ~~beckons~~ summons me as a mother does a child, pleads with me to return to her ~~arms~~ bosom. To her heart.*"

Her own heart ached with each written word she uttered. Maybe she shouldn't turn this in. What if the humans thought—

Who cared what they thought? She'd been in that position before.

She'd never put herself there again. She looked down at the next line. Spoke it, feeling its truth.

"Her heart is where mine ~~wishes~~ longs to be," she said.

Coral blew a stray hair from between her eyebrows. It floated up, then down. When she tucked it away, it fell right back where it didn't belong. After placing her pen inside her notebook, she closed it, hugged her knees, and rocked in place.

"She's never coming back," she whispered to the sea. "Never."

Coral blinked and allowed the constant thought to sink in. Shoulders hunched and eyelids heavy, she rested her forehead on her knees. She pictured the crown princess as she once was. A caring sister. A companion. A friend. But then she gave up. On life. On Coral.

For the first time since Red Tide, Coral let herself be angry with her sister. She turned that anger into new words as she flipped over the typed page and wrote new ones. They poured from her. Like a squall, their course could not be stopped. She bit her lip, dug her feet deeper into the sand, and let the words flow . . .

The soul I don't possess aches with a phantom pain I can neither ~~explain~~ rationalize nor ignore. If I could shed a tear I would, but even this is not a luxury provided ~~to me~~.

"My prince never loved me." Coral whispered her sister's words, hoping the line repeated would bring some sense of comfort. *"He never will."* It didn't. Because words wouldn't bring her sister back.

Shudders racked her body as the sun dove, then sank, then drowned beneath the horizon.

But then something warm and heavy draped her shoulders. Something smelling of summer and salt and everything warm.

"So we meet again." Merrick squatted beside her.

"Hi." She kept her eyes on the horizon, waited for the vibrant colors to sing, though they never even whispered anymore.

"I hope this isn't too stalkerish, but full disclosure, I may or may not have gone to the school to ask Miss Brandes where I could find you. She told me to check the closest beach."

She ought to tell him to go. To throw his jacket back at him and race for the pier. But she also wanted to explore the angelfish living inside her center, flapping their fins at her core.

What if my sister was wrong?

Guilt chafed her insides, killing every last angelfish flutter.

She swallowed, then found her voice. "How'd she know I'd be here?"

"She said you walk this way after school . . . and you're always taking off your shoes."

"I don't like shoes. They hurt my feet."

"That may be the best excuse to go barefoot I've heard yet." Merrick kicked off his own shoes.

They sat that way for a while. Listening to the ocean and soaking in the heat of the sun and sand. The pleasant silence between them contradicted every preconceived notion. Comfort wrapped her.

"Why did you help me that night?" She drew circles in the sand at her feet. "You could've been hurt. Duke—"

"Was that the guy's name? Duke?" Merrick buried his hands in the grains.

"My sister's boyfriend."

"For her sake and yours, I hope that's no longer the case."

Coral shrugged. "I don't know. I haven't talked to her in a while."

"Do you miss her?"

Did she? Maybe. "Sometimes."

They grew quiet again. The longer Merrick stayed, the more Coral feared his inevitable absence.

She shoved the feeling away. The Disease wanted to fool her. It wanted to make her believe in love and hope and friendship. Lies. False hope. If he ever got the chance, this human would break her.

"To answer your question," Merrick said at last, "I helped you because that's what you do when someone is in trouble. As my good friend likes to say, you'd do the same for me."

Would she?

A frustrated sigh escaped and Coral held her head in her hands. Her eyelids drooped from lack of sleep.

"Anyway, you asked me something last time. You're looking for someone. A prince? Turns out I'm looking for someone too. Maybe we can help each other."

"Maybe. I don't know." She didn't know anything anymore. *Lost* didn't cover half of it. Coral drifted without a purpose. Without an end. She existed for now. Eventually she'd be forgotten.

If she was nothing to no one, did she exist at all?

"Seems the universe keeps bringing us together," Merrick said.

"Or the ocean," she added before she could stop herself.

"Yes, that too. So, why a prince? Do you have a fairy-tale complex?"

Folks, we have a comedian. "It isn't for me. It's for my sister. The one who—" She couldn't finish. She couldn't bring herself to say the words. "I think this bracelet was a gift from him to her. It's the only thing I have left—" Again, Coral couldn't finish. The more she tried to push the words out, the larger they grew in her constricting throat. "I'd rather keep my reasons to myself."

She'd thought about her anger for so long, she hadn't actually gotten to the part where she confronted the nameless prince. Coral wasn't a murderer, though her thoughts grew murderous at times.

Would Merrick help her if he saw the Abyss inside?

He eyed her.

Coral bristled. She didn't know if she liked the way he looked at her or if she loathed it.

"Fair enough," he said. "How about this? If you help me find my someone, I'll help you find yours. Promise." He offered his pinky.

Was that fair? That he got his way first? He'd promised to help her. Would he abandon her the moment he got what he wanted?

"I have a reason for doing it this way," he said. "Trust me?"

Did she? Could she?

The sea seemed to calm, easing the worry in her heart.

Merrick's consistent gaze had the same effect.

She didn't want him to stop. "Okay." She shook his pinky with hers. His cute half smile sent those angelfish in her stomach soaring.

"So here's the thing." He released her finger and leaned back on his elbows. "I'm sort of in this predicament where I need information, but I can't go poking around too much. Otherwise people would figure out who I am, and I need to remain unseen. For personal reasons." He let out a breath as if he'd had everything bottled inside. "That's where you come in. You're not from around here. Your face isn't in the papers or online."

He had that right.

"You can ask questions and no one will give you a second glance." She lifted a brow.

"You know what I mean. Anyway, will you do it? Be my undercover journalist? You like to write." He pointed to her pages. "It works out."

"Who are we looking for exactly?" She flipped her story over so the blank side faced her. She held her pen at the ready.

"My mom."

She scribbled a note. His mom in exchange for her sister's prince? Seemed fair. "When do we start?"

Warmth spread through her. *Stop it. He's human. A human could never care for a mermaid. The crown princess made that abundantly clear.*

"How about now?" He hopped up from the sand. He offered her his hand in the same way he had the night of Red Tide.

This time she didn't back away. She took it and he helped her up.

With the sea at their backs and triumph lighting Merrick's eyes, the Disease wrapped Coral's heart with an emotion so deep and comforting, she couldn't have suppressed it if she tried.

And she didn't.

She let that feeling envelop her as spring melted into the horizon and summer led her up the shore.

Summer

"She laughed and danced with the
thought of death in her heart."

—Hans Christian Andersen,
"The Little Mermaid"

June

Dear Brooke,

I've been thinking a lot about sight lately.

Sight is more than just seeing.

It's perceiving and observing and knowing when things aren't right.

I should have seen past your forced smile into your hurting soul.

I should have heard your cries through your laughter.

I should have known while you danced, you were dying inside.

If I ever get the chance to do it all over again, I'll look with new eyes.

I'll do my best to see everything, even the things you try to hide.

I'll see you, Brooke. Sunshine and darkness and rain. Promise.

Yours,

Prince

TWENTY-NINE

Brooke

After

"Did you see my cake?" Hope barges into my room, beaming. "It's three tiers high and Mary promised to use strawberry cream cheese filling." She uses her arms to show me the cake's size. Then she crosses to my window.

I close my journal, using my pen as a placeholder, and rise from my desk. I try to smile, though it doesn't reach my eyes.

Hope checks the driveway for the umpteenth time since the sun rose. She's talked about her twelfth birthday since I returned in the spring. She remains the youngest of our girl pack but brings the most light by far.

"Maybe we should see if Mary needs help," I offer, attempting to close the curtains.

"I want to see when she drives up." Hope shoves the fabric back toward me. The curtain rings clink together across the metal rod. "She promised to come when we talked on the phone last week."

I frown. Empty promises remain an all-too-familiar concept. While Hope's dad visits at least once a month and video chats with her every Sunday, her mom remains unseen.

I hate the woman for it.

"Are you looking forward to starting school again in the fall?" I long to take her mind off the window and the empty driveway beyond.

Hope shrugs but keeps her eyes plastered to the glass. She's not herself, though today of all days ought to be about her. Instead, she dwells on the woman who hardly talks to her only daughter.

"I told Jake I don't want to go home." Hope cracks the window, allowing a summer breeze to pass through the screen. "I want to stay here."

I wrap an arm around her, knowing at this point my affection is welcome. I hate how attached I've become. She's leaving—we both are—by summer's end. Still, we need each other now. Hope is nearly six years younger and has become the best friend I've ever had.

"Aren't you excited to see your friends when you go home?" I tickle her rib cage.

She jumps. Squeals. Snatches a pillow off the bed and tosses it at me. "They're not my friends."

This is the one thing she never mentions. The thing she keeps locked away so no one can see. "You'll make new ones." When did I become the optimist of our odd pair?

She tugs her sleeves down over her arms, hiding her scars.

I wince, feeling everything she feels and sometimes wishing I could go back to feeling nothing at all.

Taking her hand, I draw her sleeve to her elbow. She resists at first, but I lock my eyes on hers. "You are not nothing," I say. "And neither am I."

Her eyes glisten, but then she turns back into her usual self and grins, all teeth. "What sage words, O Wise One."

"Indeed." I wink. "Come on. The time will go faster if we help Mary in the kitchen."

Hope hesitates but at last concedes, letting her sleeve fall and leaving the window behind.

Hope's dad brought a karaoke machine for her birthday. While we're not supposed to have our own electronics here, Jake agreed to let Hope use it for the night. Once it's plugged in and the controls light up, Hope connects her mic and waves for me to join her.

I freeze. How long has it been since I sang? My throat closes up with one glance at that dreaded machine.

"Please, Brooke. This can be your birthday present to me." She connects a second mic and holds it toward me, waiting.

I open my mouth to tell her I've gotten her a little something. Wrapped it and everything. But then she does the face that makes her look younger than she is and I groan. The other girls clap while the staff and volunteers line the walls of the gathering room.

Great. We have an audience. This ought to be loads of fun.

I rise from the couch that's been pushed against the bookcase. Chairs from the kitchen have been brought in too. Blue and yellow streamers swoop overhead, and matching balloons move across the carpet like colorful, floating rainbow fish.

The colors stand out more than they have all year.

"What shall we sing?" Hope glances out the bay window and into the evening blue.

Bitterness coats my mouth. Her mom's not coming. Her dad's here, though—a quiet man who's hardly said two words to her aside from "Happy birthday." But he's here. He showed up.

"Um, you pick." I grab the mic. Grasp tight despite my sweating palms.

Hope clicks through the choices on Jake's smartphone, connected via Bluetooth, and lands on a winner.

I roll my eyes. "This again?"

"What can I say? It's a new classic."

Hope begins the first verse of the theme from her favorite movie musical. I think I've heard her listen to this soundtrack a thousand times on the community CD player in the rec room. She never tires of it.

She sings of scars and shame and words that cut. Then the chorus ends and the song falls to me. I swallow and search for my voice. I've never liked singing. My voice was somewhat of an asset to my family. It defined me. Would they have loved me without the commodity they hoped to exploit?

I'll never know.

But here, with Hope smiling up at me and a stomach full of cake and a room stuffed with people who have never once judged me, I sing. Because I don't have to. My voice. My choice.

My heart takes flight with the first lyric. I sing of drowning and sending floods. My own flood releases through the song, and soon I'm closing my eyes and getting lost in the melody. Hope joins in and we find our harmony.

It. Is. Glorious.

The room erupts in cheers, and a high I didn't know existed encompasses my heart. Hope's right. It's going to be hard leaving this place, but we have to step out and do the things we fear most.

"Thanks, Brooke." She gives one last glance toward the window before she passes the mic to someone else.

Jake and Mary take the makeshift stage next and sing a dance song from their generation. All the girls from Hope's twelve to my almost eighteen kick off our shoes and move to the beat. We cha-cha-slide right and get jiggy with it. Because, as everyone knows, girls just want to have fun.

We're on the floor with our sides splitting by the end. When's the last time I laughed so hard I cried? A perfect day I would have thought impossible a year ago.

When the clock nears midnight, Hope's dad gives her a hug and waves good-bye to the rest of us. She watches him go, then sneaks upstairs to her room instead of rejoining her own party. I catch Jake's eye and she nods for me to follow my friend.

When I reach her door, a new kind of music begins to play.

Hope's lamenting sobs trigger a memory.

There's so much I want to say, but what would any of it matter right now? Hope's mom didn't come when that was all she wanted. The only birthday present she cared to find waiting at the door.

I retreat to my room and retrieve the thin, palm-size silver gift box tied with white ribbon. I grab the paper heart I've kept taped to my wall since the day I returned to Fathoms. Permanent marker in hand, I cover both the heart and the box, writing over the penciled lie of "nothing" Hope has believed about herself.

Worthy.

Valued.

Loved.

Twelve.

Friend.

Someone.

Something.

Everything.

The words cover every inch. Front and back. Top and bottom. I write until there's no more room. I make my final statement in the form of a favorite quote. This is what Hope would do for me. Now it's my turn.

"Courage is not the absence of fear, but rather the judgment that something else is more important than fear."

I add a few flourishes, then slip the heart beneath her door, followed by the now-graffitied box.

I press my ear against the wood. Wait. It's a few minutes before a different heart is returned to me. The once-blank space of nothing I handed her the first day we met now bears two words written in black ink.

Not alone.

I press the heart to my chest and say, "You too," through the door. "Never."

She doesn't let me in, but I sit and lean against the barrier for a while. I slip my fingers under the crack so she knows I'm still here.

She's never given up on me. Not when I pushed her away or tried to throw life to the sea.

So I stay.

I choose this. Now.

I choose after.

I can only have faith Hope will too.

THIRTY

Merrick

"You're going to see that girl again, aren't you?"

Amaya planted her hands on her hips and blocked Merrick's path to the door.

He grabbed two apples and a couple Gatorades for the road. "She's helping me find Mom. I think we're getting close."

"Close to kissing." Amaya made a face, then wiggled her eyebrows.

"It isn't like that, Maya. Her grandma's been around this town for years and agreed to let us go through her attic. She's got old yearbooks and newspapers dating back decades."

"Sure. Keep telling yourself that, big brother."

"I will, thanks."

Grim waltzed down the stairs dressed in clashing patterns of Hawaiian print. While his shorts were all green palms and orange sunsets, his shirt was hula girls and pink leis. A straw hat sat on top of his head, and he had zinc pasted beneath each eye and over the bridge of his nose. "You ready, birthday girl?"

"My birthday is *next* week." She followed up with yet another face. She seemed to notice what he was wearing because she added, "You aren't seriously going out dressed like that, are you?"

"What's wrong with what I'm wearing?" Confusion lighting his expression, Grim spread his arms and walked to the kitchen, treating the living room as his personal runway.

Amaya rolled her eyes. "Good thing Nikki's not here to see this."

"Didn't I tell you, kiddo?" Grim asked. "Nikki's meeting us at the beach."

"And here I thought you wanted her to fall madly in love with you," Amaya teased, batting her eyes.

"Why do you think I chose the ensemble, Maya girl? No one can resist the Grimsby charm!"

"And that's where you're wrong, big guy." She jumped and snatched Grim's hat. He growled and chased her around the kitchen island.

Amaya pretended to be annoyed, but the sparkle in her eyes told Merrick she'd have the perfect first Saturday of summer.

"Make sure she wears the zinc too," Merrick called from the door. While he didn't want his sister sunburned, he also wanted to remind them to keep her face disguised.

"She will go unseen," Grim promised, tugging the hat back onto his head. "Plus, she's got her own personal bodyguard." He flexed his muscles. "She'll be fine."

Merrick nodded and rolled his eyes. "Tell Nik I said hi."

"Will do, commander in chief." Grim winked. "Now go get your girl."

Merrick headed down the back steps that led to the beach. He'd almost protested that Coral wasn't his girl. She was helping him investigate things around town. They'd been getting together every weekend over the past month. Now she was out of school and the real work could begin. It was coming together better than he'd hoped. She knew all the right questions to ask and had even come across a few locals who remembered his mom. He sensed they were closer than ever.

Which was the *only* reason he offered to take her out to lunch. To thank her. This wasn't a date. Just two friends—partners—who happened to be eating lunch together. No big deal.

This time of year was his favorite. The sleepy tourist town no longer sat idly by as the rest of the world turned along without it. Businesses boomed with the sounds of bells over doors and the laughter of old friends meeting up for brunch.

The past few weekends ran through his thoughts. At first Coral remained distant. But the more time they spent together, the more she softened.

She was so easy to talk to. Did she feel the same about him?

Merrick neared the tea shop on his left—his mom's favorite place to come when they were kids. She'd brought him and Amaya several times over the summer breaks. They'd sit in the window booth looking out over the street. His mom would sip a cup of tea while Amaya and Merrick devoured the homemade scones and jam.

The cracked door invited him in, the scents of shepherd's pie and pastries escaping. Inside, rafter beams slanted up to a point in the roof and floating tea lights glowed on every white-clothed table. Mismatched china and teacups dressed the place settings, adding to the antique ambience his mom had appreciated. Fresh summer roses soaked up drinks in vases across the cozy room that wouldn't seat more than a couple dozen people at most.

When he entered, a friendly looking woman with a pink apron and cheeks to match greeted him. "You look like the sort of young man who belongs next to a lovely young lady." She winked at Merrick, then gestured toward the window booth.

His knees grew weak and he had to brace himself against a chair.

Coral hadn't noticed him yet. She sat there, her blue dress only drawing more notice to her brilliant eyes. Her attention rested on the menu before her. The sunlight streaming through the window behind the booth lit her sandy hair that had been pulled off her face and braided to one side.

Amaya was right. He was falling for this girl.

"Go on, young man," the woman who greeted him urged. "She won't bite."

Merrick checked his reflection in the window to his left and walked to the table. "Hi," he said, sliding into the booth beside her. The word got stuck in his throat and he had to cough to remove it.

She glanced up from her menu, laying those dazzling eyes on him again.

Yep. He was a goner. Denial was pointless.

He turned his eyes to his own menu and tried to focus. "Did you order yet?"

"I was waiting for you."

The tea selection printed before him suddenly became more amusing. She was nice. She'd waited for him. It didn't mean anything.

Did it?

He was way overthinking this. What was wrong with him? He'd never been so self-conscious with Nikki.

Because Nikki was not Coral.

Merrick cleared his throat. *Focus. You're here for business. A favor for a favor. Promise for promise.*

He browsed the assortment of teas, sandwiches, salads, and a schedule of daily specials. Chicken potpie. His mouth watered.

"What are you getting?" Was that his voice sounding like a twelve-year-old boy's?

The waitress—Elizabeth—returned before Coral could answer. "What'll it be, dears?"

"Scones for the table," Merrick said, finding his confidence again. "Lots of marmalade and butter, please. And a chicken potpie."

"I'll have the same." Coral folded her menu. "And hot tea."

"Excellent choices." Elizabeth took their menus, writing nothing down. "Would you like a pot for the table?"

Coral glanced at Merrick.

His smile widened. "Absolutely."

"What tea do you fancy?" Elizabeth glanced between Coral and Merrick, a gleam lighting her eyes.

Coral hesitated.

"What do you recommend?" Merrick asked for her.

"They're all fine choices," Elizabeth said. "Twinings. Harney & Sons. Tazo. I'm partial to the Savoy blends myself. Miracle Mermaid Tea is a tourist favorite."

"Sounds good." Coral nodded and placed her hands in her lap, fidgeting with her napkin.

Was she nervous? Did she think this was a date?

Merrick cleared his throat again.

Did he *want* this to be a date?

Elizabeth shuffled away, leaving them alone.

They had been alone before. But not like this. With her wearing that dress and Merrick unable to stop staring.

"My mom used to bring me and Amaya here." Merrick jumped into conversation, hoping it would rid the air of the awkwardness he was creating with all his staring. "It's been years since we've been back. This is nice. Thanks for meeting me."

Ease washed Coral's expression. "I'm out of school now, so I can help you more during the week if you want. I actually questioned a few people on my way over this morning."

His heart raced. She'd done that for him? On her own? "Wow. Thanks." He ran a shaky hand through his hair. Tried to look anywhere but directly at her. "Anything good?"

She pulled out her notebook and flipped it open. "You said your friend's mom grew up with Lyn?"

The way Coral said his mom's name, with so much care and tenderness, made Merrick's heart skip three beats. "Yes. Yeah, she did. I talked to Grim's mom a bit before she left for Denmark last week. She said the one thing she remembered about Mom was how much she loved this town. She loved being close to the water."

"Vague," Coral said, jotting down some notes.

Merrick laughed. She never failed to say exactly what she thought. "Right?"

"Anything else?"

"That having a daughter was my mom's dream."

"How is your sister, by the way?"

"She's okay, I think." He shrugged. "I'd love for you to meet her sometime."

"I'd like that." She rested her pen on the table. Her eyes crinkled and he could sense the change that had been taking place in her. She trusted him. Or she was starting to.

Please don't let me blow this.

"Did you . . . ?" He couldn't find the words. "What was your sister like? Before . . ." His voice trailed. He didn't want to venture where he wasn't welcome, but he also wanted more.

Coral looked up from her page and met his eyes. "Honestly?"

"Honestly."

"Some days she was fine—*seemed* fine."

Merrick nodded, relating to every word.

"The thing is, I knew she wasn't fine," Coral went on. "But by the time I actually did something about it, it was too late. She was gone."

"It wasn't your fault." He'd carried that blame with Amaya. It broke his heart to think of Coral taking responsibility for her sister's death.

"I don't know." She looked out the window. "It's not all my fault, I know that. I feel like there's more I could have done. Or said. She felt so unloved, Merrick."

And there it was. She'd said his name and his heart soared.

He had it bad. If Amaya were here, she'd say his blush was showing. Merrick only hoped Coral didn't notice.

"It's *not* your fault." He set his hand on the seat between them. It lingered an inch from hers. "With Amaya . . . I keep reminding myself that I'm doing everything possible to save her. To let her see how much she's loved. That's why I'm trying to find our mom. She'll know what to do. She and Amaya were close. My dad wants to send her away, but I have to believe there's a better alternative."

Coral stayed quiet for a bit. Through the tea Elizabeth brought and the three new customers who walked past them. Finally she sighed. "Did your sister start cutting before or after your mom left?"

"Before." Merrick passed her the sugar and cream, studying how she prepared her tea. Her hands were so delicate. They made him think of her name and the fragility of ocean coral. The rarity of something so beautiful and breakable.

"But that's because of our dad," he continued. "He puts so much pressure on Amaya to be this perfect daughter. If she and my mom could start over, away from him, I know things would be easier."

Coral stirred two sugar cubes and an inch of cream into her tea. "It sounds like you are putting as much pressure on your mom as your dad does on your sister."

The words stung Merrick more than they should have coming from a girl he hardly knew. "So." He fiddled with a spoon to busy his rejected hand. "You said you talked to some people today?"

She sipped her tea, then referred to her notes. He was grateful she let him change the subject, though he had a feeling it wouldn't last.

"The woman at the dance studio remembered her," Coral said. "And your dad too."

Merrick had forgotten his mom used to dance. He'd forgotten that she did anything before she was his mom.

"She said Lyn was one of the best talents she'd seen. Your dad observed every rehearsal. Every show. He even proposed to her here."

"As in *here*, here?" He laid his palms flat on the table, his excitement growing.

Coral shook her head. "In this town, I mean. Supposedly they had some secret place they used to sneak off to. They were quite the sweethearts."

He tried to imagine his parents like that. Holding hands and stealing kisses. He racked his brain for some spark of information he'd heard in passing. But his parents rarely told stories of their dating days. They'd fought for so long, he sometimes wondered what his mom had ever seen in Hiroshi to begin with.

Elizabeth returned with their food, giving Merrick a chance to imagine a life before his dad had become such a jerk. He couldn't fathom it. Whatever his father was before, it was an act. In the after, he'd shown his true colors more times than Merrick could count.

"Enjoy, dears," Elizabeth said before moving to wait on another table.

Merrick's eyes grew wide. "I forgot they served whipped cream with the scones!" He took a big dollop off the top of the cream and shoveled it into his mouth.

Coral giggled.

Satisfied with the move Grim would have been proud to witness, Merrick relaxed and waited for Coral to tell him more. He could listen to her talk all day. There was something about her voice that made everything that had happened over the past six months seem less trying. Conquerable.

"So my theory is she didn't leave town at all," Coral said after swallowing her bite of scone and marmalade. "That she's hiding in plain sight. Kind of like you."

Merrick glanced at her meticulous notes. She'd done more work than he'd given her credit for. And what had he given her? Some tea and scones and a chicken potpie? He owed her the truth. They hadn't found his mom yet, but in the weekends they'd spent side by side, poring over ideas about his mom's location and the interviews Coral had conducted, Merrick found he trusted her more than anyone.

"Coral." He would tell her everything. Now. He wouldn't do it as payment. He would do it because he—

"Have you ever considered she doesn't want to be found?" Coral set her cup in its saucer, interrupting his thoughts with a *clink*. She scooted an inch to the right. Away from him.

The sudden barrier of oxygen between them felt stifling. Why did she do that? Put up a wall the second he started to get close?

"Why does everyone keep saying that?" His frustrations got the better of him but he didn't hold back. "First Grim, now you? You don't know her."

"No. I don't. But maybe you don't either. You only *think* you know. You assume you understand. That you can fix everything with a happy family reunion or by playing Sherlock Holmes."

Where had this come from? He'd thought she was on his side.

"If your mom wanted you," Coral said, "she'd cross the ocean, search land and sea until she found you. Family doesn't abandon family. Love doesn't leave."

"Says the girl who refuses to answer every time her sister calls."

The betraying words left his mouth before he could swallow them. She'd shared that insight into her still-mysterious world last week, and now he'd used it against her. Shame fell over him, but he couldn't take it back now.

"Coral, I'm sor—"

A crash resounded from the kitchen. A dropped dish? A broken pitcher?

Coral tossed her napkin onto the table and scooted to the other end of the booth. When she rose, Merrick caught a glimpse of the withdrawn girl he'd first met.

Now I've done it. Nice work, genius.

He should have told her about the prince then. It might have fixed what he'd ruined.

But Merrick remained quiet.

Coral waited a blink before leaving him alone at the pink booth with his half-eaten scones and untouched potpie.

He watched her escape, knowing every step she took away from him was one step closer to hiding in her shell for good.

Let her go. What do I care? She's too sensitive. Can I be expected to handle her constant mood swings? Her up-and-down emotions?

The empty space beside him said everything.

It was no longer 100 percent about his mom. He liked the girl who related to him in a way no one else could. He liked her, emotions and mood swings and all, and he'd completely blown it.

"Will you be needing this to go, dear?" Elizabeth asked.

"Yes," he said. Because he needed to *go.*

He'd fight for the girl who drove him insane and made him want to be better.

He'd do the thing she'd described if it came down to it.

Merrick would cross an ocean. He'd search land and sea.

He would not abandon her now. He had pinky promised, after all.

So he paid the bill and dove headfirst into what he was sure would end up as either (a) a complete disaster or (b) the best decision he ever made.

As he headed for the beach, Merrick was certain he heard the latter calling his name.

THIRTY-ONE

Coral

What was it about being alone that grew stale after a spell?

Loneliness—solitude—was an enchantment, the curse Coral had subjected herself to and suddenly longed to break.

"True love makes life, even a broken one, worth fighting for."

Coral heard her oldest sister's words as if she were sitting in the sand beside her. She missed her desperately. Some days a new wave of grief would fold over Coral, pulling her into a tumult that was impossible to escape. Logic became nonexistent. There was no up, down, left, or right. She let that wave take her. She didn't fight. She simply allowed it to consume every part that remained.

What would happen if I dove off the pier? If I went for a swim when the tides grow strong? Would anyone miss me? Would anyone care?

Coral took out her phone and checked her rather sad and friendless social media account. No tags. No notifications. It had been weeks since she'd submitted her entry to the Young Literary contest. Miss Brandes told her she should expect to see the finalist list posted by midsummer. Now it was the first week of July and still nothing.

Not that it mattered. What difference would winning a contest make?

Maybe it would mean I'm worth something. Maybe it would give me a reason to stay.

Coral stretched her legs before her in the damp sand. Bubbling foam washed over her feet. The ocean froze her skin, her muscles, her bones in time, providing relief and the most luxurious feeling of nothing. Her eyes closed and her thoughts wound back through the past months. The day of Red Tide. The night Merrick found her. Then the night he found her again. She'd agreed to help him, believing he'd lead her to the prince. Coral held her breath and went under, diving into what began as a means to an end.

In one brief moment that Merrick probably didn't even remember, everything had changed.

They sat across from each other on the bench that day in May, a basket of sweet potato fries between them. Merrick chose tartar sauce, but Coral preferred ketchup. The inventor of all things weird and gross—Coral soon learned—Merrick decided to mix the two and create a new sauce he dubbed "tarchup."

As much as she hated the way he broke through her barriers, Coral laughed and rolled her eyes. "I'm pretty sure that's already been invented."

Merrick's expression exuded mock hurt. "How could you?" His hand flew to his heart. "Tarchup is an original creation by yours truly and I am appalled you would accuse me of plagiarism."

He spoke her writerly language and Coral's amusement betrayed her again. "Forgive me. I did not mean to offend thee, sir."

Merrick tossed another fry.

Revenge became sweet, and what was meant to be a meeting in which they discussed clues turned into an hour-long game of "Would you rather?"

"Would you rather encounter a shark in the water or a tiger on land?" He dunked a fry into his sauce mash-up and shoved the entire thing in his mouth.

Coral pondered, then answered, "A shark on land."

"You can't change it, cheater. A shark on land would be dead."

"Exactly!"

He chucked a fry at her arm.

"You're wasting them."

He shrugged. "So we'll get more. There will always be more."

Had he been referring to the fries or something else entirely? She didn't ask, instead joining in his game of fry-tossing.

He pulled out his harmonica for a while after that. His seamless playing became the perfect background to her writing.

"You're good at that." She rolled her neck and flexed her hand. "Where'd you learn?"

"Some stuff Ojii-Chan—my great-grandfather—taught me before he died. The rest I winged." He set the instrument down and nodded to her notebook. "How about you?"

"Winged it. I'm that awesome." Her own fleeting confidence startled her, but Coral didn't take the words back. "I'm ready to cool off. Up for a swim?"

They grabbed their things and Merrick followed her down to the water. Coral walked into the ocean fully clothed. She welcomed the coolness of the waves, relished each lap at her skin.

A full minute passed before she noticed Merrick had stopped short of the line separating wet sand from dry sand. He stood there, hands in his pockets and brow furrowed.

"Come on!" she called, splashing a bit of sea toward him.

He half smiled but didn't budge from his place on the shore.

She watched him closely after that. They would meet at the beach or near the beach. The water called to Coral, especially as the days grew warmer. Her clothes stuck to her skin and she had to pull her hair back in a braid or a knot by noon. But Merrick never joined her in the water. He never even dipped his toes in.

Was he afraid? An awareness overcame her. Merrick had faced his fear the night of Red Tide.

219

It was the first time Coral questioned if her sister's theory about humans had been wrong.

A new wave of grief rolled over her, but this one was not caused by a memory of her sister. Coral missed Merrick. She had pushed him away.

Why did she run from him when she clearly wanted to head in the opposite direction? Maybe she didn't know how. Or maybe it was too late to alter old habits.

A shadow passed over her and Coral's heart sang.

"There you are. You're a hard person to track down, you know."

Merrick stood a foot away, hands on his thighs, panting. "Is this where you've been hiding? Beneath the pier?"

She shrugged. "It seemed like the best place to avoid you." She bit her tongue at the forward admission. She'd been avoiding him. Would he be angry? Offended?

"And that's where you're wrong." He wagged his eyebrows and stared her down.

What in the ocean was he up to?

He backed away then, slowly.

Coral touched her parted lips when Merrick kicked off his flip-flops and walked backward into the sea.

She stood, brushing off the sand from her legs and knee-length shorts. She hadn't bothered to wear shoes, as usual. When she joined him in the water, the waves kissing their knees, she asked, "I thought you had ocean-phobia."

"I did." His honesty stormed her defenses. "I'm a grown man who never learned to swim. My father loved the ocean, so it was my way of rejecting all the things he wanted for me that I didn't want for myself."

Coral drank in every word. She related and wanted to say as much, but when Merrick turned to her in the water and peered deep into her eyes, her voice vanished.

"You love the ocean."

She nodded. How did he manage to see so much of her when she didn't say a thing?

"Those first weeks after we met, I'd watch you. Fearless. I wanted to join you, but I let my fear control me. So I enrolled in a swim class at the community center in town. I wanted it to be a surprise."

She swallowed back the emotion threatening to break her. "You did join me, though. The night in winter. My sister?" So many questions surrounded her heart. "Why?"

"Because of you. I saw you and I knew . . ." His hands moved back and forth over the moving surface.

"Knew what, Merrick?" Did she want to know the answer?

"I love when you say my name."

"Merrick," she said again.

"I wish you'd tell me yours."

Her mouth turned down. "You know my name."

"Coral. You don't respond right away when I say it. It's as if that's not your name at all. You don't trust me completely yet. You're afraid. And that's okay. I'll wait. However long it takes. I'll wait for you."

With the sea swirling around them, they drifted far away though they stood perfectly still. The Disease warred within Coral, pushing and pulling her in all directions. When Merrick's hands found hers beneath the surface, she pulled back. But Merrick stood there. Waiting for her to let him in.

"I need time." She didn't know what to believe. Would she betray her sister if she fell for a human?

"Time is what I've got. How about six o'clock tomorrow?"

"What are we doing?" The corners of her mouth twitched.

"You'll have to trust me on this one."

Though it went against everything she thought she believed, she had grown to trust Merrick in the small moments. In the still minutes when time ticked by and he waited.

And waited.

And waited.

Maybe the waiting would be over soon.

Coral hoped by then she would have more answers than she did now.

THIRTY-TWO

Brooke

After

The college campus is greener than I expect, especially for the end of July. It's hot, but not so hot everything's dead. If anything, the heat adds to the vibrancy of it all.

And green, I decide, is my favorite color today.

Wide lawns and aged trees wait between old buildings with so much history in their bones, I think I might have traveled to another time period.

But this is now. *Deep breath, shoulders back. I can do this.*

"I'll be right here when you're done," Jake says.

She drove me two hours south to get here. Unspeakable gratitude expands my chest. I know it's her job, but Jake cares. She takes an interest in my future when she could pass me off to someone else.

I don't get out of the car.

"You'll be fine," she says. "Go on. Your student mentor will meet you in the library."

I gulp and gaze out the window. "Which one's the library again?"

"You'll find it," she says. Then, "You can do this. Don't be afraid to ask for directions."

I know she knows where the library is, but she's making me find it, helping me prepare for when I'm inevitably on my own. "Why am I doing this? I can't afford—"

"No buts. You're here. You can worry about the financial part later. How are the meds?"

"Good," I say, and I mean it. "I think we found a regimen that works."

"Yess!" Jake punches the air, and I almost forget she's my therapist instead of my friend. "Glad to hear you've found your normal. Now *go*. No more excuses."

I finally get out of the car and step into the midsummer sunshine.

I'm turned around within ten minutes. I'm allowed to use my cell phone for the day so we can stay in touch. I check the time. I'm a little early and I make a beeline for the coffee cart. Caffeine fix plus directions equals my first win of the day.

A line has formed so I dig through my bag and pull out the twenty Jake gave me for food. My tote is heavier than it should be. The last-minute decision to bring my bulky and half-filled leather-bound journal, along with my sea glass bottle, is one I'm starting to regret. My shoulder aches and I still have to carry this thing around the remainder of the day. At least I have a cookie for later. The napkin Mary included bears one word written in her messy hand.

breathe.

It's identical to her tattoo and I make a note to tell Mary she needs to start her own brand. The word is a logo, a tagline, and a mission statement all in one.

Mary has officially nailed down my nutrition plan but manages to fit cookies and brownies into everyone's diet no matter what restrictions they have. This double-chunk-chocolate goodness happens to be gluten-free. Tossing the ingredient has helped my nightmares. Who knew a change in diet could also usher a better night's sleep?

When it's my turn at the register, I ask for an extra-foam cappuccino and pay. I leave a tip in the jar, relishing the feeling it brings to purchase my own drink even if Jake technically paid the bill.

Maybe I *can* do this.

My phone says I have less than five minutes to find the library. I ask the barista for directions, and she points me toward a wide white building that belongs in a museum—either that or it is a museum.

"Thanks," I say and sip at my drink.

She smiles and I head to the museum-slash-library.

Inside, my steps echo and I am pretty sure I'm not supposed to have a drink in here. Out of nervous habit I touch my wrist. But my bracelet isn't there. My heart soars. I pause and picture Hope, wearing the pearls I gave her for her birthday. She moved home last week and my heart broke. Soon I'll leave Fathoms too.

You're brave, Hope. We both are.

I promise to tell her over the phone as soon as this day is over.

I find no one who appears to be waiting for me so I step outside the library door. My coffee's still hot and I almost spill it when my phone vibrates in my bag. I'm about to peek at the screen when a girl wearing an outfit made for the runway jogs up the steps. In heels.

She passes me, then does a double take. "Brooke?"

"Nikole?"

"Nikki." Her genuine grin eases my jitters. "Sorry I'm late. I'm taking some summer electives and my human studies prof ran over time."

I beam at the way she says "prof." Because it's way too cool and I don't think I could pull it off.

Also, why is she so familiar?

She seems to think as much about me because at the same time I ask, "Have we met?" she ventures, "Do I know you?"

We laugh in sync and then she says "jinx" like we're in elementary school.

"Technically," I tease, "we didn't say the same thing, just at the same time, so jinx doesn't count."

"You're going to fit right in with the English majors, girl." She winks and leads me inside. "Welcome to UC Berkeley."

I thought the library was my favorite part of the tour until Nikki shows me the famous clock tower—the Campanile.

She flashes her student ID at the man behind the front desk, then points to me. "Potential students are free too, right, Henry?" She winks and he blushes.

"You know it," he says in an accent I can't place. "Go right on up, ladies."

"Thanks." I picture myself in Nikki's shoes next year. Anticipation stirs and hope wells to bursting. This is the first campus I've seen and I'm sold.

We take the elevator, followed by a short flight of stairs. When we reach the top I'm speechless.

"Isn't this stunning?" Nikki steps aside, allowing me a full view.

I step forward and peer through the bars at the city and campus below. The huge buildings don't look so grand from up here, and the Golden Gate Bridge might as well be dollhouse furniture. My confidence builds. Where anxiety would normally surface, I only meet a sense of calm and accomplishment. Like I could tackle anything and I don't know why I ever believed otherwise.

I can totally do this.

"So, you've seen most everything," Nikki says. "What's the verdict?"

"It's . . . big."

"You'll definitely get your steps in here."

I nod.

"So seriously, I can't stop thinking we've met before," she says.

"I know. It's been bothering me all day."

"Did you grow up in the Bay Area?"

"No, I'm actually from the East Coast."

"Oh, what brought you to Cali?"

I haven't talked about this. Not even with Jake. I've written it. But saying the words unplanned, unhindered, and unedited is different. "I moved here when I turned sixteen," I say slowly. Maybe that will be enough. Maybe she won't ask for more.

She does. "Family stuff?"

"No. Sort of. Just me and my grandma—Mee-Maw."

"How funny. That's what I called my grandma too."

It's a small thing. A tiny thing. But sharing this with her feels like the seedling of friendship. I've ruined so many relationships in the past. Broken so many bonds. Maybe this is my chance to start something that can last. While my instinct says to shrink inside my shell and offer only what she asks, I know that can't last forever. I told Jake I wanted to grow. To start over.

No going back now.

"Is your grandma here in California?" I ask.

She shakes her head. "She passed away when I was five, but Gramps is still here. I'm pretty sure he's going to outlive me at this point. He's a tough one. What about your grandfather?"

"I never knew him. Only Mee-Maw."

"And your parents?"

And here is where it gets real. My pulse picks up and I close my eyes. "My mom died and my dad—" I swallow, recalling the last time I heard his voice, feeling the disappointment in his gaze. "My dad and I had different ideas about what my future held."

"Any siblings?"

I can talk about this. I should talk about this. I push myself to get real, off the page and unscripted. "Have you heard of Jordan King?"

Nikki's eyebrows shoot up. "The singer?"

I nod.

"She has that hit song. The one that's dominated all the radio stations. What's it called?"

"'Sirens,'" I say. "That's my sister."

"She's dating someone famous too, isn't she? That music producer . . . um . . ."

"Jerome LaDuke. Duke for short." Worst man alive. "Yeah, that's him."

Nikki must sense my feelings of worthlessness and pain at the mention of their names because, for whatever reason, she squeezes my arm. "I'm glad you came today, Brooke."

"Thanks. Me too."

"Come on." She winks. "I know the best place on campus to get ice cream. You haven't had ice cream until you've had CREAM ice cream."

I have no idea what that means and I don't care. Because for the rest of the afternoon I have a new friend, and it doesn't feel forced and I'm not constantly worrying she doesn't like me or questioning if she's annoyed or doesn't want to be here. Instead, I enjoy my plain vanilla in a cup while she eats her birthday cake ice cream smashed between CREAMfetti cookies, which I would absolutely order if they didn't have gluten. I almost want to cheat, but I'd regret it later.

There will be a next time. I let the idea turn to choice. I'm already making plans for when I'll visit again.

We talk and laugh and exchange numbers. When I meet Jake at the car, Nikki's already texted. I have a text from Hope too. I skip it, wanting to tell her in person about how amazing Berkeley is.

I climb into the car and click my seat belt in place. "Hey, can we take a detour to Hope's house? It's only thirty minutes out of the way and I haven't seen her in a week."

Jake doesn't answer right away. The radio plays low over the car's speakers. I open Nikki's text. I love that she uses proper grammar and punctuation. I can tell we'll get along well.

Hey, that guy behind the ice cream counter was super cute, right? I think he was interested in you. Should I give him your number?

Nikki already has a boyfriend so I know this is her way of being nice. But I can't help that all-too-familiar feeling that surfaces when I think of boys and summer and first dates.

Thanks, but I think I need to keep my options open. Let me check Cold Stone and Baskin-Robbins and get back to you?

I add a winking face and hit Send.

She responds with four crying-laughing faces and I know I've made a friend.

It didn't even hurt.

I pull up directions to Hope's house, then turn to Jake to tell her about my campus tour.

Her deadpan expression shatters every perfect detail, shading it in gray.

This is Jake's version of crying. This is the face she makes when she doesn't want to make a face at all. It's the same face she made before I was life-flighted to the hospital in January.

"Jake?"

"The hardest part about this job," she says, "is getting attached."

I unbuckle and twist to face her fully. A new song fades in over the radio, a haunting, siren-like voice I recognize too well. I hit the power button and the music dies. "Jake. What. Happened?"

"It's Hope."

And that's all. I don't need more because that's it.

It's Hope.

And so a new normal begins.

I didn't brace for the impact this time. I fly headfirst through the shards of my flawless day. They cut me as I sail straight into the concrete finality of Jake's words. I'm lying in a pool of the blood that drains from my head. Because . . . because . . .

I close my eyes, squeeze my phone hard, wishing I could turn back time and open the text I didn't read when it would have meant something. I make myself say the words for her.

"Hope is gone."

THIRTY-THREE

Merrick

Merrick had braved the Fourth of July crowds before, but this was insane. Sweat bordered his hairline, the deodorant he'd put on this morning expired. He removed his tank and shoved the bottom end in the back of his board shorts, giving himself a nice tail.

Humans occupied every inch of the beach. Mothers slathered sunscreen on their children from head to toe. Dads threw Nerf balls. A few teen girls sunbathed on their stomachs, bikini strings untied.

A year ago, he might have whistled. Maybe even joined them in hopes of some action. Today he searched for a girl who was fully clothed and never failed to make him believe in a better version of himself.

When the pier was fifty yards off, he sensed her before he saw her. Coral's presence was a song he'd gladly play on his harmonica any day. He'd brought it tonight. He was determined to show her how he felt with more than words.

Be cool. Be cool. You've played the harmonica a thousand times before.

When had he gone from caring about nothing to caring about everything?

No, not everything. Just her. And Amaya, of course. And their mom. But that wasn't the point.

Merrick made a beeline for the men's bathroom and ducked inside. Splashed some cold water onto his face. "Get it together, Merrick."

"Talking to yourself again?"

He whipped around to find his sister standing in the doorframe.

"You left the house. Alone? Maya, not cool. Someone might see you."

"What? In the million people here?" She jerked her chin over one shoulder. "I'm nothing, a nobody, a Waldo in this sea of busybodies." She'd propped the door open with her arms and feet spread apart like a starfish. Her wrinkled nose was warranted thanks to the reeking scent wafting from every corner of the space. What was *not* warranted was how comfortable she felt to intrude here, of all places. "Relax, Brother. Grim and Nikki are with me. They went to get shaved ice."

He'd have a word with Grim again about his sister's safety. It had been over six months, but that didn't mean they were in the clear.

"Amaya." Merrick left the cracked and graffitied mirror and filthy sink behind, bolted toward her, and scooted her out before someone saw. Or came in. "This is the *men's* bathroom."

She rolled her eyes, dug her thumbs under her backpack straps, hitching it higher on her thin shoulders. She drew her sunglasses down over her nose, removed one of Grim's ball caps from her back pocket, nestled it low over her forehead. "I'm inconspicuous. See?"

Merrick eyed her. Had she lost more weight? Hard to decide when all her clothes were too baggy to begin with. Amaya's knee-length shorts hung low on her hips, and the neck of her T-shirt sagged beneath her collarbone. Maybe he'd ask Nikki to bring her some new things.

He suppressed his worry over Maya's weight and searched the perimeter for Nikki and Grim. They waved at him from the shaved-ice shack and Merrick's worries eased. He wanted to introduce them to Coral, but he was also selfish. This night had to be perfect. If he overwhelmed her with introductions, it might trigger her anxiety.

So Merrick swung his arm around his sister's neck and forced her into a hug. She *had* thinned, and the circles under her eyes said she lacked sleep. He glanced at her arms, hoping she wouldn't notice. He didn't see any new cuts. Still, his gut said his sister wasn't as okay as she seemed.

They were running out of time.

He needed to find their mom. Yesterday.

Amaya elbowed his side.

"Hey, buddy." Grim and Nikki walked up. It didn't escape Merrick's notice that they were holding hands. "Should we have gotten you one too?" Grim held up a yellow shaved ice—pineapple.

"I'm good," Merrick said. "I sort of have this thing."

Amaya rolled her eyes, her favorite pastime. "Your girlfriend again? Are you sure she exists? Are you certain she's not a mermaid you imagined?"

Merrick gave her another hug and decided he'd let her have today. Maybe he needed to loosen up, let her out more. This was a good thing for her.

It was good for both of them.

They parted ways after Merrick reminded Grim and Nikki not to let Maya out of their sight. Nikki assured him they'd stay linked and took Maya's hand. Merrick expected her to pull away, but she didn't.

Maya liked Nikki more than she liked her own brother.

He watched them go until they were lost in the crowd. Amaya had to hold up one side of her shorts to keep them from falling off. Guilt stabbed Merrick's ribs.

She'll be okay. It's one night. I'll buy her a double cheeseburger tomorrow and watch her eat it until it's gone.

The pier and boardwalk waited fifty yards off. Merrick headed to her spot. The Summer of Lights Festival was in full swing, complete with balloon-animal artists, cotton-candy vendors, and two shaved-ice trucks. A canopy booth was set up on the boardwalk where attendees could buy lanterns, markers, and lighters. Every July, people from all over showed up to write their wishes on the white paper lanterns and send those wishes afloat over the ocean. The entire sky lit up. Better than fireworks, there was a serene calm to the Lights Festival. The last time he'd sent a wish into the sky, his mom was there. Merrick was young and had wished to make his dad proud.

He'd stopped believing in wishes after that.

"But . . . I'm starting to again." The words released on a murmur as he kicked up some sand behind him.

Coral sat on a dry patch beneath the pier, hidden away from the crowds and lights and noise above. Band music played a nostalgic tune in the distance. Merrick tapped the beat out on his thighs, whistled along for good measure. The ocean approached and receded against the shore. It barely reached Coral's feet before it backed away. She wiggled her toes, shifted closer. The sun began to set, the day fading like the end of a song.

She was writing again, lost in the world she'd created between the pages of her notebook. She didn't look up, didn't even notice Merrick standing a foot behind her.

Intrigued, he stayed back and crossed his arms. Was she . . . *humming?*

The sound was soft, almost nonexistent.

Merrick withdrew his harmonica from his pocket, played the chords to match her tune. His heart swelled with each step toward her.

Coral continued to hum. She bobbed her head, tapped one foot on the damp sand. She was lost in her own world. With her, time dwindled from existence. Merrick wanted to freeze these moments before they escaped.

He leaned forward and caught a glimpse of his name on her notebook page. A diary entry? A poem? A few more inches and she'd be leaning back against his shins. But she didn't look up from her notebook.

Merrick became an intruder in the private bubble she'd created. So he pocketed his harmonica, cleared his throat, and offered a casual, "Hey."

Coral stopped humming and closed the notebook cover. "Hi."

He sat and their hands lay side by side in the sand. If he moved his pinky finger a few centimeters, they could make another promise. One that mattered more than the one they'd already made.

She lifted her hand and played with her braid.

"So . . ." He coughed. *Classy, Merrick.* "You came."

"I said I would."

"I'm glad." He inched his hand closer, hoping she'd place hers next to his again.

She didn't. "Me too. What are we doing?"

"Trust me?" He wanted her to say yes more than anything. To take his hand and let him show her that he could be her safe haven.

When she looked at him, a strange sensation in his chest took over.

"Lead on," she said.

It wasn't the answer Merrick wanted, but he'd take it.

They stood at the same time. Merrick almost offered his hand, but he didn't want to mess this up. He'd told her he'd wait and he would. He wasn't about to rush things when she'd only begun to let him in.

"I went through my grandmother's attic."

"Without me?"

"Yes."

Questions ran rampant, but he allowed her to speak first, showing her he could be as patient as she needed him to be.

"You've only shown me some recent photos of Lyn, so I can't be sure."

His ears perked. "You found something, didn't you? Tell me you found something."

"Maybe. It might be nothing."

Merrick stopped where they strode. They were both barefoot and their strides matched in pace. He tried not to get his hopes up. He didn't want this evening to be all about that. Still, she couldn't mention it and expect him not to ask questions. "What is it?"

"An old newspaper clipping. An engagement announcement. That's it."

"Did you bring it?"

She nodded, then withdrew a small square of faded newspaper from inside her notebook.

It wasn't much. A few sentences. *Lyn Camden, town sweetheart, to marry the most eligible bachelor in San Francisco. Wedding date to follow in a later edition.*

His dad's name wasn't listed, but Camden had been his mom's maiden name. This had to be about them. "How long did it take you to find this?"

Coral shrugged. "A few days. My grandmother has a lot of junk. I pulled out a stack of old photo albums too. I haven't gone through them yet . . ." Her voice trailed.

Was it an invitation?

Merrick pocketed the clipping and didn't think before he made his next move. He pulled her into a hug, picked her up, and swung her around. When her feet met sand again, she drew away, her hands sliding down his arms. When her hands found his, they stayed.

This was different from anything he'd experienced.

Merrick reached out to touch her face, half expecting her to flinch. She didn't. His confidence boosted. "You're amazing. Has anyone ever told you that?"

Questions glazed her eyes. She searched his as if looking for a flaw. It was the longest she'd ever held eye contact.

He leaned closer. Was this his chance?

She didn't move. They were so close he could feel her breath on his skin.

A popping noise resounded from somewhere to their left.

Coral jerked.

"It's okay," Merrick said. "Probably a balloon or some firecrackers or something."

But it was too late. Coral withdrew, ending the moment.

They walked down the beach, their arms brushing. After a few minutes, their fingers found the other's again. Soon they intertwined. Her hand, icy in his palm, was soft despite the chill. Merrick squeezed it, hoping to share some of his warmth. Hoping to make her see, with a touch, that he'd keep any promises he made.

When they reached the other side of the boardwalk, where a giant screen and projector had been set up, Merrick beamed. "I hope you're a movie buff."

Coral's eyes illuminated brighter than the lanterns that would soon be overhead. "I've never been to one."

Merrick's jaw dropped.

"I mean, I've seen a movie, but not like this. On the big screen surrounded by people. My father thought it was silly and common. My oldest sister went once."

"And? What was the verdict?"

"She said it was magical."

"You haven't seen anything yet." He led her to a spot he'd reserved for them earlier in the day. An oversize blanket with a picnic basket at the center. Excitement sped his pulse. He'd never taken so much care to plan a date. His father usually did that for him.

They sat and a vendor called through the crowd as the previews played. "Popcorn. Cotton candy. Ice-cold Coca-Cola."

Merrick opened the basket and pulled out a to-go container of scones from the same tea shop they'd visited in June.

Coral stared. Her eyes glistened.

"I figured since we didn't get to finish the last time, a do-over was in order. There's no whipped cream or marmalade, though. It would have gone bad."

Her lips pressed and she shook her head. "No. This is perfect. Thank you."

Merrick watched her as she ate. He watched her eyes on the screen as the opening scene brightened the night.

As she brightened the night.

He leaned back with elbows locked. Then he hunched forward over his bent knees. Then his arms were behind him again and he was basically lying down, fingers clasped behind his head.

Why was he acting like such a spaz?

While Merrick was all nerves, Coral didn't move. Her knees had to hurt after kneeling for so long. Merrick tried to focus on the movie, but stray hairs kept falling away from their tucked places behind Coral's ears. She had a tiny, brown, apple-shaped birthmark beside her left one. It could only be seen when her hair was pulled back. Every time a strand fell, the mark disappeared again.

He coughed but she didn't react. How could she remain so still? He was practically jumping out of his skin at her nearness.

What. Is. Wrong. With. Me? If this were Nikki, or any other girl for that matter, I'd have made a move by now.

Other girls were predictable. In their revealing dresses and so much makeup caked on their skin that a guy had to wonder what they were hiding underneath all that paint. Coral didn't wear makeup. Her eyebrows were so light, they almost blended in with her skin. Her dark eyelashes contrasted, framing her two-tone eyes, shocking against her pale complexion. She rarely spoke but always listened. On guard but begging to be seen.

She was something else.

Merrick didn't want to be that other guy ever again.

The air seemed to change as the final scene rolled. Merrick observed the other couples cuddle closer. An old man and woman sat in a pair of matching lawn chairs. The man leaned in and kissed the woman's cheek. His lips lingered and he nuzzled her skin with his nose. She giggled, batting him away, pretending she couldn't stand him. What a cornball.

I hope I end up like him.

The music swelled and half the audience clapped and cheered as if they didn't expect the happily-ever-after ending. Like they had zero clue the princess and her prince would end up together.

It's why Merrick loved the classics. Every time was as good as the first.

When the credits rolled and the theme song faded in, the old man took his wife by the hand. They swayed in the sand as if they were the only two people in the world.

"Shall we?" Merrick offered his hand, palm up.

She placed hers there and he guided her to stand.

Coral often seemed a little uneasy on her legs, reminding him of a toddler first learning to walk.

Merrick placed a firm hand on her waist and guided her arms into position. He drew her in, the music accelerating his confidence. "Trust me. Pinky promise."

She seemed to relax at those words. They swayed at first, nothing more than a back-and-forth rock. Merrick didn't mind. As long as she was near, they could have simply stood still.

When they locked eyes, everything in him wanted to close the last bit of distance between them.

But her expression wilted and he held back. Or maybe she held back? "You're safe," he told her. "You're safe with me."

"Nothing is safe. No one. Everyone leaves eventually."

"I'm still here."

"For now."

"What are you so afraid of?"

Her body stiffened and they stopped swaying. "You'd never understand."

"Try me." Merrick attempted to move her into rhythm with the music again.

Her resistance was painful.

"I'm here," he said. "I've been here. I'm going to be here. You can't get rid of me."

She released him and took a step back.

He tried not to let his frustration show. "Why do you do that? Why do you push me away anytime we start to get close?" The words spilled out before he could swallow them back.

Her chest heaved and her eyes narrowed, transforming her once again into the withdrawn and closed-off girl he'd first met. "You know all about pushing people away, don't you, Merrick? Your dad. Your sister."

"Don't bring Amaya into this. You don't even know her."

"I know enough. The bits and pieces you've told me. She may have stopped cutting, but she hardly eats, right? She inflicts pain on herself so she doesn't have to admit how much it hurts that your mother abandoned you both." Her breaths were short, quick, hot.

Merrick could hardly breathe.

"You walk around with your foolish ideals and dreams of your mom whisking you away to a better life. Get a clue, Merrick. There is no such thing as better. Your mom's not coming back and Amaya's going to slip away before you finally realize she's not okay."

Several of the couples near them had stopped to stare. The credits rolled in the background. They had become the main source of entertainment.

A curse left Merrick's lips. Old habits died hard.

The magic between them had broken.

Coral took her cue and exited stage right.

Was he expected to handle her constant roller coaster? One minute she was up, the next she was diving off a cliff.

"Don't just stand there, son."

At the word *son*, Merrick froze.

But his father was not the one calling him by the term he'd come to despise. It was the old man. The cornball who'd kissed his wife on the cheek.

"Go after her," he said.

His wife nodded. "You won't regret it." The elderly woman bent down. When she straightened she handed Merrick their flat paper lantern and a lighter. "We've had a lifetime of wishes. I think you need this more than we do."

She turned to her husband and kissed his chin. They gazed at each other with so much love, with so much understanding, Merrick wondered if there had ever been a chance for his parents.

Probably not.

But their story didn't have to be his. He thanked the couple, grabbed the picnic basket, blanket, and notebook Coral had left, and sprinted up the beach after her.

He would follow her. Again.

He would always follow her.

To the bottom of the sea and back.

THIRTY-FOUR

Coral

Where were tears when she needed them?

Coral wanted to cry so hard and so loud and so ugly that her father and Jordan would hear it from a million miles away.

She wanted her face to get red and splotchy. She wanted to sob until she fell asleep and then awakened again to cry some more.

She wanted her tears to fill the ocean. Because then she could walk away and finally, *finally* start somewhere new. Coral wanted to let it go. All the pain, all the hurt, all the spiraling thoughts and reliving of nightmares. She couldn't do this. These emotions, this Disease, was killing her. Day by day. Week by week.

Merrick only made it worse.

Every kind word he said, every moment he proved he was nothing like her sister's prince, only tortured Coral more. Now she couldn't stand to lose him. Now he was a part of her after. It was only a matter of time until he became nothing but before.

Fire lit the sky as it had the night of Red Tide. She didn't bother going inside the cottage when she got home. Her grandmother would be asleep, and Coral wasn't in the mood to answer her questions with fake responses like "It was fine," and "Yes, I had a lovely time with the boy I'm probably falling in love with but push away every time he gets close because I know he'll eventually leave and this can't last and . . ."

Coral kicked a potted plant over and stormed around the back of the house to the ladder that rose to the roof. She climbed the rungs, heart prepared to fall from her chest and smash on the concrete below. When she reached the top she stepped lightly, finding her balance, until she worked her way to the spot toward the middle that was flat enough she could sit comfortably.

The cottage rested on the crest of a sloping hill covered in ice plants that produced little purple flowers. A private beach in the shape of a crescent waited below. During the day the water sparkled so blue she could imagine herself in a more tropical setting. Now it bled ink. Coral wanted to dip her pen there, to write everything she felt so she could get it out and away.

But her notebook waited on the beach. With Merrick. With her heart. Without a way to escape her own whirring thoughts, she sat naked, helpless, exposed. If she couldn't write them, they stirred inside her, unable to flee.

So she watched the fireworks and let her heartache drown her. They were almost soundless from this distance. Glittering and lovely and unreal.

"Like Merrick," she said aloud, tasting the words she needed to believe if she was ever going to survive. "He isn't real."

"Pretty sure I am, actually."

Coral whipped her head toward his voice. Her heart leapt but she covered it with a look of disdain. "Did you follow me here?"

He lifted an eyebrow. "Did you want me to follow you?"

Yes. "No."

"I don't believe you." His deadpan voice was more serious than it had ever been. "In fact, I'm pretty sure you left this on purpose precisely so I would follow you."

He climbed a little higher and produced her notebook.

"You walked all the way here to bring me that?"

"Yes and no." He set the notebook on the roof and disappeared for a moment. When he returned, he carried the picnic blanket and . . . Was that . . . ?

"I felt like our do-over needed a do-over." He climbed onto the roof beside her, paper lantern in hand and blanket draped over his arm. When he joined her, Merrick laid the blanket across her legs, then opened the lantern. Next he pulled a lighter from his pocket.

"Where did you get that?"

"Questions, questions. Can't you ever be in the moment?"

Could she?

Merrick lit the lantern in silence. "Make a wish. Anything you want. Then we'll send it out to sea."

She faced the water. She used to wish upon sea stars. Her grandmother would take her to find them. When they found one, Coral would close her eyes and hope for some silly thing. But this felt real, as if she had a single chance at a wish that might actually come true. She didn't want to waste it.

"Whatever your past holds," Merrick said, "we'll get through it. Together."

Coral closed her eyes. She pictured Merrick by her side. With that image so clear in her mind, others of the crown princess and Red Tide receded.

"Got one?"

She hugged her knees and faced him, searching his eyes. Nodded. Could he see through her now? Could he know what she wanted in this moment, in the here and now?

Merrick lit the lantern, only briefly taking his eyes from Coral's. He held on to it for a moment. The warm light illuminated his skin, washing his face in an orange glow. As he released it, his gaze stayed fixed on hers. Though Coral's habit was to look away, she willed herself to stay with him. She shut the door on the past and let the future stay right where it was.

The lantern took height, soaring down and away to the water. Coral freed a breath and made her wish again.

Merrick inhaled. Their faces hovered inches apart. He searched her eyes now. She gave the slightest nod. Would he notice?

But he saw.

Merrick closed the distance between them. First his thumb found her jaw. He traced the line of it, his gaze trailing down and then back up.

Coral kept her hands laced, arms wrapped around her knees for fear she might try to escape if she let them free.

Slowly, gently, purposefully, with so much care Coral wondered if he thought she might break, Merrick pressed his lips to hers.

Warmth filled every inch of her. Her chest swelled. Fear closed in, try as she might to keep it at bay. Her lower lip quivered against his and her throat grew tight.

He pulled back an inch. "What is it? Did I hurt you?"

No, she wanted to say. *But you will.*

Coral wanted to stay there with him as he kissed her again, then drew her in to rest her head in the soft space between his chest and shoulder. They watched the lantern drift over the water until it disappeared. The sight made her think of summer. Of the bright days and warm nights that ended too soon.

She watched it vanish before she was ready to let it go.

Her sister had been right about one thing.

"Give your heart to one and you can never go back."

Why hadn't she listened? Though she no longer held the same desire to drown a prince, she still wanted to find him, if only to ask him why.

Why didn't you love her?

Why wasn't she enough?

Soon Coral would ask those same questions of Merrick. He would move on and she would end up like her oldest sister. Then Red Tide would come for her too.

Merrick never loved me.

He never will.

THIRTY-FIVE

Brooke

After

Hope's memorial takes place the last day of July. I pile into the van with the other girls. Jake and Mary have shotgun. I sit in the back, stare out the window, and ask why.

Will nothing ever change?

I've gotten into the habit of taking the sea glass bottle and my journal with me wherever I go now. The pages are packed. I'll need to start a new one soon. I open the cover and scan the now-full page of quotes Hope wrote.

"Sometimes . . . the smallest things take up the most room in your heart."

—A. A. Milne

We drive over a bump as I press the words to my chest. The smallest thing did take up the most room. She still does.

A sharp turn onto the highway has me reaching for the overhead handle. I check my bag. The bottle remains intact, wrapped and padded inside my new UC Berkeley sweatshirt. I have one month until I leave Fathoms Ranch behind and trade it for a dorm room. Jake helped me fast-track my application to Berkeley (helps when your therapist knows the dean of admissions) and even found some scholarship money that hadn't been claimed. That, plus the work-study program with the university's paper, put me halfway there.

Mee-Maw's retirement fund covered the rest.

I finally found the courage to call her again the day I learned about Hope. This time she answered. I expected Mee-Maw to be mad. Waited with bated breath for her to remind me of how horrible I'd been. Her words became the salve I needed to soothe my scarred soul.

"Hush now. We'll get through this. Together."

I hold on to those words as I stare through the glass, only the faintest outline of my flat expression visible in the window. With as much hurt as I've experienced at the hands of my family, Mee-Maw never abandoned me.

Maybe humanity isn't completely lost after all.

THIRTY-SIX

Merrick

The remainder of July was filled with quiet moments beneath the pier and stolen kisses in the attic.

Merrick and Coral had found their rhythm.

So why did he feel as if he was trying to convince her to stay?

It wasn't that she pushed him away. She kissed him back and didn't withdraw when he held her hand. He kept waiting for the right time to take her by the house, introduce her to Amaya and Grim and Nikki. But that moment never came. Anytime he'd bring it up, she'd avoid or redirect, changing the subject to his mom.

Maybe she *didn't* want to be found. What if Coral and Grim had been right all along?

The idea broke something inside as Merrick turned off the computer in the office and made his way downstairs to the kitchen. Amaya was there, *not* eating. Again.

Merrick checked the clock on the stove. Late afternoon. "Did you just get up?"

"Yeah. So?"

She hardly spoke lately. Was she tired? Depressed? What about PMS? She was eleven now, and Merrick didn't have a clue what to do. If she sent him to the store for tampons, he might lose it.

Maya needed Mom.

What now? He couldn't call his dad. The beach house was quiet. Grim was gone, off with Nikki on another adventure. Maybe Merrick could ask Nikki to talk to his sister when she came back. She'd know about that stuff, right?

Merrick studied Maya's eyes. Dark circles made her look years past her age. September would be here before they knew it, and she'd need to start her online courses again soon. How was Merrick supposed to get her to do her homework if he couldn't even get her out of bed?

"There's leftover pizza in the fridge." He grabbed a cold slice from a storage bag and tore off one corner.

"Not hungry." Maya grabbed a water bottle and moved to the stairs.

"It's a nice day. Why don't you sit on the deck and get a little sun?"

"No, thanks."

"What about—"

She rounded on him. "Which is it, big brother? Do you want me to go out or stay in? Because I'm pretty sure you've made your point that I'm safer if I stay inside so Dad can't find me, isn't that right?"

Whoa. "I didn't mean—you know I'm trying to find Mom, right? For you? This has all been for you."

"Right. This is all for me." She waved her arms in an arc. "It has nothing to do with the fact you hate Dad and love that it's killing him not to know where I am. Where *you* are."

Merrick's fists clenched at his sides, but he kept his cool. Maya was tired. Frustrated. She was allowed to lash out. He needed to let her vent.

"Did you ever ask me what I wanted? Did you ever think maybe I didn't want to come here and play board games and wear disguises while you go off with your girlfriend doing who knows what?"

She was emotional. She didn't realize what she was saying. "Myyy-uh." Merrick drew out her name on purpose. He couldn't say the wrong thing and make matters worse. "Dad was going to send you away. Remember? You didn't want to go. You said you loved hanging out with Grim and Aunt Ashley and Nikki. I'm doing everything I can so you can have a better life. So you can be free."

She laughed.

The lifeless sound sent a chill through Merrick's bones.

"You call this freedom?" She narrowed her eyes. "Maybe I don't know what I want, but it isn't this, Mer. It isn't this." She turned, her fiery hair whipping around her like a whirling flame. Every stomp up the stairs drove the nail in Merrick's resolve deeper.

No more messing around. He'd let himself get distracted.

He'd find his mom before summer ended.

Even if it meant his summer ended all too soon.

THIRTY-SEVEN

Coral

Coral's sneezes always came in threes. After the third "ah-choo," she sniffed, blinked, and rubbed the dust from her itchy eyes.

Coral had been in the attic for hours, scrutinizing old photos her grandmother kept in a box. Her notebook lay open on the floor beside her. She jotted down notes with one hand and flipped through the album with the other. She would find Merrick's mom. He couldn't possibly leave her then.

Fear festered. Coral awaited an impending disaster. Any day Merrick would wake up and realize he didn't care. That she was nothing to him.

She swallowed the lump in her throat and flipped another page.

The steps below creaked and Coral smoothed her hair. She adjusted her posture and blinked away the fatigue.

Merrick appeared at the top of the steps and her heart skipped *one, two, ten* beats. He had a way of making her forget the simplest tasks. Like how to swallow or think or string words together into coherent sentences.

Coral wished he would stop.

"Hey," he said as he made his way through the mess.

The scattered stacks of boxes and crates made it smell like a retirement home and old nails. When Merrick sat beside her, he leaned in and kissed her cheek.

Coral melted into the kiss. They never had enough time. Why couldn't this last longer?

"Find anything good?" His halfhearted words stung.

Coral placed a hand on his knee and told her anxiety to control itself for once. He wasn't sleeping enough. His distance had nothing to do with her and everything to do with the fact his mom remained nonexistent, forever out of reach.

They never found anything. Not since the newspaper clipping weeks ago.

She wanted to lift his spirits. To give him back the childlike hope he'd carried when they'd first met.

"Look in that box." She gestured toward an open one a few feet to her left. "I found it this morning stashed in the rafters."

"New stuff?" His eyebrows perked but his shoulders remained heavy.

"More of the same. Albums, newspapers, some yearbooks. It's a treasure hunt up here. I can't believe my grandmother collected all this stuff from people's estate sales over the years."

"*Hoarded* is more accurate." His tone exuded cynicism.

Coral inhaled and brushed off the comment. *He's not frustrated with me, just the situation. We're close and he's taking it out on me. It's fine. We're fine.*

Merrick crossed to the next box. The contents would probably lead them to more dead ends, but she kept quiet. She wanted *her* Merrick back. She would do whatever it took to keep his hope alive.

"Why does she take such an interest in other people's old memories?"

"She said she thinks someone needs to remember them." Coral shifted, watching him. "If they get thrown out, it would be as if they never existed. My grandmother hates that. Maybe it's because she's old and sees an end to her own memory."

He nodded.

Her heart twisted. He'd told her last week that some days he couldn't remember the sound of his mom's voice or the exact blue of her eyes.

She asked him questions, letting him remember Lyn through spoken words. When they were apart, Coral wrote those words down, hoping to save them for Merrick. Wanting to make some part of his mom permanent for him, even if the woman never came back.

Merrick picked through the box with cobwebs stuck to its corners. A spider crawled out and Merrick flicked it away. He dug deep, withdrawing book after book, dusting each one off before setting it in a pile to the side.

The final book he recovered was one of those coffee table books with a bunch of professional photos in it. The title read *Lighthouse Legacy*.

Merrick stared at it as if he'd seen a ghost.

"What is it?"

"This photo," Merrick said. "It's . . . I've seen it before." He dusted off the cover and plopped beside Coral on the floor.

They looked through the book together, with the spine resting between their touching knees. The photos on each page seemed to tell a story. Coral found herself getting lost in the images, in the captions that relayed the history of each abandoned place. One lighthouse, the same as the one on the cover, had been turned into a bed-and-breakfast and museum.

Merrick was fixed on it.

Coral stayed quiet. She didn't want to interrupt the gears that clearly turned in his mind.

"I *have* seen this before." Merrick held the page closer.

She leaned in. His scent drove her mad. She wanted to hide in his arms. She wanted him to assure her that, no matter what happened, he'd never leave.

Her own insecurities made her ill.

She moved away an inch.

Merrick didn't seem to notice. He cleared his throat and stood, leaving the book on the floor.

Why did a treasure hunt always have to end?

Merrick needs this season to end. So he can start a new one, even if it's one without his mom. Or me.

Coral rose and neared him. She placed a hand on his arm and tugged. "Talk to me."

Merrick turned but didn't meet her gaze. "This whole thing is . . . It's pointless." He punched an empty box and sent it flying across the attic.

Her hand rested over her heart. "Did something happen?" She tried to draw him in but he pulled away. Was this how he felt when she'd kept her distance?

"A lot of stuff happened."

She wrung her hands, then shoved them into her back pockets. Coral tried to forget about the pearls on her wrist. The ones that served as a constant reminder he still hadn't helped her find the prince.

He hadn't kept his promise.

"I know," she said.

"Do you?"

The words hit their mark. Because he was right. She didn't know. Coral understood his sister had struggled with depression. That his dad was a jerk. And his mom was missing—left? But what else did Coral know about the boy she'd so easily fallen for?

No, *easily* wasn't the right word. It hadn't been easy. She'd never wanted to let him in.

But then she did.

"Maybe I need a break." His heartless words fired at will.

Bursts of red splashed across Coral's vision.

Red. Red. Red.

And the tide came crashing down.

"A break." She repeated his word. It hadn't been a question. "A break from me." She held on to the wall to keep from falling.

"No." He started toward her but stopped short. "I don't know." He held his head between his hands and shook it. Too much time passed before he met her eyes.

Red turned to a cool and numbing black. Unlike the night of her birthday, Coral did not fight the shadows as they closed in. "You don't know." Her flat words tasted bitter. He didn't know.

He didn't know.

"I don't know what I mean." Merrick took one step toward her. Two. "I care about you, but—"

"But," she finished for him, "you don't want this. You don't want me."

Coral wanted Merrick to refute the statement. To assure her it wasn't that at all.

Instead, he said nothing.

She found the words for him. "You lied. Pinky promises?" She shook her head. She covered her mouth with the back of her hand. Coral couldn't go on. She didn't want to.

"I didn't lie. I care about you. I'm confused. I'm exhausted. I'm . . ."

"You're what?"

"I'm sorry." His shoulders slumped.

And that was it.

Coral glanced at the open book on the floor, then back at Merrick. "Take it. Take it and go."

She took the stairs two at a time and fled out the door and toward the beach. When she reached the water, she didn't stop. Fully clothed and heart breaking, she dove beneath the waves. She stayed under until her lungs burned and the salt water stung her throat. When she finally surfaced, Coral gazed at the empty beach and, behind it, her grandmother's cottage.

Both were empty.

And Merrick never returned.

THIRTY-EIGHT

Brooke

After

It takes four hours to reach the Church in the Forest at Pebble Beach. It's beautiful, full of light and giant windows looking out over the trees. The pews are packed so our group files into one near the doors.

I spot a familiar face a few rows ahead. Mee-Maw catches my eye before she faces the front again. We've talked a few more times over the phone this past month, but this is the first time I've seen her since I moved to Fathoms. I refused her visits at the hospital last spring. Now, as I take my seat at the end of a pew, all I can think about is how much Hope would urge me to make things right before it's too late.

Music plays and a pastor stands to speak. I lean into the aisle and spot Hope's dad at the front. He's sitting with shoulders straight and face forward. I smooth my hands over my dress and convince myself to find him afterward. No matter how awkward or difficult, I know Hope would want me to say something to her dad.

Just as everyone bows their head in prayer, a woman rushes past me and finds a place at the end of one pew a few rows forward. I watch her through the slits in my eyelids. Her hair is the first thing I notice. The color of a summer sunset—the same color as Hope's.

Her *mom*?

Rage ebbs and it's all I can do to remain in my seat. I clench my fists. So much of me wants to storm the aisle and give this woman a piece of my mind. *Now* she shows up? *Now?* She couldn't have shown up this summer when Hope needed her most? Or how about last year when the girl too young to drive a car or know anything about the world attempted suicide not once, but twice?

I'm fuming, trying my hardest to see her through the lens Hope wore. Hope, the smartest, brightest, most outgoing, encouraging, positive person I've ever known.

How did that happen? One of the few people who made an impact on my decision to stay, to try, to keep going, is the same person who left me behind because she couldn't do it anymore.

What they say is true, I guess. And by *they* I mean those who see us as statistics, as numbers, rather than as human beings. While programs like Fathoms have so much potential to help pave a path toward healing, there's still the possibility, after everything, that someone will commit suicide anyway.

"I prefer to say 'die by suicide,'" Jake said once. *"Commit implies on purpose. In your right mind. Suicide is the result of an illness, Brooke. I don't believe anyone really chooses it in the end."*

I imagine Hope. There in her bathroom. The pills she took sit on the edge of the sink. Her face is streaked with tears. She considers flushing the poison for the briefest moment. She glances at the door. She looks at her phone. She waits.

But Hope was tired of waiting.

She texted me that day—the day I toured Berkeley. I didn't respond. I couldn't bring myself to read the message until two days later. I guess a part of me feared it would be a cry for help. Something that might have altered her decision had I answered. But it wasn't.

I turn on my phone now and read the text again. I've read it so many times, tried to find some sort of secret code, a hint between the lines. But no matter how much I deconstruct it, I find zero significance in her words.

I think I'm converting. Jess isn't right for Rory. Team Logan for the win.

Had I replied, I would have argued that of course Jess was right for Rory and how could she think otherwise? I've thought about sending the text anyway, though I know she'll never respond.

Even now, I shake my head and smile. *Gilmore Girls?* That's what was on her mind the day she stopped fighting? I love and hate her for it. Why didn't she call me? Why didn't she text me a thousand times until I picked up?

She didn't want to be stopped. There was a time I felt the same.

I know how difficult it is when the world becomes overwhelming or the thoughts of numbness, the end of pain, take over. For Hope, it was too much. And no matter what I did or said or how much better things got, there was still the chance she'd choose to say good-bye.

Third time's a charm, I hear her say in my head.

I scowl at the dark joke I know she would have told to lighten this morose day. Her favorite times to laugh came during the most inappropriate moments. I want to scold her in her twelve-year-old body with her fifty-year-old mind. I want to scream her name and tell her this isn't fair and how could she and why is this happening again?

This hurts worse than the first time I lost someone this way.

Because, this time, I allow myself to cry.

This time, I feel it all the way down to my drowning, bleeding soul.

THIRTY-NINE

Merrick

Merrick kicked himself. Then he punched a throw pillow and threw it across Grim's living room.

He'd blown it. Big-time. Rather than confiding his doubts and frustrations in the one person who understood, he'd done the very thing Coral did to him. He'd run. He'd run so far and so fast he didn't know if he could find his way back.

Maybe she didn't understand him after all. She hadn't even given him a chance to explain. Coral assumed the worst. She'd use whatever excuse she could if it meant she didn't have to feel pain.

"She's infuriating!"

"Who's infuriating?"

Merrick looked up.

Maya stood at the bottom of the stairs. Completely dressed with hair done and makeup on. She looked way too old with so much dark, dramatic gunk on her face. "Where are you going?"

"Do I have to be going somewhere to get ready for the day?"

"Have you been taking selfies?"

She shrugged. "Maybe."

"And posting them online?"

"Don't be stupid."

"Myyyy-uh."

"Merrrr-ick."

Make that two females who infuriated him. "You know you're not supposed to be on social media."

"You're not my dad."

"Thank the universe for that." He regretted the words before they had completely left his mouth. "I didn't mean that. I'm sorry. You know I love you. I'm sorry. I'm sorry for earlier too."

"Yeah. Sorry." She crossed to the kitchen counter and picked up the lighthouse book he'd brought home. "What's this?"

"A book I found. I thought the picture on the cover seemed familiar."

"This looks like the painting in my room."

Merrick rose from his place on the couch and moved beside her. "What painting?"

"The one in my room," she said again. "The one of the Lighthouse Inn."

He watched her. Dark circles not even makeup could conceal lined her blue eyes. Her hair was curled but clearly hadn't been washed in days. Maya was spiraling. And Merrick could do nothing to stop it.

"We've been there before," she said.

Lighthouse Inn? He racked his brain but couldn't remember ever having gone. "Mom used to take us there?" he guessed.

Maya shook her head. "No, but Dad did once."

Merrick couldn't picture his father ever taking them anywhere that didn't benefit him.

"You don't remember?"

He usually tried to forget any time he'd spent with his dad. He couldn't remember it ever being pleasant.

"I was five. You were thirteen. Mom wanted to come here during spring vacation. We stayed at our old beach house. The one Dad sold a few years later?"

How did she remember all of this? Nothing sounded familiar.

"Mom had a meltdown the second day of spring break."

"Probably because Dad pushed her into one."

Maya pursed her lips. "I remember you took me down to the shore to search for seashells until she stopped crying."

His father had probably said something to make her that way. The man was heartless.

"Dad came and found us on the beach," Maya said. "He took us for a drive along the coast and we stopped at the Lighthouse Inn. We had lunch and went to the museum. He even showed us the spot where he proposed to Mom, right at the top of the lighthouse. I can't believe you don't remember. That was the best day ever."

Merrick sat stunned. Dumbfounded. Had he suppressed that memory? He remembered the seashells and his mom crying now that Maya mentioned it. But he'd completely blocked the part about his dad taking them for the drive.

Why?

Maya picked up the book. She said something but it didn't register.

Merrick blinked. "What?"

"Can I have this?"

"Yeah. Sure. Go for it."

She tucked it under one arm and headed upstairs while Merrick stared at the wall.

The place where his dad proposed.

It was too easy. Too close.

All this time?

He wanted to call Coral. He wanted to ask her to come with him. She might not respond, but there was no one else he'd rather tell.

Merrick texted Grim. Will you be back soon?

The response came quick. Later this evening.

He drummed his fingers on the counter. Grim was with Nikki. Later this evening could mean midnight. He texted Coral. He didn't want her to feel used, but that's how she would feel, especially after how he'd treated her. She overthought everything and it drove him crazy and made him want to scream.

There would never be anyone else who made him feel a million things at once.

He tapped out a quick sentence and sent it before he started over-thinking too. **I'm sorry. Can you meet me at Grim's? I found something.**

Merrick forwarded the address before he could doubt himself. His words would come off shallow, short, and far too distant. He looked at the ceiling. Amaya had turned on the shower. He never left her alone. She'd probably rinse off, then sleep all afternoon. He didn't want to invite her, get her hopes up in case he was wrong. He checked the time on his phone. He scanned his texts. Turned his phone off, then back on to make sure he wasn't missing anything.

Coral did not respond. She was still mad. Of course she was. He'd blown it.

One thing at a time, Merrick. One thing at a time.

He could be to the lighthouse and back in an hour if he hurried. Grim's car was in the garage since Nikki had picked him up.

I'll be gone an hour. An hour. That's it.

Merrick scribbled a quick note and left it on the counter where Maya would see it if she returned to the kitchen. He grabbed Grim's keys off the hook and headed out into the late summer sun.

By the end of the day, everything would be back to normal.

FORTY

Coral

Coral stared at the computer screen. She read the list again. Blinked. Her name remained.

She was a finalist? Coral's short story was going to the statewide Young Literary competition? She sucked in her lower lip. She should tell Miss Brandes the news. But school didn't start for another week and she doubted her counselor would be in her office.

Coral would have to wait until Wednesday when they had their weekly library meeting. She had finally started to feel comfortable around the group, and that was partly due to Merrick. She found herself searching for him now, hoping he was at the library. Dreading it at the same time.

After logging out of her email on the library's computer, Coral pushed away from the desk and walked casually down each aisle.

He's not here. You're not going to run into him.

I'm not trying to run into him. I'm looking at books.

Sure you are. Keep telling yourself that.

The argument with herself was not one she could win. She missed her best friend and it had only been a few hours. He'd hurt her, but after taking a step back, she wanted to give him a chance to explain. She should have done as much this morning, but the pain of his seeming rejection blinded her. Now all she wanted to do was apologize and try again.

His kisses were real. He was real. They were real.

It couldn't have all been a fantasy. Their story was no fairy tale, but he was kind and understanding and patient.

She loved him.

She would finally tell him so.

Coral stepped out into the sun and found a shady spot on a bench outside the library. When she turned her phone off silent mode, relief expanded her lungs. The text from Merrick nearly made her drop her phone.

I'm sorry. Can you meet me at Grim's? I found something.

Routing the address with her map app, she saw the beach house where Merrick had been staying wasn't far. She could walk the few miles easy. She could even follow the shoreline there.

No looking back. Not this time.

A tower of steps met Coral at the beach below the house. She stared up at the white wood, rolled her shoulders, and unlatched the gate to the stairs. When she reached the door, she focused on all she wanted to say, then knocked, one, two, three times.

No one answered.

She checked her phone again. No new texts from Merrick. She looked at the time from the original text. Three hours old? Sent shortly after he left her and now it was after noon. She hadn't texted him back. Had her idea to surprise him been foolish?

At first glance, the house seemed empty. Dark. She peered in through the window with her hands cupped around her eyes. Knocked again.

Nothing.

A sour feeling in her gut churned. *It's nothing. I'm sure he's fine.* Except Merrick wasn't fine. He was a complete mess. Her heart won over reason and any sense of propriety. She turned the knob and opened the unlocked door.

She cleared her throat. "Hello? Merrick?"

Nothing.

Something stirred upstairs. Footsteps padded across the floor. Had Merrick heard her?

The sound of a door clicking closed followed by the squeal of pipes sounded. She moved deeper into the house and waited for Merrick to come down.

Eventually, the water turned off. Any minute Merrick would come downstairs, say something to make her melt, and they would make up. He'd explain and she'd listen as he had listened to her so many times before. She would be for him what he had been for her. She wouldn't abandon him the moment he needed her most.

No one came.

She bit her lower lip and shot him a text. **What's taking so long?**

He responded with a question mark.

I'm downstairs at the house. Are you coming down?

It took a minute before he replied. **I'm not there. Explain soon. Amaya is home. Check on her for me?**

Despite how awkward it felt to intrude farther into a stranger's house, Maya wasn't supposed to be left alone. Coral was surprised Merrick had left her here by herself at all.

She didn't want to startle the girl, but she also wanted to make sure she was okay. Coral stepped lightly up the stairs and found herself in a long hallway. Steam seeped under the only closed door. When she neared, she knocked with a single knuckle.

"Amaya? I'm Coral, your brother's friend." No answer. She heard the water from the faucet *drip, drip, drip* into what sounded like a filled tub. "Maya?"

She stayed there for a full minute. Waiting. Listening. Coral tried the door handle. "Maya?" Nothing. "Amaya." Silence. "Amaya, this isn't funny. Come on." An emptiness filled the air, so thick Coral could drown in it. "Answer me."

For once, the presence of nothing was far from welcome.

Shoulder braced for impact, Coral shoved her entire body against the door. It only took two tries to get the old thing to open. Steam filled the room. A discarded towel lay in her path between door and tub. The half-closed shower curtain left a scarce opening where Coral could see a hand, just a hand, hanging over the tub's edge.

"Amaya?"

She didn't move.

Coral tore the curtain aside. All feeling drained from her face. She'd been here before.

She was running.

She was dying.

She was still here.

Amaya lay slumped in the tub. Her hair, soaked and matted, covered her face.

Two words formed on Coral's dry lips. She forced them out, if only to expel them from her being. "Red. Tide."

Several things happened next. Too slow and too fast and completely blurred together.

Coral dragged Maya from the bloody water, wrapped her wrists in towels. Her clothes stuck to her in soaked bunches of denim and cotton.

"Stay with me, Maya. Stay with me." Coral repeated the same phrases over and over and over again. As if they held some magic spell that could bring a person back from where Red Tide had taken them.

Coral shook and fumbled. Frantic. Her phone rested on the counter downstairs. She looked up at the sink. A phone that had to be Amaya's sat on the edge. She was able to dial 911 without a password. The operator dispatched an ambulance, then kept Coral on the line.

Time slowed. She was sure she'd waited a year before they arrived.

Her arms burned and blood soaked her clothes. She put so much pressure on Amaya's wrists, Coral believed she might send them both straight through the floor.

Then the paramedics took over. Pandemonium. Everywhere. When Coral found herself in a sterile-smelling waiting room with a hospital gown draped over her to cover her bloodied clothes, she released a sobbing breath.

Her hand shook as she hit Call. Merrick's voice mail. Why didn't he pick up?

Coral didn't leave a message. How could she tell him over a recording that his sister had tried to commit suicide? Again?

He'd blame himself for leaving her alone.

Picturing his agony left Coral hollow and broken.

So she waited.

And waited.

And waited.

Sometimes the waiting was more unbearable than anything that came before.

FORTY-ONE

Brooke

After

I tuck my phone away and study Hope's mom.

Her head hangs and she dabs at her eyes with a tissue. Every now and then, her shoulders shake. About midway through the service, she stands and hurries out the back.

Her trails of mascara stay with me as my own tears continue to fall. I haven't cried in over a year. Now I can't seem to stop.

The pastor steps down from the podium and an odd couple takes the stage. A tall, gangly guy wearing an oversize beanie and a loose tie over his plain T-shirt stands beside a girl who could pass for a supermodel.

Nikki?

She's the same as the day we met, except now she's dressed in all black aside from the white silk rose pinned to her ebony hair. *Small world* doesn't begin to cover this one.

"She was a sister to me," Nikki says.

I'm impressed by how she refrains from emotion the entire way through. Her flawless speech hits each and every heartstring, snapping them in two.

Yes, she was my sister.

Yes, she was wise beyond her years.

Yes, we lost her too soon.

But *lost* seems the wrong word choice. It implies Hope has been misplaced. That she can't be found. But she's here, everywhere. She's in the rafters and in the walls. She's in the trees and the wind. In the shaking shoulders of her mother and the impossible stillness of her father. She's in Nikki's controlled words and in my twisting, turning heart.

The guy I assume is Nikki's boyfriend squeezes her shoulders. They exit the stage together, and the pastor leaves the mic open.

"If anyone would like to say a few words, now is the time."

Anxiety grips me as my emotions war. Fear of getting up in front of a room full of strangers. Knowing I'll inevitably say the wrong thing or do the wrong thing or act totally awkward or cry hysterically and run from the room.

But I'll never get this chance again.

And if I don't stand now, I know I'll regret it.

Jake and Mary sit behind me. I glance backward and Mary offers silent encouragement. She lifts her arm and flashes her tattoo, reminding me all I have to do is breathe.

Jake leans forward and squeezes my shoulder.

I rise and make my way to the line around the edge that's already forming. A girl gets up and starts spewing off all sorts of things about how Hope was her best friend and this is such a tragedy and she'll be missed by so many.

I want to punch this girl for her plastic words and synthetic tears. My gut says she was one of the people who contributed to Hope's depression. The girl doesn't even call her Hope but refers to her as classmate or BFF. Hope would have hated that. I straighten because it's in a single syllable I see I knew her better.

She let me into her world and I'll never forget it.

When it's my turn, I fan my fingers over my heart, attempting to quiet my shuddering nerves. I try to find Jake at the back of the room, but there are too many faces and they're all staring at me. My mouth gets too close to the mic and I trip over the cord and why on earth didn't I write down what I wanted to say?

"Hi," I start. Stammer. I feel sick and I forget my line.

Hope. What would Hope do?

"You know exactly what I would do," a memory whispers in my ear.

Hope hated when things grew too serious. Making light was her defense, and a good one too. Not always fitting, but now?

Now is precisely the right time to do a very Hope thing.

I clear my throat and do what I dread. Sing. While writing has become my comfort, my own story, my voice has so much more to give. There are more stories than mine. This is Hope's story. So I tell it the way she would have wanted it told.

I find an empty spot in a pew a few rows back and imagine Hope sitting there. She'd wear all the colors, of course, no black or drab for her. I see those colors as they dance and take flight, carrying Hope with them. I keep singing though everyone is staring. I sing because she was my friend and I've failed her and hers was a life that could have been saved.

I missed my chance.

I lost a friend.

The sudden playing of an instrument accompanies me, throwing me off for a second. But I find my place and keep going. I don't stop until I've given every last note. She deserved as much. She deserved everything.

When the song ends, the music fades and I find my words again. "Hope," I say, imagining her sitting in front of me, "you are not nothing. And neither am I."

A sob catches in my throat and my gaze falls on the front row. On her dad. He's stoic, hard to read. But I think I detect a hint of gratitude in his shining eyes.

My gaze shifts and, for the first time, I see the boy sitting next to him. A harmonica rests in his lap and sadness shades his dark eyes.

I gasp and nearly drop the mic.
How did I miss it? Why didn't I see?
"Small world?" I hear Hope ask.
You have no idea.

FORTY-TWO

Merrick

The inn was exactly as he remembered. Or hadn't remembered.

Now the memory came to life. A black-and-white film restored with color.

His father *had* brought them here. Merrick could see it clearly now.

Cars packed the modest parking lot. Merrick headed inside where he found a vacant registration desk. A hostess stood outside a double door arch that led into the restaurant. She greeted him and asked, "Party of one?"

"Sure," he said, too nervous to say anything else. He glanced left and right. He didn't know what he was looking for yet. But something told him he was about to find out.

"This way." The hostess led him to a table at the back of a busy room of families, couples, and groups of women chatting away.

Merrick sat and the hostess placed the menu on the table. "Can I get you a drink?" She removed a coaster from her apron pocket and tossed it onto the smooth wood.

"Coffee."

"Cream?"

"No, thanks."

She nodded and stepped back to the kitchen.

Merrick scanned the room. This was where his father proposed? It was so not him. Merrick had pictured them as more of a Gary Danko couple than the mom-and-pop restaurant sort.

The hostess returned and set a full mug of steaming black coffee before him. "Thank you," he said.

"Your waitress will be with you shortly." The woman wove her way through the full-to-capacity restaurant, greeting the customers who had started to line up by the podium.

Merrick didn't bother looking at the menu as he sipped his hot drink. He took in each table, group, family. A little boy with oatmeal all over his face, hair, and high chair banged his spoon on the table. Two old women talked incessantly, their mouths moving a mile a minute and at the same time. A man with a newspaper, Rolex, and fedora sipped at his own black cup of joe, seemingly unbothered by the commotion surrounding him.

"Can I take your order, hon?"

He spilled coffee all over the front of his shirt at the question. Merrick scooted back and stood, fanning his chest while pinching his soaked and stained shirt.

The waitress gasped. "Merrick?"

"Mom."

Several customers stopped to watch the scene unfold. Funny how an entire room could go quiet like that.

"Merrick," she said, between her teeth this time. "What are you doing here?"

"I should ask you the same question." The statement came out with more severity than he'd intended.

"Have you ever considered she doesn't want to be found?"

He shoved away the question that came to him through Coral's voice. "Mom. I've missed you."

This was the part where she would hug him. Tell him she'd been trying to find him and Amaya for months, but their controlling father had kept that from happening.

Instead, Lyn covered her mouth with her hand and shook her head. "Merrick. I can't."

And for the second time this year, his mother took her leave without so much as a good-bye.

Leaving a five-dollar bill on the table, he made his way to the hostess stand. "Can you tell me the time, please?"

She checked her watch. "2:02 p.m."

"Thanks." He was out the front door. His phone vibrated against his leg. A text from Coral lit the screen. She was at the house. Shoot, he'd forgotten he'd asked her to come. His impatience got the better of him. He replied with a quick apology and asked her to check on Maya before pocketing his phone and circling the inn's wraparound porch.

Several mismatched chairs occupied the border, some vacant, some hosting quiet vacationers sipping Arnold Palmers. On one end of the inn stood the old abandoned lighthouse that gave the place its name. Out of use for years, it had been transformed into a museum, a tourist trap for anyone who'd never seen one before. An image of his dad with little Maya on his shoulders filled Merrick's mind. He swatted it away and entered the lighthouse.

Behind the front desk sat a quiet little man with large eyeglasses, a striped button-down shirt, and a vest. "Welcome to the oldest operating lighthouse on the West Coast." He went into a spiel about the lighthouse's history.

"How much is admission?"

The man's expression altered from joyful welcome to baffled and blinking. "Well, it's free, but we have a suggested donation of—"

Merrick slammed a ten down on the desk and sprinted up the stairs. More he'd owe Grim later.

Old framed photos dating back at least a hundred years covered the swirling stairway walls. Lighthouse keepers and their families had kept the place alive for generations, making sure sailors found their way home. This was considered modern technology back then. A beacon of light and hope for the community.

A few people lingered on the balcony at the top. Taking photos against the railing with the Pacific as their backdrop. Merrick circled the perimeter, finding his mom alone on one side next to a pair of pay-per-view binoculars.

"Mom." She'd run out of places to hide and he was out of words.

She held up a hand and her shoulders shook. Wiped her reddened cheeks.

He'd struck an emotion. He couldn't decide if that was good or bad.

"You're a waitress?" Merrick didn't mean it as a jab, but that was how it sounded.

"Tryin' to be." She shrugged. "I'm not any good." The breeze tousled her hair. She looked so much like a healthier version of Amaya in that moment.

"I can't believe that man would do this to you. That he would send you here to make scraps while he's in the city in his high-rise office."

When she turned to face him, her confused expression sent an explosion of questions across his mind. She dabbed at her eyes and nose with the corner of her apron. "Your father didn't send me here." Her lashes lowered and she turned to watch the sea again. "I couldn't do it anymore. That life with him. I . . . couldn't. I was suffocating."

His hands grasped the railing next to hers. "He's a jerk. I know. I watched how he treated you."

She shook her head.

"Would you stop defending him? For pity's sake, Mom. Look where you are!" Merrick gestured at her soiled apron. "If it wasn't for him—"

Lyn placed a hand on his, her voice soft and kind. "If it wasn't for your father, I wouldn't be able to afford to stay here, bless his heart. He comes once a month to pay my bill and make sure I'm okay. He asks about you. And Maya. He wants to know if I've seen you. Every time I have to tell him no. I see so much heartbreak and regret in his eyes."

No. This was backward. She was lying, defending the man as she often did.

"Hiro is rough around the edges. He didn't know how to be with y'all. His time in the Navy hardened him. He used to be so . . . soft. Sweet, even. All he ever wanted was the best for you both."

Merrick's eyes burned and his throat was closing in. No. *No.* He gripped the railing tighter.

"Your great-grandfather was soft on him as a boy. Your daddy didn't want you to go out into the world unprepared. He had the best intentions."

Merrick wanted to tell her to stop. To take back the words that changed his whole perspective. He didn't want to see his father as a hero. As the good guy. He was not the good guy. He couldn't be.

"Mom. What you're saying. It can't be true. He wanted to send Amaya away to some facility."

"Did you ask him about it? Did you look into it at all?"

That wasn't the point. "Don't do this. Don't make him out to be something he isn't."

She turned to him again, sadness gone. Replaced with something else—resolve. Certainty. "I'm not. He knows who he is. And so do I. We're not good for each other anymore, but he's taken care of me. He's been faithful despite the numerous opportunities he's had to do otherwise." Her hand over Merrick's, she squeezed gently. "He's never hit me. Or you. Or Maya. The night we went to the hospital wasn't the first time she cut. It was just the first time you knew about it."

He backed away. His hands found his head, held it there to keep it from spinning. "No."

"The summer two years ago when you went on that school trip? The one you begged to go on? That was when we found her cutting. Your father hired the best counselors and doctors. Maya didn't want her big brother to know."

"Dance lessons?" His head wouldn't stop shaking. "Piano? Violin?"

His mom's downcast gaze confirmed his worst fear. "Counseling. Group sessions. Doctor visits."

Everything Coral and Grim and even Nikki had been trying to

get him to see came crashing down. "Amaya isn't okay, Mom. She needs you."

Lyn shook her head again. "I can't. I'm not strong enough to watch her go through that. I never was. She needs your father." She squeezed his hand again. "And so do you."

He jerked away. The last thing in this life or the next that Merrick wanted to do was go crawling back to that man. "Mom. You have to come see her. Please." He resorted to begging, but so be it. "You're our *mom*. We need you. Both of us."

"I'm sorry." Lyn wasn't there anymore. She was far away. Lost. She'd made her decision. No amount of pleading would convince her.

Grim's words hit him like lightning, burning from the outside in. *"All the money in the world can't make a mom stop being a mom . . ."*

Coral's warning rolled through him. Thunderous as it was true. *"If your mom wanted you, she'd search land and sea until she found you . . ."*

His mom had been here, twenty minutes away all this time, and she never once tried to find them. She didn't want to know what had happened. Not to Maya. Or Merrick. She couldn't handle it.

What kind of love was that?

"I'm glad to know you're both okay." She faced the wind, an odd sort of peace wrapping her in a bubble where Merrick couldn't reach.

How would he forgive her for this? For abandoning them?

"Good-bye," he said, refusing to call her Mom because that wasn't what she was. Not anymore.

When he reached Grim's car, Merrick sat with his hands and forehead resting on the wheel. How could he tell Maya their mother didn't want them?

He couldn't process it.

When he turned the key in the ignition, he let the car idle and pulled out his phone. Merrick had three missed calls from Coral and a series of texts.

His heart pounded.

He didn't see anything but where he needed to meet her.

The hospital. She was at the hospital. With Maya.

Merrick pulled out of the parking lot and hoped he wouldn't get pulled over for ignoring the speed limit. When he sat at a stoplight, waiting to get on the freeway, he resorted to his new plan B.

He hated this plan.

Loathed it.

But what else did he have left?

Hiroshi picked up on the first ring.

Merrick swallowed. He couldn't hide the defeat in his voice when he said, "Dad?"

FORTY-THREE

Coral

The nothing began much like her first journey into the Abyss.

It was dark.

It was cold.

It was nothing.

Coral was numb. Everywhere. Things that should have bothered her didn't.

When school started in August and some of the boys came too close for comfort, she escaped into the nothing until they let her alone.

She sat in English, usually her favorite class, and stared out the window. A blank sheet of paper lay on the desk before her. While the other students had been writing feverishly for ten minutes, Coral hadn't even bothered to take out her pencil.

When the bell rang and everyone headed to the next class, Coral's teacher stopped her at the door. "Miss Brandes tells me I can look forward to some beautiful writing from you this year," he said.

She shrugged and checked her phone. Five texts from Merrick. She deleted them without reading them.

"I assume you know that means you actually have to write something." He held up the blank page she'd turned in.

"How do you know it's mine?"

"Everyone else's has a name. Yours is the only one missing."

She shrugged again.

"Of course, a blank page sometimes says a lot more than a full one."

"Such as?"

"Such as perhaps you have more to say than anyone. So much, in fact, that a single page isn't enough to get it all out."

"Is that all?" She was going to be late for her next class. Not that she cared, but still. It was better than standing here listening to Mr. What's-His-Name analyze her reasons for skipping the assignment.

"Miss Brandes showed me your writing from last year. She says you submitted it to the district writing contest. You were even a state finalist."

Why did he have to bring that up? "And?"

"And I wanted to offer any help or guidance you might need before you turn in your final entry in December."

Coral hadn't told her counselor there would be no final entry. She'd spent every extra moment of the summer trying to finish the first draft of that stupid novel. Come to find out, she had no ending. The story simply stopped. Sure, her first chapter had placed her as a finalist. But the rest?

The rest were words. They were nothing.

She was nothing.

"Thanks," she said to get him off her back. "I'll think about it."

He nodded and she left. But Coral didn't go to her next class. She wouldn't be going to her first after-school session with that new therapist Miss Brandes had recommended either.

None of it matters. None of it makes any difference. My sister died. Merrick's sister . . . died.

Coral couldn't face him. Not after she hadn't been able to save Amaya. She relived that day until it was forever seared in her mind.

The blaring sirens.

The blood and the water and the stains.

Stains on Coral's hands and clothes.

A faceless girl lying lifeless in her arms.

The nurse at the hospital explaining they were doing everything they could.

In the end, it hadn't been enough. Coral had watched as Merrick sobbed into another girl's arms at the hospital that day. Whoever the girl was didn't matter. But the pain on Merrick's face?

That was something Coral couldn't erase.

And all this time she'd believed men—human or otherwise—were incapable of emotion.

Wrong. Everything feels wrong.

How could she write the ending to her story? She'd seen too many endings, and no one wanted a tragedy. She would be disqualified from the contest when she inevitably failed to turn in a completed manuscript. Her deadline would come and go. She wasn't a real writer. She was a fake, an imposter.

I'm a failure. I am everything Father and Jordan ever said.

When she walked past her next class and straight off campus, she made her way as far from the beach and the ocean as she could.

She wouldn't go to the meetings at the library.

She wouldn't answer Merrick's calls or texts. She couldn't bear to hear him tell her it was truly over. Of course it was. If she'd been anyone else there that day, maybe Amaya would have lived.

With each step toward town, emptiness consumed Coral. She felt less. Hollow.

Nothing.

She floated outside herself. Watched life pass her by.

And why wouldn't it?

Life never waited. She'd once written that time was a ribbon. Her time had been knotted and lost and cut. She would never piece it together the way it was before.

She and Merrick would never be as they had once been.

Coral could never get him back. And even if she could, she'd forever question his true intentions. She would keep him at arm's length, doubting if she could trust. Forever second-guessing his reasons for being with her. Pity? Guilt? Shame?

Who needed the ocean when life was plenty devoid of oxygen on its own?

There is more than one way to drown. I'm drowning and no one even notices.

No. Merrick was not part of her after.

Without him, things would never be the same.

FORTY-FOUR

Brooke

After

Seeing Merrick again. Now. I'm reliving that day from a hundred years ago.

I find refuge in the trees as I make my way outside. The fresh air quenches a thirst and I find myself drinking it in with each step away from the church and closer to the sea. It's too far out to walk, though. I'm not dressed for a hike. There is no escape from this. I close my eyes and press my back against a tree trunk.

Hope was Amaya all along. I see her there, in a bathtub filling with her own blood.

Red Tide, I think. I've never been able to say the word.

"Suicide," I say now.

One word. Three syllables. The definition of pain.

Hope didn't slit her wrists as she had the last two times. She could never bring herself to cut deep enough to end it before she was revived. This time there was no blood, I'm told. But the goal remained the same. The outcome one she didn't return from.

Now I see the forest for the trees. They've surrounded me on all sides, closing in, making it impossible for me to see anything else but my own version of this story. That's the problem with one point of view. It stands alone in its limitations, unable to recognize the details until the end.

I'm there. In the hospital. Waiting for him to come. But I'm no longer Coral, the character I created as a way of coping with my own demons. I'm me. I am Brooke. And I'm watching the scene unfold with new eyes.

I wander the hospital halls because I can't stand to sit in the waiting room, waiting for news they'll never give because I'm not family. All I see is blood and a little girl tangled in a mass of hair and lifeless limbs.

I never even saw her face.

The hospital windows let in light on all sides. Even so, the place feels dark. Depressing. This is where you wait for good news, hoping you'll be part of the small percentage who walk away from these walls smiling.

When they asked me how I knew Amaya, I didn't even know what to say.

She's my boyfriend's sister?

Boyfriend. Another word that seems wrong. What is Merrick to me?

Who am I to him?

I grab a cup of tea from the cafeteria and find the elevator that leads to her floor. Every sound is heightened, every detail playing forward in slow motion.

The ding of the elevator as the doors scrape open.

The sound of my bare feet slapping linoleum.

The rush of bleach and cleaner and lemon mixing with the sterile hospital air.

The swish of a doctor's white coat as he pursues a destination down the hall.

And there. Merrick. Sitting alone on a chair, head hanging between his knees. He's been in this position before. The day his mom left. Just before my sister took her life. So many horrific things pushing and pulling us together.

Merrick once called it fate.

I labeled it chance. Nothing more. Nothing less.

Now I'm not so sure.

Relief and heartbreak take over. We've both seen too much of this. Will it never end?

I move toward him, then I stop, back away, retreat out of sight behind a vending machine.

A girl approaches him. Tall and lean and perfect. Her back toward me. A day of faceless girls, it seems. When Merrick sees her, his eyes fill with an emotion I can't name. He stands and wraps his arms around her.

They don't release each other for a long time.

"Are you with the Princes?"

I blink. Start. What did the nurse say?

"The Princes?" I swallow.

The nurse points toward Merrick and the girl. Neither have seen me yet.

"The Prince family," she says. "Amaya Prince? The paramedics said you came in with her. You're the one who called 911?"

Merrick Prince. His name triggers a memory. My sister's voice rises from the depths.

"My prince never loved me. He never will."

My Prince does not love me. So I tell the nurse that no, I am not with them.

And I walk out the door.

287

Had I waited before rushing out, I would have seen Nikki's boyfriend and Merrick's best friend and the same boy who came to my rescue at school. Nigel and Grim are one and the same.

Merrick would have introduced me to his friends and I would have met Amaya. I would have known who she was that first day at Fathoms and then maybe I wouldn't have run away and tried to end it. I would have spent more time with her instead of in recovery. I would have learned their last name was Prince.

Merrick became the prince who surprised me in more ways than I could ever count.

Shoulda, coulda, woulda.

"Hi," Merrick says. Such a simple word, *hi*. So much meaning behind it. Does he have any idea the effect he has?

"Hi." It sounds lame coming from me.

People file out of the church now. I catch a glimpse of Merrick and Hope's dad. He finds their mom sitting alone on a bench by a tree. He approaches her. Holds her for a few seconds before she pushes him away.

The sight moves and unsettles and surprises.

Merrick follows my gaze and one corner of his mouth lifts. "He'll never stop chasing her." The way he says it, I know there's more he wants to convey.

There's always more with him.

His eyes find mine. He searches them and for the first time ever I hear him say, "Like father, like son." He rocks back on his heels. "Can we walk?"

I nod and fall into step beside him. We stroll through the forest in silence, the foot between us as long as a mile. I want to tell him I'm sorry about his sister, but I can't push the cliché and not-enough words past my lips at first. Sorry seems so trivial. But what else can I say?

"I'm sorry," I say.

"Thank you. I'm sorry too." He stops and scratches his head. His hair is longer than I remember it. He seems older. Different.

The same.

"She'd talk about you," he says. "When she'd call. She never said your name. Only that she had a friend and my dad had been right all along. Fathoms was the right place for her. I should have seen it from the beginning."

I set my jaw. "It didn't change anything."

"Yes, it did."

"The outcome was the same. She's gone."

"True. But her journey was different. No matter what she chose in the end, you impacted her. Don't ever think otherwise."

I let his words simmer. No matter what, I know I never impacted her the way she touched me.

We talk then. I tell him about my grandmother and how she moved to assisted living after Christmas last year. "It was either go back to my dad and Jordan or settle for Fathoms. Mee-Maw set it up."

He nods. "I've finally started taking college courses."

"Do you have a major yet?"

"Counseling and family studies."

"Good choice." My cheeks flush and I study my shoes. "How are things with your dad?"

"Ask me again in a few months."

"And your mom?"

He shrugs. "We don't talk. I know she didn't want to come today."

"Hope—Amaya—would have wanted her here."

"She saw the best in people," Merrick says.

Before we know it we're talking about her. The memories hurt and heal. We laugh until we cry, and a few people stare at us with looks of disdain.

But that's the thing about grief. You think it looks one way. The *only* way. You don't realize you can laugh through the tears until you're living right through them.

When most of the cars have pulled away and I see Jake, Mary, and the other girls climbing into the van, I know it's time to go. Merrick walks me to the parking lot where his dad stands, shaking hands with the pastor. Hiroshi makes eye contact with me and I want to shrink inside myself. He's intimidating up close.

"Thank you," he says. Then he shakes my hand in a rather formal and "princely" way. I can see why Merrick was afraid of him for so long. But I can also see why Hope adored this man with every part of her soul.

I have no words as I hold back my tears. I nod.

He compresses his lips and walks to a black car where he climbs in the back seat.

"Some things never change," Merrick says. "I think he'll use a chauffeur until the day he dies."

He's right. Some things never change.

And some things do.

We don't ask about the future. We don't make promises to keep in touch or reconnect.

Merrick and I stay in the now. In this lingering hug. In the moment when he picks a yellow daisy from a patch of weeds and hands it to me. In this awkward closeness where I can feel his breath on my cheek, I question if we might kiss. But we don't. There's a sort of silent agreement there. One that says it isn't the time, but maybe someday.

Or maybe not.

I don't know. Because all we have is now.

And now, I watch him drive away.

Mee-Maw appears beside me. She clutches her purple handbag in her white-gloved fingers and sighs. "What a nice young man. A real prince."

She has no idea.

I face her and the last bit of resentment I've lived in for too long joins the breeze, taking flight in the wind. "Mee-Maw, I—"

"Not today." Her voice exudes kindness. Grace. "Today is about your friend. You and I? We'll have our time."

We hug and I promise to visit her soon. When I climb into the

Fathoms van with the other girls, I close my eyes and lean against the warm window. Sunshine sends bright bursts of colors dancing beneath my eyelids. I listen to their song and bid farewell to two summers.

The summer of Coral that I couldn't release until now.

And this one. The one in which I—Brooke—learned that life is more than just living.

Hans Christian Andersen had the right idea. "Just living is not enough . . . One must have sunshine, freedom, and a little flower."

I twirl Merrick's daisy between my thumb and forefinger. Tuck it into my hair the way my older sister, River, used to do. I rarely let myself think of her. I've kept her so far removed from my story, she was hardly there at all. Now I picture her as she was. I imagine her and Hope together. Holding hands and walking along a private beach I can't see.

They're free, I think.

But so am I.

Autumn

PRESENT DAY

"Just living is not enough . . ."

—Hans Christian Andersen, "The Butterfly"

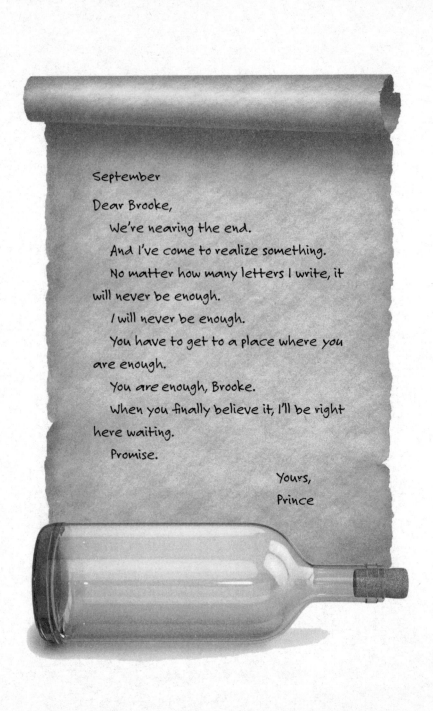

September

Dear Brooke,

We're nearing the end.

And I've come to realize something.

No matter how many letters I write, it will never be enough.

I will never be enough.

You have to get to a place where you are enough.

You are enough, Brooke.

When you finally believe it, I'll be right here waiting.

Promise.

Yours,
Prince

FORTY-FIVE

Merrick Prince

One month.

It had been one month since Merrick watched his mom leave Amaya's funeral without a word. She looked at him the same way she had the night she abandoned him—them—at the hospital.

But the regret in her eyes was never enough to make her stay.

He was not enough.

This time, Merrick no longer searched for his mom or waited for her to return.

This time, it was his dad he sought. On purpose. Who would have guessed that would ever happen?

September had nearly come and gone, but the corner office with the skyline view was the same. Photos of his dad's Navy days decorated the wall alongside an organized cluster of achievements and awards. Shaking hands with the president. Three American Business Awards in different categories. He'd even made *Fortune*'s list of 100 Best Companies to Work For.

Merrick had been intimidated by this wall. His own wall had nothing. No Little League trophies or student-of-the-month awards. Not even a spelling bee win. He'd felt average in his father's ever-present rising shadow.

Crossing to the wall of windows that overlooked the Bay Area, Merrick took in the familiar view. San Francisco's iconic Golden Gate Bridge in all its glory was lit, standing out in stark contrast to the autumn night sky. The promise of it taunted him, daring him to escape again. His life was an even bigger mess than it had been last year. When Amaya was still alive. When Merrick blew his chance to save her.

He let out an inaudible curse and stared through the city to the water beyond. He'd only hurt Amaya more by taking her away. Merrick couldn't help her. He'd waited for the inevitable then. Had been sure his dad would press charges and Merrick would face the much-deserved consequences.

But the charges never came.

He never asked his dad the reasons behind the silence over his crime. They'd hardly spoken since that day in the hospital over a year ago. Another cry for help. Another chance to save his sister.

But in the months that followed, even Fathoms Ranch couldn't stop her from taking her own life.

He avoided his dad as much as possible during her time away, stayed with Grim at the beach house rather than return to an empty home. But now, in the wake of his sister's funeral, Merrick could no longer put off facing the man who had done everything in his power to help Amaya Hope.

The office door opened and his father entered. Alone. There had been a period when every knob rattle or hinge creak made Merrick jump. Had him worried this was it—his dad was finally having him arrested.

But nothing.

He'd thought more than once about turning himself in. But with Amaya so fragile, he needed to be available, not serving time. Merrick had sent her letters and care packages and even visited her at Fathoms once. She asked him not to come again. It was then he knew his sister's healing was never something he could force.

Hiroshi closed the door behind him and moved to his leather desk chair. He opened a drawer, withdrew a file, and donned his reading glasses.

Lay it on me, Dad. Tell me what a huge disappointment I am and how I'll never learn from my mistakes.

A glance at the time set Merrick on edge. He'd arrived at 4:00 p.m. sharp, as his father asked. He sat in the lounge, thumbed through the most recent issues of *Forbes* and the *San Francisco Gate* to bide the time. It was now well after business hours.

How long is he going to draw this out? Amaya's suicide is my fault. He's disowning me. Ironic after I spent the better part of my life trying to disown him.

Hiroshi sighed, sat, and leaned back in his chair. The seat didn't groan with his weight, only serving as further proof of how tight the man kept his ship. Though it was late and most of his staff had gone home, Merrick's dad still looked pristine. His tie sat tight against his Adam's apple and his suit remained unwrinkled. The CEO of Prince Technology was nothing if not presentable.

But something else didn't fit. Exhaustion framed Hiroshi's dark eyes. A recent development? Or had it always been there and Merrick failed to see it?

He cleared his throat.

His dad released another sigh, folded his hands on top of his desk, and met Merrick's gaze. "I never expected you to volunteer to meet with me, Son. Especially not at work as you have made it clear my career is not for you. So tell me, what brings you to my side of town?"

Merrick's mouth turned down and a lump formed in his throat. He stared at the sole picture frame on his father's desk. The family featured was one he hardly recognized. One from another lifetime. From before. His father stood stoic behind his mother, the man's redwood hands resting on her willow tree shoulders. Hiroshi looked pained to be anywhere near a camera.

But Merrick's mother? She'd lived for photos. Said they were a human being's way of freezing time and capturing the soul. Her expression in this particular photo was pleasant. She held baby Amaya in one arm and had eight-year-old Merrick wrapped in the other. Mom's fiery red hair matched the reddish tuft of fur on his sister's tiny head.

There was a time Merrick had wanted to scream at his father. To blame him for the demise of their family.

Now he looked at the photo with new eyes. He saw a withdrawn man trying to keep it together. He saw a lost woman with soft, pale features and strawberry freckles that matched his sister's. Merrick studied his father's pointed jaw and tapered eyes as black as his hair. Their hair.

Merrick saw it now, how similar they were beyond genetics. They both wanted the best for Amaya. Maybe they didn't agree on what the best was, but Merrick could no longer doubt his dad had loved her.

Clearing his throat again, Merrick made his gaze steady. "I'm sorry." It had taken him too long to speak the words. Now they came across lacking and hollow. Like his heart these days.

Hiroshi gave one quick nod. "I'm sorry too."

Merrick had to work his jaw to keep it from dropping. Seemed pride was something else he'd inherited from his father. They were learning to let it go. Together.

"Was that all, Son?"

It was too easy. Exchanged apologies following the loss of half their family? He needed more. "Why didn't you have me arrested? Last year, after I took Amaya and she landed in the hospital again?"

Hiro's eyebrows arched. "Misunderstandings happen. Your sister . . . If she hadn't tried it under your care, she would have found a way at home. Which we've seen is true." The man swiveled in his chair and cleared his throat. He removed his glasses and pinched the bridge of his nose.

Merrick blinked, then peered past his father's concrete exterior, searching for the man he'd forever failed to see beneath. "Misunderstanding? Dad, you know I put her in danger. But you covered for me." It hit him then, a brick to his skull. Of course Hiroshi would be embarrassed. This was a PR thing. He couldn't have his wayward son's misdeeds showing up in all the papers. "If this is about good publicity, I don't—"

"Will I never win with you?" His dad set his glasses on the desk and sniffed. "What do I need to do to show you I am not the villain here?"

Villain. Wasn't that how he'd seen his dad? For once, Merrick didn't have a retort.

"You are my son," Hiroshi said in such a low tone, Merrick almost missed it. "I have only ever tried to raise you to be the best man you can be."

"I'm sorry you feel you failed." Merrick looked away, unable to bear the disappointment his father would no doubt share. If he hadn't taken Amaya away last year, things might have turned out differently. She would have gone to Fathoms sooner. Maybe she wouldn't have given up.

Neither of them said anything for a long time. When Hiroshi finally stood and joined Merrick at the window, he pocketed his hands and stared out at the streets below. "I didn't fail. I'm proud of you."

Merrick's heart stopped and started. Proud? Where was the punch line?

"While I don't condone your untruthful actions last year," Hiroshi went on, "I see a brother who risked everything to do what he thought would help his sister. I see a son who went to great lengths to track down his mother. I see a young man who stood on his own two feet, who was willing to sacrifice everything for those he loves. The details are foggy, but your heart was in the right place."

Merrick swallowed. His misplaced emotions jolted his system.

"I forgive you," Hiroshi said. "I hope you can forgive me too. I pushed you on Nikki. I tried to make you fit into my own mold. I take partial blame for you taking such desperate and reckless measures. While the choices were yours, I could have listened more. I should have been the person you came to rather than the one you ran from."

Merrick couldn't believe what he was hearing. He didn't know what to say except, "It's my fault, Dad."

"Would you blame yourself if your sister had died of cancer?"

"What? No. Of course not."

"How about a car accident? What if a drunk driver had hit her? Would that have been your fault?"

Merrick waited for the catch. The phrase that would show his dad's ulterior motives or need for control.

It never came.

"Nooo," he said slowly. Where was this going?

Hiroshi rocked back on his heels. His reflection in the window revealed glassy eyes and a pained expression. "What if Amaya had died of a poisonous bite? Or the flu? Or by falling down the stairs? Any of those on you, Son?"

Merrick shook his head, starting to catch on but waiting for his father to continue.

"Amaya was sick. Depression is an illness. It is a disease. Those on the outside sometimes brush it off as a choice. A simple change in mood or outlook." His dad laughed, but the sound was dark, almost resentful. "No one would ever tell a cancer patient to 'just get over it.' Why people think they can tell those with a mental illness as much is baffling and cruel."

Every word sank deep, anchoring in Merrick's core. His father understood more than he'd ever recognized.

Hiroshi turned toward Merrick. Up close he seemed less put together. More human.

The sight lent a sense of comfort.

"You messed up," he said. "No one is denying that. But you are not to blame for Amaya's death. Depression killed your sister. Not you. If you believe me on nothing else, believe this."

Merrick nodded as he held his father's gaze. It had taken him years to perfect the art of looking the man in the eyes. Now he found the task easy. There was no malice. No hatred behind his expression. They were two Princes trying to figure out how to move on from tragedy. And for the first time since Amaya Hope's death, Merrick saw he was not alone.

Hiroshi returned to his desk and Merrick glanced at his phone. He still hadn't heard from Brooke. He adjusted his perspective and reminded himself of his promises.

He would wait.

And he would find her older sister's "prince."

"What now?" Hiro asked when he sat again.

Merrick had the same question. He was at a loss for how to talk to a man he clearly didn't know at all. With an exhale, he ran a hand over his face, catching himself in the reflection of the dark window. He looked tired, eyes sunken, his hair in desperate need of a cut. "Beats me."

"I don't suppose I can ask you to work for me? To take an internship?"

Merrick chuckled. His dad had groomed him to be a businessman since Merrick was old enough to spell *economics*. "I've never had my life figured out, Dad." He'd said it. Why had he been so afraid to admit this before?

"I knew what I wanted, even at your age."

Merrick winced. *Here comes the insult.*

"Sometimes I wish I didn't," Hiroshi added. "I wonder if things would have turned out differently with your mom away from all the pressure that comes with my position."

Once again, these were words Merrick never thought he'd hear his father say.

Hiro donned his glasses. Loosened his tie. "You'll figure things out, Son. Give yourself some time." He opened another drawer, pulled out a set of keys. "I'd like you to start by driving up here to have lunch with me once a week." He set the keys on the desk. "You are responsible to pay your own insurance and fill your own gas. The car is a loan. Maybe you'll want to visit some college campuses. While public transportation isn't a bad thing, builds character, this will give you a little more freedom to explore your options. Use it wisely."

Merrick relaxed his taut fists. "I will."

"If you'll excuse me, I have some work to finish up." Hiro smiled, a look that was foreign but also familiar. It brought back memories of the day at the lighthouse all those years ago.

And Merrick found himself smiling in return.

As he grabbed his new keys and headed toward the office door, ten pounds lifted from his shoulders. He stopped at the threshold. "Dad?"

"Son?"

"I have a project I'm working on. Someone I need to track down. I'm wondering if you could help me."

"Do you have a name? An address? An email?"

"Not exactly."

Hiro glanced once at the stack of files on his desk before he shoved it aside and waved Merrick back inside. "Have a seat. Tell me who you're looking for and I'll see what I can do."

Merrick closed the door and pulled up a chair. He scanned his memories, flipping them on their heads. His dad wasn't perfect, but the man was here. He cared.

As Merrick explained in detail about Brooke and her story and her older sister and the nameless man who had broken the young woman's heart, his spirits lifted. His father nodded and listened, jotting down notes on a legal pad, then firing up the desktop computer and opening his vast database of contacts.

All this time, Merrick had seen himself as the hero his sister needed. As the son who could bring his mother home. As the one person who could get through to Brooke and fulfill every promise he'd made.

It was only now he wondered if the hero had been his father all along.

FORTY-SIX

Brooke

I choose a seat at the same booth inside the tea shop where Merrick took me for our first date. To return more than a year later is cathartic. A therapy of its own. Something Jake said in a phone call recently stirs my thoughts.

"Visiting physical places that house both positive memories and negative ones can be part of the healing process, Brooke. Seeing the negative from a new and distanced perspective is freeing. Realizing the things that once hurt you no longer hold that power? There's nothing sweeter."

I glance around, taking in the same smells and sounds that surrounded us that day. We'd talked and laughed. Then we argued. I ran off. Afraid. Pushing him away when all I wanted to do was fold into his arms.

I miss him. I miss him so much my soul aches.

Still, I know I'm not quite ready to go back there yet. Back to him. This is one step in a thousand I have to take moving forward. Save the best for last, right?

The waitress takes my order—scones with cream and marmalade and a pot of Miracle Mermaid Tea. My heart sinks an inch. Part of me hoped to see Elizabeth again.

I guess not everything can remain the same.

When the waitress who is not Elizabeth retrieves my menu and heads to the kitchen, I remove my laptop from my bag and set it on the table. While my weekdays are filled with classes and assignments and navigating the massive and overwhelming campus that is UC Berkeley, the weekends are mine.

Until finals, anyway.

A glance at my phone shows it's just before one in the afternoon. I don't need to meet Mee-Maw at the assisted living facility for dinner until four, which gives me a few good hours to punch out some words. While I prefer handwritten prose—so personal and romantic and artistic—using the computer has helped speed up the writing process by a million and one percent.

With renewed determination, I lift the laptop screen, log in, and pull up the saved doc.

One Year Ago—September

Coral stared, unblinking, at her untouched bowl of butternut soup.

She stirred and stirred until nothing but cold orange mush remained. Why had her grandmother made this? The onset of a new season had barely begun and already autumn foliage decked the cottage. Every meal they ate looked like pumpkin guts.

"Here." Her grandmother offered the basket of fresh rolls. Hawaiian sweet. Coral's favorite.

"No, thanks."

"How are you liking your senior classes?"

"Fine, I guess."

"And your counseling sessions with Miss Brandes? How are those going after the break?"

Coral pushed away from the table and took her bowl to the sink. "I'm tired. I think I'll go to bed early."

"Don't worry about the dishes, dear. I'll get them."

She didn't argue. Her grandmother lacked the energy to wash, but so did Coral. She slept eight to twelve hours easy every night. How was she still this tired? "I guess this is good night then."

"Sit down, please." Her grandmother gestured toward the sofa. "This will take a minute. There's something I want to discuss with you."

Coral's bed called to her. The state of sleep held her nightmares, but it was also the only time any sense of freedom surfaced. "I'm tired, Mee-Maw."

"I understand. I'll be quick."

Conceding but groaning, she dragged her feet to the small living room and sank between the cushions, hugging a throw pillow to her chest.

"I'm getting old." Her grandmother took the love seat across from her. "The cold weather is bad on my joints." She massaged her weathered hands. The visible blue and purple veins looked like tiny tentacles, spreading and reaching beneath her skin.

Coral stared past her grandmother to the open window beyond. A warm breeze fluttered the curtains. "It's seventy-two degrees outside."

"Yes, now it is. But winter will be here before we know it. Without you here, I won't be able to walk up and down the steep stairs. The cottage is no place for me anymore."

What was she getting at? Was she sending Coral home? There was a time she'd wanted that. But now? Now that would be worse than anything. She couldn't go back there. She wouldn't.

It wasn't home anymore.

"I'll move into an assisted living facility at the first of the year. Miss Brandes has offered to drive you to Fathoms Ranch herself." The old woman slid a brochure across the coffee table between them.

Coral took one look at the brochure's cover and blanched. A

trio of laughing, smiling girls sat on a porch swing. A green lawn made up the background. In the distance, a few horses grazed and rolling hills finished off the lush landscape.

"Is this a joke?" She shoved the brochure back the way it came. Those places were all the same. She'd never been to one, but she had a good enough idea. She wouldn't argue, but she wouldn't jump up and down either.

"It's for the best, dear." Her grandmother slid the brochure toward Coral again. "Please. They can help you heal. You've hardly talked about River's suicide since it happened. You don't take your medication consistently. I've spoken with the program director on the phone. She sounds—"

"Nice?"

"Real."

Real. Right. No such thing.

"It's for the best," her grandmother said again.

The best. Right. Okay. Fine. Whatever. She didn't have much of a choice, did she?

Perhaps the best thing would be for me to slip into the nothing for good.

The thought sank deeper and deeper into her mind until it anchored to her heart. She would stay through the early winter until her grandmother moved. And then . . . ?

Then she would embrace the nothing. For good.

"After Christmas." Her grandmother rose on shaky knees. "We'll make the transition over winter break, okay?"

Solace smoothed Coral's expression as she imagined the feeling of nothing. She longed for it. The release crept near her fingertips.

She held on to the hope she would finally, *finally* be free.

She didn't want to feel.

She didn't want to be.

She didn't want to wake from the Abyss any longer.

Coral only wanted to go back, to be one with the sea once more. The season would soon change, and the colors would fall from the trees like so many broken tears. Soon those colors would fade to winter's gray and vanish as if they never were at all.

Those colors would become nothing.

Coral would become nothing.

Nothing but a color washed up and out and away.

The Disease had finally won.

Coral became as sea foam.

And sea foam could not survive when Red Tide came.

I sit back and take three grounding breaths, focusing on each inhale through my nose. Each exhale through my mouth.

Reliving real and raw memories—emotions—from my past stirs old anxieties, setting every nerve on fire. I close my eyes. This is now. Here. The memories may be triggering, a word Jake so often uses, but they are only memories.

They happened. The feelings tied to them are valid.

But they don't have to define who I am now. Today. They are only a part of me. If anything, they make me stronger.

I close the laptop.

Tuck them away.

And save them for another chapter.

I sip at my rose-colored tea and take a bite of scone, watching as the locals walk up and down the sidewalk beyond the booth's window. To look at them, you'd think they live the happiest, most glorious carefree lives.

But maybe that man in the green ball cap with the almost painted-on smile is suicidal.

Maybe that young woman with her designer bag and eyes glued to her phone suffers from anxiety, depression, or even PTSD.

That's the thing about mental illness. It has many faces. And most of them look pretty normal. You'd never know the person is slowly dying inside.

Another sip of tea warms my throat as the bell above the shop door tinkles. My pulse forgets its rhythm when a mess of black hair appears in the corner of my vision. I turn. Can't seem to recall my name.

"I heard you were in town." Merrick sits without an invitation.

I find my words and hide my delight behind one hand. "Mee-Maw or Nikki?"

"Both." He shrugs, resting an elbow on the table. "Nikki texted me yesterday. Said she'd be bringing you with her on her weekly Grim visit. Your grandmother called me this morning."

I laugh, shake my head, and scoot to the right to give him room. I haven't seen him since the funeral. Even so, his nearness feels easy. Natural. A breath of air I didn't know I needed because I've been under for so long.

"How did you know I'd be here?"

"Because I know you." He pops a bite of scone in his mouth, again without invitation. "You can't resist a good cup of tea and the finest scones in town."

"True." Once, I believed I wanted nothing else but to be alone. To live inside that nothing my character saw as an ever-looming Abyss.

Now I see alone is not the answer. It wasn't for my sister. Or for Hope.

"What are you working on?" He eyes the laptop, dipping half a scone into the cream, then swallowing the piece whole. "I have to say I'm shocked to see you without your tattered old notebook and pen."

"I'm a little shocked too, to tell you the truth. Jake—my therapist—gave it to me." I run a hand over the shiny apple on the laptop's closed cover. "I promised her I'd use it, so I'm kind of stuck now."

He chuckles. A sound that soothes my ache for him to scoot closer. "I remember Jake. I met her the one time I visited Maya at Fathoms."

My eyes widen. Merrick? At Fathoms? When?

He seems to catch the question in my eyes. His own stare exudes meaning. Understanding. Pain. Hope?

And I know. The same day I chose to end it, he was there. Did I sense his nearness in my dreams? Is it possible I imagined him with me in the cave because he almost was? Had I stayed at the ranch house that night, instead of running away, would we have crossed paths?

Too many what-ifs.

The air falls silent between us. I sense he's waiting for me to say something, anything. But what? Do I ask how he's doing? Is it too soon to talk about his sister?

Am I finally ready to talk about mine?

"Read anything good lately?" He breaks the silence after finishing off my plate and flagging down the waitress for a refill.

The question feels loaded. The opposite of small talk.

I look down, deciding how best to answer. Is it me, or is he closing the gap between us? I swear he's a few inches closer than he was a minute ago.

But he'll never be close enough. Not until I let him in. "Have *you* read anything good?"

He tilts his head, studying my face with eyes the color of raven's wings. "I'd like to."

Don't freak out. This is happening. This is happening now. One step closer.

I open the laptop again, find an early chapter—the only one I've never edited or rewritten or revised.

Merrick peers at the heading. "Red Tide?"

I nod. He knows what happened. He was there. But to see it from my perspective—from Coral's eyes—makes him a true and permanent part of my world.

"Read it to me?" He leans back and clasps his hands behind his head.

Fear races across my pounding heart, begging me to put this whole thing in reverse. When I swallow and begin the first line, my words catch in my throat.

But then Merrick closes his eyes and I know he's taking in every syllable. Not judging. Simply waiting. For me.

Always for me.

I clear my throat. I read of my oldest sister and Red Tide—suicide. Of how she slit her wrists in the ocean on our annual family vacation to the West Coast that January. Our tradition. Our escape.

My father couldn't bear to be anywhere near our home on the anniversary of my mother's death—my birthday.

I go on about the four sisters who were miscarried before my time and the way my father never looked at me. Jordan comes up, as does Duke. I bare it all. My heart and soul and all the shattered pieces in between.

When I finish the chapter, I hesitate a moment before finding Merrick's wide-eyed gaze. He's staring at me with so much hope and promise, I almost can't bear the weight of it.

"Thank you." He reaches across the table and stops short of taking my hand.

I so want to take that final leap, to close the distance and tangle our fingers. To remember the taste of his lips on mine and drink in his summer scent and finally believe he's real.

A true Prince who puts all fairy-tale charmers to shame.

My hands fidget in my lap. Then my phone alarm blares "Hedwig's Theme," making us both jump and drawing stares from the other customers I hadn't even noticed until now. Spell broken. Moment gone.

"Time to go?"

"I have to meet Mee-Maw."

He slides out of the booth and rises.

I gather my things and shoulder my bag as he walks me out into the autumn sunshine.

I have to head right. He needs to go left.

Merrick has one foot off the curb and one hand in his pocket when he says, "I need to tell you something."

Anything. Everything. Always. "Okay," I say in the most casual tone I can rally.

"I've been holding on to this." He withdraws a piece of jewelry from his pocket.

The sight stings. My pearls stare back at me. The old Brooke wants to grasp for an accusation. Instead, I ask, "Why didn't you tell me sooner?" I reach for the bracelet.

"This was your sister's."

I nod.

"You've never told me her name."

Haven't I? "River," I say for the first time in ages. The way my father and Jordan refused to talk about her felt wrong. So I say it again. Louder. "Her name was River." She was real. She existed.

And her story needs to be told.

"Pretty. But I'm partial to water names that start with *B*."

His wink is all that's needed to send flames up my neck and cheeks.

The emotions I used to dread blossom. I don't push them away this time.

"These were so important to you. Why did Maya have them?"

"I gave them to her for her last birthday. She needed them more than I did." The heavy truth of it slices a fresh wound.

"She'd want you to have them back. But I'd like to hold on to them a little while longer. Is that all right?"

I sigh. Trust him with one more piece of my soul. "Of course."

With a final signature grin that's all Merrick, he crosses the street. First River's and then Hope's bracelet remains clutched in his right hand as he waves.

It's a common gesture but one that promises another tomorrow.

A good-bye that says this isn't forever, and I'll see him again sooner than I'd hoped.

FORTY-SEVEN

Merrick Prince

Merrick held fast to the pearl bracelet. The last piece of the puzzle.

All he had to do was take it to the jeweler his dad had contacted. If the guy could trace the original maker, Merrick would find the man who had broken River's heart. He had no clue what Brooke might do with the information. Confront the dude? Tell him off?

Or perhaps it wasn't as complicated as all that. Maybe knowing would be good enough, help her move on. Give her the last bit of closure she needed for River's story to be complete.

He hopped inside the two-year-old black Toyota Corolla his dad had loaned him. It had Bluetooth capability, keyless entry and start, and even a built-in GPS. It may not have been a Tesla—which Hiroshi Prince could totally afford—but Merrick wasn't complaining. He had a car. No chauffeur to wait on or waiting on him. Just him and the wheel and the open road.

The leather seats smelled of freedom.

With a good three-hour drive north ahead of him—if he didn't run into traffic—Merrick set his music library to shuffle and relaxed low in the driver's seat. When he pulled onto the curving Coast Highway with nothing but the ocean to his left and billion-dollar homes to his right, a sense of peace he hadn't experienced in years settled in and made itself at home.

"So this is what it feels like not to hate Dad," he said to his reflection in the rearview mirror. To the empty passenger seat.

All these years. All those hours clenching his fists, ready to take a swing the second his father dared to get physical. Merrick had spent so much time expecting the man to prove him right, he'd never faced the truth.

Hiro was rough around the edges, sure. But he wasn't the bad guy Merrick had often made him out to be.

The sun passed over the car's roof and blared through the driver-side window. Merrick adjusted his visor and donned his sunglasses. The rock song that had been playing faded out and a new one faded in.

He stiffened. He'd forgotten this song was on here. Tempted to skip to the next in line, his finger hovered over the stereo controls.

But as the lyrics played on, the singer's voice disappeared and a different voice filled his mind.

This was Amaya's song. Or one of them, anyway. Merrick could almost imagine she sat cross-legged in the seat beside him, singing at the top of her lungs without a care or worry in the world. His memories transported him to this time last autumn.

When they'd sat on their family room couch.

And for about two-point-five seconds, everything seemed normal again.

"Are you going after her or not?"

Amaya sat cross-legged on the couch. An old *Sorry!* game board rested on the cushion between them. It was missing a few pieces, but the game worked well enough. "Sorry." She slid her yellow piece into Merrick's red one and grinned.

He placed the pawn back home and looked around.

Since the summer ended and Merrick's sister had gained another chance at life, again, everything changed between them.

At home with their dad plus a new therapy and medication regimen, Amaya was herself again. She was eating. The color had returned to her cheeks and she didn't snap at Merrick between syllables.

"Have you heard from Brooke at all?"

Merrick drew a card, then moved a few spaces forward. "She doesn't want to talk to me."

"Yes she does."

"Did she tell you that?"

"She doesn't have to, big brother."

"Would you stop already?"

Maya took her turn, moving another one of her pawns inside the safety zone. She only had one left on the board that could be sent home.

He grunted. His sister—the board game queen. Even games like this one that required no strategy whatsoever. He'd never beat her. The only reason he'd agreed to play was to make her happy.

"What about a letter?" She stretched both arms above her head and yawned. "You could write to her. Girls love that."

He laughed. If only everything could be as simple as it seemed in a Disney movie. "It's more complicated than that. It wasn't our time."

Amaya took a sip of her cocoa and glanced at her phone.

Merrick eyed her. "You're staying off social media, right?"

She rolled her eyes. "Yes, *Dad*. I know the rules. Our actual dad password-protected those apps so I can't even get into them. And that new tech his team created to monitor all devices in the house basically means I can't do anything online without his approval."

Merrick was sure there were other ways his sister could get into her accounts, but he didn't push it. "I want to make sure you're not opening a window for those girls to bully you again."

"Who said they were all girls?"

"I only thought—"

"Your move."

It took every ounce of willpower he had not to press the issue. He drew a card and moved a new piece onto the board. "There."

"You sure you want to do that?"

"Yep." He stared out the bay window overlooking their street. Cars rushed past and colors changed. Fall never lasted long enough, giving in way too soon to the long winter ahead.

Amaya took her turn. Her pawn was only a few spaces behind his now. "Dad wants to do a family dinner on Friday." Her change of subject didn't help her angle. "He asked me to ask you."

"I can't."

"What's the excuse this time?"

"I have a thing."

"Oh. Right." She rolled her eyes dramatically and air quoted with her fingers as she said, "A thing."

This conversation had become more awkward each time she asked, but what was he supposed to do? Their dad was clearly making him sweat it out until Merrick believed he was out of the woods. The moment he thought he was safe . . . bam! Hiro would press charges and Merrick would be in handcuffs for kidnapping and child endangerment.

He may or may not have spent too much time googling his crime.

"Have you finished your college applications yet?" Amaya asked.

He hadn't even started them. But the pressure of his own indecisiveness wasn't what irked him. Her tone didn't lie. She was leading into something. "No," he said. "Why?"

She looked up at him, all seriousness now, which was rare for his sister. "I don't want you to worry about working your class schedules around my stuff. You know. When you finally decide to get your act together and be a grown-up." She shoved him lightly.

He raised an eyebrow. Her humor tactics weren't going to work. Not this time. "What's up, Maya?"

She pulled a brochure from beneath the couch cushion.

"Fathoms Ranch?" he asked, staring at the bright cover.

"I'm thinking about going after all." She fidgeted with her hands and messed with her hair.

How long had she been working up to telling him this? "I thought you were doing better. You told me your therapist said you were making progress. That your meds were working."

"There is better and there is best," Maya said, clearly struggling with her words. "This is not my best, Merrick." She pulled up her right sleeve and looked away. "I still think about it all the time. Death. I step outside and imagine jumping in front of a moving bus. I go to a restaurant and picture what the knife on the table would feel like slicing against my skin."

Merrick's stomach lurched. Amid the old whited-out scars on her pale, freckled skin, fresh ones stood out.

He took her hand. Where did he go from here? Nothing he could say would make her better or best. So he showed his support with a gentle squeeze.

Amaya sniffed, withdrawing her hand and swiping at her nose and eyes with her sleeve. "It's my ploy for a free vacation. Did you see where it is? They even have horses."

Merrick opened the brochure. His eyebrows shot up at all the ranch had to offer. "This is actually cool. I didn't even know they had programs like this one."

"It's privately funded. Dad and I are going up for a visit next weekend if you want to come."

Merrick smiled. "Maybe."

They were quiet. He searched for the right words. Thought

for a long time. What could he say to a person who openly admitted she wanted to die? Nothing seemed right.

In the end, he spoke the only words that felt true. "You are not nothing. No matter what anyone says. Okay? You are *not* nothing."

She stared at him, her expression blank.

Had he offended her? Said the wrong thing? Again?

"That's a good line, big brother," she said at last, blue eyes twinkling. "You mind if I steal it?"

Relief came in a whoosh of air between his lips. "Go right ahead."

Amaya's flat expression transformed into a mischievous grin. "So . . . about that letter to Brooke?"

"Stop."

"I can't help it. It's in my blood."

The mention of blood sliced an awkward silence between them. But then Amaya said, "I see you being weird and it's not cool," and Merrick realized the serious part of the conversation was officially over.

"Sorry."

"I know." She frowned. "I'm sorry too." Then her mischief returned. "See? That wasn't so difficult. Sorry isn't so hard to say. You might find it's even easier to write . . ."

"I'll think about it." Though Merrick said it to get her off his back, a part of him wondered if he should. An idea formed in his mind as he recalled his first conversation with Brooke.

She didn't believe in fate.

Merrick did.

They were all wrong for each other. Different people from different worlds.

Which made his idea all the more epic.

"Do you still have those old corked sea glass bottles you used to collect?"

Amaya eyed him. "Why?"

"No reason. Can I have one?"

Amaya laughed and knocked one of his pieces out of the way, sending it home again. "You can have all of them. There are at least a dozen."

Merrick didn't bother drawing another card. She'd basically won. No use embarrassing himself. He stood and paced the living room, his idea becoming more and more concrete. He perused the picture frames on the wall. "It feels strange without Mom here."

"She'll come back." Amaya sighed.

"You think so?"

"Dad goes to see Mom every month, and you know what he asks her every time?"

"No. What?" Did Merrick want to know?

"He asks her if she's ready to come home."

"What does she say?"

"That she *is* home. But he keeps going back anyway." Maya's shoulders sank.

They both missed their mother. While Maya was optimistic, Merrick no longer carried delusions about who Lyn Prince was.

He pictured his father in his suit and tie, walking into that quaint inn and asking a waitress to come home with him. Merrick's perspective had begun to alter. All the preset ideas he had about his dad were fading.

One by one by one.

"You should talk to him about Brooke. If anyone knows about perseverance when it comes to love, it's him." Amaya gathered the game pieces, folded the board, and placed it in the box. "And you need to do something about your hair."

Merrick shook his head at her, his now chin-length mop going wild. "What's wrong with it?"

"I hate to break it to you, but you look like a dog. One that's badly groomed and never takes a bath."

"Hey!" He finger-combed the locks away from his eyes. "That's rude!"

She stood, took the game box, and placed it inside the giant ottoman by the armchair. "If you're going to win Brooke back, you'll need to do some serious work."

His grin was too far gone to hide. To Amaya, the girl he forever talked about was Brooke. But she had given him a pseudonym when they met.

Coral.

She tried to keep her true name a secret, but he'd found her out. He never told her, but he saw her name written on the inside cover of her notebook that first night at the library. Still, he wanted Brooke to offer the truth herself.

Maybe there was still a chance she would.

"Thanks." Merrick side-hugged his sister and moved to the stairs. He paused at the bottom step. "Hey, Amaya Hope?"

"Yes, Merrick Noah?"

"I'm sorry. For everything."

She held up a hand. "I can see where this is going, and let me stop you right there, big brother." She plopped back onto the couch and pulled a blanket over her legs. "You messed up, but you don't get to take the blame for my illness. You don't get to own something that belongs to me. That's stealing." She winked. Her eyes sparkled, but a sadness remained. A memory of something that pained her.

He saw past her walls now. Had learned to look beyond. "You okay?"

"I'm trying to be." She shrugged. "Some days are better than others."

"I'm here if you need me."

"I know." She gazed out the window, closing her eyes as she rested her head on her bent knees. As much energy as she tried to exert, Amaya was tired. If they let her sleep all day, she would.

When Merrick reached her room, he found the corked bottles in green and blue sea glass lined up along three shelves above her dresser. He grabbed a blue bottle and headed to his room, where he retrieved paper and a pen.

He sat on the bed he no longer slept in and wrote. He wrote because this was her language.

Brooke may not believe in fate.

But eventually, Merrick would help her see the light.

It was dark by the time he pulled up alongside the curb before the glammed-up storefront. He paid the parking meter and leaned against his car, not quite ready to go inside. It had been a year since he'd sent that bottled message out to sea. If not for his sister, he never would have had the courage to see the rest of his plan through.

"Miss you, Maya."

A breeze picked up, lifting the collar of his shirt. It was stupid. Silly. But every time he spoke to his sister as if she were here, Merrick wondered if she could hear him.

And if she could hear him? She'd tell him to get his rear inside and fulfill the promise he'd made.

"I'm going. I'm going." He pressed two fingers to his lips and blew a kiss to the wind before he shoved off his car and headed through the glass doors.

FORTY-EIGHT

Brooke

"You got this?" Nikki looks past me through the passenger-side window. "I can come in."

I follow her gaze to the lobby entrance of the four-star San Francisco hotel. Inhale. Clutch my twine-bound manuscript more tightly in my arms, hugging it to my chest. Me and these words. These words and me.

So many times I've pressed the work of another author against my heart. Wishing they could change me. Mold me into another character. Shape me into the best version of myself.

But *these* pages. *These* thoughts and emotions and memories . . . They *have* changed me. More than any Hobbit's journey or child's venture through a wardrobe.

Because they are mine. This is my story. And I'm finally ready to share it.

"This is something I have to do on my own," I say, allowing emotion into my eyes and voice. Not so afraid to let it show anymore. "Thanks, Nikki. For driving me. For everything."

"You're a Berkeley girl now. We've got to stick together." She winks. "Speaking of sticking together, Nigel says a certain Prince never stops talking about you."

I blush and clutch the pages even tighter. I haven't seen Merrick in over a month. Not since that day at the tea shop when I let him view River's suicide through my eyes. Since I trusted him to hold on to the pearl bracelet I desperately want back. We've texted. Liked one another's posts on social media. Now it's mid-October and we haven't once hinted at meeting up again. I can't decide if he's just being nice, or if both of us are too afraid to make the first—or second—leap.

"He keeps asking me if I've read anything good lately," I tell Nikki.

"Oh?" Her dark, perfectly shaped eyebrows arch. "And have you?"

I eye her. "Is there something you're not telling me?"

She looks up at the low convertible ceiling and bats her curled eyelashes. "I don't have the slightest idea what you're talking about, girl."

I slap her arm playfully. Nikki feels more like a sister to me after two months than my own sister Jordan feels after seventeen years.

"I'm not saying anything." Nikki focuses on her phone and taps the screen until she pulls up her favorite podcast. "But I will tell you that there may or may not be something you're missing."

"As in . . . ?"

"You know, for a college girl who's written almost an entire novel, you'd think you'd catch on to things more quickly."

My jaw goes slack and I slap her arm again. "Nikki! What do you know?"

She shrugs and clips her phone into the holder beside the stereo. When the podcast host's voice plays through the Bluetooth speakers, she unlocks the doors with a *click*. "I've said too much."

I groan and gaze toward the brightly lit hotel lobby.

"Have you written an ending?" Nikki touches my arm. She knows me so well already. I love her for it.

"I can't." I think of River. How I believed her death over a year and a half ago was the last page. "The novel reads like a fairy tale but feels closer to a tragedy. I don't know how to end it on the right note."

"You'll figure it out." Nikki turns down the volume. "Personally,

I vote for a happily ever after with the most romantic kiss ever. One where the girl runs into her beau's arms. The music swells and everyone watching can't help but tear up a little."

I can't tell if she's talking fiction or real life now. "Sounds like a fairy tale."

"And who says fairy tales can't come true?"

"Maybe *you* should write the last scene," I say, and I almost mean it. "You have way more experience in that department than I do." My cheeks burn hotter. My heart beats a little faster with thoughts of summer nights and lanterns and kisses beneath the stars.

Now it's Nikki's turn to blush. "Nigel is definitely a much better kisser than I imagined. Of course, he's had an excellent teacher." She palms her chest lightly and tilts her chin. Her confidence is both intimidating and inspiring. Never arrogant. More . . . secure. She knows who she is and nobody can make her change.

I want to be Nikki when I grow up.

"Maybe your happy ending scene is closer than you think."

Again, I have no idea if she's speaking of my book or something else that warms my core and lightens my head.

When at last I step out onto the curb, I slip my manuscript inside my tote bag and adjust my focus. The October evening air is perfect. Welcoming.

I wish I didn't have to go inside.

But I have to do this. It's what my—*our*—oldest sister would have wanted.

I enter the lobby and ask a woman at the front desk for directions to the event space where the concert will be held. She pulls out a map and a highlighter, marks an X where we stand, and circles a set of elevators.

"The north elevators take you to the even-numbered floors. You'll take those to the fifty-second floor. There you'll see a new set of elevators that grant access to the roof, where the amphitheater sits. You'll need a room key to gain access to that floor, hon."

"Thanks. My sister's staying here."

She nods. "You know you're a day early. The show isn't until tomorrow."

I tuck a stray hair behind my ear. "I prefer to know where I'm going ahead of time."

Recognition flickers across her gaze. "You look familiar. Do I—"

The desk phone rings, my saving grace. When she answers, I take the map, dip my head, and move toward the elevators. Muster up the courage to continue forward even if all I want to do is flee.

A chandelier glitters overheard and marble floors give the illusion I'm walking on melted pearls. Every nook and corner radiates my former life. A life fit for royalty.

The glitz.

The glamour.

The money.

It's in the walls and ceilings and floors. This was my childhood. Watching my father, and soon my sisters, onstage, awaiting the day I, too, would make my debut.

The night I turned sixteen I sang the only song I've ever written. One that came out of anger and hurt and resentment toward the man who refused to see beyond his own pain. Jordan took over halfway through my ballad, cueing the band and drowning my voice with a fast, upbeat jam she'd performed a hundred times before.

I'd left to look for River then. When I found her at the beach, standing in the ocean with the waves lapping at her thighs, it was too late.

I was too late.

I bow my head lower, hiding my face between drapes of my beacon-bright hair. No one else recognizes me, though. No one sees. I am no longer the someday-pop-princess daughter of Jonah King—country music legend. I am as forgotten as a long-ago tale. As washed up as the foam of the sea.

I'm alone on the elevator when I step on, a low hum the only sound as I'm lifted *up, up, up*. No music plays. The elevator doesn't stop and no one else gets on. I'm taken to the floor just shy of the roof. It's another lobby, with a sitting area and a bar. The only other souls present are a bartender wiping out wineglasses and a security guard at the elevator doors ahead.

When the guard sees me, he holds up a hand. But then he pauses. And blinks. And shakes his head. "Brooke? Brooke King?"

"Hey, Will."

"Does Jordan know you're here?"

Remember who you are. You belong here. Or you did once. "I wanted to surprise her, since she's in my state."

Will considers my half-truth for only the briefest second before he steps aside and swipes a card over a reader to the right of the elevator. The doors slide open and I step inside. Seconds pass before the doors reopen. I'm on the roof, standing on the precipice of a sloping amphitheater.

It's a stellar design, housing row after row of circular bench seating swirling *down, down, down*. A whirlpool, descending into darkness. And there, at the center of it all, is Jordan.

The crew performs the sound check while my sister sings her hit single. The same song that played over Jake's car radio the day Hope died.

"I'm swimming through your head, swimming through your head.
Don't you know my voice is poison?
Can't you see you're already dead?"

The depressing lyrics reverberate, transporting me back to the emotions of that day.

But rather than crawl inside myself, I choose to face my pain head-on. I feel Hope with me now. I hear her voice. See her confident smirk and optimistic attitude. She'd tell me to rip the Band-Aid off. *"What's the big deal?"* she'd ask. *"She's a girl. Like you. You're both human. She's no better than you are."*

"Easier said than done," I say to myself.

I wish Hope had believed her own words.

I wish I'd said them to her every day.

I wish the ones who bullied her understood the depth of their damage.

"You are not nothing," I'd tell her again and again and again. *"And neither am I."*

Jordan doesn't see me yet. Beneath the hot lights and enveloped by the sound of the band and her own voice, she's lost to me. As far away as the bottom of the sea.

It's easy to feel drawn to my sister. With the San Francisco city-scape as her audience, she appears immortal, timeless. I picture tomorrow's crowd, imagine as they listen and sway, watching in silent wonder while Jordan's voice fills the air.

Keeping to the shadows of the amphitheater's dark staircase aisles, I inch closer. The sound check goes on. With each new song, Jordan's voice seems to carry farther, up and out and away. Her silver sequined halter top sparkles and her white skinny jeans appear to glow. If I angle my gaze right, I can picture Jordan with silver scales, shiny and slick, slipping beneath the waves.

When the rehearsal ends, Jordan says, "Thanks, guys," then turns off the mic clipped to the back of her jeans. She sets her guitar on a stand by the drum set and exits the circular stage.

And that's my cue.

When she heads up the steps of the aisle closest to her, I backtrack. We reach the top of our sets of stairs at the same time. She aims for the elevator and I follow, stepping out of the shadows and into the light as she pushes the down-arrow button.

I swallow every fear that whispers she'll hurt me again. Extinguish each anxious wave of emotion that tells me I'm nothing.

"Jordan."

She bristles. Turns. Squints through black-lined slits. "Brooke?"

My gut churns. I long for the courage I possessed in Nikki's car.

Instead, all I feel is the sense that this is not the beginning of something new, as I'd hoped.

This is the end.

"Hey," I say.

"What are you doing here?" She sounds tired, irritated. Overworked and overbooked.

"I wanted to see you. I saw you were on tour and I . . ." My words fall flat. "Congrats on the single. That's something."

"You've ignored my calls for months, Brooke. You left Nashville without a word."

I stare at her. Hard. Anger, rage, and maybe even a little insanity stir inside me. "Dad sent me away." Why does she do this? Why does she twist the truth to make me feel like I'm crazy?

"Don't tell me you haven't been living it up by the beach with Mee-Maw. You always were her favorite. You didn't even say good-bye."

"You told me I was nothing, Jordan. You abandoned me the day of River's funeral—"

"Don't say her name," Jordan snaps. "Don't you dare say her name. Our sister betrayed us. She went off with that lowlife street musician behind Dad's back and came back heartbroken. Served her right. She should have listened to him."

I don't know what I expected from Jordan, but this? Never. "How can you say that?"

Jordan glares. "What do you want, Brooke? Get to the point or leave."

I clear my throat. "Is Dad in town?"

Jordan blinks. "No. And he wouldn't want to see you if he was."

"Duke?"

"Off signing the latest boy band to his record label. He's an important man, you know."

I don't care about Duke's business deals or how valuable he is to my father. He could sign all the platinum recording artists in the world and I wouldn't give a shark's fin. All I want to know is, "Are you still together?"

Jordan lifts her left hand. A massive diamond sparkles from her ring finger. "The wedding is in December."

I bite the inside of my cheek. Ignore the fact I didn't receive an invitation. "I need to tell you something." Speaking it means reliving the moment, but I have to. I've been through this with Jake. Now I look at the memory with new eyes.

Duke can't hurt me anymore.

But he can hurt Jordan. If my story makes a difference for her, it's worth it.

"The night of my sixteenth birthday . . . he tried to . . ." *Swallow. Keep going.* "Before I got onstage, he found me at the pre-show party. He cornered me, Jordan. The way he touched me, it made me feel powerless."

"I know who Duke is. I don't need you to tell me."

A chill rushes my senses. "He followed me when I left to look for River."

"I told you not to say her name."

"How can you be so cold?"

"I told you." She flips her hair and checks the time on her phone. "I know who my fiancé is."

"And you're okay with it?"

A couple of band members skirt around us and load the elevator. Jordan coats her expression in sugar and they exchange good nights. When the doors close, she crosses her arms and shrugs her shoulders to her ears.

Why won't she look at me?

"He's promised me he can change." Her eyes close. "Dad thinks he can. He says I need to give Duke a chance. We could go far together. Duke knows a lot of important people in the industry. Besides, he loves me."

My skin freezes. Time seems to still. What she's saying . . . She can't possibly believe her own words. "That isn't love, Jordan."

"And what do you know about *love*, little sister?"

In the past, Jordan's condescension would have stopped me, would have eaten at my heart for days. Now, the same empathy I felt for Jordan the night of River's suicide overcomes every other emotion.

"I know enough to tell you love isn't cruel or controlling. I know true love is patient and gracious and understanding. It's the kind of love that accepts you, tears and wounds and brokenness. The kind River would have wanted us to have for one another."

The kind Hope showed me.

And Jake.

And Mee-Maw.

And maybe even Merrick Prince.

Jordan shakes her head. "You're still living in the fantasy world you've made up for yourself, Brooke. Face the music. The love you think exists, the kind our older sister ended her life over? It isn't real. Anyone who says otherwise is fooling themselves."

How can I bring myself to reconcile Jordan's words? Did I believe things would be solved in one conversation? Regret washes over me. Part of me wishes I hadn't come at all.

"You should go. It's late."

"Jordan—"

"*Go.*"

A familiar numbness courses through me. There is no closure for me here. No reconciliation. Still, I came for a reason.

And I won't leave until I make it to the end.

I reach into my tote, withdraw my manuscript, and offer it to Jordan. My heart ticks off each second that passes.

"What's this?" Jordan eyes the pages. Still, she takes them.

"Read it."

"*Coral,*" Jordan says, reading the title on the front. "Why *Coral*?"

I exhale. The name triggers a memory. Of the first time Merrick spoke the name I gave him.

"Do you know what happens to coral when it dies?" I ask.

Jordan shakes her head.

I squeeze my eyes. Open them wide. I bled my soul into those pages. Now I'm finally setting them free.

"It loses its color. It turns gray." Like my world after River died. And Hope. Only recently has the color finally begun to return.

"I don't get it."

"You will," I say. Or maybe she won't. "It's about us."

The horrified expression spreading across her face ought to drown me.

Instead, anchors lift from my shoulders. Whether or not Jordan understands doesn't matter. It doesn't change what happened. It doesn't invalidate my perspective or my feelings or make them any less real.

"Brooke."

I wait for Jordan's next words. Hope.

"You haven't shown this to anyone else, have you?"

Sigh. The story of our sister's suicide was an embarrassment to our King family name. But somehow, it also aided in helping Jordan rise to the top of the charts. Her voice has become quite the commodity. Even more than River's was. Our older sister's face was featured in all the tabloids and plastered across social media after her death. She was reality TV. She was entertainment. A good story twisted and retold a hundred times over.

But my story is different. Because, even with the mermaids and the Sorceress and the Abyss, everything I wrote is true.

Sometimes fiction speaks truth the way nothing else can.

"The first chapter was a school assignment. It even made the finalist list in a statewide contest."

Jordan gasps.

"It was disqualified when I couldn't finish the manuscript. It doesn't have an ending yet."

Her features relax. "Are you going to publish it?"

"I don't know."

"I don't think—"

"Read it," I say again.

"Do you need money? Is that it?"

Why can't she see this goes so much deeper than material things? "I wrote it because I couldn't hold on to it anymore. I need to let it go." Even without a proper ending.

I turn to leave. I've said everything. Now it's up to her.

Jordan doesn't stop me.

I press the button beside the elevator. It lights up and I stand there, alone though my sister is inches away. An awkward silence hangs in the air between us. So much left unresolved. So much pain behind Jordan's eyes.

When I step over the elevator's threshold, Jordan rushes forward and blocks the door.

"I'm pregnant."

My emotions war. I want to kill Duke and scream at my dad and do anything I can to protect the lost girl before me. "Oh, Jordan," I say, same as I did the night of Red Ti—of River's death. "That doesn't mean you have to stay with a man who is abusive."

"I know what it means." She doesn't look me in the eyes. "It means I'm connected to Duke for the rest of my life. No matter what. I've made my choice. And nothing you can say will change it."

I nod. Jordan is stubborn as a clam and twice as hard on the outside. Inside, though . . . inside there's a pearl waiting to be set free.

Maybe not today, or tomorrow, but someday. "I'm here." I let my gaze linger on hers so she knows my words are true. "I'm a call away."

Jordan's armor seems to crack before she swipes at her eyes again and allows the doors to close. The last thing I see before she's gone from my vision is the tear that slips down her cheek. The one she doesn't hide.

I wrap my arms around my middle and take the elevators back to the lobby. Jordan has to walk through her own season of darkness. I only hope she'll eventually let me help her find the light on the opposite side.

A quote Hope wrote in my journal back at Fathoms invades my thoughts. The first half once stood out more than the latter. Now I recall the quote as a whole.

> *"Life damages us, every one. We can't escape that damage. But now, I am also learning this: We can be mended. We mend each other."*
>
> —Veronica Roth

We can mend each other. So many in my life have played a part in mending me. I take out my phone and send a quick text to Jordan. It's the one thing I didn't say that I wish I had.

I love you. You are not nothing to me.

She doesn't respond, but I see the notification she's read it. Maybe someday she'll say the same. Even if she doesn't, I know I am loved. That I am not nothing. And I never will be again.

Relief washes over me when I see Nikki's red convertible sitting outside the lobby entrance. I climb inside. Exhale.

"How'd it go?" Nikki asks.

"I don't know yet."

"Did you give it to her?"

"I did."

"And?"

I face my friend. Stare at my empty hands. "We'll see. But I think I figured out my ending."

Nikki squeals, then makes a face. "You're not going to tell me, are you?"

"I thought you hated spoilers."

"True." She puts the car into drive and pulls away from the hotel. "But I get dibs as first reader."

"Promise." I can't help but picture a boy with his pinky extended, a Prince who promised he didn't read my words.

Now that's *all* I want him to do.

As we cruise through the city, the lights gazing down like so many stars, I let the scene form in my mind. I'd planned for Coral to die at the end of her story. She was supposed to die. That was her purpose. Her destiny.

Her fate.

But every time I sat down to hash out the chapter, I could never get it quite right.

Now I know why.

Now I know . . . that's no way to end a fairy tale.

Like a character created by one of my all-time favorite authors—a boy who beat the impossible odds against him—Coral would make it past her intended ending.

She would have an after.

And I would be the girl who lived.

FORTY-NINE

Merrick Prince

Merrick pulled his key out of the ignition, sat back, and stared up at the shabby downtown apartment building. The barred windows gave him a feeling of entrapment, though he hadn't even stepped foot inside.

After all his searching, the trail had finally led him here?

He almost didn't want to know what waited beyond those brick-and-mortar walls. What did this last chapter matter? The truth might hurt Brooke more.

He turned the engine over again and shifted into reverse. The car idled, ready to take him far away from the finality of this moment. He wasn't doing this. What good could come of it?

But then his phone conversation from earlier that morning replayed in his mind. Vivi King—aka Mee-Maw—truly did have her fair share of secrets.

"The bracelet was yours all along?" Merrick's detective work had ended at a custom jewelry store off the coast just north of San Jose. "The shop's records showed your name on the purchase order."

"A wedding gift from my late husband," she said through a light chuckle. "I thought I'd lost it for a time. When it showed up on my oldest granddaughter's wrist a few months later, I kept my lips sealed. She was so happy with that young street musician the summer she came to stay."

Mee-Maw told Merrick everything. About the guy River referred to as her "prince." Though Vivi only knew his alias, it didn't take long for Merrick to trace his identity through social media based on his description and where he played. Process of elimination did the rest.

Ironic that the man who'd caused so much trouble lived mere miles from the home where Merrick grew up. Big city. Even bigger state. Small world.

"What about when Brooke started to wear it?" he asked Vivi.

"She grew so attached to it after River passed, I couldn't bring myself to tell her it was mine. I didn't have the heart."

Merrick released a full-voiced exhale as the memory faded. He put the car in park, shut down the engine again, and climbed out. The strong scent of asphalt stung. He tripped over a crack in the sidewalk and cursed. He was on edge and he hadn't even started. At the top of the stoop he rang the buzzer for apartment B3, then pocketed his hands and waited.

"Yeah?" The man on the intercom sounded as if he'd been sleeping.

Merrick checked his watch. Late afternoon. Either the guy worked a night shift or he was lazy. Merrick was inclined to believe the latter.

"Hey, I'm looking for Andrew 'The Sandman' Daniels." The pearl bracelet in his pocket felt like a weight. He hoped to lift it soon. From Brooke's shoulders more than from his own.

"It's Drew. Or Sandman. I answer to both. Who's asking?"

"My name is Merrick Prince. I'm a friend of River King's."

The intercom went silent before a loud *ennnt* sounded above him. Merrick slipped inside the bar-and-window door, then took the stairs two at a time. When he made it to the correct apartment, Drew stood in the open threshold. The scent of stale air and dried sweat wafted from behind him.

"What do you know about River?" he asked before Merrick could explain. "If she's pregnant it's not mine." He crossed his arms and then one leg over the other. Everything about his stance said this guy had a certain amount of experience with pregnant girls showing up on his doorstep.

Nice. Merrick should have stopped while he was ahead. He still could. Instead, he withdrew the bracelet. Held it up into the harsh, flickering fluorescent light. "Recognize this?"

"Ah, a jealous boyfriend, then?" Drew shrugged a pair of bony shoulders. "Figures she'd go for a rich one. Good for her, man."

The way he said *man* rubbed Merrick the wrong way. It was so far from Grim's casual terms of endearment. Was Drew covertly insulting him?

Merrick glanced down at his retro jacket, ironed shirt, non-distressed jeans, and white sneakers. Did his clothes give away his—his *father's*—status? So what if they did? Who was this guy to judge him? Currently, Drew modeled a pair of Santa cat pajama pants. At three o'clock in the afternoon, for crying out loud.

Plenty of insults bombarded his mind and played on the tip of his tongue. *This isn't about clothing or status or who drives what car. This is about River. And Brooke. I'm not leaving until I get to the bottom of this.*

"I'm not River's boyfriend." Merrick almost said he was dating her sister, but that wasn't quite true.

For now.

"I'm trying to help her sister find closure," Merrick started again, trying to figure out where the conversation had gone south.

"Closure?" Drew asked, tone drenched in sarcasm. "It didn't work out between us. How much more closure does she need?"

It hit Merrick then. Full force.

He doesn't know.

Merrick cleared his throat and swallowed. "River died."

Palm to his forehead, Drew slumped against the doorframe. "Oh, wow—" He slid down the frame to a crouch. "When?"

"January before last. She left this bracelet to her sister. Brooke."

Recognition shone in Drew's green eyes. Had River mentioned

Brooke to him? He rose, pushed his bleached hair off his forehead, and took the bracelet. The way he stared at it made Merrick wonder if the guy was seeing another scene entirely.

When Drew finally spoke again, Merrick's theory solidified.

"We met the summer before that. She was visiting her grandmother in that little tourist town. You know the one off the Coast Highway? The one named after a dessert topping?"

Coastal tourist towns were in full supply here. But yeah, Merrick knew the one. He nodded.

"I would play my harmonica on corners," Drew continued, "hoping to earn a few bucks, maybe even land a gig with a band."

"You play harmonica?"

Drew blinked as if it hit him Merrick still stood there. He stepped inside the apartment and returned with a brass instrument. It was a little beat up but still much newer than Merrick's hand-me-down one.

"Do you mind?"

"Not at all." Drew handed the harmonica over.

Merrick wiped it with his shirt, then pressed the instrument to his lips and played a few simple chords. It produced a clearer sound than his grandfather's, but the latter was more authentic. Or maybe it made him nostalgic. He handed the harmonica back to Drew and waited for him to say more.

"Anyway," Drew said, "River found me on whatever corner I chose. This bracelet ended up in my tip hat around mid-July. I figured some tourist had dropped it by mistake, so I held on to it. Played at that same corner for a week straight, waiting for the owner to claim it. But no one ever did."

"So you gave it to River?"

"She called me her 'Prince Charming.' Can you believe that? I wanted to sell it, see if it was worth anything. But she was so sweet. It was almost like she needed me. So, yeah, I gave it to her. To be honest, I felt bad for her. She seemed so . . ."

"Sad?"

"Yeah. And lonely. Being around her started to get depressing. Cramped my style."

The tone in which Drew said it, like it was no big deal, told Merrick more than his words had. "What happened between you, if you don't mind me asking?"

Drew cast his gaze to the concrete floor. He didn't have to say anything else for Merrick to get the gist. Typical. "Another girl?"

"River lived across the country." Defense coated his words. "I thought it was a fling, you know? When she showed up on my doorstep in the fall with her bags packed, I wasn't prepared. You have to warn a guy. You don't show up at his apartment unannounced."

"You told her you loved her." Merrick knew this much from what Brooke had told him.

"You know how it is. I've probably told at least a dozen girls the same thing. Who hasn't?"

Merrick hadn't. He pocketed his fists and worked his jaw. This guy had "player" written all over him in scarlet ink. If only River had waited. If she could have seen what true love looked like. Maybe things would have turned out differently.

Even so, how could he blame this loser who clearly needed a shower and a shave and probably didn't have more than five bucks to his name?

"Depression is an illness," his dad had said. *"It is a disease . . . You are not to blame for Amaya's death."*

Merrick sighed. He hated Drew on principle. But there was more to River's suicide than her broken heart. Of course this piece of work had made things worse, poured acid into an already open wound, but she was sick, same as Amaya had been.

"Thanks," Merrick said. "I think I have what I need." He held out his hand for the pearls. They were done here.

"She was a sweet girl," Drew said, as if that was any consolation. "I'm real sorry she died." He placed the bracelet in Merrick's hand and closed the door, taking his old-sock scent with him.

"Yeah," Merrick said to the peeling maroon paint. "Me too."

After taking a moment to collect himself, he made his way back outside. The day was uncharacteristically warm for the first of November, and his light jacket suddenly stifled him. After shrugging it off, he sat on the curb across from the apartment steps. Dead leaves littered the gutter and the barren branches above him offered little shade.

"So that's your story, huh?" He turned the bracelet over in his hand. "That was the prince River fell for?" A dark laugh escaped. "Some prince."

His phone buzzed. He answered without checking the caller ID. "Hey."

"Did you find him, compadre?" Grim's voice provided the grounding Merrick needed.

"Unfortunately."

"Bad news, my friend?"

"I wanted to punch the guy."

"Ouch." He pictured Grim's wince. "I knew I should've come with you."

"Nah," Merrick said. "This was something I had to do on my own."

"I'm proud of you, man."

"Thanks. I'm kind of proud of me too."

They made plans to grab burgers and shakes later that night for their final exam study session, then Merrick hit End and tucked both the phone and the pearls inside his pants pocket. He exhaled and hung his head between his knees.

What would he say to Brooke? How could he explain that the epic and tragic love story she'd imagined for River was nothing more than a case of deadbeat-itis?

Merrick made a silent promise to himself then. He would live up to the name he bore. A name he'd once hated, but now found described exactly who he needed to be.

A prince.

Did she still want him? Their texts reeked of small talk. The moment they'd shared in the tea shop last month never came up. After all this time, after all the heartbreak and hurt, could the damage that had created a chasm between them be undone? Could they rebuild and find their way back to one another? Brooke was still healing.

But so was he.

Even if they couldn't make it work, Merrick would be the prince Brooke deserved. And if it turned out she didn't want him as part of her world?

He would still be a Prince.

Merrick would stand by her side until the very end.

FIFTY

Brooke

Thanksgiving break brings with it the final phase of changing leaves and all things pumpkin and pecan and cinnamon.

Nikki and I stroll side by side past the charming shops and quaint businesses you'd only ever find in this town. We've found our way back once again. To this enchanting corner of the West Coast where time slows and life pauses. We can't keep ourselves away, it seems. Nikki for Grim, of course. And me?

Mee-Maw is here, the life of the party at Ocean Gardens Assisted Living. Or so she claims. She never fails to work her magic, casting a spell on everyone she meets. There's never been a soul who's met her who didn't immediately fall in love.

I drink in the cider-tinged air as a breeze swirls around me, lifting the hem of my skirt, reminding me why I wear leggings. I feel River here too. This is where she died. Though a stirring inside my heart says she'll never really leave this place.

"I'm here," I sense her whisper through the wind. *"I'll always be here."*

I take a moment to remember her voice. I picture her and Amaya Hope off on an adventure somewhere. Splashing in the waves, pretending to be mermaids for a day.

"Take care of each other," I want to tell them.

I can almost hear Hope's response. *"You guys take care of each other too."*

A shiver runs through me as her brother's smile takes up every inch of my thoughts. My heart twists. I check my messages. Nothing from Merrick, but my eyes widen when Jordan's name lights the screen.

Happy Thanksgiving.

I shoot her a quick reply and include all the turkey and pie emojis I can fit. Jordan's words are few, but they're real. For now, that's enough.

Nikki and I stop at a cart and order three spiced chai lattes. I treat her since she drove, then we head across the street where my grandmother waits at a table on the patio of a crepe shop.

"Thank you, dears," she says as she takes her cup. Her gloved hands tremble but still when she rests them on her knees. "This is my favorite time of year. I love the fall festival. Thank you for coming to see me."

Nikki squeezes her arm. "I've been so excited to meet you, Mrs. King."

"Please, call me Vivi. Or even Mee-Maw, if you like. As far as I'm concerned, you're family now."

Anyone else might be put off by Mee-Maw's immediate outpouring of love. But not Nikki. "All right, Mee-Maw. I guess this means I'll need to introduce you to Nigel soon. The fall festival is his favorite too. You two would get along nicely, I think." She blushes. "Speaking of which, I promised to meet up with him. See you both later?"

Mee-Maw and I both nod. We watch my unlikely best friend wrap a scarf around her neck and round a corner in her high-heeled designer boots.

"Nice girl," Mee-Maw says after a steadied sip of her chai. "I'm glad you're friends."

"So am I." A glance down at my flat but cozy UGG knockoffs stirs new emotions. I contrast Nikki in so many ways on the outside. In another life, another world, I never would have been friends with her. Or rather, I never would have believed she *wanted* to be friends with me.

If I hadn't been so quick to judge others before they had a chance to judge me, some things may have turned out differently. On the inside, Nikki and I aren't so opposite. Inside we're two human souls who value friendship. Authenticity. Love.

"I was horrible to you last year, Mee-Maw." Each wave of emotion ripples into a new one. All at once I can't stop from speaking what's weighed heavily on my heart since Hope died. "I'm sorry. I saw you as a villain when all you tried to do was help me survive."

"You don't worry about me." My grandmother winks, as is her way. "I'm no worse for the wear. I wouldn't have brought you here unless I was ready to face everything with you, Brooke. Sometimes you have to swim through a bit of darkness . . ."

"If you're ever going to surface in the light." I finish her coined phrase that belongs on a mug and sip my chai, careful not to let it burn my tongue. "How are you liking Ocean Gardens? You've been there almost a year now."

She shrugs. "Well, it's no beachfront cottage, but I can still see the ocean from my window." Mee-Maw pats my hand.

I cover it with my own and hold tight.

Her forehead wrinkles soften as she gazes out over the busy street. She looks older, weathered, more fragile than the last time I saw her about a month ago. Did a time truly exist when I didn't want to be anywhere near her? A time when everything seemed black or white or stained in shades of gray?

A leaf flutters to my lap. I examine its gradient hues—a sunset of oranges, yellows, and reds bursting between each vein. Winter nears and colder days lie ahead. The world will dull, and the days will seem bleak. But I won't forget the warmth of summer.

And if I do?

Then Nikki will tell me about her latest date with Grim, or Mee-Maw will call to gush about the strapping young physical therapist she insists has a crush on her. I'll have those I love to remind me that even the slightest bit of good holds more weight than any of the bad.

My drink warms my throat. Soothes my anxiety. Maybe it will never fully go away, but I am learning how to face it. Finding new ways to cope every day. Things do get better. And sometimes they get worse. But that's okay. One day at a time is all anyone can be expected to give.

"Shall we walk?" Mee-Maw asks.

I want to tell her she's already walked me through so much and I'd rather sit here and enjoy her presence as long as I can. I know there's a day all too soon when she'll leave me behind. But I also know she will have spent every last twinkle in her eye loving me. Real love. The kind that heals even the deepest wounds.

So I say, "We shall," and I link my arm with hers.

We bask in the atmosphere of the beachside town I've grown to love. Pumpkin wreaths, leaf garlands, and paper turkeys with pilgrim hats hang from every shop window. The streets burst with life. People from near and far graze the sidewalks, doing some early Christmas shopping or pausing to chat with a familiar face or two or three.

Mee-Maw is one of those familiar faces. We can't walk a few yards before someone else taps her shoulder, asking about my dad or turning to tell me how much I look like my mom. Mee-Maw gives them the novella instead of the whole novel and we continue on.

"You must have better things to do than hang out with your old grandmother all day."

I pat her arm. "Not at all." I mean each word. I've wasted too much time away from her already. And I'm making up for it every minute I can.

We move to the next storefront and sweet smells bombard my senses. A candy shop owner passes out goody bags filled with candy corn and business cards and coupons. Hand-dipped caramel apples line display tables and local artists create caricatures on the next corner. Face painters, acrobats, street dancers, and musicians have all come to celebrate. Summer of Lights comes to mind.

Part of me wishes it didn't.

My heart squeezes. I allow myself to think of Merrick and how he helped me believe in after. The more days that pass since the last time I saw him, the more I wonder . . . do I need to let him go?

Mee-Maw's walk slows as we pass an Italian restaurant. I can almost taste the meatballs and four-cheese lasagna and tiramisu. But Mee-Maw doesn't appear to be thinking about food. She peers down a brick alleyway lined with ivy and vine. "Goodness, I haven't seen this place in ages. I'd almost forgotten it was here." She releases my arm and ambles down the narrow path.

When we reach the end, a hidden garden surrounds us, a paved brick path curving toward a quaint-looking shop that appears to have once been a cottage. A few easels out front display magnificent paintings depicting the most beautiful settings. Landscapes and sunsets and valleys and oceans. Beyond the windows waits a small art gallery, colors bursting to life, singing a melody of their own.

My heart swells. Today is a color-song day. I couldn't ask for more.

Out of the shop walks a woman with strawberry hair and a smattering of freckles across her nose and cheeks. Even if I hadn't seen her at the funeral, I would know her in an instant.

She's the spitting image of Hope and my lids brim with tears.

The woman doesn't notice us at first. She's too busy watering the golden poppies in the window boxes. The way the light hits her hair just so and the manner in which her blouse rests across her delicate shoulders makes her fit perfectly within this scene. She is as timeless as the paintings on display.

I step close enough to smell her perfume. As floral as her surroundings.

She doesn't startle when she notices me. She straightens and smiles.

"You're Amaya and Merrick's mom," I say without pretense.

"I am." Why doesn't she seem surprised to see me?

"I'm Brooke. Hope—*Amaya*—and I were at Fathoms Ranch together." Did she know Hope was at Fathoms? She must have, right?

"Yes. I saw y'all at my daughter's funeral," the woman says, southern accent subtle but present all the same. "I'm Lyn."

I don't tell Lyn I sort of met Hope before our time at Fathoms. The second time she tried to take her life in the bathtub of Nigel's beach house. Instead, I tell her what a good friend her daughter was and how she impacted my life. I say everything I didn't say the day of the memorial. All the things I should have said and more.

"Bless your heart." Lyn turns her attention to Mee-Maw. "I don't know if you remember me, Vivi."

"Of course I do. How are you, Lyn?"

"Wait . . . You two . . . know each other?" I'm flabbergasted but somehow not surprised. My grandmother has been in this town longer than a few spells and knows almost everyone.

"Vivi gave me my first job in high school." Lyn closes her eyes a moment as if pausing in reminiscence. "Do you still have an attic full of everyone's junk?"

"I like to refer to my things as treasures, thank you. When did you move back to town?"

Lyn studies a painting by the door, avoiding the question in my grandmother's eyes. "Almost two years now." She doesn't elaborate. Doesn't explain about the husband and two children she left behind. She waves us toward the cottage gallery. "Come on in. We have some wonderful pieces on display."

Her purposeful change of subject does not elude me.

Still, we follow her lead. Inside the gallery, rich mahogany walls make the space feel grander than it is. Individual lamps cast a warm glow over each painting, bringing out the lively hues and playing on the use of positive and negative space.

"This one's a favorite." Lyn pauses beside a scene depicting a lighthouse on a hill. "It's a duplicate, but as lovely as the first the artist painted."

The lighthouse reminds me of the one Merrick found in the coffee table book. The one that led him to the woman standing before me now.

She moves on, giving us brief spiels about each painting in turn. When she rounds the last corner of the miniature gallery, time slows. The painting ahead is a rendering of a mermaid sitting on a rock, human prince at her side. The scene is one I've imagined in my mind—my heart—oh so many times before.

"Here we have one of the artist's final creations prior to his death. He loved the Danish author's tragic fairy tale but was also partial to the more modern, animated retelling." Lyn's fingers linger on the painting's frame. "He believed in the innocence that comes with first love and how true love overcomes even the most impossible things."

She couldn't possibly know how deeply those words sink. How hard they hit home. I spent so much time looking for the worst. The deceptive Sorceress I saw in my grandmother. And Lyn—the witch who left Hope and Merrick behind. Even Jake and Miss Brandes played villains for a time, only to be revealed later as heroes. Mentors. Friends.

Now I see them for who they are.

Mee-Maw who loves me so much, she walked with me through darkness.

And Lyn. A lonely and lost woman who still searches for the best way to stand on her own two legs.

Jake, who checks in every week, and Miss Brandes, who still encourages me to write an ending to the story I never finished.

Hope and River, who live on in my memory.

And Merrick. Does he understand the change he induced by accepting me as I am?

When I look at Lyn again, I watch as a single tear travels from the corner of her right eye to the tip of her chin. In that tear every preconceived judgment I have harbored falls away. It's in this tear I am reminded she is human.

We all are.

I pull a Kleenex from my tote bag and offer it to the mother of two of my favorite people. Has Merrick been here? Has he seen her since that day at the forest chapel?

"You should call him," I say.

She blinks and smoothes the tissue over her open palm. "Who?"

"Merrick."

"He doesn't want to talk to me. I messed up. Wasted my last chance. It's too late now."

"It's never too late to let someone know you love them." This time it is Mee-Maw who offers her wisdom.

Is she talking to Lyn alone? Or are her words meant for both of us?

More tears spill from Lyn's eyelids. They form streams down her freckled cheeks. Sing a song of mourning splashed with ripples of hope.

My gaze finds the mermaid painting again, so full of color and promise. The tune it plays is one I'd long forgotten. One I want to remember again.

"Here." Lyn thumbs through a basket of postcards. "I want you to have this." She hands me a postcard with a copy of the mermaid painting printed on it. "Maybe this will inspire your own love story someday."

I take it, tracing the image with my fingertips. "I think it already has."

Mee-Maw remains quiet until we're outside. When our eyes find one another, she's beaming. "That's your ending." She nods toward the postcard. "All you have to do is choose it."

I glance over my shoulder. I don't tell Lyn I forgive her for abandoning my friends. It's not *my* forgiveness she needs or wants. It's her own.

She nods at me through the window. She will call Merrick. Maybe not today, but soon.

Mee-Maw and I walk back through the gallery's garden, following the path away from the hidden enchantment and out to the street once more.

When we reach a nearby bench and Mee-Maw sits to rest, I don't join her.

"Go on, get out of here." She shoos me with her hands. "Write that ending."

I bite my lower lip, then give her a quick kiss on the cheek. When I pull away she catches my eye. Do I sense a little magic in her after all?

Yes. Of course I do. There's nothing more incredible than unconditional love.

I head for the pier then. When I reach the sand, I'm already kicking off my boots and pulling out my notebook. I always keep one on hand and this one is brand new. Never been written in. Well . . . almost.

This is the last gift Hope ever gave me.

A golden mermaid silhouette decks the teal-and-white-striped cover. *"I saw this on our beach field trip in the spring and thought of you,"* she said on her last day at Fathoms. *"I held on to it for when you returned."*

I open the cover to reveal an inscription written on the first page. As was her way, Hope penned a quote that seems written for me. For now.

"When we are at the end of the story, we shall know more than we know now . . ."

—Hans Christian Andersen

I sit, dig through my bag, and withdraw the only writing tool I can find—my red editing pen. It'll have to do.

At last I dive in. My hand flies across the pages, the words spilling out faster than I can capture them in ink. With each new curve of an *s* or loop of a *y* I hear a new sound, each note lovelier than the one before it.

Red doesn't have to be poison. It doesn't always mean pain.

Red can also show warmth and passion. And maybe even . . .

Yes. I see it now. Hear it. Red is a symphony blossoming before me.

The color of light.

The song of love.

I stare at the red words at the bottom of the last page.

The End.

I can't speak or control the elation tingling to my toes. Because I finished it.

I only wish Hope were here to read how it all turned out. Would she be proud? Would she have chosen to stay?

I close the notebook and rest my head on my bent knees. I can't help the tears that come now. Fast and free and falling. I say good-bye to a final chapter. With only fresh pages ahead, where do I go from here?

That's the beauty of life, isn't it? Every day is a new page, waiting to be written.

When I stand and stretch, I stuff the newly filled notebook into my bag and walk along the beach, padding over the line of damp sand where the sea rushes my soles. About halfway between the shore and the sidewalk I see it. A corked, frosted blue sea glass bottle. My heartbeat ceases to exist.

The bottle is nearly identical to the one I found in the ocean the day I turned my own world upside down. I've carried it with me as a memorial token of the choice I made to keep fighting. Could it be more than just a bottle?

I whip my head left and right. It's Thanksgiving Day. Of course the beach is abandoned. Everyone is stuffing their faces with turkey or enjoying the fall festival in town.

I give the area another once-over before kneeling in the sand beside the bottle.

It's crazy. We were together little longer than a summer. A moment. A single scene within hundreds. But that moment? Somehow it became my air. A way to breathe through the hurt and the pain and the grief I couldn't cope with and that all at once consumed me.

Merrick was the first person I didn't hide from. I opened the door for him. My beacon of light in a raging storm.

This is more than a bottle.

This is Merrick's way of keeping his promise.

"I'll wait. However long it takes. I'll wait for you."

It takes some work to pull the tight cork free, but I manage. I peer through the hole with one eye. Have I missed what was right in front of me all along? I tilt the bottle until the rolled paper reaches the lip, rip the edges as I tug, but . . . there! It's free.

I know it's a message before I unfurl it. When I do, I stare at the words. The note is signed "Prince" and my heart can't handle the conflicting joy and sorrow within.

Winter can't last forever. I'll wait for you through the storm, Brooke. Promise.

How could I ever have questioned him? Why did I push him away when all this time he would have welcomed me into his arms?

I don't swallow my emotions when I look up. Don't bother masking my heart behind a blank expression any longer. I see the other bottles then. Spaced every ten feet or so, creating a trail over the sand up the shore and back down again. I rise. Take my time as I kneel beside the bottles one by one. Each letter is dated and signed. One letter for every month over the past year. I follow their path. Read. Relish. Remember. At the end I'm exactly where I began. At my favorite spot beneath the pier.

Our spot.

He's standing there, waiting. The final bottle in his left hand.

"How'd you know I'd be here?" I ask, though I already know the answer.

"Nikki. Mee-Maw." He shrugs. "Take your pick."

"What is all this?"

Another shrug. "You said you don't believe in fate."

"I don't." Didn't. My smile reaches my hairline. "I'm starting to reconsider."

"I knew it was a one-in-a-million chance you'd ever find the original bottle I sent out to sea. So I decided to give fate a little push." He hands me the last bottle, fingers brushing mine for an instant.

I try to control the wave ready to break loose at his touch. I take the bottle and read the final letter. The short and sweet and perfect letter that says more than all of his messages combined.

Today

Dear Brooke,
    I love you.
    Promise.

                        Yours,
                        Merrick Prince

"We choose our own ending," he says when our eyes meet. "And, Brooke?"

My lips part at hearing him say my true name aloud for the first time.

"I choose you. For all the endings and beginnings and in-betweens."

We sit beside each other in the sand, the way we did many summer nights ago. Our fingers weave between the grains, sliding closer to the other's with each second.

We say nothing for a moment. When the silence is so long neither of us can stand it, he leans close. His shoulder against mine is a pillar. Though I've learned to stand on my own, I've also found there's nothing wrong with relying on others.

I can have both.

The sea creeps closer. When the foam reaches us, the past urge to take refuge there lingers. "Once upon a time I believed everything was better underwater," I say. "Where sounds and colors collide. Where my body becomes weightless."

His pinky finger finds mine. I link my own with his, relishing the way it feels to make this silent promise with him again. I turn to face him. "Merrick, when this year began, I wanted the freedom I believed only the ocean could bring."

I wait for the information to register. Watch as understanding settles in his gaze.

My fingers slide over his, pulling back, then pushing in and holding tighter. "I tried to end it." I find his eyes and hold faster still. "But you saved me." My shoulders rise and fall in a ripple. I dig through my purse and withdraw a sea glass bottle.

Not one I found today.

The one I clung to nearly a year ago when everything was gray.

His eyes grow wide.

I uncork the bottle now, discover his very first letter from last November. Why didn't I ever think to look inside sooner?

November

Dear Brooke,

You are not nothing.

You never have been.

You never will be.

353

You are something to someone.

You are everything to me.

Promise.

Yours,

Prince

Merrick draws a quick breath. "Is that—"

With moist eyes and a full heart, I try to find the words. But, for once, they're lost to me.

Because Merrick found them first.

"You said it would be a one-in-a-million chance I'd find this." I draw the message to my heart. "But I did. I found it. And it led me back to you."

I tell him of the storm and finding the bottle in the sea. Of hypothermia and hallucinations and the night in the cave. It had all been a dream. But now it's my ending.

"True love"—I choke on the words, so raw and real—"makes life, even a broken one, worth fighting for."

"If you ever find true love, hold on to it." River's voice comes back to me. I think of everything she believed she lost. Of all she left behind.

A tear slips down my cheek. Then another. I can't stop them. I don't even try. I sniffle, but I won't wipe them away. "I once saw emotion as a curse or a disease. I thought love was a fairy tale."

"And now?" He lifts his hands to my cheeks, catches my tears with his thumbs. He takes care to remove each one, touching them to the ocean and letting them dissolve with the foam as it recedes.

"Now I know my emotions are what make me human. And that love is as real as the healing, incredibly human tears on my face."

"Spoken like a true writer."

"You would know." I wink. "You have a way with words yourself."

"I had a good teacher."

We stay in this place. I take in his summer scent and he holds my gaze, challenging me to keep the intense stare without looking away for fear of what he might see. I match his stare with everything inside me, unafraid for the first time to let him look into who I am.

"I found him." He reaches into his pocket. Withdraws my bracelet. "The guy who broke River's heart."

"When?" My pulse picks up as he slides the pearls over my wrist.

He doesn't draw back, instead wrapping his fingers over mine. "A few weeks now. I couldn't figure out how to tell you at first." Merrick hangs his head, regret shaking his shoulders. His story spills out in run-on sentences and whispered curses. At the end, he doesn't meet my gaze.

Now it's my turn. I place my palm to his jawline, nudging him to look at me.

When he does, his dark but forever warm eyes express more emotion than a hundred thousand words could. "I'm sorry. For what he did. For not finding him sooner."

"Thank you. For keeping your promise." Our foreheads meet, tips of our noses barely touching. "He doesn't matter. River wouldn't want me to dwell on revenge. She would hate to know I wasted my time on someone who didn't value hers."

"I've never seen you like this." His admission warms my cheeks. "So calm. Present."

I close my eyes and linger on his words. "Now is all we have. And right now I am completely in love with you, Merrick Prince."

My heart sets the truth free and a moment of terror grips me. How could he love me when I still struggle every day to love myself? Then again, a life without love—without Merrick—is a life of drowning. I'd rather struggle together than face another second apart.

I push aside the old voice of fear and uncertainty and close the distance between us, matching my lips to his. He doesn't need to speak the words. He's written them, made them permanent on a page, and etched them over my heart. Besides, Merrick's soft response now speaks more than words ever could. Our lips part and join, like the waves meeting the shore. We don't come up for air for a while. We kiss until our breaths aren't our own and there's no telling which one of us draws back first.

"You stole my line," his lips say against mine. "That was from one of my letters."

"Are you going to arrest me for plagiarism?"

"Most definitely."

We share another long embrace and several more tentative kisses before the sun fades. When we stand and walk hand in hand up the beach, we collect the bottles until our arms are as full as our hearts. We walk back to town, ready to celebrate together. Our holidays will always be bittersweet, missing the faces of those no longer with us. Sorrow remains an unwelcome companion in the days ahead.

But joy follows close behind. And laughter. We can take the journey side by side, find healing in sharing every heartache. Discover hope in every tear we freely shed.

And maybe—just maybe—our own version of happily. Ever. After.

Enden.

(Which, in Danish, means "The End")

"When we are at the end of the story,
we shall know more than we know now."

—Hans Christian Andersen

AFTER

I never thought I'd get here.

To the beginning.

To the place where everything starts over. Fresh. Bursting with new life, and color, and love.

I soak in the light that seems to drown me now. Though the darkness is never fully gone, I've learned how to fight it. It only takes one drop of sunlight to break through an Abyss.

It might be impossible to change the past. But who said starting over had anything to do with going back?

No matter where after begins, there's always a chance for a new before.

Before starts right now. Because I choose after.

And after will never be the same again.

AUTHOR'S NOTE ON
HANS CHRISTIAN ANDERSEN'S
TRAGIC TALE OF TEARS AND
TORTURED SOULS

Oh, Dear Reader, welcome to the end.

And, as it turns out, the beginning.

This tale has been a journey, to say the least. When I began writing this book, I had no idea it would be about mental health. The Disney girl that I am wanted . . . well, *Disney*. But something happened during the writing (and rewriting) process that took me down a path I never expected. A road of learning about myself and others who have experienced trauma and heartache. There are more of us than we know.

"But a mermaid has no tears, and therefore she suffers so much more."

This single line from the original tale sent my mind spinning. While I'm a Disney girl through and through—and allude to the 1989 film that brought Disney animation back to life throughout this book—I was also heartbroken that these words were somehow lost in the film adaptation.

For those who aren't familiar with the story as it was first told, Andersen wrote of a little mermaid who longs for a human soul.

Because mermaids do not possess a soul, they become as the foam of the sea when they die. And without a soul, mermaids cannot cry.

This simple concept got me thinking about life as we know it. About stoicism and the idea of being tough or "just getting over it." As if it were that simple. For those who have never experienced depression, anxiety, or trauma (physical and emotional), it can be difficult to explain the concepts of numbness or dissociation.

I cannot represent every situation, and I won't claim to. I am also not a licensed counselor or therapist. But I do know something about grief and loss and being told to "get over it." When I assumed I'd cried every last tear an ocean could hold, I reached a point where I felt removed from my own life. As if all the things that had happened to me were happening to someone else. I couldn't cry and I couldn't feel. There were no more tears to shed, and that was a new kind of suffering. A suffering inside myself that no one else could see.

And that is why this story hangs on this single line written by an author I could only aspire to be like. It is a story not necessarily retold, but rather reimagined.

If you have been or are in a place where your tears no longer fall, I relate to your suffering. And it's a suffering far greater than many could ever understand.

There is much more I want to say on this topic. Ways I want to explain why this novel took the direction it did. But there are not enough pages and never enough words. So I leave you with this—reach out to someone. A family member. A friend. A counselor. You have a voice. You don't have to drown alone. Talk to someone you trust and let those tears come.

I'll be right there with you in spirit.

You are not nothing. And you are not alone.

With all my heart,

Sara Ella

ACKNOWLEDGMENTS

This novel has only reached its end by the unfathomable grace of God. After three rewrites and countless tears, he finally helped me find the heart of this story. For that I have no words.

My momma in heaven introduced me to "The Little Mermaid." She encouraged me to believe in fairy tales. I will never stop thanking her for reminding me what true love looks like.

My husband deserves at least 50 percent of the credit for this book. This man never complained through each soul-wrenching deadline. Caiden, you are a true prince if there ever was one.

My darling children have more patience than any mom could ask for. I love you, babies. You are my world.

My parents on all sides: Dad, Mom (Jodi), Paul (other dad), Jen (other mom), Erika (also other mom), Tosh (also other dad), and Aunt Terri (might as well be my mom)—all of you deserve more thanks than I could ever give.

Jim Hart—my agent—thank you for supporting, for listening, for serving.

Nadine Brandes, Mary Weber, and Ashley Townsend—your friendships have blessed my heart. For all the insecurities you validated and the doubts you snuffed, thank you. I love you.

To my AMAZING group of Phoenix writer friends: Liz Johnson,

Lindsay Harrel, Tina Radcliffe, and Jennifer Deibel. You are priceless—I love you all.

To my sisters in life and love: Madisyn Carrington, Brooke Larson, Janalyn Owens, Mandi Alva, Elizabeth VanTassel, Kayla Kunkel, Gabrial Jones, Carolyn Schanta, Deena Peterson, Laura Pol, Arianna Fourt, Anna Fehr, Cheryse Ligabo, Vanessa Uphoff, and Tiffany Barlow—so many words and so little space. Thank you for always caring and encouraging. Hugs!

To my team at Thomas Nelson: Becky Monds, Amanda Bostic, Jodi Hughes, Allison Carter, Paul Fisher, Matt Bray, Kristen Ingebretson, Kristen Andrews, Julee Schwarzburg, Whitney Zapffe, and everyone else I am failing to mention both in the states and internationally—thank you for your tireless efforts to get this story into the hands of readers.

My writerly folks without whom I could not survive this crazy career: Sarah Grimm, Lindsay A. Franklin, C. J. Redwine, Beth Revis, Marissa Meyer, RJ Metcalf, Shannon Dittemore, Dana Black, Kara Swanson, Kayla Grey, Taylor Bennett, Katherine Reay, Kristy Cambron, Christen Krumm, Stephanie Warner, Heidi Wilson, Katie Phillips, Lauren Mansy, Annie Sullivan, Brianna Tibbetts, Melissa Ferguson, Emilie Hendryx, Emileigh Latham, and the many others who have given me their precious time over the years—thank you.

My #Bookstagram family—there are too many of you to name within my word limit! I see you. I am so grateful for you! For every gorgeous photo, shout-out, or kind comment—each one of you makes a difference. You bring light and joy to my life.

My influencers and street team (aka Bookish Belles) who never fail to support me—you are the reason my books are seen. Without you, *Coral* would be lost on a back shelf at the bookstore. Thank you for your time and energy and unfailing faithfulness.

Finally, to my sensitivity readers, including Dr. Michael Callaway—you saw this story at its very worst. Your experiences are more valuable to this story (and to me) than I can express. Thank you for helping steer these characters in the right direction, despite any triggering it might have caused. You believed in this story enough to risk reliving your own pain. You are seen. You are loved. You are not alone.

DISCUSSION QUESTIONS

WARNING! SPOILERS AHEAD

1. Several themes from the original, dark fairy tale of "The Little Mermaid" are addressed throughout the book. Hans Christian Andersen wrote, "But a mermaid has no tears, and therefore she suffers so much more." Discuss what you think this means on an emotional level for Brooke, Coral, and Amaya Hope. Does Merrick experience this type of "suffering" in his own way?

2. Coral has forms of *synesthesia*—sounds and emotions are linked to colors. Discuss the contrast between Coral's vibrant world in the beginning and the gray world Brooke sees throughout the story. What did you notice regarding how the world they see changes based on where they are in their journeys?

3. Jordan and Jonah are closed off, stoic, and cold—they see emotions as a "Disease." Discuss Coral's/Brooke's growth as she learns the value of emotions and allows herself to feel and process the things she has faced.

4. The topic of mental illness can be a difficult one in our culture. There is a lot of negative stigma surrounding

words like *suicide*, *depression*, *PTSD*, and *anxiety*. Do you believe mental illness should be approached from a different perspective? If so, how can you be a part of that change?

5. Merrick, who suffers from survivor's guilt, blames himself for Amaya Hope's death. How did his perspective alter following the conversation he had with his dad in chapter 45?

6. Compare and contrast the characters in *Coral* with the well-known characters we have come to know in both Disney's and Hans Christian Andersen's "The Little Mermaid." How are they the same? How are they different?

7. Explore the symbolism of the elements such as "Red Tide," the "Abyss," and even the name "Coral." Did you find deeper or multiple meanings behind each one? If so, discuss what you believe they represent for each character.

8. Which character did you relate to the most and why?

9. Discuss what you believe the line "there is more than one way to drown" alludes to.

10. Fairy tales are often made up of heroes and villains, though sometimes they are more obvious than others. Who or what did you find to be the main hero or villain in this story?

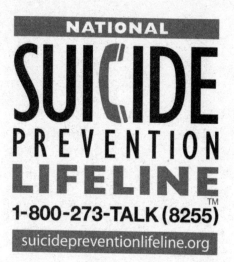

NATIONAL SUICIDE PREVENTION LIFELINE™
1-800-273-TALK (8255)
suicidepreventionlifeline.org

If you are thinking about harming yourself or attempting suicide, tell someone who can help right away.

- Call your doctor's office.
- Call 911 for emergency services.
- Go to the nearest hospital emergency room.
- Call the toll-free, 24-hour hotline of the National Suicide Prevention Lifeline at **1-800-273-TALK (1-800-273-8255)** to be connected to a trained counselor at a suicide crisis center nearest you.

Ask a family member or friend to help you make these calls or take you to the hospital.

For more information, visit suicidepreventionlifeline.org or nimh.nih.gov.

THE UNBLEMISHED TRILOGY

Eliyana can't stand looking at her own reflection. With a birthmark covering half her face, she just hopes to graduate high school unscathed. But what if this is only one Reflection—one world? What if another world exists where her blemish could become her strength?

"A breathtaking fantasy set in an extraordinary fairy-tale world, with deceptive twists and an addictively adorable cast who are illusory to the end."

—Mary Weber, award-winning author of the Storm Siren Trilogy and *To Best the Boys*

available in print, e-book, and audio!

THOMAS NELSON
Since 1798